FIC   McShea, Susanna
             Hofman.

             Ladybug, ladybug.

$21.95

DATE			

 NOV TAYLOR

L A D Y B U G

A HOMETOWN HEROES MYSTERY

L A D Y B U G

PREVIOUS HOMETOWN HEROES MYSTERIES BY
Susanna Hofmann McShea

The Pumpkin-Shell Wife
Hometown Heroes

SUSANNA HOFMANN McSHEA

LADYBUG

A HOMETOWN HEROES MYSTERY

LADYBUG

A THOMAS · DUNNE BOOK

ST. MARTIN'S PRESS · NEW YORK

This is a work of fiction. The characters described have arisen from the mind of the author and are not intended to represent specific living persons.

Design by Junie Lee

Library of Congress Cataloging-in-Publication Data
McShea, Susanna Hofmann.
    Ladybug, ladybug / Susanna Hofmann McShea.
        p.   cm.
    "A Thomas Dunne book."
    ISBN 0-312-11017-0
    1. Hometown Heroes (Fictitious characters)—Fiction.   2. Private investiga-
tors—Connecticut—Fiction.   3.   Women   detectives—Connecticut—Fiction.   4. Aged—Connecticut—Fiction.   I. Title.
PS3563.C8L33   1994
813'.54—dc20
                                                                                    94-1120
                                                                                    CIP

First edition: July 1994

10   9   8   7   6   5   4   3   2   1

For my stepmother,
Jeanne Meskill Hofmann,
so giving and good.

We sympathize with his parents.
They seem like nice people.
>   —Ronald Reagan, after having
>   been shot by John Hinkley, Jr.

. . . How indistinct! How blurred!
Yet within are images,
How blurred! How indistinct!
Yet within are things.
>   —Lao-tsu

CHAPTER ONE

EARLY JUNE

The smell of wet wood hung in the air and mud sucked at his feet. He moved slowly, carefully, the tip of his cane black with ash. Every now and again a stray ember popped and he fought the urge to duck.

A voice called out from ten o'clock. "Gonski! What the hell're you doing here?"

He stared in the right direction. Tommy McKnight wasn't mad, just surprised. Gary had been keeping a low profile of late. He heard the squish-slap, squish-slap of McKnight's clodhopper boots and then McKnight was grabbing his left hand, pumping it up and down, saying "How ya been?"

"Getting by, Tommy. Doing okay."

"Tough break, Gary. We all felt for you. Well, at least they got the sonuvabitch, right? So what you doing here?"

"Just out for a morning stroll. What happened anyway?"

"Electrical short. Behind the sofa in the living room, it looks like."

"A bad one from the sound of the sirens last night."

"The family never had a chance. Smoke detector didn't help, it went so fast. The central AC kept pumping fresh air. A fire loves fresh air."

"Anyone make it out?"

"No. I've seen a lot in my time, Gary, but *Christ*." Gary pictured Tommy running a hand through his red hair. "They were

1

huddled together. *Welded* together. The parents, kids. Even the grandmother, who was visiting."

Gary raised his nose and sniffed, inhaling burned scrapbooks and Raggedy Anns and six lives gone up in smoke.

"Come by the firehouse sometime, why don't ya?" Already Tommy McKnight was edging away. Couldn't wait.

"Yeah, sure," replied Gary. But he knew he wouldn't.

CHAPTER   TWO

The nurse walked ahead in marshmallow shoes, the rest of her brisk and official and starched to the bone. She stopped at the entrance to the day room, jutted her pointy chin in that direction and said "She sits by the window. Won't participate in any activities." An accusation.

Dumb nurse. That's why she's here, I could have replied. She won't participate! Because she's ruined! What do you people expect!

But I didn't say a word. She was someone beneath me, and I remained gracious. I smiled and bobbed my head as though I followed her stupid line of shit.

"Be careful not to get her excited," said the nurse in a commanding voice.

Oh, don't I wish! To see her dance on your clay-smeared tables. To see her unravel those stupid potholders. To see her strangle you with a poorly woven lanyard. To see a glimmer of recognition, never mind happiness, in those vacant blue-gray eyes. A little excitement might do the trick. But no. She's had enough excitement to last a lifetime. Look where it got her.

I waited, not wanting to speak more than necessary. Finally the pillowcased battle-ax left us alone.

"Deanie?" I whispered. "Deanie, darling?" I sat and took her hand. Of course she didn't recognize me. Under the best of circumstances I wouldn't have expected her to, and these were the worst. "Deanie, it's me." I preened.

"Unga, unga, unga."

Chief Thunderthud on Howdy Doody used to say exactly that, I could swear it. No, I'm wrong. He said "Kowabunga." Buffalo Bob Smith and Clarabell and Princess Summer-Fall-Winter-Spring. And Mister Bluster, who was one mean son of a bitch, just like I am.

"Come on, Deanie, you can do better than that." Please! "Pucker up and sing 'It's a Beautiful Morning' just like the Young Rascals used to do."

"Ahoooga! Ahooga!"

I tried to joke. "You sound like one of those auto horns." Just for the fun of it I repeated her. "Ahhhooooogah!" Deanie's eyes clouded and she looked confused. Well, more confused than usual. And to think that at one time she made such strides. She was tutored to death, then mainstreamed. And look where it got her.

"Never mind, Deanie. Much as I'd like to sit and chat, I can't tarry. There are things—important things—that need to be said before I leave. I'm going away. I took care of those Boardmans, like I promised." I stopped. Was she getting any of this? "You remember those bad Prescotts? The ones in the boat last summer? Well, now the Boardmans are gone too. Not quite the same way, but gone just the same. Done to a turn, you might say."

I took a deep breath, afraid it wouldn't register and more afraid that it would, then plunged on. "So now—if you're counting—we have two families down and one to go. Which is why I'm going away. They've moved, you see, and it's getting complicated. They're not even all together anymore. The boy's gone to school. Summer session, the little sneak. But I have a plan, don't you worry." I stopped and became shrill. "Are you getting any of this, Deanie?"

The hell with it. I was running out of time and had to go. I kissed her on the cheek for the last time and fled the room. As I hurried down the hall I heard her wail "I get it!"

Or maybe I just imagined it.

CHAPTER THREE

LATE NOVEMBER

The boy's body was found by a drunk.

It was two days before Thanksgiving and Lester Brooks was fishing the Housatonic River. Brooksie was in a foul mood. Maybe it was the cold. November that year was the coldest since '55. On top of that, he was out of work and almost out of booze. Being out of booze was worse than out of work, of course. A man needed a pull on a pint of Mother Fletcher's every now and again just to keep himself straight.

In any case, here he was, wearing leaky waders and a pair of grease-stained leather gloves he'd scavenged off the counter at Pearl's Luncheonette, reeling in a frozen line, fishing out of season on posted property.

Of course the game warden knew about Brooksie. He knew Brooksie'd been canned by the college, knew he could use the catch, so he looked the other way. Besides, the raggedy old geezer with the snot-crusted mustache probably wouldn't catch a damn thing. Everyone knew trout and bass didn't bite this time of year. Everyone except Brooksie. Man's got to be desperate to stand in freezing rain, teeth chattering like castanets.

Desperate, yeah. Or crazy.

Folks said the latter. He talks to himself, Brooksie does.

So far all he'd caught was a snow tire, a rusted tricycle, and a silt-covered doll with glassy unblinking eyes. Betsy Wetsy or Tiny Tears. Who the hell could remember and who the hell cared?

"Keeeee-ryst, Sadie. Cold as a sonuvabitch, ain't it?"

Sadie was his wife. She'd been dead going on seven years and was the only one Brooksie talked to at any length. He liked her much better now that she was dead. She didn't ride him, didn't interrupt and didn't talk back.

Needles of sleet stung Brooksie's cheeks. He thought of the pint of Mother in his hip pocket (there was one good pull left) and decided it was high time for a break. He remembered a place about a hundred yards downstream. Our Lady of the Pines, it was called. A rustic chapel made of logs with a fieldstone floor. It was owned by the college and hardly anyone used it this time of year. It would be creepy tipping a bottle in front of the Blessed Virgin but, what the hell, she'd probably seen worse.

He reeled in his line, anchored the hook and picked his way toward shore. Icy water churned around his legs. At the embankment he grabbed hold of a blueberry bush, hoisted himself up, then he made his way toward that chapel pushing through brambles and brush.

As he got closer he heard music. Rock music from the oldies station, WKLB 10.95. Roy Orbison singing about a pretty woman. Damn it to hell! Someone was in there. A couple of horny college kids probably. Playing rock music in a church. Screwing their brains out. Had they no shame?

Brooksie crept to a stained glass window for a look. He shoved his eyeglasses up the bridge of his nose. The image inside was wavery. It took a moment to make out what was going on.

First off he noticed candles, dozens of them, flickering all around. Then he noticed a fella. He wasn't praying and he wasn't screwing. He was leaning back in a pew, head tipped back, like he didn't have a care in the world. His hair was copper colored. It looked like he was taking a snooze.

Then Brooksie spied an object on the floor. Glory be, a bottle of Jack Daniel's. The kid wasn't sleeping—he was drunk. Dead drunk. Ha!

The bottle was half full. Thank you, Jesus!

Maybe the kid had a wallet. If he was drunk, he'd never feel Brooksie's hands skim his pockets.

You'd steal from a man in church, Brooksie? You'd stoop so low?

"Bet your ass."

Brooksie pushed open the heavy oak door and music spilled outside. He slipped in, ready to bolt should the kid wake up. Roy Orbison broke to a commercial. Bath Magic can make your bathtub like new! You have to see it to believe it! Call now for a no-obligation demonstration!

As Brooksie crawled down the aisle feeling like a horse's ass a thought crossed his mind. The boy was awfully still. He wasn't snoring. He hardly seemed to be breathing. Obviously passed out, Brooksie reassured himself, which was good because he was beyond hearing or feeling anything. Brooksie moved more boldly. He would make it to the promised land. He would grab the bottle. He would lift the wallet. He would—

"Holy Mother of Jesus!"

The boy was dead. Candlelight danced on his pretty hair and the lashes of his half-closed eyes. His lips were stretched, revealing orthodontically corrected teeth. Spanky and Our Gang let fly with "Sunday Will Never Be the Same."

"I've lost my Sunday song, he won't be back again!"

He was young. Not a child, but not a man either. His face was smooth as marble, his flesh as white, as stiff, as the clerical collar under his chin. He was from the seminary, eighteen years old or thereabouts, and he would never see another birthday.

"Sunday will never be the same!" Chime-chime-chime-chime!

Brooksie struggled to get up and in the process jostled the

6

body. A precarious balance was disturbed. The boy pitched forward as though to say "Howdy!" He was so close Brooksie could have kissed him.

Instead, he screamed.

CHAPTER FOUR

In Raven's Wing, Connecticut, about eighty miles south of the dead boy, sleet pelted frozen ground, forming glaze thick as shellac. The mournful honks of Canada geese could be heard overhead. Christmas lights were already strung along Main Street and wreaths hung in every window of the wedding cake mansion that was the Community Center.

On High Ridge, Forrest Haggarty cursed Jack Frost and tossed more rock salt on the sidewalk. Irene Purdy baked a pie, the third and final in a series of apple, mince, and pumpkin for her Thanksgiving table. Mildred Bennett and Trevor Bradford worked on the *New York Times* crossword puzzle and sipped honeyed coffee from flowered cups.

Over in the Cannivan house at Ten Covered Bridge Lane a twenty pound turkey sat in the refrigerator, and children dressed for the last day of school before the eagerly anticipated Thanksgiving break. Someone shouted "Where's my homework!" and someone else, "Mom, you forgot to sign my report card!"

"Daniel, hurry up! You're going to miss the bus! Again!"

Louise Cannivan slipped a piece of French toast off the spatula onto Daniel's plate and added two strips of bacon. Even at this hour, she tried to look nice. She wore a white terrycloth robe from Talbot's monogrammed "LCC." Her blond hair was brushed into soft waves that framed her face. She was slightly overweight, the result of twenty years of marriage and five children. Once upon a time her husband told her she looked like Marilyn Monroe, and once upon a time it had been true.

Louise smiled, remembering the time little Michael Logan, a friend of Daniel's, looked at her in amazement and blurted "You're pretty!" It was the nicest compliment she'd had in a long time, heartfelt and true. She'd laughed and given him a hug.

Where Louise was a child, pretty didn't count. Grit did. Her father was poor then, scratching out a living on a dusty farm in Ohio. He never could afford much and was unimpressed by her looks and the grades she brought home from school.

"Think you're really something, don't you, Weezie?"

"No, Daddy. Schoolwork comes easy, is all."

"Well let me tell you something, just because they put you in that gifted and talented class, don't go getting ideas. There's no money for college."

"I know."

"There's lots needs to be done around here. The hen house needs a new roof. We got to get combination storms and screens. The heating bills are bleeding me dry. I need a new tractor. The silo is leaking . . ."

And on and on and on.

"You think money grows on trees?"

"No."

Then he'd snap open another Pabst and crush the old can in his fist. Sometimes he'd cuff her on the head for good measure. And if she cried, he'd laugh and tell her it was just his way of being affectionate. She was too sensitive, he'd say. She didn't have *grit*.

"Got to be tough to make it in this world, Weezie. Got to be tough."

In time she learned to change the As to Bs. It was easy enough. And not to cry, she learned that too.

Maybe she wasn't tough, but later on she got lucky. She married a man who took her away from chickens and squashed beer cans. She married a man of refinement, if not integrity. A man who gave her things.

I never expected to have the life I do, she would have told you. Living in a house like this, belonging to a country club, having all these fine things. It's the American dream and we're lucky ducks. My children have advantages I never had. Ballet lessons. Summer camp. Winter vacations at Stowe or Vail or the Bahamas.

Louise took absolutely none of it for granted. She tried to do everything perfect. Tried to be a good wife. Tried to raise her children right. Tried to make her home like something out of *House and Garden*. And she tried to spread her good fortune around too. The Cannivans supported a Save the Children child in Ecuador. They gave generously to the United Way. On Wednesdays Louise visited shut-ins at the nursing home. She read the paper to them, took them on drives. On Fridays she played the piano at the Senior Center.

She tried to deserve what she had, tried very hard.

I appreciate all this, she would have told you, waving her hand at all *this*.

Lucky ducks.

Sometimes she could hear her father's voice. A fool's paradise, that's where you live, Weezie. A fool's paradise.

His voice played on. *A fool's* . . . She forced herself to ignore it.

She drizzled real maple syrup over Daniel's plate, all the while keeping one ear trained to the local radio station.

Why on earth hadn't they cancelled school? It was sleeting outside, for heaven's sake. When she'd awakened that morning in the king-sized bed that was half empty and heard the crackle of sleet against the window, she rolled over for another forty winks, thinking the kids could sleep in too. Thinking there wouldn't be any school today, or if there was school, it would start late, right?

Wrong. The superintendent was reluctant to call a snow day so early in the year. Cancellations were mentioned for New Canaan, Darien, and Wilton but not for Raven's Wing.

"Daniel!"

"Relax, Mom." Daniel's older sister, twelve-year old Marty, spoke between gulps of orange juice. "He'll be down at the last minute like he always is."

Marty made a grab for Daniel's bacon and Louise smacked her hand with the greasy spatula. "Quit that!" She sat down between Marty and Samantha, her youngest. "I'd feel better if you were both on the same bus, like last year." Marty, who went to middle school, started a full hour later than Daniel. "Why they have the little ones starting first is beyond me. Look at it outside—it's still dark, for heaven's sake." Without thinking, she fed a forkful of French toast into Samantha's gaping mouth. At four Samantha was too old to be fed, but she was a placid child and accepted motherly attention without protest.

Pete Cannivan crashed down the stairs and into the kitchen. "Anyone want a ride this morning? Cannivan's limo service is ready to roll!"

Louise looked up at her number two son. He had just gotten his license and seized every opportunity to use it. "No driving today, Pete. Not in this weather."

"Aw, Mom."

"I mean it. Besides, Dad took your car to the station."

"He what?"

"Don't look so outraged. Dad paid to put that car in running order, remember?" When I was against it, she didn't add. "His has a flat."

"He could have taken the wagon."

"Oh sure, and left me high and dry."

"Jeeze," muttered Peter. "Here I am trying to do everyone a favor." He thought for a moment. "Maybe I could take the wagon."

"Never mind. No one's driving. It's a sheet of ice out there. I'll breathe easier if you all take the bus. They have chains. They have reinforced steel walls. They have experienced drivers."

"The Volvo is a safe car. All the commercials say so."

But she hardly heard him. She looked out the window. "I just hope the weather clears before Kevin starts for home."

"Nothing," said Pete, "will keep Kevin from missing Thanksgiving."

"I get to sit next to Kevin at Thanksgiving dinner," interrupted Marty. "Right, Mom?"

"Right," replied Louise absently. "Peter, please go get your brother. Carry him down bodily if necessary. He's going to miss the bus, and I don't want to drive him today."

She watched Pete upend a bowl of runny oatmeal and pour the contents into his mouth. He hardly seemed to swallow as it traveled uninterrupted into a vast gullet. Almost as an afterthought he swiped a napkin across his lips. "You bet." Then he burped.

Where did they go—the manners she had taught them so patiently? Where? Louise had devoted herself to motherhood. She had come from modest means, from a family who thought nothing of putting a carton of milk on the supper table or reaching in front of your nose to grab a kaiser roll. In high school she studied etiquette books while other students studied for SATs. She learned how to navigate through a bewildering maze of manners and later passed them along to her children. She taught them all the little niceties . . . which fork to use, to keep their napkins in their laps, to ask to be excused at the end of a meal. But with the advent of adolescence manners vanished into a black hole.

"Jeeze," mimicked Samantha.

"Don't say Jeeze, Samantha." Louise called after Peter, "Now see what you've done?"

Marty looked up from her French toast. "You gonna drive Daniel to the bus stop again, Mom?"

"I don't know. Maybe."

"You really should quit that. It's only at the end of the road. The other kids call him a mama's boy."

"Let them." Louise wiped Sam's chin. "He's the only one on this road who goes to elementary school. I don't like him waiting out there by himself."

"I don't know why. This is hardly the South Bronx."

"Souse Bonx!" cried Samantha through a mouthful of strawberry jam.

No, it surely wasn't the "Souse Bonx." It was a desirable cul-de-sac of million dollar homes in Raven's Wing, Connecticut. It was a place Brendan had wanted to move to. An appropriate place, he said, for a newly minted advertising agency president. The man across the way was president of Save Rite Stores and the one next door was a senior partner at Peat Marwick and the one of the other side . . . Well, nobody talked about what he was. He was overextended, that's what. His wife was having panic attacks and breathing into paper bags because they couldn't meet their mortgage payments. She thought she was having heart attacks and didn't believe it when doctor after doctor told her it was all in her head. She confided this to Louise. Everyone confided to Louise, who was an open, friendly midwesterner.

A midwesterner who sometimes felt out of place in this New England town. Of course, she kept quiet about it. Bouts of the blues were to be ignored. You stood up straight and put one foot in front of the other. You smiled and nodded and listened to what Brendan referred to as "women's-trouble talk."

You didn't tell tenuous new friends that your mother died the previous summer, died of lung cancer and drowned in her own blood. They didn't want to hear it. You didn't tell them how much it frightened you that someone so caring and good could be devoured by something so painful and ugly. You didn't tell them that it planted an ember of fear inside you, fear that all *this* could be lost. That now you watched your family with fiercely protective eyes. You managed your house with organizational skills worthy of General Patton. You watched out for your children. You protected them. You drove them to the bus stop. You had them call when they arrived at a friend's house. You felt a twinge of panic when they got a nosebleed because last summer little Nathan Schuster had nosebleeds and it turned out to be leukemia and, my God, what if it had happened to one of your own?

"You worry too much," Brendan would scoff. "Especially when it comes to the kids. You'll smother them, Louise. Let them go. Let them grow."

"I let them grow," she said back. "Look at Kevin. Off to college." She sighed.

Brendan gave her an absentminded squeeze. "You miss him."

"Yes."

He was a good husband in many ways. A hard worker, a good provider, a leader of corporate battalions. But Brendan was gone most of the time. He got up at 5:00 to catch the 6:15 train to New York so he could be at his desk at 7:30. On days when there were no late meetings or client dinners, he managed to get home at 7:15, gulp a martini, and rush to the dinner table so they could eat as a family at 7:30. It was late for Samantha and Daniel, but Louise had a thing about families eating dinner together. So many children in Fairfield County saw their fathers only on weekends. She didn't want Brendan to be a stranger to his own kids. Or to me, she thought. She sighed. It was a little late for that.

"Hey, Samantha . . . look!" Marty stuffed an entire hard-boiled egg into her mouth and peeled back her lips. Samantha shrieked with delight.

"Marty, that's for your lunch."

Marty spat the egg into her hands. "I'll buy lunch today. They're having pizza."

"I thought you didn't like school pizza."

Pete bounded into the kitchen carrying Daniel over one hip like a sack of grain and dumped his little brother into a chair.

13

Daniel's shirt was buttoned crooked and his belt had skipped over two loops. Louise looked at him and couldn't help but smile. He was Robin Williams in miniature. Daniel her clown, Daniel her dreamer.

"They put pine needles on the pizza," said Daniel. "Yuck."

Louise pushed the plate toward Daniel. "Here honey, eat your breakfast."

"Spice," corrected Marty. "I asked the cafeteria lady, Mrs. Marinelli, and she said that's what it is. Spice." Her eyes lit up. "But if you don't like their pizza, you can have this egg." She held it out to Daniel, deftly concealing the tooth marks. "For your lunch. Go ahead, it's never been used."

Daniel eyed the egg warily. Any gift from his sister was automatically suspect.

"Never mind," said Louise. She snatched the egg from Marty's hand and stuffed it down the disposal. She unhitched Daniel's belt and re-inserted it through the loops. She tied his shoe and rebuttoned his shirt. "You have an egg of your own in your lunch bag, Daniel. Now eat. Please."

Daniel stabbed four bite-sized pieces of French toast with his fork and stuffed them in his mouth.

I live with human garbage disposals, thought Louise. It's a losing battle. She went to the fridge and took out Daniel's lunch bag. She put it on the counter. She flipped through her mental Rolodex of today's after-school activities, then realized that today was Wednesday, the day before Thanksgiving, and all after-school activities had been cancelled. No cub scouts, no karate, no drum lessons, no Catechism class.

Thank goodness for that. She could use a break from dour Sister Theodora, a.k.a. Attila the Nun. Daniel was always getting in trouble in that class. He was supposed to make First Communion next spring but had almost gotten excommunicated at the age of seven for making fun of Sister. "It looks like brrrrrrread. It tastes like brrrrrrread. But it isn't brrrrrrread. It's that hooooooooooly sacrament!" Then he would writhe around like some kind of evangelical minister covered with snakes. It had become a family joke—"It's that hoooooooly sacrament!" Everyone made fun of Sister Theodora, "a relic in her own time" Pete liked to say. All of them except Kevin, who was very grim on the subject of religion lately. Kevin, always so glib, until recently. Just before he'd gone away to that school he'd become sullen and gloomy.

"You know what Daniel put on his list?" asked Marty as though reading her mind.

Louise set her mouth. Marty liked to stir the pot. As part of his preparation for First Communion, Daniel had to learn how to make a good confession. The children were in the process of considering possible sins that might be confessed. They were supposed to make a list.

"No," replied Louise, "and I don't want to know, young lady."

"You looked!" cried Daniel.

"Well," said Marty with a sniff, "you left it on your dresser. I didn't see any sign telling me not to look. And since when did you commit adultery anyway?"

"Mom!"

"That's enough, Marty." Now where, thought Louise, did he get that?

"Well, it's true, Mom. He put down adultery. And coveting his neighbor's ass. He put that down too." She snickered.

"Shut up!" cried Daniel.

"Oh, Daniel." Louise ruffled his hair. "Maybe you'd better go over your list with me tonight, okay?"

"But I can't think of any sins."

"It's all right. I'm sure we'll come up with something." She decided to change the subject. "What are you taking for Show-and-Tell?"

Daniel's answer was lost in a mass of bread and egg.

"Oh gross!" cried Marty. "You're not gonna let him, are you Mom?"

15

She'd missed it. "Let him what?"

"He wants to take the glass eye."

Pete grinned. "Holy shit. I'd like to be a fly on the wall when he pulls that out."

"Peter!" Louise looked at the clock. She had approximately forty-five seconds to talk Daniel out of taking his grandmother's glass eye to Show-and-Tell. The eye was Daniel's prize possession. Patience had worn a series of them since childhood, when a chicken blinded her right with a well-placed peck. Over the years the artificial eyes had become more and more lifelike, down to tiny red capillaries embedded in the lower half around the pupil. People would peer intently and ask which one was fake. Patience would reply with a smile, "The one with kindness in it."

When Patience lay dying, she asked Louise to tell Daniel he could have anything of hers he wanted. He chose the eye, and Patience found that hilarious.

Wherever she was, Patience was probably having a good laugh about this right now.

"Honey, I don't think it's a good idea."

Daniel's eyes opened very wide and his lower lip stuck out, both bad signs. "How come?"

"Because some people might find it disturbing."

Pete tried to suppress a grin.

"Because some people might find it disgusting!" corrected Marty.

"It is not disgusting! It's Gramma's eye!"

Louise shot a glance at Marty that said hush. "I know, Danny, but some of the children might find it a little unnerving when you pull what looks like a real eye out of the bag. They might get scared."

Marty leaned into her brother's face. "They might throw up."

"Shut up!"

"Martha Cannivan, go brush your teeth. Now!"

Daniel's face flushed and Louise could see tears on the horizon. "I've got to take the eye! I told Mark Hollinger I was bringing it and he didn't believe me! He called me a liar!"

"I see." Daniel had a point. Mark Hollinger was a bully and a braggart. His mother had a big job at Salomon Brothers and left his upbringing to a housekeeper and a nanny. They were both wrecks.

"Besides," wailed Daniel, "I don't have time to think of something else!"

For once Pete spoke up reasonably. "Let him take the eye, Mom. I mean, it could turn out to be educational. The teacher can segue into parts of the body and handicaps and stuff like that."

"What's segue?" asked Daniel.

"Deviate. Veer." Louise looked at the clock. Daniel should have been at the bus stop two minutes ago. She threw up her hands. "Oh all right."

"Jesus," said Marty, "I don't believe this."

"You will stop with that language, young lady!"

Quitting while he was ahead, Daniel ran to the closet and put on his ski jacket. Louise followed at his heels. "Here, put on your slicker too. Over your parka."

"Can I go by myself?"

She wavered. She hadn't finished feeding Samantha. Maybe Pete could drive Daniel to the bus stop.

"Please!"

"Oh all right," she said.

"Goody!"

"You know the rules. Walk on the shoulder of the road. Don't cross the big street. Wait under the covered bridge until the bus comes and the red lights are flashing and Mrs. DeLorenzo motions for you to cross."

"I know, I know." He whirled toward the door.

"Don't I get a kiss?"

"Oh. Yeah." He planted a syrupy kiss on her cheek and ran

17

off. She watched him through the icy windowpane. He carried a paper sack in each hand, one with his lunch and the other with the precious eye. The visor on his rain hat hid his eyes. His red boots slapped against the salted pavement. He vanished around the bend in the road.

Ten minutes later the front doorbell rang.

"You see, monkeys?" said Louise cheerfully. "He missed the bus." She wiped her hands on her apron and went to let Daniel in.

"Mrs. Cannivan? Mrs. Brendan Cannivan?" The state trooper held his hat in his hands.

Louise stared at him blankly, not getting it. Then her heart skipped a beat. Calm down, she told herself. It's probably nothing. She nodded.

The hat turned round and round, like a wheel. The man cleared his throat. "I'm Trooper Stoudt. May I come in for a moment?"

Something in his eyes told Louise that this was not nothing. No, she wanted to say, you may not come in. You may leave this instant. You may let me go finish breakfast with my children, with my—

"Danny!" She tried to push past Trooper Stoudt.

He grabbed her shoulders. "Please, Mrs. Cannivan." Without waiting for permission, he guided her back inside.

He stood in the foyer dripping on her immaculate quarry tile floor. "Is someone here with you?"

She gestured vaguely toward the kitchen. "The children."

"Is there someone you can call? An adult?"

Her lips felt wooden. "About what?" She felt like giving Trooper Stoudt a good shake. She pictured a pea-sized brain rattling inside an aluminum cranium.

Somewhere behind her she heard Pete. "Mom, is everything okay?"

Trooper Stoudt answered for her. "Everything's fine, son. Go call your father. Tell him your mother needs him."

"Mom?"

"Do as he says!" she snapped. She waited until Pete was gone. "Tell me. It's Danny, isn't it? He's been hit by a car."

"I don't know anything about any Danny, ma'am. I'm here about your boy Kevin."

Her hand went to her heart. The weather. He was coming home in a car full of students. Oh God . . . "Has there been an accident?"

"I'm afraid so. I'm sorry, there's no easy way to say this. They found him this morning. He's dead."

CHAPTER FIVE

She awoke in her bedroom, a prison of cabbage roses. A silver-haired man with worried eyes was leaning over her.

"Who are you?" she heard herself say.

"Trevor Bradford. I'm a doctor. Retired. I live down on Main Street. You fainted."

All at once she remembered. "My son is dead." She waited for him to say she had it all wrong.

"I know. I'm sorry."

"How did it happen? I asked, but . . ."

"I don't think they're sure yet." Dr. Bradford looked pained. He patted her hand.

She rolled onto her side and faced the wall. "Never mind. I don't want to know."

The next days were a blur. Louise sleepwalked through them, making motions, feeling as brittle, as empty, as spun glass. Dr. Bradford called the Sunshine Society, which sent a sitter so she and Brendan could drive upstate. They had to identify the body. It's just a formality, said Trooper Stoudt, a legal thing.

She gazed at frosted fields and leafless trees. "Just a formality. A legal thing."

Brendan looked bone weary. His rugged face was deeply lined and his hazel eyes fixed on the road. He couldn't seem to look at her. Every once in a while he would blink in rapid succession like a rabbit or run his hand across his mustache as though trying to smooth it down.

"This doesn't seem real," she said.

He didn't reply.

"I don't understand. Why won't they tell us what happened? He's our son. He died. They should tell us."

"They have to be sure. The pathologist—"

"What is this?" she sneered. "Some kind of puzzle?"

"Louise. They're trying to treat us gently." He took a deep breath. "They think maybe he committed . . ." His voice trailed off.

"Suicide?"

"Yes."

"Stop the car."

"Louise?"

"I'm going to be sick."

He pulled over and waited while she threw up on dead leaves.

When they arrived at the hospital, Brendan left her sitting in the lobby. He vanished behind swinging doors. When he came back, he was holding his body very tight, as though it might break. He nodded once, took her by the elbow and began to maneuver her outside.

She stopped, refusing to cooperate. "Did you see him?"

Brendan looked at her as though she were crazy. "Yes."

"And?"

She wanted him to say "It's all a mistake, Louise. Can you believe it? It's not Kevin at all. Some other boy, a boy that looks like him, yes, but not our Kevin. Thank God."

But he didn't. He looked at her with angry red-rimmed eyes.

"He's dead," he said, biting off the word. He sounded almost glad.

"Brendan, please."

"He looked fine. Just fine."

He always was a handsome boy! Perfect as always!

"But he's not fine! You're telling me he's dead. How can he be fine?"

"Louise."

She had always behaved, always been a good wife, but this was asking too much. She spoke slowly so there could be no mis-understanding. "This is a mistake, Brendan. It's not Kevin. It can't be." She opened her purse and rifled through it. She withdrew her wallet. She ripped out a plastic accordion file and let it spill open. A chain of family pictures trailed to the floor, with recent ones of the children exposed and old ones from years gone by, ones she couldn't bear to part with, sandwiched underneath. With trembling fingers she extracted prints from the plastic compartment reserved for Kevin . . . high school graduation . . . Kevin smiling in a football uniform, his helmet with the snarling tiger cradled in his arm . . . standing next to Meg Cravin in a white tux for the senior prom . . . and there on the bottom, grinning widely for a grade school portrait, his curly red hair clashing against the garish floral backdrop, his face a mass of freckles, his new front teeth too big for his small face.

"No," she repeated. "He's not dead!"

"Louise."

"Look at this letter." She waved it like a flag. "It came the day before yesterday. It's Kevin's handwriting. He's coming home. It says so right here. Read it, Brendan. Please."

"I've read the letter, Louise." People in the lobby were starting to stare. Brendan hated it when people stared. He ran a hand through his hair. "Louise, I think we should go back to the hotel. I think you need to—"

"No! Everyone's lying! Why is everyone lying! I'm going to see for myself. This is an unfortunate misunderstanding, do you hear me? Some poor child is dead, but not mine. I'm going to go in there. I'm going to take a good hard look at what will turn out to be a stranger." She turned to the gawkers in the lobby. "And you can all go to hell!"

"Damn it, Louise, isn't this hard enough?"

She broke past her husband and rushed down the hall. She pushed through two sets of swinging doors and into a white tiled room where she encountered three long tables tipped at a slight angle. They had heavy-duty wire mesh on top and open aluminum troughs underneath. Each trough had a faucet at one end, a drain at the other.

A sheeted form lay on the middle table, head high on a block of wood.

Why so many tables? She wondered. Do people die in threes? Is it some kind of magic number?

Then she realized it was because of tragedies. Car wrecks. Fires. Shoot-outs at Dunkin' Donuts. Stack 'em up, roll 'em in, move 'em out.

But Louise's family didn't have tragedies. They were special. Blessed. Her family lived in Raven's Wing, Connecticut. They went to St. Mary's Church on Sunday. Her children played Little League and belonged to scouts and caught frogs at Great Pond. Her children didn't die alone in some *godforsaken* chapel in the middle of—

She lifted the sheet.

"Brendan, what are the kids doing?"

"I don't know, honey." He was stretched back in the chaise, a straw hat tipped rakishly over his eyes. *"Building a sand castle or*

something. *How about seizing the opportunity for some connubial bliss.*" He pushed the hat up, leaned over and nibbled her ear.

"*Not here, big boy.*" She put a cold can of Diet Pepsi against his stomach.

"*Yikes!*"

She craned her neck, looking for the others. They'd been joined by two other families, the Matthews and the Wylies, for a one-week vacation at Myrtle Beach. It was a luxury for everyone. They all had little children and money was tight. But by pooling resources they'd been able to afford a slightly dilapidated cedar shingled house five blocks from the beach.

"*I don't like it,*" she said. "*They're too quiet.*"

"*How can you tell in this crowd? Come on, Louise, they're fine. Dottie's with them.*"

"*I'll just be a minute.*" She stood up and readjusted her bikini bottom. "*Watch Petie, okay?*" Louise waved at her youngest who was seated in wet sand at the water's edge, shovel in hand.

"*Maaaaaa!*" He waved a streamer of seaweed.

"*As long as you're up, get me a lemonade, okay?*"

She picked her way through the maze of oiled bodies.

"*Okay?*" he called after her.

"*Right,*" she called over her shoulder. "*Lemonade.*"

She saw them as she jogged over the crest of the dune. Dottie was standing there like a drill sergeant or camp counselor, hands on the hips of a bathing suit with a pleated skirt designed to minimize her thighs. Mickey, Roland, Paulie, and little Marybeth were kneeling in a circle, building some kind of enormous mound with sand.

Where was Kevin? She scanned the group again and felt a tingle of alarm.

She ran down to them, sidestepping beach blankets, kicking sand, dodging Scotch coolers. "*Kevin!*" she cried. "*Kevin!*"

Dottie turned with a big smile on her face. "*They wanted to bury—*"

"*Where's Kevin?*" she demanded.

"Relax, Weezie." Dottie stepped back. "He's right here."

Louise looked at the elongated mound of damp sand. Sticking from the base of one end was Kevin's head. His little feet poked through the other. He was laughing hysterically.

"The kids wanted to bury someone, and Kevin volunteered."

She felt relieved and slightly foolish. "Oh." She tried to smile.

She watched as the children piled on more sand. Small hands flew in the air. Roland worked with a sprinkling can, dampening the mound, then tamping it with pudgy hands into cake-like firmness. Kevin's head bobbed up and down as he laughed and laughed.

Kevin has a heart murmur. *It was a whisper.*

The doctor had said it was nothing to worry about. Lots of children have heart murmurs, he said. They grow up fine.

Was she imagining it, or did Kevin's lips look blue?

"Kevin? Honey?"

He looked up and stopped laughing. His eyes locked with hers. Suddenly he gasped. She watched in horror as his eyes rolled back and he went limp. His head flopped sideways.

She clutched Dottie's arm. "Dottie!"

"What's wr—, oh God!"

The two of them fell to their knees and began digging frantically. The children shrank back, bewildered. Marybeth started to whimper.

"Kevin!" cried Louise. "Kevin!"

They clawed through the wet sand, scraping knuckles, ripping manicured nails. Please God, she thought. Please. Let him be all right. Her mind raced. She would scoop him up and carry him to the lifeguard. No, there wasn't time. She would breathe air into his lungs. She would—

"Does anyone know CPR!" she screamed.

"I'll go get help," said Dottie. She stumbled once in the sand, then raced toward the boardwalk.

Louise brushed sand from Kevin's inert body. She grabbed him by the shoulders. Please, she thought, please be all right. "Kevin!" she cried. "Kevin!"

His eyes opened. He grinned. "Fake out!"

She wanted to smack him, to kiss him, to shake him like a rag doll. But all she did was hug his sandy body to hers and blink back tears of relief.

"Don't you ever do that again! Do you hear me? Do you?"

She touched his unshaven cheek. She ran her finger across his lips.

Fake out.

She smoothed back a thatch of red hair. She leaned down and kissed him for the last time.

"Aw, Mom."

The words hit her in the stomach. She froze, waiting to hear him again. But the only sound was the muffled drone of the hospital intercom.

"Paging Dr. Kearney. Dr. Tom Kearney, line eight. Paging Dr. Fishman. Dr. Hal Fishman, line two . . ."

She had imagined the whole thing. Kevin was gone. She let the sheet drop.

"Kevin Cannivan. Dr. Kevin Cannivan, line six."

Her hand flew to her mouth and she stifled a cry.

She felt Brendan behind her. "Louise?"

She turned and buried her face in his shoulder. "I think I'm losing my mind."

"We'll get through this, Louise. I don't know exactly how, but we will."

"Had he been drinking?"

He hesitated. "Some."

"I see." As if that explained anything.

"The doctor wants to talk to us. Do you feel up to it?"

She lied and said yes.

The doctor turned out to be a wiry Puerto Rican named Ramírez. He looked about fifteen and had brooding dark eyes. His voice was kind and patient. He looked into their stunned faces and explained everything. There would be an autopsy, he said, but the medical examiner felt certain it would confirm his preliminary findings. He named the cause of death. The words sounded like Latin. Louise asked him to translate, and he did, elaborating in some detail. "No," she said. "Kevin couldn't have died like that. Kevin wouldn't have—"

"There's nothing to be ashamed of," interrupted Ramírez. "This happens more often than you think. Families hush it up. But they shouldn't." His voice became gentle again. "It's an accident. A tragic, terrible accident. Don't, for God's sake, be ashamed."

But they were.

C H A P T E R   S I X

Brendan drove her to a seedy hotel in the center of town. The Coldwater Arms. It smelled of Lysol and mold. The management seemed determined to celebrate Christmas early. Or perhaps the hotel was a broken record, playing Christmas over and over again all year long. To Louise, everything seemed out of place—the twinkling Christmas lights in the lobby, the desk clerk with an overly made-up clown face, the tinny carols piped into the hallways.

The room was a knotty pine coffin. Louise studied a card which informed her that, if she was willing to rent a VCR, a selection of tapes was available, all of them old: *A Kiss Before Dying; Defending Your Life; Ghost.* On regular TV, Channel 5 in a marvelous twist of irony was once again showing *It's a Wonderful Life.*

Brendan would go to the school to accept condolences from Kevin's advisor, pack Kevin's things, and fill out forms.

Does one have to formally withdraw from school, wondered Louise, even if one is dead? Will Kevin get failing grades if we don't fill out proper paperwork? Should we advise Selective Service? Is there a book I can turn to for guidance? Are there any rules?

He looked at her. "You'll be all right?"

"I'm going to take a nap," she replied, not answering the question.

"We'll go to dinner when I get back, okay?"

Once upon a time she would have been delighted to have an evening alone with him. Once upon a time she would have looked forward to dinner out, just the two of them. Now she felt nothing.

"Sure." She waited until he got to the door. "I've got a question."

His hand poised on the glass knob. "Yes?"

"Was it an accidental suicide or a suicidal accident?"

"Louise."

"I want to get it straight."

He turned away—"I'll be back soon as I can"—and closed the door behind him.

She stared at the door for a moment, then closed the curtains and took a pill. Dr. Bradford had prescribed them reluctantly, reminding her in a voice so infuriatingly reasonable that sedation "only postpones grief."

Louise lay on the lumpy bed and closed her eyes. Sometimes, she thought, sedation is good. Like last June. We could all have used some sedation then. That was when this whole thing started.

She remembered finding Kevin in the kitchen one night at two A.M., sipping a glass of ginger ale. At least she assumed it was ginger ale. She poured herself a brandy and sat down.

"So," she said lightly, "can't sleep?"

He took a sip from the glass and nodded.

It's the pressure, she assured him. College admissions. The

heavy course load. Those AP courses. Baseball and track. The job at Friendly's on Saturdays. All of it. She suggested he cut back, try to relax a bit, enjoy the finish of his senior year.

"It's not that." He looked away.

"What is it then, Kevin? You haven't been yourself since the prom. You've got to put that behind you. Stop blaming yourself. It was an accident. Not your fault. Meg's going to be fine. I saw her in town the other day. The bruises are almost gone and her smile will be pretty as ever." It was amazing what good dental work could do.

"I'm not blaming myself!"

Don't be so sharp with me, she almost snapped. But she bit her tongue. Of course he was blaming himself. She could see it. And it wasn't right. It hadn't been his fault. On the way home from the prom, a deer jumped in front of the car. Kevin veered off the road and into a stone wall. Meg, not wanting to wrinkle her pretty dress, hadn't been wearing her seat belt. She slammed into the dash. When Louise got to the emergency room, Meg's pink prom dress was covered with blood. And her face . . . Louise winced remembering what her face looked like.

"I'm not going to Yale."

He jumped tracks so suddenly she wasn't sure she'd heard correctly. It was two A.M. She was tired. "Excuse me?"

"I've been accepted at St. Sebastian's College." His jaw hardly moved as he spoke. "Into their seminary program."

She waited for some kind of punch line. Somewhere he'd hidden a camera for America's Funniest Videos. She leaned forward and grinned. "April Fool, right?"

But it wasn't April Fool. He meant it. She could tell, the way he wouldn't look her in the eye. Her smile dissolved and her fingers wrapped themselves around the brandy snifter. She breathed evenly. Something was askew here. Something wasn't right.

"Look," she said, trying to remain calm, "it's late and we're both tired. We'll talk about this in the morning, okay?"

"Now's as good a time as any. You may as well know. Dad too. It's what I'm going to do."

"Kevin . . ." Her voice edged up shrilly and she forced it back down. He never responded to displays of emotion. "This is crazy. You never talked about this before. You've been accepted at Yale, for heaven's sake. We had a party celebrating that fact." She hammered that point home, as though the party cast his acceptance to Yale in concrete. "It's where you said you wanted to go. You didn't even apply to this St. Sebastian's place." She knew this because she'd labored over all his applications. She'd visited all the campuses. Colby, Dartmouth, Middlebury, Yale, and not some podunk Catholic college called St. Sebastian's, God only knew where.

"I changed my mind, okay?"

"No," she said, "it most certainly is not okay. If you want a Catholic college, we'll consider a transfer to Georgetown or Notre Dame after your first year at Yale."

He slammed his hand down on the table. "No!"

A kitty-cat saltshaker went spinning and she grabbed it. Suddenly Louise was afraid. Everything was out of whack.

"Kevin, you're talking crazy."

"It's what I'm going to do. I've made up my mind."

She stood up and steadied herself on the edge of the table. She set down the saltshaker as though it might explode. In her mind she groped for an ally. "What about Meg? What does she think about this?"

He looked at her like this was the biggest joke of all. "Meg? She's glad, Mom." He stood up and shoved in the chair, hard. "Glad!"

He started to leave, then stopped. He turned and gave her a kiss on the cheek. "Don't worry. It's not the end of the world. Some parents would even be proud."

But Louise didn't feel proud, not at all. She was confused and angry. He was throwing his life away. It was all wrong. It wasn't what they'd planned. She took the empty glasses to the sink. She looked into his and sniffed. She thought maybe it did smell like ginger ale. It slipped from her fingers and shattered on the tile floor.

Brendan wasn't any happier than she was.

"I've never heard of this school," he said the next day.

"It has a good reputation in some circles," said Kevin.

"Not any circle I'm aware of."

"It's got the program I want."

"Program?" repeated Brendan evenly. "What kind of program?"

"St. Sebastian's is affiliated with a seminary, Dad."

"Christ," exploded Brendan, "give me a break."

She and Bren decided not to pressure him. Kevin would come to his senses over the summer. Young men entering the seminary at St. Sebastian's were required to attend a summer session. Let him have a taste of that, said Brendan. Getting up at 5:00 A.M. Going to Mass daily. Studying Catholic theology, for God's sake.

Nobody became a priest anymore, for crying out loud. Yes, the Cannivans were Catholic but not to that degree. They kept their religion neatly compartmentalized. Louise and the children went to church on Sunday and, if it was convenient, on holy days of obligation. Brendan went with them at Christmas and Easter. Louise sang in the choir. The children received religious instruction. Children need some kind of foundation, after all. But Louise and Brendan kept things in perspective. They didn't wear religion on their sleeves and certainly never intended to raise a family of fanatics.

So they didn't tell Yale. They waited for Kevin to come home with his tail between his legs. "Just wait," said Brendan. "He'll be back by the end of July."

But he wasn't. July dissolved into August. When the bill from Yale arrived for first semester fees, Brendan was finally forced to write a letter saying that Kevin Cannivan was withdrawing. And Brendan was finally forced to accept Kevin's choice of school, if not his choice of vocation.

"At least this school is co-ed," he muttered one night as they got ready for bed.

"I thought seminarians were supposed to be cloistered or something."

"It's a pilot program. They attend the regular college and mingle with other students. The seminarians are a small part of the student body. There are less than twenty of them. The others are all normal kids."

"Our kid is normal," said Louise.

"I know." But the words sounded hollow.

"I suppose we should look at the bright side," said Louise. "He could be on drugs. He could have gotten some girl pregnant."

"That might have been preferable. At least we could fix it."

Louise was incredulous. "Fix it?"

"Come on, Louise. We've always paved the way for the kids. Made things easier than they were for us. Don't pretend. We'd damn well fix it if he got some girl pregnant. You know we would."

"Well," she said primly, "this appears beyond fixing."

Now she lay on a lumpy bed in the Coldwater Arms, staring at a stain on the ceiling. I thought things were beyond fixing then. But look at us now.

It took a long time to fall asleep, a long time wondering how her son could do this to himself. And to her.

CHAPTER SEVEN

It didn't take long for the light to go out in their room. Ten o'clock they went to bed. I wondered what they were doing up there. The nasty, no doubt. That's what people do in hotel rooms, don't they? They do the nasty and leave pecker tracks. But never mind. Best not to think about that. Best to work fast.

The wire worked well—practice makes perfect—and the door of the Volvo swung open with nary a creak. A dusting of snow fell away from the hood as I lifted it up. They'd parked under a streetlamp, which was helpful but not imperative. I've studied Volvos, you see. I know their insides like the palm of my hand. I knew right where to go.

I could work in the dark, if I had to. I could work blind-folded.

I removed the air cleaner and went to work replacing the Cotter pins.

"Car trouble?"

Dear God. I shoved in the pins with trembling fingers and wheeled around, the screwdriver tight in my fist. A fat police-man floated toward me like a blimp. Snow muffled his footsteps. He drifted closer, aiming a flashlight at my face. I blocked the beam with my ungloved hand.

"All fixed," I said, trying to breathe easy.

"Let me have a look. I'm a car buff."

"It's fine. Really. I heard a rattle on the Turnpike, but there's noth—"

"Won't hurt to have a second opinion. Volvo, huh? An oldie but goodie. These things run forever."

He shined the beam under the hood, then put his head in. I thought about plunging the screwdriver into his back. I could have done it quick and easy. The street was deserted. No one would have heard.

"Looks okay to me . . . Hey, wait a minute. Your air cleaner's missing."

"Yes, I have it right—"

"You got a potential problem here. I almost missed it. See there . . ." He aimed the beam into the guts and waited for me to join him. "There." He wiggled a pin with his fingers. "These need to be replaced. They're loose. Corroded."

"I'll see to it, officer. First thing in the morning."

"Try the Texaco on Main Street. They'll fix it in a jiffy."

"I will. Thanks."

Should I kill him or should I not? He's seen my face.

"Where you headed?"

"Burlington." He's seen my face.

"Hmmm. Well, you can stay at the hotel for the night. They're never booked, 'cept parents weekend at the college."

"I already got a room. Thanks for your help, officer."

"Don't mention it."

I touched my face. Maybe it wouldn't matter.

He turned and walked away, not knowing how lucky he was.

CHAPTER EIGHT

As he backed out of the parking lot Brendan's eyes went reflexively to the rearview mirror. The view was obstructed by piles of Kevin's clothing and cartons of books, cassette tapes and compact disks. On top of the heap lay a tennis racket, a lacrosse stick and a pair of ski poles. "Can't see a damn thing."

"Stop then. I'll rearrange—"

"No. I'll manage. When we get to Raven's Wing, we'll drop this stuff at the Thrift Shop."

"We will not!"

"I'm trying to make it easier for everyone, Louise. Easier for you. Easier for the kids."

"Never mind easy. This will not be easy. There is no reason it should be easy. We are going through hell."

He twisted the wheel and backed out. "Whatever you say."

She dozed for a while and woke up as they were pulling onto 95. "We should talk," he said.

"About what?"

"About what we're going to tell people."

She didn't get it at first, and when she did the words came in a rush. "Dr. Ramírez said we shouldn't be embarrassed. He said it happens more often than people know. If people knew about it, he said, it would happen less. Boys would be careful. Boys wouldn't—"

"I *know* what he said, Louise. Easy for him." He gunned the car and shot into the center lane. Brendan was always aggressive behind the wheel. Behind them a semi screamed. "Shit, just what we need. It's starting to sleet. We'll tell them Kevin fell. That he broke his neck."

A lie.

Autoerotic asphyxia. She'd been saying it in her mind. Practicing. It sounded exotic. Foreign. Not deadly, not really. If she said it enough, maybe it would become meaningless and bland like *stubbed toe.* She said it: "Autoerotic asphyxia."

"Louise."

"Explain it to me, Brendan."

"Dr. Ramírez already did. Thoroughly."

"Well, explain it again. I'm a slow learner."

His mouth compressed. The car rocked into the fast lane. They never discussed things like this. Private things. Sordid things. He took a deep breath. "Sometimes when boys masturbate—do you really want to hear this?"

"Yes."

He emitted a long-suffering sigh. "They intentionally cut off the flow of oxygen to the brain."

"Hence," she said it hard, "the rope."

"Yes. It heightens the pleasure of orgasm, or so they say."

They. "Have you ever . . . ?"

"No! For God's sake. I didn't even know about this. It's crazy. A goddamn dangerous trick. A boy can pass out. If no one's there to remove the rope—"

"The boy dies."

He nodded grimly as if to say "Satisfied?"

"But I don't think Kevin would—"

"He would. Believe it, Louise. Kids are crazy. They do dumb things. They think they're immortal. And that celibacy crap didn't help. Kevin liked the ladies. He was a normal boy with a healthy sex drive. So he sought . . ." He groped for words. ". . . other outlets."

She looked out the window and blinked hard.

35

"We mustn't discuss this again. Ever. We have other children to think of. He fell. He broke his neck. We'll keep it simple."

A lie should be simple.

They drove in silence for a while. He was going awfully fast, but Louise didn't care. "Brendan, I have a thought."

"What?"

"Maybe he was with someone. I mean, it could have happened that way, right?"

"No. Dr. Ramírez said there was no evidence—"

"Dr. Ramírez," she shot back. "He seemed awfully eager to tie this up in a neat little package. Get it out of the way quick. God forbid the college should be embarrassed. What about that advisor Father Reilly? What was he like?"

"Father Duffy. He was nice. Very sympathetic. It was awkward. He's probably worried about a lawsuit. Everyone sues these days. Not us, though. Not the Cannivans. I assured him—"

"Brendan, please slow down."

He eased up on the gas, but the car sailed on at breakneck speed. "Jesus!"

"What, Brendan?"

The pedal was flat on the floor. "I can't stop!"

"Well, do something!"

"I'm trying, Louise! Jesus!"

They were all over the road. Brendan pumped the brake frantically and fought with the steering wheel. They narrowly missed a van, then a truck, then a Jeep. Horns screamed.

"The key!" cried Louise. "Remove the key!" She clawed at it, missed, then clawed again. Finally she made contact. She pulled, but it wouldn't disengage. Then she remembered and twisted it counterclockwise. The key came free in her fingers. Triumphant, she held it up.

But Brendan's face was white and his eyes were fixed on the

road ahead. The steering wheel was locked in his hands. His eyes widened. Louise followed his gaze and gasped as the car plunged into the back of the tractor-trailer they'd passed just minutes before.

CHAPTER NINE

"Amazing," was what the trooper had said over and over again. Amazing. And "lucky," that too. If the truck hadn't been moving to minimize the impact, if they hadn't been driving a Volvo, if another car had rear-ended them . . . if, if, if . . . they would have been dead. Seriously maimed at the very least. As it was, they escaped without a scratch.

"Totalled," said Brendan as they drove home in a rattletrap rental from Budget. "That's supposed to be lucky?"

"Kevin's things are ruined," added Louise miserably. They were stashed in the trunk, broken and soggy.

"I know, honey." He reached over and squeezed her hand.

"I should have had the car serviced. It was due. I was distracted, getting ready for Thanksgiving."

"I know."

"What did he say it was?"

"The linkage. It can go in an old car." He almost added that the linkage would have been checked had the car been serviced, but stopped himself.

"I should have—"

"Shoulduv, woulduv, coulduv. Let's forget it, Louise. Put it behind us. Put . . . everything . . . behind us."

* * *

"I'm sorry to be a pest, officer, but surely you can appreciate my concern . . . That's right. Brendan and Louise Cannivan. They were due home hours ago, and what with the roads as slick as they are, I'm beside myself . . . Yes, I'll hold . . . Hurry up, you stupid son of a bitch . . . Yes, I'm here . . . An accident! Dear God! Are they . . . They what? . . . *Survived?* . . . No, I'm fine. Overcome with emotion. Such wonderful news. Praise God. What hospital did you say? . . . None? No injuries whatsoever? . . . A miracle, yes indeed. Thank you, officer. Thank you very much."

I set down the phone. "God damn them to hell!"

Survived.

"We'll see about that. We'll just see!"

CHAPTER   TEN

Three days later they had the funeral service. Faces loomed and she felt her hand being squeezed. Meg Cravin wore a dark green dress and a tiny gold neck chain. There were no scars, no bruises. Her teeth glinted under a latticework of braces.

You survived, Louise wanted to say, and my son didn't. I hate you. "How good of you to come, Meg."

"I'm so sorry, Mrs. Cannivan. I . . ." She faltered, fighting tears.

Teenage girls, thought Louise. Always so emotional. Spare me.

"I thought St. Sebastian's would be good for Kevin."

Louise attached no significance to these words. "St. Sebastian's killed him," she said, not batting an eye.

Meg burst into tears and fled.

After the funeral Louise fell apart. For one thing, she heard voices, voices going round and round in her head. Kevin talked to her. As did Meg Cravin. As did Kevin's teachers. She felt like a convention center. And when she wasn't having internal dialogues, she was hearing bells. She would run to the front door and no one would be there.

Brendan said she needed rest. Dr. Bradford said she needed to be with people. And therapy, she needed that too, a suggestion she flatly rejected. She hugged her grief tight. It was her only comfort.

Her courtesy was gone and so was her patience. When the woman next door resumed her tearful litany about heart palpitations, Louise suggested that she trade her paper bag for plastic. And one day she smacked Samantha across the face for not eating her breakfast. Afraid she might do it again, she enrolled her youngest child in day care, something she'd sworn she'd never do.

As soon as the children were off to school she would head to Kevin's room to do her morning's work. She vacuumed, dusted, and washed windows. She did it again and again. There was always a speck of dust, a shred of lint, or the ghost of a smudge that caught her eye. She wanted the room to be perfect and told herself cleaning was therapeutic.

When she wasn't cleaning, she was sorting. She sorted through remains of Kevin's childhood—the photos on the dresser, coins from the family's trip to the Caribbean, baseball cards and a slinky and Bazooka bubble gum wrappers and cans of stale tennis balls. She listened to his records. *Iron Maiden. Kiss. Def Leppard.*

One of his merit badges was coming off the sash so she sewed it on with heavy-duty thread. Before she knew it, she was cutting his clothes into neat little squares and sewing a quilt. She would create a masterpiece of memories. The first fish he caught. The trumpet he played for a month and then abandoned. The Camp

Hidden Valley logo. It made sense to her. Quilts were very "in." There was a quilt for AIDS and *People Magazine* had a story about a woman who made a quilt about her divorce. A therapist husband bought it for his therapist wife for five thousand dollars.

But Louise would never sell her quilt. Not for five thousand, not for five million. She kept it hidden in a closet.

When she wasn't cleaning, sorting, or sewing, she was searching, going through his dresser and closet, looking for reasons that weren't there. She unearthed stray socks, a Batman mask from some long ago Halloween, and stabbed herself on a geometry protractor. She sucked her finger and rocked back and forth.

Afternoons were devoted to serious drinking. It started off with a cocktail after lunch. To calm her nerves, she said. Soon she was having two, then three, then . . . well, who was counting?

One day she was sitting on the floor, Brandy Alexander in hand, when she became aware of bells. This, of course, was nothing new. She set down the drink and pressed her hands to her ears. "Oh, shut up!"

The ringing continued relentlessly.

She edged over to a window and peered through the sheers. Just as she expected, no one was there. Then she realized it was the phone. This was a new trick, a new torment. She reached for the sleek white Trimline, intending to rip it from the wall, but changed her mind at the last second.

"Hello?"

"Mrs. Cannivan?"

The voice was a whisper, a hiss.

"Yes?"

"I'm calling about Kevin . . . I'm . . ."

"What?" snapped Louise. "What are you?"

"Sorry."

Another condolence call, that's all it was. "So am I," she replied. "Thank you for calling."

"Wait!"

Louise paused.

"I probably shouldn't be saying this. It won't bring Kevin back and will probably make things worse. But you should know. You have a right."

"Know what? Who is this?"

"Never mind. You should know . . ." The person took a deep breath.

Louise waited, scarcely breathing.

"It wasn't an accident."

She clutched the receiver. The line was eerily silent. She tried not to whimper. "Please," she said. "What are you saying?"

"I'm saying someone did it to him."

"But why?" she wailed. "Why would anyone do such a horrible thing?"

The person hesitated. "Kevin had a few enemies."

"Who? Please! You've got to tell me!"

"I shouldn't have told you this much. I'm sorry. I—"

"Don't leave! Please!" She started to cry.

"Maybe you and your husband should come up. To ask some questions, you know?" Very gently, the person hung up.

Louise stood there listening to a dial tone. Finally, she set the receiver in the cradle. She went to the kitchen and made a pot of strong coffee.

She had a germ of an idea. She didn't know how she would accomplish it. She had to think it through. But first she had to sober up.

As soon as Brendan got home she told him about the call. It was a mistake.

"You were drinking again, weren't you?"

"No."

"All right. What time did this person call?" He waited, arms crossed. "Five o'clock? Four? Three? Two? Well, Louise? Well?"

"I don't know."

"Was it a man or a woman?"

"A woman. I'm pretty sure."

"Did you record the call on the machine?"

"No." It had never occurred to her.

"Very well. You didn't record the call. We get a crank call and you have no proof."

"It wasn't a crank call. It was real."

"Right."

She realized he didn't believe her. He didn't believe there had been a call at all. He believed she was cracking up. She never should have told him about the voice in the hospital. Ever since then he tiptoed around her and talked about psychiatrists.

"There was a call, Brendan. The caller said it wasn't an accident."

"I've read the police report. There is no doubt, Louise, no doubt at all."

Louise's voice escalated shrilly. "Well, I have doubts! I have plenty of doubts! Do you think the way Kevin died was normal?"

"Of course not. But we have to accept it."

She hardly heard him. "There are lots of ways to die, Brendan, lots of ways people do themselves in. I'm aware of them. I've considered them for myself. They're listed in this." She thrust a book in his face. *The Enigma of Suicide.*

"Where the hell did you get that?"

She flipped to page 235. "People jump into volcanos, vats of beer, crocks of vinegar, retorts of molten glass, white-hot coke ovens, or slaughterhouse tanks of blood."

"Stop, Louise."

"They throw themselves on buzz saws, thrust hot pokers down their throats, suffocate in refrigerators or chimneys, lock themselves into high-altitude test chambers, crash airplanes, jump from airplanes . . ." She inhaled.

"Louise, for God's sake—"

". . . lie in front of steamrollers, throw themselves on the third rail, touch high-tension wires, place their necks in vises and turn the handle. They hug stoves and climb into lions' cages. They blow themselves up with cannons, hand grenades or dynamite."

"The children, Louise. The children will hear—"

But Louise wasn't finished. "They bore holes in their heads with power drills, drink Drano, swallow poisonous spiders or firecrackers, pierce their hearts with corkscrews—"

He slammed the book from her hand.

She crumpled to the floor like a marionette with cut strings, and he stood there, looking down at her. Finally he knelt. "You've got to get help. We can't go on like this."

"You never loved him," she whimpered. "You've always hated him. Ever since—"

"How can you say that? I *helped* him, Louise."

Daniel appeared at the door.

"Go to bed," snapped Brendan.

"Did Mommy have a bad dream?"

Eyes of father and son locked. The bewilderment in Daniel's matched Brendan's. "Yes."

"Is Mommy sad?"

"Yes."

"Is she sad about Kevin?"

"Yes! Now go to bed!"

Cringing but determined, Daniel edged over and planted a kiss on his mother's cheek. "You still have me, Mommy."

How can I be doing this? she wondered. How? "I know, sweetie." She rose to her knees determined to pull herself together. She gave Daniel a hug. "You want me to tuck you in?"

His face lit up. For the past two weeks Brendan had been performing bedtime duty—listening to prayers, fetching glasses of water, tucking him in—with a lack of enthusiasm that was all too apparent. "Uh huh."

When she came to bed, Brendan lay staring at the ceiling. "We have to do something, Louise."

43

"I know."

"I think you should see a professional, someone who can help."

"You mean a shrink."

"Someone who understands."

"No one understands."

"There's nothing shameful about counseling. We could all go, if that would be easier. The whole family."

"You keep talking about easy."

"No I don't."

"Always trying to make things easier. Well, it wouldn't be easy, Brendan. Do you really want to open Pandora's Box? We'd have to talk about more than Kevin."

"What are you getting at, Louise?"

"We'd have to talk about our marriage."

"I don't see why."

She sat up and looked at him. He was actually serious. "We haven't had sex in more than a year."

"That hasn't been my choice."

"No." She rolled over. "Lisa is your choice."

That shut him up quick. Perhaps he was stunned that she'd finally said it out loud. She didn't really care.

"She's nothing, Louise. I'll get rid of her."

He spoke of his secretary as though she were a stray cat or a case of the clap.

"Do what you want. I don't care anymore."

CHAPTER ELEVEN

The next day a woman in a mink coat materialized on Louise's doorstep. She had elegant frosted hair and sympathetic blue eyes. She looked like Gena Rowlands. The bulldog at her side wore a red knit sweater monogrammed "WLB." Ropes of drool hung from bulbous pink gums.

Louise eyed the woman warily.

"Mrs. Cannivan?"

"If you're from Welcome Wagon, I'm not in the mood."

"Oh no. I—"

"Or if it's about those tickets to the AAUW Christmas luncheon, I know I said I'd sell them, but I can't. You'll have to take them back."

"Mrs. Cannivan, I'm from neither of those organizations. I—"

"Well then, what is it? Spit it out. What do you want?" She waited for the woman to dematerialize. Waited to see her lipstick smile compress into a thin line of outrage. Waited to see her flee. But she stood her ground.

"I'm Mildred Bennett. Dr. Bradford told me you were having a hard time."

"The old blabbermouth. What is it with this town? Doesn't anyone mind their own business?"

Mildred didn't flinch. "I also heard about your son from someone else. A young friend of mine. Cameron Maine."

Kevin's roommate. Louise feigned indifference. "So."

"So I wanted to pay you a visit. I wanted to offer . . ."

"What?" Louise looked at a white bakery box in the woman's hand. "Condolences and coffee cake? I don't want them. I don't need them."

"I think you do."

"And what do you know about it?" She started to shut the door in the woman's face.

Mildred inserted the box between the door and the frame. "Quite a lot, I'm afraid. My son committed suicide. A long time ago."

Louise stared at the crushed box.

"It might help to talk about it. With someone who's been there."

Louise opened the door and backed into the foyer.

To Mildred Bennett, Louise Cannivan looked like a crazed possum. Her raggedy terry robe was stained . . . her hair frizzed on the ends with the remnants of an old perm . . . her eyes peering from puffy pockets . . . her feet bare against the cold tile floor. Mildred had seen suburban women like that before. She called them the Double D's. Daytime Drinkers.

She busied herself wiping Winston's paws, then removed his sweater.

"WLB?"

"Winston Leopold Bennett. Winston, after Churchill. Leopold because it means king."

"I see." The dog didn't look very regal. He looked old and arthritic. He lumbered painfully toward a heating register and collapsed on top of it. "He looks old."

"Twelve in February, poor dear. But he's doing fine. Aren't you, Winnie?"

At the sound of his name the dog opened an eye and lifted his massive head, leaving a trail of saliva on the floor.

"Oh dear." Mildred swooped down and wiped away the glop with a Kleenex. "He's not as tidy as he used to be, I'm afraid."

"That's okay," said Louise. "I have five children, a dog and a cat, and God knows how many gerbils, hamsters, and snakes.

I'm always cleaning up after them." She plucked the mink and the sweater from the deacon's bench, not realizing she'd said five instead of four. The label on the sweater said Saks Dog Toggery. She stuffed both among a mass of ski jackets in the closet.

Mildred eyed all the jackets. "Your children live at home?"

"Of course. Where else would they live?"

"Mine went away to school. From the age of twelve on. They got excellent educations but not much family life, I'm afraid."

"You had other children? Besides the one?"

"A daughter. She was eleven when it happened."

"Didn't you hate it when people said you were lucky to have her? Like having her made the loss less."

"Yes, I hated it a lot."

"I have four others. I suppose that makes my loss four times less painful."

"People don't know what to say, Louise."

"Well I do. I finally figured it out. After years of being Miss Nice I'm saying 'Go to hell.' " She picked up the squashed box. "Come on. I'll make us some bitter coffee."

They sat in the kitchen on stools at a center island of ceramic tile where children's drawings were preserved under glaze.

"I stopped drinking yesterday, in case you were wondering."

"Oh no," protested Mildred.

"I could see it on your face. I know how I look."

Mildred didn't know what to say. She wasn't good with blurted truths. She wrapped her hands around her mug and tried not to look at the coffee cake.

"Aren't you going to have any?"

"At my age even raw carrots turn to fat. I'm constantly battling the pounds."

Louise cut her a piece anyway. "If you're going to talk to me, you're going to pay with some calories." She slipped the slice onto a plate and pushed it toward Mildred. "How long did it take anyway?"

"How long did what take?"

"Until your taste buds came back." She chewed mechanically. "For me, this might as well be styrofoam."

"I know. I felt like a zombie. My senses shut down. And people kept expecting me to get over it. I could almost hear their feet tapping impatiently, and it made me want to scream. The only one who seemed to understand was an elderly Jewish lady I met in the park. I ended up telling her the story of my life. Sometimes it's easier with a stranger, you know? She said when someone dies in a Jewish family, there is a prescribed period of mourning—so much time for a spouse, so much for a parent. But for the loss of a child no length of time is stipulated, because it's not supposed to happen. It's unnatural. And when it does happen, you mourn forever. Somehow that made me feel better."

"You seem fine now."

"I have my moments, Louise, but for the most part, yes, I'm fine. It took a long time but things kind of crept up on me. Sensations. Tastes. Smells. Bit by bit life came back. Of course, I was determined that it wouldn't. I did my best."

Louise looked at her questioningly.

"When my son died, I felt as though I died too. I didn't want to be alive, and I was outraged that others went about their daily business as though nothing had happened. I never told anyone this, but . . ."

"But what?"

"Sam was my favorite. Isn't that terrible? Mothers aren't supposed to have favorites. But he was mine. I tried not to show it. Molly knew though, especially afterwards. That's part of the reason things are difficult between us to this day. She was the one who was left behind, and she always knew she wasn't enough."

"Kevin was my favorite," said Louise. "I never told anyone that either. My children certainly don't know."

"Don't let them find out. Protect them from that. That much you can do." She sipped her black coffee. "What happened to Kevin?"

"Dr. Bradford didn't tell you?"

"He said there'd been an accident, that's all."

Louise swiped a clump of stray hair out of her face. When it fell right back, she reached for a pair of scissors and snipped it off. Mildred said nothing but was alarmed by this self-destructive gesture.

"An accident," repeated Louise. She placed the scissors back in a ceramic container stuffed with Ninja Turtle and Barney pencils.

Mildred hoped Louise wasn't going to say it was murder. She'd had enough of that to last a lifetime. Other retired people took up sensible hobbies such as golf or sewing or stamp collecting. But not Mildred. Along with Forrest, Irene, and Trevor, she repeatedly found herself being dragged into episodes of death and dismemberment, each more sordid than the last.

She thought of the stack of mail on the kitchen counter, letters from police chiefs, from families, from well-intentioned third parties asking the four of them to lend a hand solving some horrendous act of violence perpetrated by one human being on another. As though solving a crime was nothing. As though it wasn't dangerous. As though it wasn't heartbreaking too.

No, she thought. Not me. I've had enough. Forrest almost died the last time, and the time before that I almost did. So please, don't say it was murder.

Fortunately, Louise didn't. At least not right away.

"Autoerotic asphyxia," she said.

"I beg your pardon?"

"That's what killed him. At least that's what the coroner said." Louise explained what it was.

"How devastating." Mildred reached out and patted Louise's hand.

"I don't believe it was an accident, Mildred. I believe it was murder."

And there it was. Mildred kept her voice reasonable. "Now why on earth would you think that?"

Louise's voice dropped to a conspiratorial whisper. "Can you keep a secret?"

Mildred looked around, wondering who might be listening. Now I'm getting paranoid, she thought. "Of course," she replied. It was an unintentional lie. She couldn't keep a secret worth a damn.

Louise told her about the phone call.

"Good Lord."

"Brendan says it was a crank call. Or that I imagined it." She arched an eyebrow. "Brendan thinks I'm crazy. My own husband."

Mildred looked at Louise and thought Brendan's perception might well be correct.

"Kevin was murdered and people up there know something." She put her face in her hands and stared into the folds of her fingers. "I've been trying to develop a plan. Trying to think of what to do. But I can't."

Minutes passed. "Listen," said Mildred tentatively, "I don't mean to meddle, but . . ."

"Don't tell me I need a shrink."

"All right, I won't. Maybe you should try to find the person who called. Or if you imagined the call—and I'm not saying you did—it might help to confront reality. Look around. Talk to people who knew Kevin."

It was probably poor advice, but when Sam died Mildred let Connor handle everything. Over the years that followed she learned the hard way that retreating was no way out. Loss gets you one way or the other. Loss is patient. Loss says pay me now or pay me later. If you don't look Loss square in the face, Loss hangs on and bleeds you dry. Mildred didn't want Louise to suffer the way she had.

"Oh," said Louise, "I don't know. I mean, I'd like to but I just don't see how. I have responsibilities. People depend on me, Mildred."

"The children?"

"And Brendan. They all need care. Meals have to be prepared. Laundry has to be done. Food shopped for. Beds made. Homework supervised." Her voice edged up hysterically. "Christmas is coming, for God's sake. Gifts have to be bought! How can I forget that?"

"Perhaps a break from responsibility would do you good. The Sunshine Society could send someone to look after things while you're gone. There would be a modest fee, of course."

"Oh, I'd pay. I wouldn't expect someone to do it for free." She stopped herself. "I don't know what I'm talking about. This is nonsense." She shook her head. "No. I can't possibly go to St. Sebastian's. Not alone. Brendan would hit the roof. He already thinks . . . well, you know what he thinks."

"Maybe . . ." Mildred stopped.

"Maybe what?"

Don't, she thought. Don't get involved. It's harebrained. The woman is probably delusional and here you are encouraging her. And besides, you haven't even talked to the others.

But Louise Cannivan was a woman in trouble, a woman on the brink, and Mildred couldn't resist reaching out to pull her back. Surely Trevor would agree. He was the one who encouraged her to come here in the first place. He was the one who'd said Louise Cannivan could use a friend.

"Maybe we could go with you. For moral support."

"We?"

"My friends and I. Trevor you already know. There are two others: Forrest Haggarty and Irene Purdy."

"Purdy," murmured Louise. "The name sounds familiar."

Mildred hoped Louise hadn't heard gossip about Irene's eccentricities.

"That other man you mentioned—Forrest Haggarty. Who's he?"

"Why, he's the former chief of police. A master at investigation. Very experienced, very knowledgeable."

"Perfect!"

"Oh, I didn't mean he should investigate Kevin's death, don't misunderstand me. He's retired. I'm sure he wouldn't agree to—"

"Of course he would! If he knew the background." Her eyes gleamed brightly. "That's what we'll do. We'll go up there and investigate. We'll even have an expert. This Haggarty person. It couldn't be better!"

Oh dear, thought Mildred. Me and my big mouth. Now I've fanned the fire. Quickly she tried to backpedal. "Maybe it's not such a good idea after all. Even if Forrest were to agree, he can be very *dis*agreeable. He's cantankerous. Abrasive. Headstrong. Bossy. He's difficult, even for those who know him well. Believe me, you don't want any part of him."

"That's just what I need. Someone difficult."

"And he's old." Forrest, forgive me.

"How old exactly? Not that I'm quibbling."

"Seventy-five."

"I like a man with experience."

Mildred sighed. "You're not going to let me off the hook, are you?"

"Not on your life. Don't look so glum, Mildred. There's work to be done." She reached for a pad and started making a list. "I've got to call the Sunshine Society. I've got to get myself cleaned up. Do you think I can get an appointment at Hair Today on short notice? Oh, and I've got get to the market so I can get food to make meals—stackable, packable, freezable meals. Lots of them. This family eats like an army, believe you me." She looked at Mildred. "How are you at making casseroles?"

CHAPTER TWELVE

Mildred and Winston staggered up the front steps at her estate on High Ridge late that afternoon. Her head whirled with visions of mozzarella, macaroni ribbons, and ground sausage. She had baked three dozen oatmeal cookies. She had churned two quarts of ice cream. She had frozen two trays of lasagna. Never in her life had she cooked in such volume and in such a frenzy. She felt like a cross between Sara Lee and the Bride of Frankenstein. Louise had been a woman possessed, flipping through cookbooks, barking orders like a mess sergeant, building a tower of Tupperware.

Good Lord, thought Mildred, what have I gotten us into? What will I tell Forrest? That we're going to college with a crazy woman? A woman who hears voices? A woman who refuses to accept the death of her son? Mildred had seen Kevin's room. It was a shrine, a tabernacle, a moment frozen in time, not a thing out of place. She'd seen the quilt too, a perfectly ghastly creation. Louise had shown it to her, full of pride.

She's out of touch, thought Mildred, clearly out of touch. Trevor said the woman needs a friend. She needs more than that. She needs a rubber room. And now I've committed us to her deluded mission. Perhaps I'm the one who ought to be committed.

Still, Mildred felt sympathy for Louise Cannivan. Maybe a little trip to St. Sebastian's wouldn't hurt. What was the harm?

Now you're the one who's crazy, Mildred.

We have nothing else to do, she reasoned.

There's lots to do. Christmas shopping. Caroling on Main Street. Volunteer work at the Thrift Shop. Trevor's work at the blood bank. Irene's baby-sitting. The birdfeeder has to be filled every morning.

Nothing exciting. Nothing like this.

Being old is not about excitement, Mildred. It's about settling down. It's about contentment. It's about acting your age.

"Rubbish!" she snapped.

She paused on the uppermost step, waiting for Winston. The elegant house with its enormous wraparound porch and five acres of formal gardens had been left to Mildred by her mother. Sometimes it felt like home and sometimes it drove her crazy. As she tugged on Winston's leash, she feared today would be one of the latter times.

She and Trevor Bradford divided their time between Mildred's Manhattan co-op and their houses in Raven's Wing. Since they had become romantically involved, the two rarely spent a night apart. Having two houses in the same town seemed not only extravagant but ridiculous. Trevor was trying to sell his Victorian on Main Street but the market was down. Consequently he was forever running back and forth to unlock the door for realtors and prospective buyers. He refused to have a lockbox installed. He refused to allow open houses. He refused to budge on the price either. It was no wonder the place wouldn't sell. But Mildred knew Trevor was sensitive about her wealth and wanted to carry his own weight financially, so she held her tongue.

Their friends Forrest Haggarty and Irene Purdy served as caretaker and housekeeper at the High Ridge mansion. Of course, that was merely a ruse devised by Mildred so Forrest and Irene would accept free accommodations. Yankee pride would have prevented them from doing so otherwise.

Forrest and Irene were what Mildred's father had called "local yokels." They were salt-of-the-earth farm-type people. Forrest had grown up on Lookout Mountain in Tennessee and relocated to Raven's Wing as chief of police after World War II. Irene had lived in Raven's Wing all her life. For forty years she'd been married to Earl Purdy, a good-hearted plain-speaking farmer, who allowed Irene to keep a goat in the kitchen. They were childless, not by choice. Irene busied herself practicing veterinary medicine and midwifery without a license.

When Earl died, Irene buried him in a meadow before developers took over. She still visited his grave once a month, provoking a family (who were unaware that Earl Purdy was planted next to their septic tank) to complain repeatedly to the police about a "strange looking woman lurking around the hemlocks." "She rocks on her knees and talks to herself," they said. "It looks like she's praying." The police knew Irene and looked the other way. The family of newcomers finally got used to their eccentric visitor. Irene was the sort of person who took some getting used to.

Forrest and Irene both lived on meager social security checks. Forrest had a modest pension, which helped, but he needed watching because of his heart condition. With her unorthodox nursing experience, Irene was good at watching, but the two of them living in her West Mountain cabin was out of the question. It was two miles up a slippery dirt road that was impassable in winter and prone to mudslides in spring. Besides, the cabin had no electricity or indoor plumbing. Logs had to be cut for the wood stove. It was just too much for people in their seventies. So here they were. A caretaker who took care of nothing and a housekeeper who didn't clean worth a damn.

"Come *on,* Winston. I know you're tired. So am I." Mildred pictured herself next to a crackling fire, a Manhattan in hand, listening to soft classical music. She opened the door and the vision evaporated. There stood Trevor, Irene, and Forrest, in a semicircle, glaring at her.

"Where you been?" demanded Irene, her hands on ample hips, her voluminous breasts rising and falling under a plaid flannel shirt.

"We were starting to worry, Mildred," said Trevor.

"What's that on your nose?" asked Forrest. He pointed a callused finger. "Is it snowing again?"

"Snow?" Mildred looked at her disheveled self in the foyer mirror. She brushed a finger against the tip of her nose and held it up. "Flour."

"Flour?" repeated Irene. "What were you doing?"

"Working on a new case," she replied. "Such as it is."

CHAPTER THIRTEEN

"Brendan, I have something to tell you."

They were lying in bed. His nose was in a book. He answered without looking up. "Ummmmm?"

"I'm going."

He turned a page. "Going where?"

"To that school." She could hardly bear to say the name. "To St. Sebastian's."

Taking care to hold his place, he looked at her over his half-glasses. "For God's sake, what put that idea in your head?"

"I want answers. I want to find the person who called."

"I thought we agreed to forget that."

"You agreed. I never had a say. I want to talk to Kevin's advisor, to his roommate, to his friends. I want to talk to all of them. You said they made themselves scarce when you packed his things."

"That was understandable. It was uncomfortable for everyone."

"Especially Kevin. Well they're not getting off so easily. I need to know what happened, Bren. I need to understand."

"You're consumed by this, Louise. We've had troubles, I know, but don't do this just to spite me."

"You have nothing to do with it."

They didn't discuss it again until the next night. Louise knew Brendan. He was biding his time, confident he could talk her out of it.

"It's hours from here," he pointed out. "Where would you stay?"

She refrained from telling him about Mildred and her friends just yet. Somehow she didn't think that would help. "I don't know. In one of the dorms perhaps. We paid for room and board for the year. They wouldn't refund the money, remember? Cheap SOBs."

"Louise, what has gotten into you? You never used to talk like that. And what about the family? What about Pete and Daniel and Samantha and Marty? Yes, what about Marty, while we're on the subject? She had her first period this week, did you know that?"

Guilt shot through her. So that's where her Tampax had disappeared to. How had Marty even known how to put a tampon in? And the cramps . . . nothing is worse than those cramps when you're twelve years old.

"Well she did. And you were—"

"I was what?"

"Too self-absorbed to notice."

Guilt was replaced by anger. He was a fine one to hurl accusations. "I'll talk to Marty," she said evenly.

"It's a little late for that."

"You don't care about Marty's period. What you care about is who does the laundry, who makes the meals, who carpools the kids."

"That's not true, but all right, who will? Someone has to take responsibility. I have an ad agency to run."

"How could I forget? Well don't worry about anything intruding on your evening 'meetings.' I've arranged for help around here."

"We already have help—a cleaning lady, a laundress, a landscape service, window washers."

"I've hired a housekeeper from the Sunshine Society. Mrs. Cranston. Just for a few days." A lie. It might well be longer. "She'll keep things on an even keel until I get back."

"I don't believe this. You hired someone without even consulting me?"

"I didn't see the point. Someone from the Sunshine Society stayed here before. When we went to get Kevin's things. You were agreeable then."

"Before we had no choice. Before we were trying to get through a tragedy. Now it's over. Now you belong home."

"It's not over, Brendan. That's the whole point."

"Louise, I'm not going to discuss this further. I refuse to allow you to go traipsing up to St. Sebastian's on your own."

"Allow me?" The words rang in her ears. She had always done what he wanted, always. "I'm going, Brendan. Whether you like it or not." She paused, to let that sink in. "But you needn't worry. I'm not going alone."

That snagged his attention. "Who's going with you?"

"A woman named Mildred Bennett, for one. She's very nice. She wears a mink coat."

"That's a hell of an endorsement."

"It's the kind of thing that impresses you."

"I see. You said 'for one.' Am I to presume there are more?"

"She has three friends. It so happens they're experienced at doing investigations. Irene Purdy—"

"I've seen that woman around town. She's a nut."

"She's an old Connecticut Yankee."

"She hangs around Young's Feed Store. She dresses like Ma Kettle."

"So she doesn't shop at Lord & Taylor. Big deal."

"She's also shacking up with some ex-cop. An old coot named Haggarty. Did you know that?"

"He was chief of police before he retired, not 'some ex-cop.' And he's going too." She couldn't help but smile.

"Jesus!"

"The last one you'll approve of. Dr. Bradford. He'll come in handy in case I go off the deep end."

Brendan got out of bed and thrashed around for his robe and slippers.

Her face softened and she reached out to him. "I'm trying to put myself back together, Brendan."

He brushed her hand away. "And what about the rest of us?"

She winced as the door slammed behind him.

CHAPTER FOURTEEN

Mildred, Trevor, Irene, and Forrest went to fetch Louise two days later in Trevor's cavernous black Lincoln. The intervening time had given Louise the chance to prepare the household for her absence. As Trevor drove, they rehashed the mysterious phone call Louise had received.

"A call from beyond," proclaimed Irene.

Mildred looked at her friend. "I beg your pardon?"

"Don't get her started," said Forrest. "It's that New Age crap."

"It is not. Remember Josie Dunlap? Used to do nursing at Craigmoor?"

"How could we forget?" smiled Mildred. "She took such good care of Forrest."

"The hell she did," said Forrest. At one time he'd been an unwilling guest at Craigmoor Convalescent Home, railroaded there by his well-intentioned children. It was a time he'd just as soon forget.

"Josephine died last spring," said Trevor. "Massive heart attack."

"And I was sorry about that," put in Forrest quickly. "The woman wasn't one of my favorites but I never wished her dead."

"I went to her funeral," said Irene. "Saw her all laid out, pretty as a picture, hair fixed just so. A lot of the girls were asking Bob Kane what number the color was.

"Anyway, there she was, dead as a doornail. Or so I thought. Then lo and behold, what do I get in August but a birthday card. From Josephine! Four months after she passed! I was taken aback, I tell you, mighty taken aback."

"Taken aback?" laughed Forrest. "Reenie acted like she'd seen a ghost. Carried on, hooted and hollered. The whole neighborhood heard her."

"I'm glad I missed it," said Mildred, who'd been cruising the Rhine with Trevor.

"I didn't sleep for days," said Irene. "Nights neither. I just kept seeing that card. Kept seeing Josie's signature. Her handwriting. Honest and true. *Birthday greetings from the great beyond* it said. Lordy."

"I was the one who figured it out," said Forrest. "I saw an ad in *Yankee*. 'You passed away months ago . . . but on every occasion that's important to those you left behind they receive a BEAUTIFUL CARD!' The ad said a person would have the joy of knowing they'd be in folks hearts after they died. 'Til they were together again. The outfit was called Heavenly Sentiments."

"A curious concept," remarked Trevor.

Forrest was more to the point. "A racket, a real racket."

60

"Maybe that phone call was along the same line," said Irene. "A Call from Heaven." She proceeded to sing. "You've got to make the choice to share your heart and voice. We're aaaaalllllll connected! New York Telephone!"

Mildred laughed. "Irene! This wasn't a call *from* Kevin Cannivan, it was *about* him." Honestly. Sometimes Irene had the mind of a bird.

"No," said Mildred, "Louise Cannivan is traipsing about in a mental minefield. Other than giving us a chance to visit Cameron, this trip is a wild-goose chase, if you want my opinion."

"Oh, I don't know about that," said Irene.

Forrest eyed her keenly. "Why's that, Reenie?"

" 'Cause think about it. It really could be the perfect crime."

"A boy dies," said Forrest, "with a rope around his neck and his thingamabob in his hand. What's so perfect about that?"

"Honestly," muttered Mildred. "Your choice of words . . ."

"What's wrong? What'd I say now?"

"Nothing," sighed Mildred.

Trevor spoke up. "Why is it the perfect crime, Irene?"

"Well, it certainly could be, yes indeed. Picture this . . ." She held out mittened hands. "A young seminarian. Homesick. Alone. No physical contact with the female persuasion."

"So he takes things in hand," said Forrest.

"I give up," muttered Mildred, "I really do."

"Anyway," Irene glared at Forrest, "he's lonely. Then along comes some girl—a hotsy-totsy—who lures him to her love nest."

"A chapel in the woods," corrected Mildred, "is hardly a love nest."

"You take all the romance out of things," sighed Irene. "Okay, so she lures him to this chapel. The chapel of love, like in the song. Where she has in mind to murder him. It's all preme-diated."

"Premeditated," said Mildred.

"Whatever. They have a few drinks. They put on some

mood music. And one thing leads to another. He's only human, after all. He's a young man with raging hormones. She gets him all hot and bothered. Then she tells him about this sex game, this autoelectric thing, with the rope. She convinces him to try it. Maybe he's even tried it before."

"Or maybe it was his idea," said Forrest.

"That doesn't fit with my premediated picture, but I guess it could have happened that way. Whatever. Anyway, she puts the rope around his neck. Soon he's out of control, and at the moment of truth—she strangles him!"

Mildred shuddered. "A ghastly scenario!"

"But possible. It's a perfect setup. Even a little bit of a girl could kill a man in that manner. It's like Samson and Delilah."

"It does make sense," said Trevor finally.

"Yes," agreed Mildred. "After he's dead she puts the rope in his hand."

"Then she leaves," added Forrest, "and it looks like an accident. Something he did to himself."

"Exactly!" exclaimed Irene. "Like I said, the perfect crime." She leaned back and looked smug.

"The caller did say Kevin had enemies," said Mildred.

"Then again," added Trevor, "maybe Kevin's death was an accident. Two kids fooling around and one of them dies. It's happened before. But in this case the girl—maybe it was even the caller—panics and runs. It looks like an accident, and she feels guilty afterwards. So she calls Louise."

"No one feels that guilty," said Forrest.

"I would," replied Trevor.

"I see it another way," said Irene. "I think the caller knows someone did it to him, maybe even saw it happen. That's what I think."

"Accident or no," said Forrest, "a woman was probably involved for him to be vulnerable like that."

But Trevor shook his head. "Not necessarily. It could just as easily have happened during a homosexual encounter as a heterosexual one."

Forrest made a face. "Jesus, give me a break."

"Well," said Mildred, sighing, "there's certainly a great deal to sort out."

Trevor parked in the Cannivan driveway. Mildred and Irene walked to the front door, leaving the men in the car with the engine idling.

"We shouldn't be long," called Mildred over her shoulder.

"Better not be," replied Forrest. "I don't like the looks of that sky."

Winston accompanied Mildred, his movements stiff and labored. Irene's arms were wrapped around a cat carrier and a bulging shopping bag dangled from her hands. When the door opened, Mildred was relieved to see Louise had indeed made an effort to pull herself together. Her hair was washed and styled so the missing clump was barely noticeable. She was wearing gray wool slacks and a peach cashmere sweater. Her fingernails were shaped and pink nail polish applied.

Irene followed Mildred inside. Her eyes took in the overhead chandelier, the deacon's bench, the hooked rug and the brass umbrella stand. "Nice place you've got here, Mrs. C. Real homey. I get good vibrations here, indeed I do."

Louise was nervous about the trip. Except for the time of her mother's illness, she'd never left her family. She forced a smile. "You're clairvoyant?"

"Claire who?"

"Never mind," said Mildred. She smiled at Louise. "It's good of you to allow Winston and Walter to stay here while we're away. With five of us going, we simply can't fit them in the Lincoln, and besides, the hotel doesn't accept pets."

"I just hope Mrs. Cranston survives," whispered Louise. "I'm going over last minute instructions now. She seems a bit overwhelmed."

A grandmotherly white-haired lady stepped out of the kitchen. She wore rimless glasses, lace-up orthopedic shoes and a flowered apron over a white uniform. She wiped her hands on the apron and smiled uncertainly. Introductions were made.

"Mavis and I know each other," said Irene. "We go way back. This here's Walter, Mavis. A genuine Siamese. Isn't he pretty? We inherited him on our last case. You leave him alone, he'll leave you alone. You want to pet him, put on some leather gardening gloves."

"My word," said Mavis. She looked from the cat to Louise to Winston. "And what's that?"

"A prizewinning bulldog," said Mildred proudly. "Winston Leopold Bennett. He's very old and sleeps most of the time. He won't be a bit of trouble."

Mavis eyed Winston's hyperactive jowls. "Does he always drip like that?"

"Only when he's excited. If that's happening and he starts to shake his head, just hustle him outside."

" 'Cause he slings it around," said Irene. "And the stuff is potent. I've seen it eat through lampshades, through wallpaper too."

Mildred hastened to reassure Mavis. "If you get him outside it's not a problem."

"The Sunshine people didn't say anything about additional pets."

"The children will help you," interrupted Louise. "You'll be fine."

"Speaking of which," said Irene, "I brought these here games for the children. Board games make for fine entertainment, don't you know."

Louise and Mavis peered into Irene's bag and saw *Chutes 'N Ladders, Go to the Head of the Class, Candy Land, Sorry,* and *Twister.* Games nobody played anymore.

Irene didn't care that no one played these games but her. They were classics. "You'll be glad I brought these games, Mavis, believe you me. Children like them fine, once they get used to them. And besides, playing board games is a whole lot healthier than watching trash on TV like *Hard Copy* or *Current Affair.* "The best thing you can do with a TV is throw a brick through the picture tube, take it from me."

"Perhaps," said Mildred, ignoring this latest outlandish opinion, "you should finish with Mavis in the kitchen, Louise."

Louise smiled at Mavis reassuringly. "Of course. We need to review the menu."

"Menu," whispered Irene to Mildred. "La-de-da."

Louise went to the kitchen with Mavis and flipped open a spiral-bound notebook. "Everything is written here in explicit detail. Breakfasts are eaten on the fly. I usually make a raft of pancakes or waffles or scrambled eggs and keep them warm. Brendan eats first—his train is at 7:05. Daniel has to catch the bus at 7:40. It's a problem getting him up, but Pete will help you. You should take Daniel to the bus stop and wait until he gets on. Marty or Pete will watch Samantha while you're doing that."

"Who's Samantha?"

"The baby. You remember, Mavis." She waited. "Mavis?"

"Yes." The woman said it with such lack of conviction that Louise was certain she was lying. Not only did Mavis not remember Samantha, she probably wouldn't remember any of these instructions. She probably had Alzheimer's. The family would starve. Bedtimes would be forgotten, curfews broken. The house would burn down.

I can't go, thought Louise. I just can't.

But I must.

There was no time to find another sitter. Mavis would have to do.

"Marty and Pete will fix their own lunches if they want to take them, but if Daniel doesn't like school lunch that day, you'll have to make his. Peanut butter and jelly is fine, with an apple and a cookie." She lifted the lid from a stoneware crock. "Cookies are in here."

"Mrs. Cannivan?" said Mavis.

"As far as dinner is concerned . . ." Louise whirled and opened the freezer. ". . . everything is in here."

Mavis gazed in wonder at a solid wall of intricately packed plastic containers, each bearing a number on masking tape. Her expression changed from wonder to panic. "How long are you going to be gone?"

"As you can see, the containers are labeled by numbers, which correspond to days noted in this . . ." Louise held up the notebook. "It's really quite simple."

"Mrs. Cannivan?"

Louise rattled on. "For dessert they like something sweet. I tried to avoid sugary stuff and serve fruit or something healthy but discovered that the kids were smuggling Ring-Dings, Twinkies, and Devil Dogs into their rooms, hiding them under the beds, which caused an infestation of ants. Now I find it's easier to make something wholesome for dessert and monitor the portions. Carrot cake. Angel food. Strawberry short." She opened a cabinet revealing every cake mix known to man. "These serve as backup in case you run out of the cookies and the homemade ice cream in the freezer." She consulted her notebook. "Cookies in containers sixteen and seventeen, ice cream in nine, ten, eleven, and twelve."

"Mrs. Cannivan," said Mavis, more forcefully this time. "Mrs. Cannivan!"

Louise felt herself derail. She gripped the counter for support. "Yes?"

"Hold on a cotton-picking minute. Please."

"Okay. I'm holding."

"How long are you going to be away?"

"Why . . . I don't know."

"You don't know?"

"I mean, I'm not sure."

Mavis Cranston reached for her handbag. "I'm very sorry, Mrs. Cannivan. The Sunshine Society didn't tell me this was an

66

open-ended assignment. There's more than I can cope with . . . so many people, so many animals, all those containers. I'm not as young as I used to be."

"It won't be so hard," said Louise lamely.

"You have enough food in there to last for weeks. I didn't plan on being here weeks."

"I don't think it will take weeks," said Louise quickly.

"A day or two is what I had in mind."

"It might take longer than that."

"That simply won't do, Mrs. Cannivan."

Louise latched onto Mavis Cranston's arm. "Please, Mrs. Cranston. Mavis. I'm begging you. Don't leave me in the lurch."

"I'm sorry, Mrs. Cannivan. This assignment is far more taxing than I was led to believe. It's simply too much. I simply never expected—"

Louise blurted magic words: "I'll pay double."

Mavis froze. Her eyes brightened. "Really? Double the daily rate?"

"In cash. The Sunshine Society doesn't have to know."

"Well then . . . I suppose I can reconsider."

"Bless you." Louise gave the elderly extortionist a hug and started for the door before she could up the ante.

"Oh!" Louise whirled around. "I almost forgot!"

"Forgot what?" said Mavis warily.

"The phone. Do not answer any phone that is white."

"I see," said Mavis, not seeing at all. "White phones."

"Yes. Those phones are on Mr. Cannivan's and my line. There is a machine to answer incoming calls, a machine that records them. I may get an important call, Mavis, from someone at Kevin's school. If so, it must be recorded. I have to prove that it's real, you see."

Mavis nodded, not seeing at all.

"The machine will take care of it automatically. You can call out, of course, but I repeat: Do not, under any circumstances, answer a white phone. Is that clear?"

67

"Yes." She looked at the white wall phone as though it were a device from hell. "But what if the children answer?"

"They won't. They know the rules. They know all about white phones, believe me."

"What if someone tries to call me?"

"Have them call on Marty and Pete's line. The so-called 'teenage line.' Theirs are red phones. Here's the number." She scribbled it down. "Samantha and Daniel have no phones. They're too young to care about getting calls."

"Who's Daniel?"

Louise swallowed a scream. Before she could have second thoughts, she rushed to the foyer, reached into the closet and yanked on her camel coat. She pulled on boots and gloves. She slung her handbag over her shoulder and grabbed a suitcase with each hand.

She turned to Mildred and Irene. "Let's go, for God's sake!"

Then she walked out the door and out of her children's lives.

CHAPTER FIFTEEN

Trevor hated to contend with trucks on the superhighway, so they took the more countrified Route 7. The Lincoln pushed its way north like a black turtle through a blanket of snow . . . past Danbury, through Kent, Falls Village, and Cornwall.

Trevor peered through the snow-crusted windshield. "I hope this doesn't turn to sleet." He turned on the wipers and defroster. He and Mildred sat in front, with Louise, Irene, and Forrest wedged in back.

Louise stared at the rural landscape. "I don't know," she said to no one in particular. "Maybe I should have gotten him into therapy."

"Why?" asked Irene. "Was he depressed or something?"

"No," said Louise quickly. "Nothing like that."

Forrest hitched up one eyebrow. His white hair, combed into some semblance of order before they left, now looked electric. His hatchet face was deeply lined, his nose sharp and beak-like. His blue devilish eyes darted this way and that and didn't miss a trick. The teeth in his mouth, though his own, were crooked and stained with nicotine from cigars he'd been forced to give up two years before. They'd been on the road for nearly two hours and he'd dozed off, but the word "therapy" snagged his attention like a vaudeville hook.

"I don't hold with headshrinking. Have you noticed how they've turned everything that's a weakness into a disease?"

Mildred's knitting needles clicked away. She glanced over her shoulder. "Don't get him started, Louise."

"No," said Louise, "I haven't noticed."

"Well it has. Take alcohol, for instance. Used to be if a fella drank himself silly, he was a drunk. He was weak. But not now. Now he's got a disease."

"Well it is," said Louise.

"Yeah maybe. But then things got out of control. Before you could say Doctor Joyce Brothers, all kinds of other stuff jumped on the medical reimbursement bandwagon. Drugs. Gambling. Sex. Even shopping, for God's sake. And some silly ass thing called co-dependency. Now if that isn't a crock, I don't know what is. And chronic fatigue syndrome, I almost forgot that. Well I've got a syndrome of my own, and it's a beaut."

"What's that?"

"Louise," whispered Irene, "don't encourage him. Really."

"Compassion fatigue. Isn't that a pisser? I'm going to have it patented. I'm going to start a Disease-of-the-Month Club and offer it as a main selection."

Though Mildred had warned her, Louise was taken aback

69

by these cranky opinions so freely offered. Maybe it was because Forrest was old. Maybe his arthritis hurt. Maybe—

"I'm sick and tired of all these cockamamie ailments. I don't want to see, hear, or read about them anymore. I can't even go into Encore Books without tripping over a pile of garbage about the latest psychic affliction. People Who Love Too Much. People Who Hate Too Much. People Who Screw Too Much, pardon my French. You want to know what I think?"

This time Louise didn't ask.

Forrest answered anyway. "It's a conspiracy. By the therapy industry."

"The therapy industry?"

Irene leaned forward and whispered to Mildred. "Louise don't know when to quit, does she?"

"Yes. There's a headshrinker factory that reworks everything into a disease. So they can get insurance money. They have a book with numbers. They assign each disease a number." He nodded knowingly. "That's how it works."

"I see." Louise tried to change to a more pleasant subject. "Do you have children?"

"Yes. And a more ungrateful lot of louts never walked the face of this earth."

"Forrest," said Mildred, "why don't you go back to sleep?"

"Louise asked about my children, Millie, and I'm trying to tell her. If you don't mind."

"Very well." She feared Forrest might be working up to one of his rants. For occasions when there was no escape, she kept a fresh pair of foam rubber earplugs handy in her purse. She hoped she wouldn't have to resort to them now.

"They tried to put me in a home. Can you believe that?"

"Yes," replied Louise.

"Very funny. You're a real card, you know that? Now where was I? Oh yeah, my kids. There's LuAnne, she's the oldest. Got a Maaco body shop in Danbury and a do-nothing husband who takes freely from the till. Then there's Billy, he's on the force in South Salem."

The Force. Louise pictured some sort of intraterrestrial organization, creatures with green skin, horns, and warts.

"The police force, that is. And of course there's Scott . . ."

"Of course."

Forrest looked at Louise sideways, wondering if that was another smart-ass remark. "He lives with his family right in Raven's Wing. The only one who could afford to stay there. He's a numbers cruncher. Calls himself a certified financial planner, whatever the hell that is."

Louise was becoming irritated. "Don't you love any of them?"

He looked at her curiously. "Sure I love them. They're my kids, aren't they? But that doesn't mean I like them. Jeeze. Anyway, I wasn't finished. You keep interrupting."

"Sorry."

"Smokey's the youngest, lives in New York City. Works at the Metropolitan Museum of Art as an authenticator. I don't know what the hell that is either, but it sounds impressive."

"It is impressive," said Trevor. "Smokey has an amazing job."

"I should say," added Irene.

"The Museum flies her all over the world," said Mildred.

"So she tells me," said Forrest. "Says she looks at paintings, tells folks who painted them, tells folks when. Anyway, Smokey's okay. Got more sense than the other three combined. Know what she gave me last Christmas?"

"It was in poor taste," said Mildred. "I'm sorry to say it, Forrest, but it was."

"She gave me a book. *Final Exit*."

"How awful!" blurted Louise.

"No it isn't either. It's practical. It's a gift I can use. Smokey's got a head on her shoulders. She's okay. She comes to visit sometimes."

Louise pictured a lonely old man waiting for the doorbell to ring and felt a pang of pity. "The others don't?"

"Not if I can help it."

She decided to try another subject. "Mildred said you all know my son's roommate. Cameron Maine."

"I can't wait to see him!" cried Irene.

"Now there's a boy!" said Forrest. "A fine fella. A mite too serious, but a boy with substance. A real piece of bread."

"His family lives next door to Mildred," put in Trevor.

"What about you, Louise?" asked Trevor. "Do you have folks?"

"I'm an only child. My mother died last winter, but my father's still alive. He lives in Warren, Ohio. You probably never heard of it."

"I have," said Forrest. "Nice town."

"It's a pit."

"What's your daddy like?" asked Irene.

"You don't want to know." God help me, thought Louise. I'm sounding just like Forrest.

"That bad?" said Forrest.

Mildred looked up from her knitting. "We shouldn't pry, Forrest."

"It's all right," said Louise. "We were poor when I was growing up. My father really had to struggle. He was a farmer. Was—and is—very tidy. Always planted his rows extra straight, you know? A place for everything and everything in it's place, that's his motto. He and my mother were an odd match. She collected clutter, went to every flea market and garage sale in three counties." She paused, remembering iridescent zodiac figurines, Egyptian mummy tins, quilted toaster cozies, and mobiles made out of bottle caps. "Her debris drove him crazy. It was a constant source of friction between them.

"Then one day out of the blue she began discarding. She

started in the attic and worked her way to the basement. It took weeks. She had the garbage company position a dumpster by the window and just heaved things in. She still had her strength at that point.

"We should have known something was wrong. This was very out of character. She was throwing her life away, and we couldn't even see it. My father, of course, was quite pleased. He thought she'd finally seen the light."

"Maybe she had," said Irene. "Folks see a light when they're about to die, you know."

"What was it?" asked Forrest. "A brain tumor?"

"Lung cancer. She knew and she was cleaning house. That's when she said Daniel could have her eye after she was gone."

Mildred dropped a stitch. "I beg your pardon?"

"It's glass. Anyway, Mother gave or threw everything away. Except for one thing." Louise smiled.

"What?" asked Irene.

"An old print of some fat nymphs dancing around a Day-Glo fountain. Lord knows where she got it. It was awful. Garish colors that would give you a headache. But for some reason she liked it. She kept it over her bureau and looked at it right until she gasped her last breath. She called it 'my little bit of heaven.' After she was gone—I swear, she wasn't even cold—my father took it down and tossed it in the trash. As an afterthought he decided to retrieve the frame. He thought maybe it was gold leaf." Louise smiled again.

Forrest looked at her. "What's so funny?"

"What was behind the nymphs: an original copy of the Declaration of Independence. One of six in existence. It had been there all the time. I think my mother knew. I think she did it to show him trash can be treasure. Telling him not to always take things at face value."

"The Declaration of Independence," said Irene. "Fancy that."

"It was worth a lot of money. Nearly three million."

Forrest's head jerked back. "Dollars?"

"No," quipped Trevor. "Yen."

"Don't be such a smart-ass."

"Today my father is a man of comfortable means."

Forrest nodded approvingly. "Having money's better than not, I always say. A man can take comfort in money. A man can travel. See the world."

"Are you kidding? The world is his enemy, not his oyster. He still lives in the same white frame house, wiping smudges off the counters and cleaning the top of the ketchup bottle. At night he sits in his rocker on the porch. He drinks Beefeater martinis instead of Pabst. The money did that much for him."

"Well, maybe he's content," said Mildred.

"In his way I suppose he is. He's a very negative person, always has been. He hates people. He used to say that another fellow might give him the shirt off his back, but he wouldn't want it. He never goes anywhere." She stopped. "He didn't even come to Kevin's funeral."

"That's not right," said Irene. "Families ought to stick together."

"If he does venture out, there's always something wrong. The air conditioning is too cold or not cold enough. His martini has too much vermouth. There's a noisy child or, never mind noisy, just seeing a child makes his skin crawl. He hates things that are unpredictable, things he can't control."

"Sounds like a man after my own heart," said Forrest.

"What heart? Sorry. I didn't mean it. I'm sure you have a heart. I don't know what's gotten into me. I used to be nice. I used to be sweet. But not anymore."

Trevor turned off Route 7 and onto a country road. "We're almost there. This is the main drag, if you can call it that. Not much of a town, is it?"

For once everyone was in agreement. Coldwater, Connecticut was a hamlet hit by hard times.

"I read an article about Coldwater," said Mildred, "in *New England Monthly . . .*"

According to the article, Coldwater was an old mill town. It had been prosperous during the first half of the century and served as a springboard for the children of Irish, German, and Italian immigrants who worked the mill. Over time they made the transition to steadier, more secure jobs. They became policemen, UPS drivers, plumbers, postal workers, exterminators, and Kmart clerks. They escaped from the dank row houses that circled the mill to developments of tidy ranches, capes, and bi-levels that sprouted like pastel mushrooms on surrounding farmland.

These escapees were proud of their newfound middle-class status and clung to it with a vengeance. They worked overtime. They made their mortgage payments and managed to scrape up tuition to send their children to the local parochial school. They put pink flamingos or wooly sheep ornaments in the yard and looked forward to retirement to Florida. They planned on sending their children to college.

But some of their cousins, those less intelligent or less ambitious or just plain less lucky, never made the transition to the cookie-cutter developments. They remained in the row houses in the section called Braytown and worked at the mill like their parents, aunts, and uncles had before them. They tried to be what they thought was middle class. The women bought lipsticks from Avon, put plastic slipcovers on the furniture, and purchased seven-hundred-dollar Kirby vacuum cleaners on time. They tended gardens of twisted geraniums in front and hung clothes on crisscrossed lines out back. The men worked in shifts, drank beer at Rudy's, and bowled every Saturday night. Annual league tournaments were a very big deal.

When the third shift was eliminated, some of the stragglers felt a shiver of apprehension, but most ignored it. They made ends meet as they always did, by hunting and fishing out of season, by switching from ground round to ground turkey, and by resorting to food stamps. When hours were cut back even further, many muttered among themselves. But none were prone to action.

What action could they take, after all? The mill was the only place an unskilled man could get work. To drive UPS you had to be able to operate one of those newfangled hand-held computers. The closest a mill man ever came to a computer was the video games at Bowlarama.

They told themselves things would get better. They told themselves that the mill would always be there. They told themselves their union would protect them and that everything would be okay in the end.

They told themselves wrong. One day a disembodied voice on the PA system announced the mill was moving to North Carolina. Two weeks later the gates were padlocked. There was no time to prepare, no time to retrain, no time to do anything but fill out the forms to collect unemployment and finally, the ultimate disgrace, welfare. The men from the mill were on the dole. It was beyond belief.

In astonishingly short order the industrial core of Coldwater slid into decay. It became the economic hole in a doughnut of middle-class suspicion and disdain. Alcoholism was widespread. Forty percent of core inhabitants remained chronically unemployed. Those lucky enough to work did so as pump jockeys or alongside despised Koreans who tediously assembled tiny electronic components at a plant two towns away.

A few of the core inhabitants, women mostly, tried to keep things nice. They swept the sidewalks and pulled weeds that grew through the cracks. They strung colored lights at Christmas and hung plastic eggs on the trees at Easter. They kept doing their wash with Tide. But it was a losing battle. There is just so far you can stretch food stamps, after all. It became painfully obvious that Wonder Bread wasn't any wonder and it sure as hell didn't build strong bodies twelve ways. Children skipped school and joined gangs. They disappeared into Waterbury or

Bridgeport and returned carrying mysterious wads of cash. Some of them ended up in prison, some ended up pregnant. A lucky few ended up in the army.

"I know all about places like Coldwater," said Louise. "Warren was like Coldwater. A poor town where people hope for pie in the sky by and by when they die. I told Kevin not to go to a college in such a place. A place like that is full of frustration, I said, full of envy. I told him there was still time to change his mind."

"Coldwater isn't all poor," said Mildred. "The college has always been a lifeline for the community, providing students who spend money and jobs for the locals. And lately new people have been moving in."

As the brown stain on the map marking New York City and its suburbs spread outward, the Housatonic Valley was discovered as a picturesque region midway between Manhattan and New England ski slopes. As such, it made an ideal country retreat. Hoards of real estate agents descended on Coldwater and started transforming old mill buildings into restaurants, condominiums, mini-malls and tanning salons. They bought up farms not yet subdivided, slapped new wallpaper on the farmhouse walls, filled the interiors with fake plants and chintz-covered furniture, painted the exteriors in trendy earth tones, and sold them at greatly inflated prices, driving up real estate values and taxes, making Coldwater's poor even more so.

As developers worked their magic, Coldwater was invaded by new money, Eurotrash, minor royalty, bicoastals and bisexuals to whom price was no object. Many were successful people in the arts—actors, movie producers, playwrights—seeking a safe haven to sample simple country pleasures when the spirit moved them. They maintained homes in Beverley Hills, Manhattan, and now Connecticut. They flipped from residence to residence the way their social inferiors flipped through TV channels. They showed up at St. Sebastian's in expensive foreign cars, knowing only that it was Catholic and alien, expecting to buy jellies and wine from Trappist monks. They sent their children to private schools—Hotchkiss or Kent or Choate—and never to local public or parochial schools. Their children didn't live at home anyway. They lived away.

Residents of the doughnut and the hole saw the escalation of prices, the shining prosperity that never rubbed off on them, the ostentation, the BMWs, the Range Rovers, the gleaming new Jeeps and Trackers used just for fun. And they saw that to these newcomers everything in Coldwater seemed to be one marvelous kick.

The article quoted Patrick Rooney, chief of the volunteer firemen. "I'll give them a kick," he said. "A kick in the kiester."

One day a weekender was surveying a pile of moth-eaten quilts at Grandma's Trunk and exclaimed "Isn't this fun!" In short order this expression became a grim joke. Old time residents belted it out as they greeted one another in the unemployment line, at Elks meetings, or in the Stop & Shop. The expression even spawned the headline of the article—"IS THIS FUN? COLDWATER RESIDENTS DON'T THINK SO."

"Here we are," announced Trevor. "The Coldwater Arms."

The others looked out and blinked. It was a crumbly brick building with a broken rocker on the front porch.

"This is it?" said Irene.

"I'm afraid so," said Trevor.

"The only place in town," explained Mildred. "It gets no stars in the Mobil Guide, but I didn't expect it to be like this."

Louise looked at her watch. "It's not very late. I'd like to go to the college. To go talk to Kevin's advisor."

Mildred got out and stretched. "Louise, we're all tired from the drive."

"Donahue's going to be on any minute," said Irene.

"Might as well start in the morning," said Forrest. "When we're fresh."

"In that case," said Louise, "I'd like to borrow the car."

Everyone protested at once. Forrest said she shouldn't be

running off by herself. Louise said she was a grown woman. Trevor said he would drive Louise if she was really set on going. Louise asked if he was afraid she would smash up his car. Trevor said no.

"It's just up the hill. If I can't have the car, I'll walk."

Mildred was tired and only wanted peace. "Oh for heaven's sake, let her go."

Louise snatched the keys from Trevor's curled fingers before anyone could protest further.

Forrest watched her drive away. "Mildred, are you nuts? Why'd you go and let her do that?"

CHAPTER SIXTEEN

Gary went around the living room turning on lights. It unnerved Bea to come home to a dark house. Johnny was off in the Navy and Sally was late at school for play rehearsal. Or maybe it was yearbook. This was her senior year, full of activities. Next fall she'd be gone.

He had told Bea she could leave too if she wanted. The kids will be gone. You don't have to stay on my account. She hauled off and smacked him and he burst into tears. They fell into one another's arms, holding tight, survivors at sea. "Don't say that again," she said. "Don't even think it."

She was working two jobs—teaching business science at the high school and sales clerking at the mall for two hours after. "Just for the Christmas season," she'd promised. He hoped it wouldn't turn into more than that.

He heard the box outside clank and wished he'd remembered to pick up the mail. It would have been a small enough thing to do. Like the song says, little things mean a lot. Lately his days were filled with little things. Setting the table. Feeding the dog. Scouring the tub. He could do that pretty well. Once he tried doing laundry and it had been a disaster, their underwear flamingo pink. Now there were two hampers and it was easy. But ironing was hard. He left that to Bea.

The front door opened. "Hi, honey!"

She was breathless, glad to be home. Her cheek was cold when he kissed her. "I put that casserole in the oven," he said.

"Oh, Gary." She protested when he did domestic things, but was grateful. "Thanks. Kay Bee was a madhouse. I wish they'd cancel Christmas. It brings out the worst in people. That new dinosaur doll, you wouldn't believe. Women were shoving each other out of the way. One grandmother grabbed five. She was absolutely crazed. You should have seen her. Let me hang my coat, I'll toss a salad and—"

"Already done."

"Oh you."

She hung her coat and came back with glasses of wine. They sat in the living room. He took a sip.

"What first? National? Local? Sports?"

"Whatever."

"Come on, Gary. Choose, or I'll read Dear Abby."

He'd already listened to the national news on the radio. "Local then."

It was their evening ritual. She turned to Section B and started reading. "The clerical union at Town Hall has filed a grievance protesting the lack of convenient parking spaces . . ."

"Let them walk."

"My sentiments exactly."

Bea read on . . . a new cineplex was being built on the west side of town . . . six candidates were slugging it out for seats on the school board . . . a teacher with twenty-three years' experience was being fired for slapping a student . . .

80

"He probably deserved it," said Gary.

"And more," said Bea. "I know that kid. He's a monster. 'Another student, who declined to be identified, commented that the slapped teen "has a bad attitude." ' That's putting it mildly."

"If people would slap their kids around more—"

"Like we do?" she laughed. They'd always been unfailingly gentle with Johnny and Sally. Gary never raised a finger. On rare occasions when it was warranted, Bea was the disciplinarian.

"The world would be a better place."

Bea read a while longer. "Same old stuff," she said. "Nothing earthshaking."

"What about the obituaries?"

"Gary."

"Just see if there's anyone we know. Ron Thiebault had that heart attack last week. I'm kind of wondering about him."

"I shouldn't encourage your morbid side." But she turned to page two and scanned the obits. Her voice fell. "Oh, what a shame."

"What?"

"Kevin Cannivan died. He was in Johnny's class, remember? The family moved to Connecticut?"

"No."

"Well, he wasn't in Johnny's crowd. He was a preppie. Hung out with Skipper Boardman and that group. Good student. Really handsome. And polite."

"What's it say?"

" 'Kevin Cannivan, former resident of River Bend, died in an accident on November 22 in Coldwater, Connecticut, where he was a first-year seminarian at St. Sebastian's College.' " Bea stopped. "Seminarian? I never would have figured him for that."

"Go on."

" 'Before his family moved to Raven's Wing, Connecticut in 1992, Kevin was a member of the class of 1994 at River Bend High School. He was co-captain of the track team, treasurer of the National Honor Society, and president of his class. He is survived by his parents, Brendan and Louise, and four siblings: Peter, 17, Martha, 12, Daniel, 7, and Samantha, 4.' "

Gary sat there, thinking.

"I should send a note to his mother. Losing a child. I can't imagine."

"Bea?"

"Yes?"

"Tomorrow morning, get me up early, okay? I want you to drop me at the station on your way to school."

"Why?"

"Just something I want to check out."

"Something like what?"

"You said he hung around with Skipper Boardman."

"Among others. That doesn't mean anything, Gary."

"I know. But I've been meaning to see the guys anyway. It's long overdue."

"You're right about that. But how will you get home?"

"One of the guys'll drive me. Or I'll hitch a ride."

"Don't you dare."

"All I have to do is wave my cane and a beautiful babe will stop the car and—"

"That's what I'm afraid of." She leaned over and kissed him.

"The casserole," he murmured.

"Let it wait. I'm in the mood for an appetizer."

CHAPTER SEVENTEEN

By the time Louise passed through the gates of St. Sebastian's it was twilight. Fresh-faced students hurried by, heading back to dormitories and dining halls for dinner. Neon ski jackets flashed against a backdrop of snow.

In spite of her aversion to this place, Louise had to admit that the campus was beautiful. Once the estate of Laurence Sturdevant, owner of the mill, St. Sebastian's was situated along the river on three hundred acres of pristine hillside property overlooking the town of Coldwater. Classrooms and dormitories were housed in tidy clusters of white-columned clapboard buildings. There was a modern new gymnasium with olympic pool, a stone and glass arts center, clay tennis courts, well-maintained playing fields, and a small but reputable arboretum. At one end of the grounds was a stone church adorned with genuine gargoyles imported from France, its dour medieval countenance defiantly out of character with the colonial charm of the rest of the campus.

Though tuition was relatively modest, buildings and grounds bore evidence that funds were not lacking. Shrubs were tightly pruned and stone walkways free of weeds. Brass postlamps along walkways were polished to a high gloss.

Louise gravitated toward a bulletin board in the center of the main quadrangle. She scanned a hodge-podge of notices about meetings, summer internships, and on-campus interviews, hoping to find a campus map.

"I could just scream."

Louise glanced sideways. The words were spoken by a startling young woman with coffee skin, ice blue eyes, and wiry blond hair that ascended in a tightly sculpted inverted pyramid. Her ears were studded with multiple rhinestones in a variety of colors. She wore a pink fur-trimmed parka and had a backpack slung over one shoulder.

"That's what I get for trying to play by the rules. Well, if that's how they want it, fine."

Louise blinked. "Are you speaking to me?"

"I talk to anyone who will listen. Have one of these." She thrust a flyer at Louise. The headline referred to something called the Women's Resource Center. Louise stuffed it in her pocket.

"I followed all their rules and it's still not here."

"What rules? What's not here?"

"Rules about posting notices. There are plenty, and I followed them to the letter. I had to get all kinds of prior approvals. I printed my notice on white stock instead of neon raspberry that was my preference. I made it eight by ten, instead of eleven by fourteen. I toned down the wording. I met them halfway—more than halfway—but do they return the courtesy? No."

"I'm afraid I don't know what you're talking about."

"The WRC—Women's Resource Center. Read the flyer, it's all there. I'm in the process of setting one up, and it's no easy task, let me tell you. You wouldn't believe the apathy on this campus. No one cares about harassment. No one cares about freedom of choice. No one cares about date rape. Sometimes I don't know why I bother."

"I think you've chosen the wrong school if you want freedom of choice," said Louise.

"I didn't have any in that regard. Choice, that is. It's the only college my parents would pay for. They wanted a conservative environment. A place with values. At least that's what they said. So I'm here, making the best of a bad situation."

"I see."

"I've always tended to go against the flow. If I'd gone to Antioch like I wanted, I'd probably have become a skinhead . . ." She snickered. ". . . or a Young Republican.

"My mistake was caving in on the name. Women's Resource Center sounds so antiseptic—like a mini-mart stocked with feminine hygiene products. Resource for what? People have no idea. I should have trusted my instincts. I wanted WAR, but Dean Quillan said it was too inflammatory."

"War?"

"Women Against Rape. Or Repression. I couldn't decide which. Of course it's inflammatory. It's supposed to be inflammatory. It gets people's attention. It got yours, I can see that."

"I think it's a bit extreme."

"As well it should be. You don't know the half of it. I could tell you stories about this place—don't get me started. But hey, I'm forgetting my manners." She held out a pink-mittened hand. "Angelique Whiting."

"Louise Cannivan. My son—"

"Kevin. God, I'm sorry. We were all sorry."

"You knew him?"

"Not really. I saw him around, part of the seminary pack." Angelique's eyes bored into her like ice picks. "It must be rough. You here to get his things or what?"

"No. I'm here to ask some questions. To investigate."

"Really? Why?"

"I have reason to believe Kevin was murdered."

Angelique's eyes widened. "I heard it was . . . you know."

"The coroner called it autoerotic asphyxia. It may have been asphyxia and it may have been erotic, but the auto part I don't buy, not for a minute. I don't believe it was self-inflicted."

"Ah, you think someone killed him by accident?"

"No. I think it was deliberately staged."

"My God, but why?"

"When I know that I'll know who."

Angelique started stuffing flyers in the backpack. "You said you have reason to believe. Any reason in particular?"

"Let's just say a little bird told me."

"Not saying which bird, huh?"

"It's not that I won't," admitted Louise. "I can't. Someone called me—I don't know who. Whoever it was said Kevin had enemies. She said it wasn't an accident."

"I see." Angelique seemed to process this information slowly. She glanced at a Swatch on her wrist—"Hey, I've got to run"—and brandished a staple gun. "Got to get posting, since going through proper channels obviously didn't work. Nice to have met you, Louise."

"Wait—what's your hurry? Maybe we could have coffee or something. Maybe you can help me."

"I'd like to, I really would, but—hey!"

Louise was clutching Angelique's sleeve. "I've got to start somewhere, Angelique. You must know a lot of people, what with your Women's Resource Center and all."

"I don't know anything about this, believe me." She wrenched free and rubbed her arm.

Louise gave up. "Sorry. At least tell me where I can find Father Duffy. He was Kevin's advisor."

Angelique waved toward a granite mansion with two turrets on a hill some distance away. "Sturdevant Hall. He lives in one of the towers. A bat in the belfry."

Angelique tried once again to leave but Louise yanked her back. "And another thing . . ."

"Yes?"

"Spread the word, Angelique."

The pyramid of hard-packed hair tilted to one side. "What word?"

"Whoever killed my son won't get away with it."

"Sure," said Angelique uneasily. "Whatever you say."

The young woman edged away and was swallowed up by the

passing throng of students. Louise watched the sea of faces, then turned and walked up the snow-shoveled path.

Like somber sentinels, Sturdevant Hall and the old stone church faced each other from opposite sides of campus. Once the home of Laurence Sturdevant and his family, Sturdevant was an imposing three-story early Renaissance-style structure that now housed a couple of classrooms, miscellaneous administrative offices, and a faculty apartment or two. It retained the flavor of a private residence, and Louise felt like an intruder as she pushed through the heavy oak door.

She told herself she would try not to fly off the handle. She would try to be calm and rational. Clutching at Angelique hadn't been wise. If anything, it had frightened the young woman away.

She stepped into a statue-rich foyer worthy of the Medicis. St. Joseph glared accusingly. The Blessed Virgin looked sad and miserable. Jesus held up his hand as though mediating. Louise felt as though she'd interrupted a terrible family fight. She dropped her car keys and bent to retrieve them. The floor was cold. Maybe this visit was a big mistake. Maybe she should have stayed at the hotel with the others. Maybe she should have waited until tomorrow . . .

"May I help you?"

Louise screamed. The voice was a croak. A moon face cross-hatched with wrinkles hung above her. Sagging jowls hung loosely from the chin. Raisin eyes, magnified by steel-rimmed glasses, peered under tissue thin lids. It was a nun, an ancient one, in billowing layers of black fabric, coffee bean rosary beads swinging at her side and a convex silver heart bobbing on her chest.

"I am Sister Gabriel," she said in a voice as ragged as old parchment.

Louise stood up and tried to look sane. "I'm sorry. You startled me. I'm Louise Cannivan." She flipped through her mental Rolodex. "You sent a condolence note."

The nun's face softened. "It was the least I could do."

"Well thank you. People have been very kind. We got dozens of notes. Flowers too. And mass cards. I have the notes back at the hotel. I keep meaning to answer them, but I never do." She looked at Sister Gabriel and felt like an eight year old. "I didn't know nuns wore habits anymore."

"Conservative orders like mine do." She smiled, exposing teeth brown with age. "There aren't many of us left. I'm a throwback, I suppose, and admittedly a bit out of touch. I led a contemplative life for decades. Now I'm out of the closet, so to speak. I do housekeeping, office work, anything that needs doing."

Clearly she wasn't capable of doing much. She was old and frail and her breathing was labored.

"What may I do for you, Mrs. Cannivan?"

"I know I should have called first, but I had to come. I have to talk to Father Duffy, have to tell him . . ." She stopped.

"Tell him what?"

Louise hesitated, and then it came out. "Murder, Sister. I have reason to think my son was murdered."

Sister Gabriel clasped her hands together. "My, what a remarkable conjecture!"

"It's more than conjecture, Sister. It's conviction."

"But they said it was an accident."

"And they were wrong. I really must discuss it with Father Duffy. So if you'd kindly direct me—"

"He's saying Mass right now. But good gracious—this will upset him, it certainly will." She wrung her plump ringless hands. "He should be back in twenty minutes. You can wait if you like. Is your husband out in the car?"

"No."

"Ah. Back at the hotel, is he?"

"No. He's home."

Sister Gabriel seemed to find it remarkable that Brendan hadn't accompanied her. She looked at Louise almost sternly. "You made this journey by yourself?"

Louise smiled. "Women do that these days, Sister. Travel without chaperones. But actually, I have four of them. Four friends—senior citizens—accompanied me. They're back at the hotel. Resting."

"I see. Well. You can wait in the parlor, if you like."

She followed Sister Gabriel into a wood-paneled room that smelled of sealing wax. The predominant color was burgundy. A fire crackled in the marble fireplace and a stained glass window cast shards of light from the setting sun. She sank into a wing chair by the fire. Suddenly she felt bone tired.

"Would you like some tea?"

"That would be wonderful."

But Sister Gabriel seemed in no hurry to leave. She hovered and chattered. "I simply can't get over this. Murder at St. Sebastian's! My, my, my. Father Duffy has a surprise in store. This is terrible news!"

She didn't sound like it was terrible; she sounded enthralled. "Goodness, now I'm going to see shadows lurking in every corner! It was such a tragedy. And now to hear that someone may have murdered—"

"Did," corrected Louise. "Someone did murder."

"As you say." She seemed to turn a thought over in her mind. "You know, Mrs. Cannivan, I have quite a bit of time on my hands. They have professional cleaners for the offices, and Father Duffy's apartment never gets very dirty. And the vestments require very little care, what with the synthetic fabrics they use today."

Louise waited, wondering what she was driving at.

"I just mean I'd be glad to help you any way I can. I could look into student records and the like." She leaned forward conspiratorially. "I'm not without access, you know. It might be useful to have help from someone on 'the inside,' as it were."

Louise was undone. "That would be wonderful, Sister! What a kind, generous offer!"

"Not at all," said Sister Gabriel primly. "If indeed it was

murder, whoever did it should pay, shouldn't they?" That said, she left to get the tea.

Louise closed her eyes and leaned back in the chair, already anticipating the sweet taste of vengeance.

CHAPTER EIGHTEEN

"Ah, Mrs. Cannivan!"

She hadn't expected him to be so handsome. He was tall, in his late forties or early fifties near as she could tell, with a ruddy face, unruly brown hair and piercing blue eyes behind tortoise-shell glasses. He took her cold hands in his warm ones and smiled.

"I'm delighted you've come. I can't tell you the number of times I thought about calling. But I didn't want to intrude. I told myself if you wanted to talk, you would come to me. And so you have."

"It's good of you to see me, Father. I know I should have called first but—"

"Francis," he said and winked amicably. "The students call me Father, but I don't stand on formality when it comes to adults."

"All right. Francis." She had never been on a first-name basis with a priest. "I'm Louise."

"And a lovely name it is. A name of character and grace. I'm pleased to see you've made yourself comfortable by the fire, Louise. Ghastly weather we're having. I wish I had some pull there . . ." He glanced up. ". . . but I'm in sales, not management." He smiled at this little joke.

"We managed fine."

"We?"

"I came up with friends—two gentleman and two ladies. They're back at the hotel. They came for moral support. And it so happens they know Kevin's roommate."

His face lit up. "Cameron Maine! A fine young man. One of our best." He glanced at his watch. "It's close enough to five— what do you say? I'm going to pour myself a scotch. Would you like one too? Or a sherry? Or perhaps you'd prefer to stick with that noxious brew Sister Gabriel foisted off on you."

Louise smiled. "She scared the daylights out of me."

"Sister has a habit of creeping up on people. It's those tennis shoes she wears. She's old as Methuselah but still full of vinegar. Never ceases to amaze me. She was in a cloistered order. Hardly spoke a word for sixty years. It's no wonder her vocal cords atrophied. At least that's my theory. I've been urging her to see a doctor, but she won't go.

"In any case, she's a blessing. We never had nuns at St. Sebastian's until Sister G. Of course, that's the way I wanted it. Nuns nowadays tend to be radical. Always raising rabble in Latin America or demanding to serve Mass. But not Sister Gabriel. She's a traditionalist after my own heart. No short skirts or polyester for her, no indeed."

"How did she happen to come here?"

"She arrived at our door one day with a sad tale. Her convent had gone bankrupt. Oh, it happens, I'm sorry to say—convents going bust right and left, leaving nuns high and dry. They have no pensions, no retirement plans, no nothing. I call them Nun Boat People.

"So here she was, seeking a safe haven. Ordinarily I'd have turned her away, but by purest coincidence we were in dire need of a housekeeper. The previous one had quit. Just up and left, most abruptly, I might add. Gave no notice, never said a word to me." His face clouded. "Well, never mind that. Sister G. is a fine replacement. She takes things in hand. Does whatever needs doing. I just wish she'd stay."

"She's leaving?"

"Can't stay beyond the first of the year. Illness in the family or some such. I don't know what we'll do without her." He shrugged his shoulders. "Well, we'll have to manage somehow. Now how about that drink?"

"Scotch would be fine. Over ice."

"A woman after my own heart." He opened a mahogany cabinet, revealing a mini-refrigerator and built-in bar well stocked with Chivas, Beefeater, Seagram's VO, and Dry Sack. "Laurence Sturdevant thought of everything, God rest his soul."

"I understand he left his estate to the college."

"Not to the college." Francis handed her a weighty prismed glass and hoisted his own as though making a toast. "To the church."

She returned the salute. "To the church!"

He seemed to find that very amusing. "I wasn't making a toast, Louise. I was simply saying that Laurence Sturdevant left his estate to the church. Then the church built the college."

"I see." She should have felt foolish, but she didn't. To her surprise she felt quite comfortable with Father Francis Duffy.

"In fact, Sturdevant left more than these grounds. He left stocks, bonds, factories, a foundry down in Chattanooga, Tennessee, real estate scattered from here to kingdom come. Cut his children off without a dime, bless his flinty heart. And him a Protestant, would you believe it? But a marvelously perverse Protestant.

"But never mind that. You want to talk about Kevin."

"Yes. No one talks about him anymore. It's as though he never existed." She swallowed hard. "People find it embarrassing, I guess. The way he supposedly died."

Francis blinked. "Supposedly?"

"You haven't talked to Sister Gabriel?"

"No. She had her face buried in a file cabinet. Was she supposed to tell me something?"

He seemed like such a nice man. Louise decided to put off telling him for the moment. "No. Just tell me about Kevin. Please."

Francis Duffy was at a loss. He wondered what to tell this woman. He searched her eyes for a clue, something to build on, something that would help her. And at that moment something quite unexpected happened: He felt a pang of longing. He wondered what it would be like to comfort her, to hold her hand, to touch her hair, to . . .

"Francis?"

He was so flustered he almost dropped his drink. He took a sip and tried to regain his equilibrium. Good Lord, what was happening to him? The church encouraged priests to have female friends and many of them at that, as a safeguard against becoming sexually attracted to any one in particular. Francis had always dismissed such suggestions as poppycock. He had always been strong, totally self sufficient, at least until . . . Well, never mind that. It was over. Done. He'd been a damned fool and it would never happen again.

He took a deep breath. "Forgive me. I was woolgathering . . . thinking about Kevin. He had so much promise. I pinned my hopes on him, more than I should have perhaps. But he was a find, Louise. A real find." This was all true.

He rattled on. "Frankly, we don't get applicants like Kevin anymore. Boys have other goals today. I make the trek year after year, recruiting at secondary schools up and down the East Coast. Every year I go to your Raven's Wing High School, even though others have told me it's a waste of time. It's a secular school in a prosperous town where boys have a plethora of worldly options. They see no appeal in a religious vocation. That's what I've been told."

He thrust his chin forward. "But I can be determined. You see, I remember not so long ago when Raven's Wing provided a stream of applicants from its devout Italian community. And now, when times are tough, when spirituality is on the decline and the world wallows in a cesspool of situational ethics, I firmly believe there has to be a light in the darkness."

Louise nodded.

"I have taken it upon myself to be that light. So I had to be at Raven's Wing High School. I had to be everywhere."

"I understand."

"You do? Good." He took a deep breath. "Therefore, I forced myself to endure booth duty at the college fair, a most demeaning experience, I can assure you. I stood out like a sore thumb. I set up my card table next to the likes of Amherst and Brown and Swarthmore. I suffered sideways glances and snickers from the students I sought to recruit. I groveled. And I hated every minute of it.

"No one touched my stack of pamphlets. It was as though I had a contagious disease. But I didn't care. I was there, you see, and that's what mattered."

Louise nodded again. Francis Duffy was a man with values, and she admired him for it.

"I knew someone would hear the calling, just knew it. And, sure enough, in time someone did."

She sighed. "Kevin."

"You weren't happy about it, were you?"

"Not very."

Francis hastened to reassure her. "I want you to know that we treasured your son. We appreciated him. Kevin was special, Louise. Very special." He closed his eyes for a moment, trying to conjure up a suitable memory.

What really happened, Francis? Did the boy disappoint you? And did he deserve such punishment? A boy only eighteen years old?

The ruddiness drained from his face.

"Francis, what is it?" Without thinking, Louise touched his hand. It was cold as stone.

"Nothing!" Her hand burned into his flesh. It was a most exquisite sensation. He pulled his away with a pang of regret. "Where was I? Oh, yes . . ."

Kevin had come for his admission interview after the deadline. Acceptances had already gone out and the seminary class was, at least in theory, closed. But when Francis saw Kevin Cannivan's transcript he knew he would make an exception. The boy's record was stellar—athletic star, National Honor Society member, delegate to Nutmeg Boys' State, Rotary Student of the Year . . . the list went on.

In fact, Kevin Cannivan looked so good on paper that Francis braced himself for disappointment at the face-to-face meeting. Surely there would be a glitch. A flaw. A defect of character. But there wasn't. The boy's manner was polite and deferential. He was earnest. He was pious. He said all the right things.

Francis thought Kevin Cannivan was just the sort of young man the church needed. The kind of young man who could help put the church back on track.

Getting the church back on track was important to Francis, for underneath his genial informality he was a bedrock traditionalist. He believed in the Virgin Birth. He believed in the infallibility of the Pope. He believed in celibacy for priests. He believed in all of it absolutely and unequivocally.

But the price for his beliefs was high. Over time Francis built a wall of faith, a wall fashioned with bricks of dogma and ritual, a wall held together by the cement of tradition, a wall that excluded all but the perfect, the pious, and the pure. A wall that excluded everyone but Francis Xavier Duffy.

If you had asked Francis, he would have told you he felt no sense of isolation. He was surrounded by people, after all—students, seminarians, faculty, administration, poor folk he helped through the Good Works Program. He wasn't alone; he was surrounded.

But lately he had trouble sleeping. Some nights he would get tipsy watching the eleven o'clock news and fall asleep in the chair. Later he would awake with tears burning his eyes and have no idea why. On nights like that he would get up. He would wander about the campus, a ghost in a black coat, checking windows, relocking gates, making lists, looking for something, anything, that might be amiss.

He had a sense of foreboding. A sense that something evil was lurking at the gate, something that no lock could exclude. It would come inside, into his heart, and steal him away.

Francis told himself that this sense of foreboding was not entirely unjustified. Just look around. Everything has run amok. The church is crumbling, and no one seems to care. Liberal Catholics denounce the Virgin Birth. Homosexuals get "married." Bishops father nasty vindictive children who expose them on national television. Teenagers pass around condoms as though they're baseball cards. Where will it end?

Francis saw himself as a man at sea, adrift in a leaky lifeboat—a lifeboat that was the seminary program at St. Sebastian's College. This lifeboat was the only good thing left in his life, and now it was taking water fast.

Once St. Sebastian's had been a grand and glorious place, an oasis of goodness and virtue dedicated exclusively to the preparation of young men for the priesthood. But over time, as worldly options multiplied, the number of applicants dwindled.

Francis winced inside. In his day seminarians had been the cream of the crop. Now it was a croppy cream. He blamed that croppy cream on the crushing shortage of manpower. More than once the bishop had sent him candidates of lesser quality. More than once Francis had rejected such candidates. And more than once the bishop had forced him to reconsider. The bishop made it quite clear that if Francis did not take all the men he sent, he would find a place that did. If that happened, enrollment in the seminary program would dwindle to nothing and the program would close.

Francis sighed. Unfortunately if a fellow wanted to become a priest and was not too educationally unfit, psychologically aberrant, or flagrantly homosexual he could usually find a diocese that would sponsor him and a seminary that would accept him. Lately St. Sebastian's Seminary accepted any slug who applied.

Worse yet, as the number of applicants dwindled secular students were allowed to enroll at the college to make up the difference. Francis fought this tooth and nail, but to no avail. Secular students soon outnumbered seminarians. Lay faculty—a grossly appropriate appellation, thought Francis—replaced most of the clergy.

But that wasn't the worst. The worst was the admission of females.

Several years back they'd been cursed with a bishop who was a liberal thinker. He was gone now, but his damage was done. He'd seen admission of girls as a practical solution to pressing financial problems of the college and he sold the board a bill of goods. He demeaned himself, lobbying like a huckster. Girls would actually help the seminary program, he said. Contact with females would make seminarians more worldly-wise, more sophisticated—and less susceptible to breaking the vow of celibacy. Contact with females would sensitize seminarians to the needs of parishioners they would be called on to counsel later.

Sensitivity? thought Francis. Stick it up your pointy hat!

The bishop painted a glowing picture of St. Sebastian's Seminary as a pilot program within the college, a program that would be replicated at Catholic colleges and universities across the nation. "Think of it," he said, putting his arm around Francis's shoulder. "Seminary programs at Notre Dame, Georgetown . . ." His voice reached a crescendo. ". . . at your alma mater Holy Cross! Seminarians studying alongside lay students."

Seminarians getting laid, thought Francis sourly.

"We face a financial Waterloo," said the bishop. "Girls must be admitted or your seminary will go bankrupt."

Francis had no choice.

After that it was simply a matter of time before his precious seminary became an odd-ball curiosity—twenty misfits in black shirts and starched white collars relegated to a decrepit cracker-box dormitory on the edge of campus.

He turned his attention back to Louise. "Kevin was a cut above others in our program. For one thing, he was more sophisticated. The others are a bit awkward socially. Kevin was polished and poised. He mixed well with everyone. We don't encourage boys who've heard the calling to be recluses, you know. We want them to participate in college life. We want them to be sure, very sure, before they take their final vows."

"We were surprised by Kevin's choice," said Louise. "And we didn't encourage him. The life of a priest is . . ." She considered the word "abnormal" and rejected it. ". . . lonely."

Francis felt a sudden and disconcerting urge to tell Louise Cannivan just how lonely it was . . . about Christmas dinners unshared and masses said in empty churches . . . about making a marvelous soufflé and eating it by yourself . . . about relying on friends like Johnny Walker and Jack Daniel's for company on long Sunday afternoons . . . and the worst, the very worst—playing Game Boy, an addictive computerized gadget, in the dim light of the confessional because no one bothered to show up. Sometimes he thought he would go crazy.

"It can be lonely," he admitted. "For some."

That's why part of him, the lonely part that had almost given up, couldn't believe his eyes when Kevin Cannivan appeared for an interview. A boy with the grades to go anywhere. A boy who could become a lawyer or doctor or stockbroker. A boy with an easy smile and confident yet respectful demeanor . . .

"I don't remember seeing you at the college fair," said Francis gruffly. He leafed through the boy's file and didn't bother looking up. "So. Why do you want to be a priest?"

It was a question he asked every applicant, and the answers were invariably boring. Heartfelt but boring. Callow young men mouth-

ing platitudes about serving God. Adam's apples bobbing above constricting neckties. Flaming whiskerless cheeks and youthful eyes burning with intensity. Sometimes those burning eyes were red flags. Zealots were to be avoided. There was a young man a few years back, a white-knuckled fellow with a pinched face and bloodless lips. He talked about "the good old days" and upon further probing Francis realized the boy was referring to the Inquisition. That boy had been culled. Several years later Francis heard he was in the state mental hospital after having torched a Planned Parenthood clinic.

Kevin Cannivan sat ramrod straight in his navy blazer, pinstripe shirt, and red tie with blue pin dots. "I wish I had an answer for you, Father. Something nice and pat and sensible. But I don't. I only know that as I live and breathe, it's what I must be." He paused. "It's as though I have no choice in the matter."

This snagged Francis's attention. "Why? Do you have visions? Is someone or something compelling you to do this? Someone in your family?" He arched his eyebrows. "Someone dead perhaps?"

Young Cannivan shook his head. "My family doesn't even know I'm here. They won't be thrilled, believe me. And I'm not crazy. I have no visions, no dead people confronting me in the night. I say prayers, but most of the time it feels like no one is listening. Or worse, like no one is there at all."

"Most of the time?"

"There are moments—few and far apart—when . . ." He shrugged his shoulders. "When I'm sure. Absolutely sure."

Francis nodded.

"I want more of those moments."

Without realizing it, Kevin Cannivan had struck a nerve. Francis would never admit it, but he himself hardly heard from God anymore. As St. John of the Cross had written in the sixteenth century, Francis was enduring the "dark night of the soul," when believers doubt the existence of God. For a deeply pious priest such as Francis doubt can be particularly devastating. If prayer has no answer and no meaning, his life's work, his very existence, is all for nothing.

Francis felt a surge of jealousy. Who did this boy think he was? To have such grand and glorious moments—to want more of them yet—when he, Francis, stopped experiencing them long ago.

"Most of the time we pray into a vacuum," said Francis shortly. "At least it feels that way. That's what faith is all about."

"Yeah," said Cannivan. "Faith." As though it was nothing.

"Are you homosexual?" Francis tossed the question out suddenly.

"Hell no!" The boy caught himself. "Sorry. I mean no."

"It's all right if you are. Homosexuals are in the clergy in the same proportion as the general population." This was debatable, but Francis went on. "The church simply forbids the practice of homosexuality. Or, when it comes to the clergy, the practice of heterosexual sex for that matter."

"Well I'm not. Homosexual. I've dated enough to be sure. Had enough girls."

Francis looked at him hard and Cannivan's poise cracked for the second time. "I didn't mean it like that," he said. "I meant I've had experiences, shared experiences. With girls. You know. At dances, on picnics. Things like that."

Even to Cannivan this sounded lame. He glanced around the room. "This isn't going well, is it?"

"It's going fine."

The boy looked desperate. "Look, I've got to get in here."

Francis eyed him curiously. "Why?"

A veil came over Cannivan's face. "I just do." He tried to make light of it—"To save my soul?"—and smiled as though making a joke.

Francis played along with the joke. Worse, he trivialized what had been a distinct warning. "Ah. So there's a dark secret in your soul, Kevin Cannivan."

"Don't I wish," joked the boy. "But seriously, I've never done anything for which I'm ashamed. Ever."

He was a far better liar than I, thought Francis, far better.

Louise folded her hands. "So my son was remarkable. But

now he's dead, and being remarkable doesn't matter very much."

He set down his drink. "It was a tragedy, Louise. We've made strides. We counsel our seminarians. We have a sex education program. We just never considered the possibility of what happened to Kevin. I blame myself for that to some degree."

"There's something I must tell you, Francis."

"Oh?" He pushed his glasses up the bridge of his nose and waited.

"Kevin's death wasn't any accident."

"I beg your pardon?"

She told him about the phone call. "Now you understand," she said, "why I'm convinced it was murder."

"Louise, that's simply not possible."

"Oh, but it is, Francis. Think about it . . ." She proceeded to describe in graphic detail just how Kevin's death could have been arranged.

He drummed his fingers on the arm of the sofa, buying time. His mind was reeling. "Who do you suppose called you?"

"I have no idea."

"You say it was a young lady?"

"I think so. I might recognize the voice if I heard it again."

"What do you have in mind? Surely you don't intend to interview everyone on this campus?"

"Maybe."

"I can't allow it. It would be disruptive. It would be—"

"I have to do *something*. My son was murdered."

"*May* have been," he corrected. "You don't know it for a fact. And I'm not asking you to ignore it. I'm merely asking you to tread lightly. There are people out there, Louise . . . people who have no use for traditional Catholic values. People who'd just as soon see the seminary program close. This would be grist for their mill."

"I can't believe they'd use something like this to shut you down."

"Oh, wouldn't they? Murder? Think about it." He gazed

into his glass. He needed time to think, time to plan. It would not do for Louise and her friends to start poking around. It wouldn't do at all.

Louise stood up abruptly. "I'd like to see where Kevin died."

"Now? But we haven't finished our drinks. It's bitter cold and dark besides. Let me take you in the morning."

Once again Louise was determined. "I don't want to be a bother, Francis. Just tell me the way, and I'll find it."

Francis set down his glass. He had forgotten how stubborn women could be, especially mothers when it concerned their children.

He took one last sip. "No bother," he said shortly. "I'll get our coats."

CHAPTER NINETEEN

"Where the hell is she?"

"Calm down. She'll be all right."

"We never should have let her go off like that."

Forrest was a worrier and Irene refused to encourage him. She continued the ritual of unpacking. She withdrew a tangled mass of clothing from Forrest's bag—underwear, flannel shirts, a pair of dungarees, socks, handkerchiefs, and a jockstrap. She arranged them in his side of the bureau. She hung two pairs of blue jeans and a pair of dress trousers in a crypt-like closet that had no door. She put his toilet kit in a bathroom that featured a cracked sink, slimy shower curtain, and mold that streaked down the walls like entrails.

"Bathroom's disgusting," she pronounced. "No amount of Lysol will fix it neither."

Loretta, the desk clerk, had assigned the group to three connecting rooms, with the hallway accessible only from the middle one—Forrest and Irene's—a convoluted configuration that caused Forrest to dub it "The Lizzie Borden Suite." Forrest, who made a hobby of the famous forty-whacker, pointed out that the upstairs rooms of Andrew J. Borden's house had been similarly arranged.

"Folks are gonna be traipsing in and out of our room at all hours," he groused.

"What do you care?" said Irene. "You won't be sleeping anyway. You never do during a case."

"Well, I might want to do something else."

"Really?" she said hopefully.

Forrest tested the bed, finding it soft and lumpy. He flipped aimlessly through the inevitable Bible left by the Gideons. He turned on the TV and turned it off. He stared at the rotary dial on the old ebonite phone. "I suppose she'll call if she runs into any trouble."

"Of course she will, Forrest."

"After all, she's a grown woman." His stomach growled irritably. "Let's get some dinner." He slipped his new sheepskin jacket from a plastic bag. The jacket was a recent birthday present from Mildred and he hadn't worn it yet. He'd wanted to keep it nice. It made him look rugged, like the Marlboro man. Or Lorne Green before he was reduced to doing Alpo commercials. He strode down the hall with Irene on his arm humming the Bonanza tune and almost felt young.

"Shouldn't we get Mildred and Trevor?" asked Irene.

"They're talking to the coroner. Guy's a GP. Has a storefront clinic right down the street."

At the desk downstairs Loretta batted clumpy eyelashes at Forrest. "Evening, Mr. Haggarty. My, what a fine jacket. What can I do for you this evening?" She arched a penciled eyebrow.

Forrest was tempted to tell her exactly what she could do and in what position, when Irene's elbow shot into his ribs. "We're looking for dinner," he managed to say.

"And nothing else," added Irene pointedly.

"Pearl's Luncheonette is across the street," drawled Loretta. "It's not fancy but the food's hearty and the prices reasonable. Or if you're thirsty, there's Rudy's Pub next door, but all he serves is chili dogs and pizza. When our guests eat there we save on heat later, if you get my drift." She smiled broadly, revealing the gift of gums.

Forrest considered the alternatives: separate formica tables of Pearl's versus the camaraderie of the bar. It wouldn't hurt to get to know some of the locals. He wasn't really supposed to drink, what with his heart and all, but what the hey, one beer would be okay.

"Maybe we'll have cocktails at Rudy's and then transfer to Pearl's for the main course." He gave Irene a squeeze.

"Cocktails? Mister, you're a sketch." Loretta touched a strand of her plastic hair and winked.

"Come on, Forrest." Irene pulled him away.

They stepped outside into a blast of frigid air. Main Street was drab and gray. A neon sign over the pharmacy blinked DREXEL   UGS. A card in the window of the Sir Speedy Print Shop said you could have a second color free on Tuesdays. An enormous hand hanging over the sidewalk announced that you could have your fortune told or your handwriting analyzed by Miss Monique. Bleached faces peered from old photos in the camera shop window. A Salvation Army Santa leaned against a soggy cardboard chimney and jerked his bell listlessly. Thirty feet down the street a portly man cried, "Sonuvabitch stole my dime!", kicked an offending meter, and cavorted about in an agonized little jig.

"Another day in paradise," muttered Forrest.

Rudy's Pub smelled of beer and sweat and pepperoni. There was sawdust on the floor and a moth-eaten moose head on the wall. Two overhead fans festooned with oily spider webs turned lazily. The place appeared empty except for a portly man in a stained apron washing glasses behind the bar.

Forrest helped Irene onto a stool and stood at her side. "You must be Rudy," he said.

The man wiped hands the size of hams on his apron. "Nope. Rudy retired three years back. I'm his nephew, Owen Quick."

"Forrest," said Forrest, "and this here's Irene."

"Pleased to meet you folks. What'll it be?"

"I'll have a daiquiri on the rocks," said Irene. "With a cherry."

"What's on tap?" asked Forrest.

"Bud, Pabst, Ganset." Each brand was a grunt.

Forrest made a face. "Christ, I haven't had a Ganset since Lord knows when. Not since a buddy of mine showed me a bottle with a mouse inside, all black and decomposing. Someone did it at the factory. Sheesh. That was years ago. I'd forgotten all about it."

"So," said Quick, "Bud or Pabst? Now that we've narrowed it down."

"I'll have a Ganset. For old times' sake."

Quick filled a glass, thinking it took all kinds. These folks were clearly from out of town. Probably wandered off Route 7 on their way south for the winter. From the looks of things the fellow had money, what with that fancy jacket. Quick served the drinks and noticed the man's hand tremble slightly as he reached for his beer. Parkinson's, maybe. Or booze. Or maybe just old age.

"Thought this place'd be packed at the end of the day," said Forrest. He took a sip. Christ, the beer tasted like horse piss. What the hell had happened? Years ago he liked Ganset just fine. Maybe they'd changed the formula. They changed everything these days the minute your back was turned. And when they weren't changing, they were discontinuing. Once he'd caused a hell of a ruckus in Stop & Shop because he couldn't find his favorite cereal, Raisins Rice and Rye. It was gone, they told him. Finished. Before he could even stockpile. A few years later they did the same damned thing with Oat Bran Options. Oat bran is out, they told him. Discontinued.

"Use to be crowded," replied Quick, polishing a glass. He held it to the light of the plastic Tiffany lamp. "That was before they closed the mill. Now we get a crowd the first Friday of the month when the welfare checks arrive and that's about it. Except for Brooksie." He gestured with the towel toward the back.

Forrest and Irene looked. It was like peering into a cave. In the darkness they saw a man, facedown on a table.

"Looks like Brooksie's had one too many," remarked Forrest.

"You know what they say. One is too many and a hundred is never enough. Brooksie's always had a taste for the grape, but it's been worse since he lost his job."

"Worked at the mill, huh?"

"No, at the college."

"Is that right?"

"Yeah. He was janitor. Then they canned him. Last October, it was." Quick lowered his voice. "He was the one who found that kid."

Forrest leaned forward. "Really?"

"Yeah. The seminarian. The one with his pecker—" He glanced at Irene. "Sorry, ma'am."

"Apology accepted," said Irene. "Now, as you were saying . . . ?"

Quick turned and began stacking steins, continuing the conversation with his back to them. "Brooksie found that kid. In the chapel. It shook him up something awful. Not that anyone sympathized. You'd think he'd done it, the way folks treated him. I suppose they were upset because it affects the reputation of the school. This town depends on the college, at least the locals do. No, it wasn't easy for Brooksie, seeing that kid, then being the messenger of such grim news. He says he has nightmares. That's why he's drinking more than usual. Any excuse, right?" He turned from the steins and looked at the empty space where Forrest had been. "Where'd the hell he go?"

"Back there . . ." Irene pointed. "To talk to Mr. Brooks."

CHAPTER TWENTY

"Careful," he cautioned, "it's icy. The path is salted, but we're plagued by the freeze-thaw syndrome."

She stepped gingerly, following the erratic beam of the Black and Decker. He gripped the flashlight tighter and reached for her elbow with his free hand. "Doing okay?"

"Fine, Francis." He was the one huffing and puffing. "What about you?"

"I know. I sound like the little engine that couldn't. I have emphysema and—"

She stopped in her tracks. "Emphysema! For heaven's sake, why didn't you say so? I never would have asked you to do this."

"It's all right. Really. I just have to take care of myself. Not smoke anymore. That kind of thing." Not drink either, but he didn't say that. Some doctor's orders were simply too much.

"You're sure?"

"I'm sure. Come on. We're almost there."

After a while the asphalt started to incline downward and she heard the river. In spite of the cold, she felt herself perspiring under her coat. Suddenly she slipped and her knee smashed on the pavement, tearing pantyhose and flesh. Tears sprang to her eyes. "Damn!"

Francis turned the flashlight on her. "Oh my." He knelt and dabbed the wound with a white handkerchief. "That's a nasty scrape, Louise."

"It's all right."

"Want to go back?" he said.

"No."

"Okay." He sighed.

"Francis?"

"Yes?"

"Please stop sighing."

"All right, but this isn't such a good idea. We can't see a thing. Morning would have been better."

"I can see fine, Francis. Just fine."

"Very well. But please hold the railing."

Finally they reached a small promenade by the edge of the river. He gestured with the flashlight. "The chapel's over there . . . Our Lady of the Woods. Rather desolate now, I'm afraid. There's no heat, no electricity. No one comes here in winter. In summer it's quite lovely. A place of solitude, a place of prayer. We never dreamed it would be a place of . . . Louise?"

She walked up a ramp for the handicapped and pushed open the door. "Francis," she whispered, "someone's inside."

He hurried to her side. "That can't be." He brushed past her, stepped inside, walked through the vestibule and shone the flashlight down the aisle.

"Father Duffy!"

"Deirdre! What on earth . . ."

The girl blotted her eyes with a wad of Kleenex and maneuvered toward them. The spokes of the wheels on her chair glinted in the light of the Black and Decker. She stopped and tried to compose herself. "Sorry, Father Duffy. I didn't mean to scare you. I come here sometimes. To be alone. To think."

He looked at her in amazement. How she'd made it all the way down here was beyond him. "You really shouldn't be coming down here, Deirdre. Not with the path as icy as it is. Not alone."

"I'm fine." The words came automatically. It was what she told everyone all the time. That she was fine.

Louise came forward. "Francis?"

He looked at her and she realized he was embarrassed that she called him by his first name in front of a student. "Louise Cannivan," he said stiffly, "meet Deirdre Canfield. Deirdre is one of our students. A member of our freshman class, I believe?"

"Yes," replied Deirdre. *You know damn well I'm a freshman, asshole.* "Pleased to meet you, Mrs. Cannivan. I'd heard you were on campus."

"Word certainly gets around," said Francis a bit sourly.

"People talk," explained Deirdre. "I'm sorry about your son, Mrs. Cannivan. Really sorry."

"Did you know him, Deirdre?"

"Louise, I doubt Deirdre would have—"

"Yes!" Deirdre stopped, as though surprised that she had blurted this truth. "I mean, well, we had a couple of classes together. We were friends."

"You were?"

"Yes. And I miss him, Mrs. Cannivan. I miss him a lot."

Louise looked down at the young woman and felt a pang of compassion. "We all miss him, honey. But thank you for saying so."

"Well," said Deirdre, "I'd better be going."

"Wait in the vestibule," instructed Francis. "We'll walk you back."

"Father, I really don't need—"

"I said *wait.*"

She glared. "All right."

When she was out of earshot, Francis turned to Louise. "Now, what is it you'd like to see?"

"I'm not sure." Her eyes searched the room. "May I have the flashlight?"

"Of course."

She shone it all around. Everything was immaculate . . . the plain white altar up front . . . a simple wooden statue of Mary to the left . . . the baptismal niche to the right . . . a row of twenty pews of unvarnished pine.

"Nothing has been touched since Kevin died," said Francis. "There were no signs of disturbance when Kevin was found. Nothing was out of place, except for the radio and the candles. You heard about the candles?"

"Yes. And the radio. Kevin hated oldies music. He liked heavy metal and rap."

"I don't understand."

"We were told the radio was playing songs from the sixties. Kevin would never have listened to that music. So that's one more piece in this puzzle that doesn't make sense."

"Perhaps. And what about the bottle of bourbon?"

"What about it?"

"If someone was here with Kevin—a young lady, for example—wouldn't there have been cups? I hardly think he'd expect her to drink from the bottle."

Louise looked at him almost pityingly. "Francis, I'm afraid you're a bit out of touch. Boys will be boys, as they say. Kevin was a gentleman most times. But an illicit tryst with a girl? I doubt he'd think to bring glasses."

"Oh."

"Or if he did, maybe she took the cups away. Whoever it was had great presence of mind."

"There were no prints on the bottle other than Kevin's. None on the radio either."

"So she wore gloves. Or wiped the prints clean."

"You're seeing things the way you want to see them, Louise."

"We'll see." She stalked up the aisle with Francis following at her heels. She shone the light on the altar, on Mary's face. She got down on her hands and knees and directed the beam under the pews.

"You'll get all dirty, Louise." He waited. "What are you looking for?"

"Clues."

He lost patience. "Oh honestly! There's nothing here!"

"Yes there is!" She struggled to her feet and held her hand up triumphantly.

"What's that?"

She turned a small white plastic jar round and round in her gloved hand. The label said DERMA COLOR CAMOUFLAGE CREAM.

"Oh that," he said as though it were nothing. "Stage makeup. Probably left by a student in our theater group."

"It's a clue!"

"You're grasping at straws, Louise. We have an active theater arts program. The students stage three productions a year. Many participate. Any number of people could have left it here."

"But the chapel is in perfect order, you said so yourself. And nothing's been touched since Kevin died. You said that too. Your maintenance people would have picked this up if it was here before then."

"Perhaps they missed it. Perhaps some other visitor—someone like Deirdre Canfield—dropped it after the fact."

"And perhaps not. Perhaps it was dropped when Kevin was murdered."

"You're a stubborn lady, Louise Cannivan, a very stubborn lady. What am I going to do with you?"

"I don't know."

"If it will make you feel better, I'll ask around about it." He held out his hand.

"Ask around, if you like, but I'll hold onto this for now." She slipped the jar into her pocket. "I'm not giving up. This is only a start. I don't have any answers yet, but I will, Francis. Mark my words."

"We should head back, Louise."

"All right. But tomorrow my friends and I will talk to Kevin's roommate."

He nodded grimly. "If you like."

He wheeled Deirdre back to her dormitory in silence. After dropping her off, he walked Louise to her car.

She turned to him. "Francis . . ."

"Yes?"

"You've been very kind. Thank you."

He waved away her gratitude. "I haven't done anything."

"Yes you have. Oh, you've been skeptical—but you've also been understanding and sympathetic. And you made that walk to the chapel. You took the time."

He patted his stomach. "I needed the exercise. And time? Well, I have plenty of that, Louise." He considered how he would spend his evening, rattling about in his small apartment in the tower.

"Louise?"

"Yes?"

"I was wondering . . ." He brought himself up short and shook his head no. "Never mind."

"What?"

"I was wondering if you might like to join me for dinner. It would be very proper, of course." He could not believe he was doing this. He willed himself to be silent, but his mouth rattled on with a will of its own. "Nothing fancy. If memory serves, there's some leftover beef stew. And a nice beaujolais. I'll toss a salad. And make some crescent rolls, the kind that come out of a tube."

He was chattering like a magpie. *Stop, Francis. Stop this minute. Stop . . . right . . . now.* "But never mind. I forgot. Your friends await you. Some other time perhaps." There. He had invited her and declined for her all in one breath. Thank God it was over.

"I'd love to have dinner with you." Without thinking, she leaned forward and kissed him on the cheek.

He touched the spot. His face flamed in the darkness. He felt a disconcerting tug in his private parts. His voice was hoarse and reproachful. "Louise . . ."

"It's okay, Francis. It was only a peck on the cheek. A platonic kiss. I'll behave, I promise."

"I hope so."

But did he really want her too? Did he? He saw himself holding her hand. That would be enough.

No it won't Francis. You'll want more.

This time will be different. I'm stronger now, much stronger. This time I'll be able to handle it.

Sure, Francis. Sure.

Gently he took hold of Louise's elbow.

"Francis?"

"Yes?"

"It would be easier if you took my hand."

He looked around. It was dark. No one would see.

"Very well," he said.

She slipped her gloved hand into his and they walked together along the ice-crusted path.

CHAPTER TWENTY·ONE

Lester Brooks sat propped across from Forrest and Irene in a booth at Pearl's. He was so drunk he was one step from comatose. He kept listing right, then left.

"Easy there, Mr. Brooks," said Irene. "Easy. What you need is a good meal."

"Damn right. A good feel."

They felt a shadow and looked up to see none other than Pearl herself. She wore a tightly packed red-checked blouse with a rhinestone-encrusted nameplate on the pocket, a white lace-trimmed apron, and an all inclusive heavy-duty frown.

Forrest smiled winningly. "Anyone ever tell you look like Delta Burke?"

"No."

"Well you do. You could go to Hollywood and be her double."

"And leave all this?" Pearl rolled her eyes, taking in ruffled cafe curtains, mother-of-pearl formica tables, red leatherette benches, and day-old doughnuts sweating under plexi. Then she glared at Brooksie. "Why'd you bring him here?"

"The man needs a good meal," said Irene.

Pearl rested a hand on her hip. "You folks some kind of do-gooders or what? This here's Brooksie. He drinks. He smells. He drives away customers. You want to do some good, take him out of my place. Otherwise you'll drive me out of business."

"Have a heart," protested Forrest. "Bring us some coffee, why don't you? No, bring us a whole pot. And some food. Whatever's hot, whatever's good."

"Cheap, hot, good," muttered Pearl. "Pick one." She wedged the pad back into her breast pocket and shuffled toward the kitchen.

Forrest dipped his fingers in a glass and flicked water on Brooksie's face. "Rise and shine, Mr. Brooks!"

"What the . . . !"

Pearl returned, juggling a glass globe of coffee and three mugs. "I'll bring you the special of the day. But I don't want him throwing up in here."

"Don't worry about a thing," Forrest assured her. "I'm in perfect control."

"I heard the same line from my high school sweetheart and now I've got a twelve year old."

"Here, Mr. Brooks . . ." Forrest pushed a mug into Brooksie's callused hands. "Drink up."

Lester Brooks drank reflexively, then recoiled and spat a spray of muddy coffee into their faces. "Shitfire!" he cried. "You trying to kill me or what?"

Irene started to sputter. "Jesum crow! That's disgusting. Yuck!"

With deceptive calm, Forrest reached for a fistful of napkins and wiped his dripping face. He then extracted a fresh fistful from the dispenser and wiped off Irene. Then he mopped the leatherette seat. Then he reached across the table and grabbed Lester Brooks by his grime-crusted collar. He turned the fabric into a constricting noose and twisted. He spoke through clenched teeth. "Now you listen here, Mr. Brooks."

Brooksie's gin-flushed face became more so. "Ungh."

"Forrest," cautioned Irene, "don't kill him. At least not yet."

He waved her off. "I'm trying to do you a favor. I'm buying you a meal, treating you with respect, see?"

Brooksie managed a nod.

"For that I want a little something in return."

"Uhhh!"

"I want you to sober up. I want you to behave. And for starters, I want you to drink this goddamn coffee." He let go of Brooksie as though he were a bag of horse manure, wiped his hand on his flannel shirt, and poured another cup of steaming java. "Now you drink this nice."

This time Brooksie drank without pause. Forrest winced and hoped the man's insides weren't being scalded. He poured another mugful. "Drink it slower, Mr. Brooks. Take your time. We got all night."

Pearl chose that moment to slam down thick plates heaped with meat loaf, mashed potatoes, peas, and carrots, all swimming in greasy gravy. Three sides of slaw followed, spinning like little dervishes. She glared at Lester Brooks, as though debating whether to ram his face into the meat loaf.

"Christ," muttered Brooksie, "what're you trying to do to me? I can't eat this . . . this . . . shit!"

"I told you it was a waste," said Pearl.

"Never mind," responded Forrest. "We're fine, Brooksie and me, just fine."

Brooksie shrugged. He examined the food intently, as though looking for vermin. He aimed and fired a forkful into his mouth. Words followed shortly thereafter, pressed through a cloud of mashed potatoes: "What you folks want with me?"

"We're here to investigate an untimely death, Mr. Brooks."

"Show me a death that ain't."

"The man's got a sense of humor," said Irene. "You got to give him that."

"The kid you found a few weeks back," Forrest went on.

"Kevin Cannivan," grunted Brooksie. "Damn shame." He poked the meat loaf with his fork, as though testing its explosive properties. "I found him, that's right." He eased a chunk of meat onto his fork with a blackened thumb. "He shoulda been looking over his shoulder, if you ask me."

Forrest's eyes narrowed. "Why?"

"Someone had it in for him, that's why. The writing was on the wall plain as day." Brooksie's appetite was making a comeback. He snatched up a Parker roll and commenced to sop up gravy.

"What writing?" asked Irene. "What's he talking about Forrest?"

"The writing that got me fired, that's what writing. Didn't tell you about that, did they? Humph. It don't surprise me. Don't surprise me a bit." He stuffed the soggy roll in his mouth.

"What writing!" demanded Forrest.

Brooksie chewed once or twice, then swallowed the roll in a lump. "There was a message. About him. Kevin Cannivan.

Written in black marker on a ladies' room wall. It happened in October. Duffy about had a fit."

"Duffy?" said Forrest. "Who's Duffy?"

"The priest in charge of the seminary program. It happened in his building. Sturdevant Hall. There's a ladies' room in the basement. That's where it was."

"What'd it say?" asked Irene.

Brooksie mashed his peas and fashioned them into a neat little brick. "It was written real tiny. I don't remember exactly what it said. Only that it was a rhyme—some kind of nursery rhyme. And it said he should die. I'm sure about that."

"Holy Moly," breathed Irene. "So someone did kill him!"

"I'd say so," said Brooksie. "But my opinion don't matter much. All I know is that itty bitty rhyme got me fired. I kept on top of things, see? I was gonna paint over it and someone beat me to it. Did a lousy job, too—the letters showed right through. Duffy thought it was me who done the painting. He said I messed up. Said I was too drunk to hold a paintbrush. Then he fired my ass."

CHAPTER TWENTY·TWO

Victor Ramírez was tidying up. He staggered the magazines on the coffee table so the titles showed: *Field & Stream; Consumer Reports; People; Seventeen; Smithsonian*. He tugged the rug to smooth the place where it always buckled. He straightened the green vinyl chairs that circled the room. He put away the toys in the kiddie corner. Blocks, an Etch-a-Sketch with a cracked screen, manhandled dolls, and innumerable pieces of Legos. Someone had snapped the head off Barbie again. A sociopathic kindergartner or maybe even a parent.

If you don't stop that whining, I'll decapitate Barbie. There! See what you made me do!

Coldwater was a hard town. When he first came here, Victor thought he was prepared for anything. He'd grown up in Spanish Harlem and thought setting up a clinic in Connecticut would be a piece of cake. Uncle Sam had paid for medical school and part of the deal was Victor would go wherever the government told him to go for five years. It seemed well worth it at the time.

He figured they'd send him to Chicago's South Side or to Appalachia or south central LA or even home. When they told him he was being assigned to a town called Coldwater along a river he couldn't pronounce in Connecticut he almost laughed. Connecticut? Connecticut was where rich people lived.

But the joke was on him.

When Victor arrived, the first selectman, a stooped old man of Portuguese descent, met the bus. Eight kids from the high school band played an excruciating rendition of La Cumparcita on dented trombones and trumpets—a tribute to his Latino heritage, he supposed. Two of them, at least two, were high on something. All were so malnourished they could hardly blow their horns. He made a mental note to give them TB tests.

They were white and they were poor, a combination Victor hadn't anticipated.

Some of the Main Street shops were boarded up back then. When they showed Victor the wooden triple-decker that was to house his clinic and apartment and one more besides, he could see nail holes where the plywood had been. The first selectman told him they'd fixed it up. He was proud. Everyone pitched in, he said.

Of course, they didn't know they were doing it for a spic. Portuguese was all well and good, but Puerto Rican? That was a horse of a different color. The first selectman skirted the ethnicity issue, but it would rear its ugly head soon enough.

He presented Victor with keys to a car, the color of which was primer. He'd need it to get back and forth to the hospital. And for his coroner work, he'd need it for that too. The county would pay fifty bucks for every stiff Victor pronounced dead. It's a good deal, said the first selectman. Lots of people die here.

The first selectman saw the look in Victor's eyes and started to plead. Coldwater doesn't have a doctor, he said. Last year a man died from a burst appendix. Kids aren't inoculated. There's no prenatal care. And rich people are moving in every day. You can make money off them.

Which turned out to be true. Four days later a lady with a tightly stretched face and thunder thighs emerged from a 450 SL demanding liposuction. But she was not the norm. The weekend set tended to rely on doctors in Palm Beach, Beverly Hills, and Manhattan. Real doctors. Victor's clientele remained mostly poor. They came to him slowly, grudgingly. After a while they came steadily, which was good because it kept his mind occupied.

He missed the sights, the smells, the action of the city. During his first year nostalgia led him to make the mistake of getting married. To LaDonna, granddaughter of the first selectman. LaDonna had made something of herself, just like Victor. She was a nurse. He thought they had something in common. He had been wrong. LaDonna helped him at the clinic but was counting the days until their departure.

"One thousand two hundred and twenty-four," she would say, flipping red lacquered fingernails. "Until we're out of here." She announced a fresh new number daily, as though pulling balls from a lotto machine. He pictured himself suturing her mouth shut.

Somewhere between thirteen hundred and ninety-one and eleven hundred and seventy-two Victor realized he didn't want to leave. He liked it here. They needed him. It was a feeling he never had before, and it was like a narcotic. Their gratitude was heartfelt and tangible. They gave him what they could . . . fresh vegetables . . . jars of homemade pasta sauce . . . new soles on his shoes . . . a five-pound rainbow trout.

He hadn't told LaDonna yet. He was saving it. LaDonna wanted to be a rich doctor's wife and didn't know he would never be one. You might say she wasn't playing with a full deck. This made him smile.

He would tell LaDonna soon. Tomorrow perhaps, or the next day. He picked up a sodden tissue from the floor and tossed it in the trash.

There was a knock on the door. "It's open."

"Dr. Ramírez?"

"Yo!"

A lady stood there all prim and proper, wearing a mink coat. Female fur, the best, considerably more expensive than male. Victor knew about things like minks. And Ming vases. And stamps and coins and antique silver.

"I'm Mildred Bennett," she said. "And this . . ." she gestured with a hand in kidskin gloves ". . . is Dr. Bradford." Victor wondered if he should genuflect.

"Trevor," said the silver-haired gent, trying to be pals.

Victor shook his hand. Suddenly the room looked shabby, the magazines old and tattered, the toys chewed and grimy. It was the same feeling he had when he was fourteen and delivering groceries. A lady on Sutton Place had given him a big tip. Before he could say thanks she smiled, exposing thick teeth. "Use it for soap," she said airily. The next day he returned for the mink and the Ming vase and the silver.

He shoved the memory from his mind.

"Excuse the mess. When you're a country doctor—the only one in town at that—things get hectic."

"Don't I know it," agreed old silver hair. He straightened a crooked print of some dogs playing cards on the wall. "Reminds me of my own place when I was starting out . . . waiting room always jammed, people calling at all hours. There was no such thing as an answering service and house calls were a fact of life. I never got enough sleep. Those are the days I miss most."

Lady Mildred pulled off her gloves. "You look so . . ."

"Dark?" supplied Victor with a grin.

"No! Gracious, I wasn't going to say that at all. *Young,* was what I was going to say. You look too young to be a doctor."

"Only kidding," he said. "Leave your coats here. We can talk in my office."

He led them into what had once been a dining room and sat behind a cluttered desk. "So you want to talk about the Cannivan kid, he died before Thanksgiving?"

He ran his words together in a higgledypiggledy jumble. Fortunately Mildred had learned to understand Spanish people to some degree from Elena who cleaned her Manhattan apartment. She looked to Trevor, wondering if he understood. Apparently he did.

Trevor held out a paper. "I've got a release here, signed by his mother."

"Good." Victor glanced at it briefly and handed it back. "You'd be surprised how many people think they have a right to look at records without the family's say so. As though it's the public domain or something." He reached into the clutter and extracted a file. "Here's copies of the death certificate and autopsy report. As you probably know, autopsies are automatic when it's anything other than death by natural causes, and this one was hardly natural."

Trevor buried his nose in the file. "Who did the autopsy?"

"Medical examiner over at the hospital. Jake Lorensen. A good man. Knows his stuff."

Victor seemed determined to convince them. Syllables rolled off his tongue. "Autoerotic asphyxia . . . recent ejaculation, capillaries broken under the eyelids, larynx crushed . . . It all fits."

Mildred's stomach churned. She hated listening to these details. "I think I'll get a drink of water."

"Got some right here," said Victor. He handed her a paper cup and grabbed a pitcher off the file cabinet.

She had a sudden urge to dash the water in his face. If she wasn't mistaken, Victor Ramírez was well aware of her queasiness and was deliberately thwarting her escape.

"The crushed larynx . . ." murmured Trevor.

"What about it?"

"It doesn't seem right. Think about it. Oxygen would be cut off, but the larynx wouldn't be crushed. If that happened, it would appear more to be death by strangulation."

Victor's eyes shifted away.

"And look here . . ." Trevor shuffled through some Polaroids. "There's a bruise on the back of the neck. As though that's where the slip knot was." He pushed the grisly photos across the desk.

Victor hardly looked at them. "Look, I'm not the expert. The ME is. And that's what he ruled."

"But surely you have an opinion," pressed Trevor. "Could someone have strangled him? On purpose?"

"The rope was in his hand and so was his penis."

"Put there after the fact? Possibly?"

Victor drummed his fingers on the desk, thinking. When he spoke, he chose his words carefully. "The thought crossed my mind. I mentioned it to Dr. Lorensen. He disagreed with my opinion."

"Ah," said Mildred.

"His opinion is what counts," insisted Victor.

Now it was Trevor's turn to choose his words carefully. "Is there any conceivable reason, Dr. Ramírez, for Dr. Lorensen to rule this death an accident? When it might have been murder?"

"Christ," breathed Victor. He looked around the room as though searching for an appropriate answer.

"Please," said Mildred. "It's important. Someone called the boy's mother. They said it was murder."

"Oh, man," said Victor. "Just between us?" Trevor nodded. "Okay. Many of us feel an obligation as decent human beings to protect the reputation of the college. The locals are in a bad way. They rely on St. Sebastian's for jobs and the money students spend in town. They rely on the church for charity and for spiritual comfort. I'm not saying Lorensen would deliberately lie. But subconsciously his judgment might have been clouded."

"I see," said Trevor.

"I'm not saying is was murder," Victor hastened to add. "I'm only saying that it could have been."

"What about the rope?" asked Mildred suddenly. "I mean, we should look at it too, don't you think? If there is anything distinctive about it, it might provide a clue."

Victor seemed relieved to get off the subject of lying. "It was different, all right." He went to the closet and rummaged around inside. "Jake gave it to me after the autopsy. Said it was too nice to throw away. Said maybe I should to give it to the family—can you believe it? Pathologists are out of touch when it comes to the effect death has on people. But he was right about one thing—it certainly is special."

He held it up like a dead snake. It was thick and burgundy colored, with a satin sheen. Tassels dangled from both ends. "Looks like a pull rope you'd see in a mansion or something. The kind they used to call servants with."

"Indeed it does," agreed Mildred. She had such relics in her Manhattan apartment. "May we borrow it?"

"Be my guest."

"Maybe it will tell us something," said Trevor and slipped it into a zip lock bag.

CHAPTER TWENTY THREE

"When I was a girl the nuns used to tell us 'pray for a calling.' I'd run home and fall to my knees. 'Don't call,' I'd pray. 'Please don't call. My line is busy!' "

Francis laughed heartily and refilled Louise's wine glass. How many had they had? He'd lost count, he was having such a good time.

They sat at the kitchen table in his tiny apartment squirrelled away in one of the two towers of Sturdevant Hall. Louise felt good. Dinner had been marvelous. Francis, it turned out, was quite a cook. And the wine, that had been marvelous too. She bit her lips and found they were numb.

He'd said everything would be very proper, and it was. But she'd assumed that others would be present, and they weren't. She couldn't decide if that was good or bad. Maybe it was good.

"Where is everyone?" she asked.

"Everyone?"

"You know. The other priests."

"There aren't many, not anymore. The few that remain live down in Aquinas with the seminarians. As director of the seminary program, I get my own apartment. Such as it is." Suddenly his smile collapsed. "I'm sorry. You assumed others would be present. I've put you in an awkward position." He started to get up. He would get their coats and walk her to her car. And that would be that.

"Francis."

He paused. "Yes?"

"Sit down. You're putting words in my mouth, imagining what's in my mind. And you're imagining all wrong."

"I'm a little out of practice where women are concerned."

"Well stop worrying. I'm fine. I'm enjoying myself—for the first time in a long time, I might add."

"You're not worried?"

"About what, for heaven's sake?"

He studied his wine glass. "I guess I'm not much of a threat, am I?"

"I don't find you a threat. But I do find you very attractive."

Now is the time to get up, he thought. The time to fetch coats and walk her to her car. But instead he went to the casement window and started fiddling. "Blasted thing won't stay closed. The mechanism's broken."

She proceeded to tell him about her marriage. She told him that she and her husband hadn't been intimate in a year, that he was committing adultery with a young woman at his company. She told him how humiliated she was, how she would have walked out had it not been for the children. She told him she was sad all the time, even before Kevin.

"It's the crank. It's been stripped. I've been trying to fix it." He picked up a screwdriver and started to fuss with it.

She went to him and touched his sleeve. "Francis? Have you heard a word I've said?"

"Please go," he whispered.

She leaned forward, unsure what she'd heard.

He set down the screwdriver and faced her. "You must leave at once. I'm sorry to put it so abruptly." He did not trust himself to be alone with her one minute longer.

"I don't understand."

"I can't provide the kind of relationship you seek."

The confusion on her face turned to shame.

"Louise, I'm sorry."

She looked away. "No, I'm sorry. I don't know what's gotten into me. I seem to have lost the ability to censor myself. I keep blurting out terrible truths."

"Not terrible," he assured her. "Understandable. You're upset. You've been through a lot. Please, Louise . . ."

She fumbled for her purse. She wouldn't look at him.

"Don't go, Louise. Not like this."

"Like what then?" To his horror, she started to cry.

He couldn't bear it. He touched her cheek and wiped away a tear. He wanted to kiss her more than anything in the world.

Her voice pleaded. "Francis."

"I'm sorry, Louise. I can't . . ."

She looked at him, disappointed but no longer ashamed. "It's all right, Francis. I understand."

He sighed. "I hope so, I really do."

He got their coats and hustled her to the car. He watched her drive away and felt like crying.

CHAPTER TWENTY · FOUR

Cameron Maine stepped carefully between piles of old newspapers. He spied a headline: WARREN COMMISSION REJECTS CONSPIRACY. And another: FDR DEAD! NATION MOURNS.

Something alive brushed against his leg. He jerked back, thinking it was a rat, and a nest of muffin tins clattered to the floor. Not a rat, he realized, but a cat. One of what? Twelve? Twenty? He shifted the stack of groceries to one arm and placed his free hand against a pillar of newspapers. It came up black.

He was doing his best not to breathe too deeply. Dust was everywhere, and the pervasive smell of uric ammonia was enough to make your eyes water. The kitty litter boxes hadn't been changed in weeks. Years maybe. Old litter hard as cement lined the pans. You could cut bricks out of it with a jackhammer and build a smelly hut. He tried breathing through his mouth and could taste it.

"Father Maine?" A crinkled face framed in a halo of white hair floated in a patch of light at the end of the hall. "Is that you?"

"Yes, Mary." He'd told her until he was blue in the face that he wasn't a priest. "I'm a P.I.T.," he would joke. "A priest in training. Not ordained yet. Not for years." But she never seemed to hear. She could be stubbornly and selectively deaf when it suited her. Then over the past year he came to realize that she needed to believe he was a priest. She needed to think he was strong, needed to believe she could rely on someone. Anyone. Him. She looked past his whiskerless chin and into his clear blue eyes and saw what she wanted to see.

"Bring the bundles here, if you would."

"I'm trying." Believe me.

He continued to navigate through eighty-odd years' worth of debris, leading the way with the grocery bag. He tried to cleanse his mind of uncharitable thoughts. He reminded himself that it hadn't always been like this here. At one time Mary Finn had been a little girl. At one time the house had been clean, less crumbly, with organdy curtains in the windows and an Oriental rug in the parlor. At one time Sean, Mary's father, had given piano lessons on a Knabe upright on the rug in the parlor.

But then everything fell apart, like the house that Jack built with everything connected to everything else and the cord breaks and the connections collapse. Now Mary and her bedridden brother remained, bickering survivors among stacks of newspapers and cardboard cartons filled with outdated coupons and scraps of soap.

"Set them down there, Father." She pointed at a vacant spot

on a table littered with pots and pans and splattered recipes. She pounced on the bag and gleefully removed each item in turn. Rice Chex, oatmeal, Bounty paper towels, chicken parts, lamb shanks, red potatoes, broccoli, asparagus, and, perhaps most appropriate, Cracker Jacks.

"Fresh asparagus!" she cried. "Fergus'll be tickled. You shouldn't have, Father. Really." She stopped herself short and reached into an empty pocket of her house dress. "Now what do I owe you?"

It was a ritual. "Nothing," he said.

"Don't tell me that, Father. Surely all this cost you a pretty penny. Five dollars at least."

Try fifty, Mary. Fifty and change. "They were free. Costas at Shop Rite gave them to St. Sebastian's and we're giving them to you. All the years your family helped, the years you ironed the vestments, the years your sister kept Sturdevant Hall so spotless. It's the least we can do."

"I miss Kathleen."

He could have kicked himself. He hadn't meant to mention her.

"Where is she, Father?" Mary clutched his hand. "Where?"

"I wish I knew, Mary."

"Why'd she leave? Why'd she run off like that?"

"You said she liked to gamble."

"Only lotto. And bingo. That's not really gambling. And it's sanctioned by the church, bingo is. She never missed a Thursday night. Then one night she didn't come back. Why? She never would have left Fergus and me, not like this, not without telling us where she was going."

Maybe it was too much for Kathleen, thought Cameron. Taking care of a cancer-ridden brother and demented sister. Too much, seeing her meager wages swallowed up by prescriptions and booze and cats. Too much, never having any money for fun. Or maybe she ran off with a lover. She was a pretty woman, much younger than Fergus and Mary. The youngest child. The caretaker.

Gone now. Fled. Living in sin. If she's lucky.

"Never even a postcard!" hissed Mary.

"You'd best put away the groceries. Before they spoil."

She nodded dully. "Yes. And you'll look in on Fergus?"

Cameron's heart sank. "I'm expected at morning Mass."

"Bah! You can bend the rules once in a while. You're an important man! And he perks up so after he's seen you. When I told him you'd be by so bright and early he had me wake him up. He refused his medication so he can talk lucid. Made me position the mirror so he could watch for you coming up the walk."

"Of course," he heard himself saying. He spied a grimy crucifix over the stove. His shoulders slumped inside his starched black shirt and the points of the short sleeves jutted out like wings.

He turned, went to the sick room, and forced himself to sound cheerful. "So Fergus, how's it going?"

The wasted man managed to raise his head from the pillow. Tendons in his neck stood out like vines. His voice was reedy. "Fine, laddie . . ." The voice trailed off. The head slumped back. "Just . . . fine."

Mary crept up behind Cameron. "He's not fine. Last night he was screaming into his pillow, thought I couldn't hear."

"Mary," said Cameron gently, "please leave us alone for a few minutes."

"But—"

"Only for a few minutes. I think I let one of the cats out when I came in, and—"

"Not Angus! Was he white with black paws?"

"Yes."

"Oh no! He's supposed to be confined! He nipped the Wagner boy the other day, and with the rabies epidemic spreading from Jersey, he's supposed to be—" She bolted from the room in her red high-top Keds.

Cameron closed his eyes. Rabies. And she's got the cat mixed in with God knows how many others. None of which have had vaccinations. He made a mental note to call Jordan Trip and ask him to come over and vaccinate the whole lot. Jordan would give a discount, but so many cats would still cost plenty. He shoved the thought from his mind and turned back to Fergus.

"So you've been feeling poorly."

Fergus looked him in the eye and managed a wink. "Had any girls lately, laddie?"

"Don't try to change the subject."

"You're pretty enough," he wheezed, "to be a girl."

Cameron flushed. He should get up and leave. He didn't have to take this. It takes one to know one, he could have said. But he didn't have it in his heart to taunt a dying old man.

Instead he said "You were screaming into your pillow."

Fergus sighed and turned his face to the wall. "I don't want her to know."

"That you're sick?" Cameron looked at the array of medications on the bedside table. Lord only knew if Mary was giving Fergus the right ones in the right doses at the right times. "I think she knows, Fergus. I think she knows very well."

"That I'm dying. I don't want her to know that."

"Oh," said Cameron. "I see." Fergus had resisted facing his own mortality until now. "Would you like me to say a prayer, Fergus?"

"You mean now?"

"Yes."

"No thanks. I'm all prayed out. Hold my hand."

Cameron took the frail hand in his.

"We won't tell."

"Right."

"So," sighed Fergus, looking at the ceiling, "let's talk about Mary. I'm worried about her. She says if I die she doesn't want to live either, that's what she says. She's talking crazy. I'm afraid . . ."

"Of what?"

"She won't be able to manage. She doesn't have a lot of friends, what with Kathleen gone."

"We'll take care of her. St. Sebastian's and the town too. They have services. Agencies."

"Mary doesn't trust agencies."

"Meals on Wheels," Cameron went on. "Things like that. Someone will look in on her every day. She'll be all right."

"She'll be lonely."

Cameron patted his hand. "Maybe. But now what about you? You're in pain all the time now."

Fergus seemed relieved to be able to admit it. "Yes."

"Have you thought any more about the hospice?"

Fergus grimaced. "People die in there, in the hospice."

"No, Fergus. People live there. They live better than you're living now. They're comfortable. Free of pain. They're able to think more clearly. They remember the good times. And the time that's left, well, it's better time."

Fergus sighed again. "I could use some better time. Would they give me something for the pain? Something stronger than all that?" He waved at the arsenal of bottles on the bedside table.

"Yes."

"Would they let me have a drink if I want one?"

"Yes." If you can keep it down.

"Would you visit?"

"Of course."

"Would you love me?"

The pain was making him talk crazy. "Yes," promised Cameron.

Fergus started to laugh and became lost in the grip of a coughing fit. When he was finally able to speak, he said "All right, I'll go."

Cameron hid his surprise. They'd been discussing the hospice for over a month, and Fergus was always adamantly opposed. The pain must be excruciating, Cameron realized. He gave Fergus's fragile hand a squeeze. "I'll tell Father Duffy. He'll make the arrangements."

Fergus looked toward the door. "Will you tell her? For me?"

"Yes."

Mary was waiting for him in the hall. "How is he?"

"I think you know how he is, Mary."

"He's dying?" she said tentatively.

"Yes. Not today. Probably not tomorrow. Maybe not next week. It could take a long time."

"Thank God for that at least."

"God doesn't want to be thanked for prolonging agony." He stopped himself and tried to speak softly. "He's in pain, Mary, a lot of it. This isn't a life, what he has."

She put her hands to her ears. "Stop."

"He wants to go to the hospice."

"No."

"It's what he wants. What he needs."

Her jaw set stubbornly. "I'm what he needs."

"You're mixing up his medicines. You're forgetting to refill prescriptions. This isn't a sterile environment." *It's filthy!* But he didn't say that. "Infection will get him before the cancer does."

She flinched and averted her face.

"You can't feed him intravenously, and he'll need that soon. You can't administer morphine, and he needs that right now." The words were like nails in a coffin. "He needs a respite, Mary. He's enduring this pain for you."

"No!"

"Yes! He doesn't want to worry you. He doesn't want to leave you. So he's forcing himself to spend what little time he's got left . . ." He jerked his head toward the closed door. ". . . moaning into his pillow. Hear that?"

She swayed, and he feared she would topple. "I had no idea."

"I know."

She hung her head. "All right. If you think it best, I'll let him go."

"I'll tell Father Duffy. He'll make the arrangements."

"Will everything be okay?"

He said what she wanted to hear. "Yes."

Cameron held himself very tight as he walked down the dark hallway. He reached for an old ski jacket hanging on a peg by the door and put it on. He stepped outside into ice cold air. He wondered if she would still call him "Father" after Fergus died.

His thoughts were interrupted by the strident blast of a horn. "Get in, Maine."

Cameron looked up. "Father Duffy!"

"I said get inside. It's cold as a witch's tit out there." The window of the old Cadillac ascended soundlessly.

Cameron wondered if the priest spoke from experience. *And how cold is a witch's tit, Father? How cold indeed?* The thought of Father Duffy bedding a witch made him suppress a smile. Father Duffy was the Pope's ideal cleric, repressed and asexual. Cameron reached for the door.

"Not in back. I'm not your chauffeur, Maine."

Cameron cringed. The old boy was fuming. He walked around, fumbled for the front door and sank into a darkened interior that smelled of stale cigarettes. The car was the only place Duffy allowed himself to smoke. He glanced at the digital clock on the dash. Six thirty. He noticed that Duffy's glasses were askew and his eyes looked very tired.

"I looked for you in your room. When you were gone at this hour, I knew you'd be here."

"I was assigned to the Finns," Cameron reminded him. "Part of our Good Works Program."

"Not at this hour, you weren't. Curfew is in effect. And you were told explicitly not to deliver any more groceries." Before Cameron could protest or, worse yet, lie, Francis reached into the glove compartment and pulled out a dented tomato. "I found this on the sidewalk."

133

"Oh." *Damn.* He was sure he'd picked them all up. "They need the food, Father."

"There are organizations to help unfortunate souls like the Finns. The church helps them too."

"I know, but—"

"But nothing. It's not your place, running around playing the holy benefactor just because you have family money. It's prideful, that's what it is. There's nothing generous about it."

The words stung. Cameron said nothing. He hadn't thought of it from that angle.

"When you take your vows, family money will be a thing of the past. In the meantime, you will not be running off willy nilly performing *your* perception of good works. Is that clear?"

"Yes." Cameron slumped into the seat. "Fergus says he'll go to the hospice."

Father Duffy took his eyes off the road for a moment. "Oh? Well. At least you accomplished something." It was the closest Father Duffy would come to a compliment. "I'll make the arrangements." He turned the wheel at the fork leading to the college. "Aren't you wondering why I've come to fetch you?"

"Well, yes."

"Yesterday I had a visitor." Francis paused. "Mrs. Cannivan. Kevin's mother."

Cameron pressed his head back against the seat and closed his eyes.

"She's staying in town. With some friends of yours. A man named Forrest Haggarty and three others."

Cameron's heart leapt. "Forrest? Really?"

"Yes, really. Who is this man Haggarty?"

"A neighbor from home." He paused, then finally said the other. "He's retired from the police department. Former chief."

Father Duffy let out a long sigh.

Cameron pressed on. He might as well give it all to Duffy at once. "Do you read *People* magazine? Or watch *America's Most Wanted*?"

"Certainly not."

"Forrest Haggarty has been featured in both. Not as a criminal, of course. As an investigator. He's solved some tough cases. He's even been invited to speak at police academies." He smiled in spite of himself. "He's an intuitive person, not scientific. But he gets results."

"Wonderful." Francis turned the car into the gates of St. Sebastian's. "This is turning into a fine mess." He glanced over at Cameron. "They want to talk to you."

"Somehow I thought you were going to say that."

"You were Cannivan's roommate. It's quite logical on their part. I don't see how I can stop them." He slowed down to a crawl and eased the Cadillac over the first in a series of speed bumps. He stared straight ahead as he spoke. "I know you and Cannivan had your differences, Maine."

Cameron barely nodded.

"Mrs. Cannivan is a nice woman. A very nice woman. There's no need for her to be hurt any more than she already has been."

"What does she want?"

"The truth," replied Francis. He brought the car to a stop and looked at Cameron steadily. "And you better think hard about what you're going to tell her."

CHAPTER TWENTY · FIVE

"Hey, Gary! Good to see you, man! Here, have a chair. Right here. That's it."

"Thanks, Ralph." He eased into the oak chair that faced

Chief Ralph ("My-middle-name-is-*not*-Waldo!") Emerson's desk. Gary had occupied this chair many times, reviewing cases or sometimes just shooting the breeze. His perspective was different now, but some things never changed. "Cookies?" he said.

A plate scraped across the desk. "Have one. You've got some sense of smell, you know that?"

"Not really. Martha always sent cookies on Fridays."

"Right. Guess I'm a creature of habit. So how's it going? The disability checks coming through all right?"

"Right as rain."

"Family okay?"

"Doing fine."

"Good." The chief sat there, not knowing what else to say.

"I wanted to ask you about the Boardman fire. Happened last June, remember?"

"How could I forget? A damned shame. A real tragedy."

"Tommy McKnight said there was an electrical short behind the sofa."

"That's what caused it, yes."

"Could it have been anything else?"

"Anything else like what?"

"Like arson."

"Jesus, Gary. No. Why would anyone do that? The only time we had a deliberate case of arson was back when Nunzio Oregano or whatever the hell his name was—"

"Argenio," corrected Gary.

"Yeah, Argenio, was going bankrupt and set fire to his own place. But no one *died,* for God's sake. You have too much time on your hands, Gary. You're dreaming stuff up."

"Maybe. But humor me, okay? Take a look at this . . ." Gary reached in his pocket, handed the clipping in Ralph's direction and waited for him to read the obituary.

"A shame, but I don't see your point."

"Kevin Cannivan and Skipper Boardman hung around together, Ralph."

"So you're saying somebody killed them?"

"I'm not sure. I'm following my gut on this. Admittedly I'm—" he smiled "—flying blind. But you tell me. Wasn't there some kind of flap a couple of years back? It wasn't my case, but several teenage boys were involved. And Skipper Boardman and Kevin Cannivan were among them, if I'm not mistaken." Ralph said nothing. "It was something about a retarded girl."

"Charladene Poultice," he replied. "It didn't amount to squat."

"What happened, Ralph?"

"She claimed three boys molested her. It was ugly. She said they used a pool stick. Said they did it in the basement of one of the boys' houses. She was retarded, Ralph. A highly unreliable witness."

"But she named names? Gave a location? A time?"

Ralph Emerson's answer was grudging. "I guess. Yeah."

"Kind of a stretch for a retarded girl, to make all that up. Don't you think?"

"Look, these were good kids she was accusing. The captain of the basketball team. President of the senior class. A National Merit Scholar. And you should have seen her. She . . . well, she was—"

"A tramp?"

"Confused! Obviously confused! Deranged, if you want my opinion. No way were we going to get anywhere with that case, Gary. The fathers of the boys already had a high-priced lawyer. The DA wanted nothing to do with it, believe me."

"What about the girl's family?"

"There was a father. Edgar or Edwin. Owned a beauty parlor over in Kmart Plaza. He was a pain in the ass. Badgered us to death for a while. Then he gave up and disappeared. Sold his shop and moved away. Thank the good Lord."

"And the girl?"

"Who knows? She didn't go back to school, that's for sure."

"So," said Gary, "two of the boys involved in that case are dead."

"Accidental deaths, both of them."

"What about the third?"

"Off at school, I imagine. I forget his name."

"Would you look it up for me, Ralph?" Gary waited. "Please."

"Sure. Why not?" Emerson left the office and returned a few moments later. He threw a file on his desk. "Want me to read it to you?"

"Just tell me the name of the third boy."

The chair creaked as Ralph tipped back and scanned for the name. "James Prescott," he said at last, and Gary knew instantly something was wrong.

"What is it, Ralph?"

"Shit."

"What!"

"It's probably coincidence. Like I said, you've got too much time on your hands. With what you've been through—"

"He's dead, isn't he?"

Ralph Emerson let out a long sigh. "There was an accident at Crystal Lake the summer before last. A boat went over the falls. The whole Prescott family died."

Gary stood up. "Thanks, Chief."

"You're not on the force anymore, Gar."

"I know that. Don't worry. I won't do anything crazy."

The lie came easily. He didn't even care if it was convincing.

CHAPTER TWENTY-SIX

"I should have known better," grumbled Forrest as they ate breakfast at Pearl's the next morning.

"Better than what?" asked Louise.

"Better than to include you in this investigation."

"Forrest," warned Mildred.

"Listen, it's always been tough with four of us pulling in different directions. Now we've got a fifth wheel spinning out of control. A fifth wheel that didn't roll in until dawn, I might add."

Trevor looked up from his French toast. "That's her business, Forrest."

"No it isn't," conceded Louise. "I had your car, Trevor. I know I should have called, but I didn't want to wake you. I got talking to Father Duffy and then I—"

"Partying 'til dawn," muttered Forrest into his eggs.

Irene mopped up yolk with a biscuit. "For gosh sakes, Forrest, the man's a priest. I'm sure he and Mrs. C. have a purely plutonic relationship."

"We don't have any relationship," snapped Louise, "and we weren't 'partying.' Francis invited me for dinner. It was all very proper. There were lots of other people there."

"So it's Francis now, is it?" said Forrest.

Mildred took a piece of cold toast from the plastic basket. "You don't have to defend yourself to us, Louise. What you choose to do is your business." She turned to Trevor. "I hate jelly in little packets, don't you? Tomorrow I'm bringing my own Bonne Maman."

"I didn't choose to do anything!" said Louise.

"Right," grunted Forrest.

Mildred held up her hands. "Stop it, both of you."

But Forrest wasn't going to give up. "It was a dumb move, telling everyone that call you got. Duffy, the nun, that girl Angelina . . ."

"Angelique."

"Sounds like an angel with a bladder disorder. Is there anybody you didn't tell?"

"People will find out anyway. St. Sebastian's is a close-knit community. We can't snoop around without people knowing. I had to tell Francis. And besides, he and Sister Gabriel can be a help."

"Sure," said Forrest, totally unconvinced. He studied his orange juice for a moment and reconsidered. "What the hell. Maybe it's not such a bad idea, cozying up to the priest."

Louise slumped in the seat. He was hopeless. "I wasn't cozying."

"Priests are human. They get lonely. They like a little company as much as anyone."

Irene nodded. "He's got a point, Mrs. C."

"Yeah. Shack up, if you want. We might get some good information that way."

"That's outrageous," sputtered Louise. "I told you nothing happened. If you must know, I wasn't even with Francis most of the time."

"Then where were you?"

"On a mission."

Irene leaned forward. "A mission? Really?"

"Yes. As I was driving away after dinner a realization came to me."

"What kind of realization?" asked Trevor.

"The realization that there was something only I could do. A contribution only I could make." She waited. "I realized that I could identify the caller!"

"Oh no!" groaned Forrest.

"Oh yes! Because only I can recognize the voice. That whisper is burned into my memory. So I decided to conduct my own little audio investigation."

Trevor glanced at Forrest. "And how did you manage that, Louise? In the middle of the night."

"I turned the car around, drove back to the college and went door to door."

"Like the Avon lady?" blurted Irene.

"No, not like Avon. Like Jack Webb. Or James Garner. Or Kinsey Milhone."

"I'm afraid I'm not following," said Mildred. "Door to door? You mean you canvassed students in their dormitory rooms?"

"Like the census?" asked Irene.

"Only the women," said Louise. "I figured it would be easy. Dorms at St. Sebastian's aren't coeducational, so I decided I'd focus on those with female names. St. Mary's Hall, St. Katharine's Hall, St. Rose's—"

Forrest was unable to contain himself any longer. "Jesus night! I don't believe it!"

"Don't believe what? It made perfect sense. Of course, it wasn't always easy to gain access. At first I used a pizza box I found in the trash. I may not look like your run-of-the-mill delivery person, but I don't look very threatening either, so I just bluffed my way in. It was frustrating at the beginning because so many of the girls were at the library or wherever. Later on, after curfew, the situation improved. Except then the dormitories were locked and I had to climb through windows."

"You did what?" said Mildred.

"Climbed through windows. Don't look so shocked, Mildred. The girls were cooperative. After I explained why I was out there tapping, they let me in."

"You explained?" cried Forrest.

"Of course I explained. How else could I gain access? Then, once I was in, I simply proceeded down halls, knocking on doors. I asked each young lady to repeat after me: 'Kevin had enemies.' Short, simple, to the point." She smiled broadly.

Forrest put his head in his hands.

Mildred toyed with her napkin. "And did you find the mystery caller?"

Louise buttered her toast briskly. "Not yet, but I only spoke to forty-eight girls. I have three hundred and fifty-two more to go. What's wrong with him anyway?"

"As if I had to explain," said Forrest. "I give up. The whole thing's off. We're going home."

"We are not!" cried Louise.

"Aw, Forrest," said Irene, "you don't mean it."

"I most certainly do mean it. Trevor, pay the check."

"Now look," said Mildred quickly, "it's not such a bad idea, Louise talking to the girls. It would be a big help to find that person, and Louise is the only one who can do it." She lowered her voice. "And it will give her something to do, Forrest. It will keep her occupied."

He chewed on that thought. It would keep Louise out of their hair. "Maybe you're right," he agreed. "The damage is done in any case. No use crying over spilt milk."

"Damage," scoffed Louise. "Listen, I want whoever killed Kevin to know we're on their trail. I want them to squirm."

"Oh, yeah? You want them to kill again? You want that too?"

"I never said that," she said quickly.

"You announce our intentions, you corner them, and they just might. Think about that."

Trevor didn't like the idea of Louise talking to people on her own. She was grief-stricken, fragile. But what could he do? He shoved aside his concerns and moved on to another subject. "What about the rope, Forrest? Do you think it will help?"

"Don't know. Maybe Duffy can tell us where it came from. We'll show it to him and see."

"Why don't you send it to your friends at Quantico?" asked Irene.

Mildred perked up. "What friends at Quantico?" she asked innocently.

"Forrest has friends in the FBI," beamed Irene. "Friends in high places. Friends who can analyze the rope. Go ahead, Forrest. Tell her."

Everyone looked at Forrest, who for once seemed to be at a loss for words. "Well, they're not friends exactly. Just fellas I talk to from time to time."

"He's just being modest," said Irene. "They call him for advice all the time."

"Well, I wouldn't say exactly that," muttered Forrest, who seemed to be sinking in his seat.

Irene rolled on, oblivious. "Those guys owe you a lot of favors, Forrest. Don't be shy about asking. Send 'em the rope. They'll be happy to oblige. Those FBI fellas are real polite."

Mildred didn't miss a trick. She smiled devilishly. "Why, that's a marvelous idea! The FBI has a wonderful laboratory. Who knows what they'll turn up? And to think you have connections there, Forrest! What a stroke of luck." She nudged Trevor under the table.

"I really don't want to take advantage of their friendship," hedged Forrest.

Trevor joined in. "Nonsense. You've helped the FBI. Give them an opportunity to return the favor. Send the rope on down. To Quantico." He grinned.

Forrest was trapped. "All right, I will. But don't get your hopes up. FBI agents are busy fellas. We might not hear from them for a long time."

"Nothing ventured, nothing gained," said Irene.

Louise, who didn't realize Forrest had been caught in one of his monumental exaggerations, plucked the jar from her pocket and placed it on the formica table. "If you're sending the rope, you may as well send this along with it."

Forrest snatched it up. "What is this?"

Irene read over his arm. "DERMA COLOR CAMOUFLAGE CREAM."

Louise explained about finding it in the chapel. "Francis says it's stage makeup."

"Sounds like makeup used to hide something," said Forrest.

"Do you think the killer dropped it?" asked Mildred.

"I don't know," replied Louise. "Maybe."

Irene studied the jar. "Wonder what she'd want to hide?"

CHAPTER TWENTY · SEVEN

Trevor parked the Lincoln in front of a crumbly brick building the color of rust with a crooked cement cross on the roof. "This is it—Aquinas Hall."

Irene's face fell. She had been anticipating the glitter of stained glass and gold leaf. "Not exactly what I pictured."

"Hardly the Vatican," agreed Mildred.

"Inside it's worse," said Louise. "Like a prison. There are no posters, no rock music, no laughter in the halls. I half expected to find a rack of hair shirts lined up in the foyer."

"Listen up," said Forrest. "Before we go inside I want to say one thing."

"That'll be a first," said Irene.

Forrest ignored the jibe. "After we've said our hellos, I want a minute alone with Cameron. I've got something I want to ask him—"

"And I know what it is!" cried Irene.

Forrest shot her a glance

"Sorry," she mumbled.

"—in private," finished Forrest. "I've got a line of questioning I want to pursue, and if everyone's hovering about he's liable to clam up."

"I suppose it's all right," said Louise.

Suppose? thought Forrest. Did she think he was asking for permission? Clearly Louise Cannivan had a misconception about who was in charge.

He stifled his irritation and led them inside. They passed through a cramped foyer lined with mailboxes into a bare beige room at the heart of the one-story building. Orange polystyrene chairs were scattered about the linoleum floor. One of them was occupied by a young man hunched over a book. His fair skin contrasted with his neatly pressed black shirt and pants. He looked up and rose to his feet.

He was taller than Forrest remembered, and the white blond hair had matured to a sandy tan. Gone was the spiky crew cut. Gone were the braces. Gone too were the shy downcast eyes. He strode toward them, an unabashed grin on his face.

Forrest reached out his hand. "You've grown."

Cameron hesitated, then clutched Forrest to him in a hug.

"Whoa there, boy, you're gonna crack my ribs."

Irene pushed between them. "Never mind him, Cameron! I've been waiting to hug you for months." He wrapped his arms around Irene's barrel body and whirled her around.

Louise watched and felt a lump in her throat. How good, she thought, that Kevin had a roommate like this young man.

Cameron set Irene down and gave Mildred a hug. "No twirling," she laughed, "not for me." Trevor slapped him on the back and gave his shoulder a squeeze.

"This here's Mrs. C.," said Irene. "Kevin's mother."

Cameron shook her hand. "Please to meet you, although I'm sorry it's under such sad circumstances."

"So am I, but it's good to meet you anyway. It's good to know Kevin had a friend like you."

Cameron didn't correct her. He looked from Forrest to Trevor to Mildred to Irene. "I can't believe you're here. I've missed you. I've missed you all so much."

Forrest wasn't about to let that slide by. "If you missed us so much, why didn't you visit? We kept waiting, you know. We figured you'd come home last Christmas, but you didn't. Then we figured Easter, and again you didn't show up. By summer vacation we'd about given up. Of course, you didn't come home then either."

Irene rushed to Cameron's defense. "Let him be, Forrest. I'm sure he had important things to do. Friends to be with. You know how young people are."

"I sent letters," Cameron reminded him. "Every week."

"Bah! Letters don't take the place of face-to-face. You can't talk to letters." You couldn't hug letters either, but Forrest wasn't about to sound sentimental.

Trevor spoke up on Cameron's behalf. "They discourage home visits the first year."

"Yeah? Well this is the second year, and unless my calendar's wrong, Thanksgiving's come and gone. I should take this fella over my knee."

Cameron grinned. "I bet you could too."

"Don't think I can't. I'm stronger than I look."

"Don't I know it." He cuffed Forrest gently on the arm.

Forrest slung his arm over Cameron's shoulders. "Let's you and me have a little talk before we continue this reunion." Without waiting for Cameron to agree, he steered the young man out to the foyer. "Where can we talk in private?"

"My room. It's as private as a crypt now that Kevin Cannivan is gone." He turned and walked through a swinging door into one of two dormitory wings. "And if I know you, that's what you want to talk about."

Forrest hurried after him. "Damn right."

Cameron pulled a wooden chair from his desk. "Take the chair, Forrest. For your back." But Forrest was already easing himself onto the edge of a sagging bed. The springs were shot. He had to lean forward, elbows on his knees, to keep from sliding back.

"Nah, I'm okay." Forrest sought to put Cameron at ease. He eyed the textbook on the desk. "What's that you're studying?"

"This? Principles of Geology. My worst course. All about plunging, asymmetrical, overturned, and recumbent folds. Normal, thrust and strike-slip faults. Basal conglomerates. Disconformities, angular unconformities, and nonconformities."

"I'll take your word for it."

"And eskers." Cameron sat back in the chair. "Know what an esker is?"

"Sounds like a girl I dated once. Esker Pettyjohn. She was quite a number. Her legs went all the way up."

"An esker," said Cameron, "is a long winding ridge of stratified sand and gravel."

Forrest winced. "Man could abrade himself fooling around with something like that."

"You haven't changed a bit. Still salty as ever."

"Yeah. Now that you've grown some I can talk plainer than I used to." He turned serious. "So that Duffy fellow told you why we're here."

"He said you're helping Mrs. Cannivan cope with the loss of her son. And he said . . . well, he said she thinks maybe it wasn't an accident. That someone set it up."

"What's your opinion?"

"I can't believe anyone would have killed him."

"Why? What was he like?"

Cameron chose his words carefully. "He was a model seminarian."

"And you're a lousy liar."

"Huh?"

"Look, Cameron, I'm asking for help here. I've got a bunch

of pieces and they don't fit worth a damn. Mrs. Cannivan gets a call saying Kevin had enemies. The autopsy says his larynx was crushed. Someone could have strangled him. So we're looking at a possible murder, not an accident. I want you to be straight with me. What was the guy like?"

Cameron chewed his cheek. "I don't think I'm the best one to judge Kevin Cannivan."

"Why the hell not? You were his roommate."

"Not for much longer I wouldn't have been. I may as well tell you, Forrest—we didn't get along. I was going to move out."

"How come?"

Cameron shrugged. "It was nothing. He spread a rumor, that's all. A rumor about me. It was a lie, not really a big deal, but Father Duffy thought it best I move into a single."

"What was this rumor exactly."

The words came slowly. "That I was gay."

"Jesus, what a thing to say!"

He swallowed hard. "Yeah. What a thing." He looked away and Forrest had to lean forward to hear. "Especially since . . ."

"Since what?"

"Since it's true."

Forrest emitted a bark of a laugh. "My hearing must be going. I could have sworn you said—"

"I did. I said it's true."

"Jesus night! Don't go saying things like that! You are not either!"

"I thought you realized by now."

"I sure as hell didn't!"

"It's not the end of the world." He tried to smile and failed.

"Pretty damn close. Jesus."

Forrest didn't know much about people of the homosexual persuasion. None of his friends were homosexual, that was for sure. And Raven's Wing was a conservative, family-type town, so there weren't any homosexuals there. Except maybe at Hay Market. Yeah. How could he forget? That was where he had his first experience with homosexuals . . .

Hay Market was a fancy gourmet grocery located where the old Grand Union used to be. They sold exotic cheeses, hand-polished vegetables, Godiva chocolates, truffles, and meats in a glass case that would have had the word Deli overhead in any other store. It was a trendy place, a place Forrest made it a policy never to frequent. Reenie, on the other hand, went almost daily to eat free samples. A taste of this, a taste of that, and before you knew it she'd scarfed down lunch. It was a wonder the place didn't go bankrupt.

Then one day last winter Forrest had a hankering for a tomato that wasn't wax, and someone told him Hay Market had tomatoes you wouldn't believe. All the way from Florida, they said. So he went.

He was shocked to find the place bustling with rich queers. They walked by practically arm in arm, sashaying this way and that, piling paté and brie in plastic baskets slung over arms like designer handbags. He eyed them with distrust and disgust.

Raven's Wing was changing, and Forrest didn't like it one bit. It might have been named the number one town by Connecticut Magazine, *but in Forrest's estimation it had slid into the bung hole since the fifties, along with the rest of the country. Gourmet food. Izod shirts. Mercedes parked at the feed store. And now homosexuals. Where would it end?*

He'd walked past a wall of cheese and a stack of paté that looked like Saran-wrapped baby shit, his eyes fixed on the pyramid of tomatoes in the center of the store. It beckoned him like a god.

He studied a sign dangling from the base of the pyramid. Written in ornate calligraphy, it was. His eyes weren't what they used to be. Why the hell couldn't people write plain anymore? Palmer penmanship, that's what the world needed. He squinted—fifty cents a pound, which wasn't too bad, not too bad at all. He snagged a plastic basket and started loading up.

"Look, Lance. These tomatoes are gorgeous."

Gorgeous? *The hair on the back of his neck stood up.*

"I'll say. They make those tomatoes at the Food Emporium look like plastic."

From the time he visited Mildred's co-op in Manhattan, Forrest decided that these were City folks. Up for a weekend in the country, most likely, wearing checked shirts and trailing those Laura Ashley sheets behind them. Invading his space. Changing his town. He shot them a Haggarty glare.

"But, Lance . . . five dollars a pound! Don't you think that's a bit much?"

Five dollars a pound? *Forrest blinked.* "The hell you say! They're fifty cents a pound! It says so right here!"

The man didn't bat an eye. "I wouldn't kid about something as serious as produce, sir. The sign says five dollars, and I for one think it's absolute highway robbery."

Forrest looked at the sign again. He supposed maybe it did say five dollars. Flustered, he started unloading tomatoes from his basket and putting them back.

Something shifted and the pyramid started to tremble. A lone tomato rolled to the floor . . . then another . . . and another . . .

"Oh no!" *cried Forrest. He scrambled to recoup and restack, but tomatoes were coming too quickly.*

"Oh my God!" *shrieked Lance.*

Now fruit really started to fly. Tomatoes tumbled down in dozens. Forrest, Lance, and Peter sidestepped this way and that, grabbing nimbly. Then Forrest planted a foot on one, skidded, and he fell backwards into the arms of Peter.

"Christ almighty!" *he bellowed.* "Lemme go!"

"Easy, sir, easy." *Peter's arms were sinewy and strong. They were arms that worked out. They held tight. Forrest felt himself being set upright.*

Lance hovered at his elbow. "Good Lord, are you all right?"

His heart was racing a mile a minute and skipping beats. He mopped his face with a handkerchief. "Uh, maybe I better . . ."

"Here." Lance shoved a wine crate under his fanny. "Do you want me to call a doctor?"

"No. I just need . . . to catch . . . my breath."

"Take deep breaths," instructed Peter. "Try to relax. It could have happened to anyone." He turned to Lance. "Let's put these things back, shall we?"

While Forrest waited for the dizziness to pass, Lance and Peter scurried about like rabbits on an Easter egg hunt, picking up each and every tomato. They polished them with monogrammed hankies. They stacked them meticulously into a new and better pyramid. And by the time they had finished—it took a good twenty minutes—the display looked even better than before.

Onlookers applauded.

"We hid the bruises," whispered Lance.

Forrest stood up. "Thanks," was all he could say, "thanks a lot."

They offered to give him a lift home, but he assured them he could make it all right.

On his way out he purchased a single tomato.

"Will that be all?" trilled the cashier.

"It's all I can afford."

"That'll be a dollar fifty."

"How can you say that with a straight face?"

"Forrest?" said Cameron. "Forrest?"

"Oh," he said quickly, "I was just thinking." About a couple of gays. Who were nice to me. But I'll be damned if I'm going to tell you.

"If it makes you feel better, I'm celibate. I'm not a practicing homosexual. I never will be."

"I didn't know it was something to be practiced. Jesus night, how did this happen? You were fine when you left Raven's Wing, just fine." He shook his head, trying to understand.

"It didn't *happen*. I've always been this way."

"Is that why you entered the seminary?"

"No." He slumped back in the chair. "Never mind. I knew you wouldn't understand."

"That's true," said Forrest. "I don't, and I'm too old to try."

"No you're not."

"Yes I am. You expect too much. There are some things I'd just as soon not deal with. At my age a man's entitled to his opinions. I wish to hell you hadn't told me."

"I had to. You may hear it anyway, and I'd rather you heard it from me."

"I guess," sighed Forrest. "This doesn't look good for you, boy. Let me tell you how it plays." He cracked his knuckles. "I've seen pictures of Kevin Cannivan. He was a handsome fella. And you . . . well, I guess given the way you are it's only natural that you'd be—" he made a face, "—attracted to him."

"No way!"

"You weren't?" He was genuinely surprised.

"That's how you think it works? Just because a guy's gay, he's attracted to any male with a pretty face?"

"I don't know what I think! I'm just learning about this stuff. And I don't know why you call yourself gay anyway. You sure as hell don't look happy. You look miserable."

"Forget semantics. The point is, I wasn't attracted to Kevin Cannivan, not in the least. But he told people I was. He told them I'd made a pass. That was the rumor."

"Why the hell would he do that?"

"I'm not sure, but I'll tell you one thing: He wasn't what people thought. They thought he was great. He was good-looking and smooth, real smooth. But he had a special talent. He could sense weakness. Vulnerability." He shrugged. "Somehow he sensed mine."

"How?"

"Beats me. I'm not effeminate."

"Damn right. Girls'd be all over you, if you gave them half a chance. You can switch back, Cameron. It's not too late."

Cameron looked at him almost pityingly. "Forget it, Forrest. Anyway, Kevin figured it out and he'd bait me. At first it was like he was joking. 'Want to get it on, Maine?' 'Headed for the shower, pretty boy? Don't bend down for the soap.' Stuff like that. I tried to ignore him, but underneath I could sense real hostility. A core of meanness. It scared me, Forrest, it scared me bad."

"So you moved out?"

"No. I'm tougher than that. I turned the other cheek. I went out of my way to be polite, which drove him nuts. Then he told Duffy I'd made a pass at him. And Duffy believed him." His voice was filled with stunned disappointment.

"Jesus."

"I couldn't believe it. Nothing I said in my own defense seemed to matter. As far as Duffy was concerned, Kevin Cannivan's word was gospel."

Forrest nodded.

"I've tried to forgive them, tried to forgive them both. I knew Father Duffy's judgment was clouded by his devotion to the seminary program. He has no other interests, no friends, no family. The program is his whole life—and it's in real trouble. Not enough fellows apply to begin with, and lots who are accepted drop out. Father Duffy prays for perfect candidates, and when Kevin Cannivan walked in the door, he saw what he wanted to see.

"Besides, why should Duffy think Kevin would lie about such a thing? It was safer for him to believe Kevin than not, safer to split us up. He could have had me expelled. That would have been safest of all. I suppose I should be grateful he didn't." But Cameron didn't sound grateful; he sounded bitter.

"Wait a minute. Why *did* Kevin lie?"

"He wanted me out of the way. I knew he had a relationship

with a girl and told him I'd have to report it. So he beat me to the punch and destroyed my credibility in the process."

"He was seeing someone, huh?"

"Oh, yeah. I found this." He opened a drawer and pulled something out. "Actually I think he wanted me to." He handed it to Forrest.

"It's a watch."

"Oh, it's more than that," corrected Cameron.

It was expensive, a Rolex Oyster. Forrest turned it over in his hand. *To K.C.,* it said, *with all my love.* The initials underneath had been obliterated.

"He scratched away the name. He didn't give a damn about the girl who gave it to him. The watch was a trophy. And it had monetary value. He laughed and told me he was going to sell it. He acted like it was nothing, until I said I was going to report him."

Forrest slipped the watch into his pocket. "So who died and left you God?"

"It was wrong, what he was doing," said Cameron. "He was breaking the rules. He had no business being here."

"I see. And you weren't a little jealous?"

"No!"

"Okay, okay. So you threatened to go to Duffy and Cannivan made a preemptive strike. He spread a rumor—and it worked. Why didn't you just tell Duffy about the watch?"

"I did. Kevin must have denied it or something, because it didn't seem to matter. Duffy was pissed at me. For causing trouble, I guess."

Forrest closed his eyes. "Cameron, why'd you get involved in this watch thing at all? Why not let it go?"

"As his sophomore roommate I felt responsible for his behavior."

"You can't make people behave as you'd like. Don't you know that by now?"

"I'm a slow learner. Anyway, the joke was on me. My reputation was ruined and I was set to move into a West Wing single."

"Then as things turned out, you didn't have to."

He looked Forrest in the eye. "I know what you're thinking."

"That you had motive?" Forrest shrugged. "What Cannivan did was pretty rotten. No one would blame you for wanting to get even. Still, murder would be an extreme measure. But never mind that. Did you have opportunity? If you have an alibi for the time he died—say, between 6:00 and 8:00 P.M. on November twenty-third—you're in the clear." He spread his hands and waited expectantly. But an anxious look crossed Cameron's face. "What's wrong?"

"I don't have an alibi. I was out jogging. No one saw me."

"Damn it, Cameron. *Damn* it!"

Cameron crumbled. "I didn't do it, Forrest! You've got to believe me! Besides, I couldn't have staged such a murder. It would have been a woman who killed him! Kevin was straight. Straight!"

"We don't know that for a fact, do we? But if we can find the lady—or person—who gave him the watch, we can find out more. And there's another thing."

Cameron was beginning to think it was hopeless.

"There's this janitor named Lester Brooks . . ."

"A drunk. He was fired."

"He says there was a message on a wall in a women's lavatory before Kevin died."

"So?"

"He says it was a threat. Against Kevin."

"What did it say?"

"He doesn't remember."

"Figures."

"It was painted over, he says, but you can still see the words. It was written. Handwriting's distinctive, Cameron. If we can see it, maybe we can find out who wrote it." It was a long shot.

"You think it's still there?"

"It's worth a look-see. Will you take us? It's in the basement of some building called Sturdevant."

Cameron jumped up. "Let's go."

"This is Officer Gary Gonski of the River Bend Police. I've been working on a case that concerns your son. I'm sorry to alarm you, but you may be in grave danger. Please call me as soon as possible. Call day or night. And call collect. The number is—"

Samantha pressed a button, put her ear to the machine and laughed with delight. The man was gone. Back in the box. Maybe tomorrow he'd come out again.

CHAPTER TWENTY-EIGHT

Forrest and Cameron joined the others downstairs and went outside. It was a crystal clear day and snow glittered like a blanket of mica. Cameron led the way across the campus . . . past the columned library . . . the new student center . . . the gymnasium.

"Will someone please explain why we have to look at some wall?" asked Louise. "We have an appointment with Francis. He's expecting us."

"This won't take long," said Forrest.

Mildred's breath billowed out in frosty clouds. "I must say," she huffed, "you're being very mysterious."

"Hey, Cameron!"

Deirdre Canfield motored toward them, her gloved hand playing at the elaborate console on the side of her wheelchair. She planted herself in their path. Cameron introduced her.

"We met last night," said Louise.

Forrest shook her hand. "That's quite a grip you've got there, young lady."

"Deirdre works out at the gym every day," said Cameron. "All the Nautilus machines—"

"Only the upper-body ones," added Deirdre. "Obviously."

"She's stronger than a lot of guys. She can benchpress one hundred fifty pounds."

"Lordy!" said Irene. She looked at Deirdre with concern. "What happened to your legs, honey?"

"Irene!" said Mildred.

But Deirdre handled the question graciously. "I don't mind. I've lived in this chair for years. I accept it. I just wish others would. It happened playing football."

"No game for a girl," said Forrest.

"So my mother tried to tell me, and I guess she was right. It was only touch football but someone 'touched' me too hard. I slammed into a tree and never got up."

"You poor dear," sympathized Mildred.

"It has advantages," said Deirdre philosophically. "My Nikes last forever." She veered away from the subject of her disability and asked if they were making any progress on their investigation.

"Word certainly gets around fast," grumbled Forrest.

"If someone did it, I hope you get them." Deirdre gave one of the spokes a snap with her thumb. "Kevin and I were alphabetical neighbors—Canfield, Cannivan—so I got to know him at freshman orientation, during exams, when grades are posted. He was a nice guy." She stopped, remembering . . .

"What're you thinking?" he asked.

"That I wish they assigned roommates alphabetically." There, she'd said it.

He looked at her, puzzled. Her cheeks flushed with embarrassment. "Never mind," she said. "Only kidding."

He realized it wasn't. He touched her cheek with the back of his hand. "It must be tough, Deirdre."

She closed her eyes. No one ever touched her.

"Have you ever . . . you know."

What answer would be best. "No," she said.

"Maybe we could—"

"Where?" she pressed. "When?"

"I couldn't believe it when I heard what happened," she said. "No one could."

"Do you know anyone who might have wanted to hurt him?" asked Mildred.

Her answer was quick, as though she'd anticipated the question. "No. Everyone liked him."

Forrest moved to cut the chitchat short. "We have to get going, folks."

"Where to?"

Louise shoved her hands in her pockets. "He wants us to look at some women's room wall. I don't see the point, but—" Forrest shot her a glance that said shut up, but Louise's attention remained on Deirdre. "Is something wrong?"

She shook her head. "What wall are you talking about?"

"In the women's room in the basement of Sturdevant," explained Cameron.

"Oh. What's the big deal about it?"

"Nothing," said Forrest. "Nothing at all. Nice meeting you, Miss Canfield. Come along, folks. Come along."

Deirdre put her chair in gear. "Catch you later, Cameron."

"My," said Mildred after Deirdre was gone, "something certainly took the wind out of her sails. You shouldn't have asked about her disability, Irene."

"It wasn't that," said Forrest. "It was Louise mentioning the wall." He turned on her. "Can't you hold your tongue?"

"I didn't think it was important."

"It might be. For gosh sakes be careful from now on." He turned to Cameron. "Now where the hell is this wall?"

Cameron pointed to the side of the administration building. "Down those steps."

They proceeded under a vine-covered arch into a musty basement room that appeared to be some kind of horrible lounge. Moldy couches lined walls slick with condensation. Trunks were piled in corners. A pot of silty coffee steamed in the corner. Corridors branched off like tentacles. Somewhere in the distance the voice of an instructor echoed eerily.

"Anybody home?" called Irene.

"Hush!" hissed Forrest. "This place gives me the creeps."

"Ugh!" cried Mildred. "Cobwebs!"

"Look!" exclaimed Trevor. "The Bride of Frankenstein! Only kidding."

"Oh, you!" said Irene.

Cameron threw up his arms. "This is where the Theology Department is based, an indication of its stature within the college hierarchy."

"Just show us that ladies' room," said Forrest. "The sooner we're out of here, the better."

Cameron led them down a corridor. "Here," he said. Without waiting for permission, Forrest ducked inside.

"Forrest!" hissed Mildred. "What if someone's in there?"

"No one is," he whispered back. "Come on in."

"I still don't get it," muttered Louise as they all slipped inside.

Forrest surveyed the blank walls. "I don't see anything."

"What are we supposed to see?" asked Mildred.

Cameron ran his hand over the surface of one wall. "Looks like it's been painted. Recently, too."

Louise became shrill. "Will someone please tell me what we're looking for!"

"Apparently someone wrote a message on one of these walls," said Cameron. "A threat. Directed at Kevin."

"Graffiti?" asked Mildred. "Is that what we're talking about here?"

"Better" said Cameron. "A *handwritten* message."

"If that's the case," said Forrest, "by comparing the handwriting we'd have a shot at tracking down who wrote it."

"Fat lot of good it does us now," said Cameron morosely.

Louise wrung her hands in frustration. "You mean evidence has been deliberately obliterated?"

"Looks like," replied Cameron.

"Not evidence," said Forrest. "A clue. A significant one too." He studied the wall thoughtfully.

"Damnation," said Irene. "Out of luck."

"Well," sighed Trevor, "that's that."

Forrest put a finger to his chin. "Maybe not."

"Trevor's right, Forrest," said Mildred. "We'll simply have to pursue other avenues. Other leads, as it were."

"Just hush a minute! Let me think!"

"I don't know what it is with this man," said Irene. "Sometimes he's stubborn as a mule. Look, Forrest, there's nothing we can work with here. You can do a lot of things, but you can't walk on water and you can't see through paint."

A smile blossomed on Forrest's face. "Don't be so sure about that, Reenie. Don't be so sure."

As Forrest pondered the paint-covered wall, Smokey Haggarty slouched in a chair in an office at the Metropolitan Museum of Art. Smokey had inherited her father's wiry build and nervous energy. At this moment she felt like a caged cat.

She pushed her short brown hair behind her ears. She twisted a loose thread on her blouse. She wished she had a cigarette. She wished a lot of things. She wished she were outside walking through new fallen snow before it turned to city sludge. She wished she were independently wealthy. She wished Michael were still alive.

She eyed the fish tank and saw that it needed cleaning. A bewildered angelfish peered through algae thick as Jell-O. Smokey sighed. *I'd trade places with you, fish. In a minute.*

"Now, Miss Haggarty . . ." Randall Moffett, executive director of the museum, smoothed his hair down. His toupee looked like road kill. He was a graduate of Exeter and Princeton, and indigo blood trickled through his veins. Yet like so many people born with old family money, he was inherently cheap and it showed in the shabbiness of his clothes. Smokey eyed the frayed collar . . . the stain on the tie that dry cleaning couldn't conquer . . . the cracked belt. Even his skin looked shabby. Unwashed. Greasy.

Go to bed with that man and you wouldn't need Vaseline. The thought made Smokey want to vomit.

"I want to be fair," Randall went on. "I'm giving you the

benefit of the doubt, the opportunity to tell your side. Philippe Tremblant was distraught on the phone, almost incoherent—"

"Oh, you know those French." Smokey managed a smile.

Randall's mouth puckered and he looked as though he was holding back painful gas. "That's neither here nor there, Miss Haggarty. In any event, I put him off as gently as I could and have waited to hear your side of the story." He leaned forward, expecting her to kowtow.

Smokey was enveloped by an overwhelming sense of lethargy. It happened whenever she faced authority figures. She felt her eyelids droop and fought the urge to smack herself in the face. She opened a glassine envelope and slapped yet another nicotine patch on her arm, upping the ante to three in a risky abuse of the prescription.

"What's that?" blurted Randall.

"Nothing. I just have these lesions."

Randall pulled back into the chair like a turtle.

"My doctor says they're probably not contagious, but he's running some tests to be sure." She smiled. "Now where were we?"

Randall tried to inhale sideways. "Your side," he said at last. "I'm waiting to hear your side."

"I have terrible jet lag. I only just got back last night." Messages had been flashing on her machine, angry red. Randall had called repeatedly, racking up four messages among six. "Couldn't this wait until later?"

Randall forgot about contagion. "Later? Later! Miss Haggarty, apparently the gravity of this situation escapes you. Let's lay our cards on the table, shall we? The Louvre is on the verge, the very verge, of filing suit! Of charging us with fraud!"

She watched his forehead turn pink. Not us, Randall. The museum. And perhaps thee. But not me.

"I wasn't here when the painting was sold," she pointed out. She refused to call it "the Titian." It was before her time, a highly controversial sale and Randall Moffett's glorious coup of the '80s. A six-by-nine oil titled the *Resurrection*. Unsigned, but clearly a masterpiece of Titian's old age—shapes emerging from semi-darkness, impasto, shimmering translucent surfaces that lost every trace of solidity, and the tell-tale glow from within. Experts at the museum dated the painting at 1573, postdating Titian's *Christ Crowned with Thorns*. The Louvre had Titian's earlier work, including *Man with the Glove* c. 1520 and *The Entombment* c. 1525. They had lost *Thorns* to the Pinakothek in Munich and desperately wanted the *Resurrection*.

Upon the recommendation of Randall Moffett, then a lowly assistant curator, the Metropolitan sold *Resurrection* to the Louvre for the then-unprecedented sum of thirty million dollars. Matching funds were pledged by the Wisch family and others. A new wing was built. Randall Moffett's career was made and he was named executive director. He started going to parties, sucking up pledge money like a vacuum. He became a practiced ass-kisser with patrons, but was excruciatingly pompous and dictatorial with subordinates. He liked to make his inferiors squirm and waited for Smokey to do so now.

But Smokey was not a squirmer. To the contrary, she was too honest for her own good, another trait inherited from her father. "I didn't do anything wrong," she said.

Randall took a deep breath. "My understanding—correct me if I'm wrong—is that you went to the Louvre—invited as an emissary of this museum—to deliver a lecture on the latest advances in dating techniques."

Comebacks flashed through her mind like summer lightning: Dating's not easy, what with AIDS everywhere. A hard man is good to find. Why do women fake orgasms? Because men fake foreplay.

"And during the lecture," Moffett continued, "you used the Titian—"

"The painting," she corrected before she could stop herself.

"The Titian." He was glaring at her now. "For a little demonstration."

"Of the infrared camera," she supplied. "That was the whole point of the trip, Mr. Moffett."

"Yes. And during that demonstration of this unproven and totally unreliable device, you said that the Titian was . . ."

She held on to her chair and stifled an outburst, but inside she was railing. It's not unproven! It's not unreliable! The infrared camera is technology at its best, science working with art, peeling away layer upon layer, to expose . . .

". . . a fake!" He spat out the word as though it were a dung beetle.

"I didn't use that word," she said quickly. "I simply said that upon close scrutiny it appeared that the work was not by Titian himself but, rather, by one of his students. You know as well as I, Mr. Moffett, that Titian did a very basic preliminary sketch in broad uninhibited strokes. The underlying sketch in this case was tight and constrained. Painstaking. Tentative. It was, most likely, the work of Pontormo. Under Titian's direction, of course."

Randall Moffett's cottage-cheese face turned the color of catsup, and she feared, no, hoped, he might have a stroke. "You can't be sure of that!" he bellowed. "These newfangled gadgets, what do they know!"

Smokey flinched as a tiny projectile of saliva lodged on her eyebrow. In an effort to be discreet, she checked her watch and wiped the droplet away with her sleeve in one efficient motion.

"You would presume to threaten the reputation of this museum on the basis of a piece of hardware, of a . . . a . . ."

". . . gizmo?" she supplied. She couldn't help but smile. It was a word her father would have used.

"You think it's funny? Well, you listen to me, Miss Haggarty . . ."

Moffett droned on while Smokey hid her bewilderment behind a smirk. How could this be happening? She had always hated science, always avoided it if she could. In college she flunked chemistry and never even took physics. And now here she was, called on the carpet, because of something incredibly technological and scientific—an infrared video camera. Who would believe it?

The camera system was actually several components joined together. Smokey thought of them as gifted, eccentric friends and not as intimidating electronic equipment.

In her mind she called the camera Boris. It was easier for her to deal with it on that level.

Boris's function was actually quite simple. All physical phenomena—all matter—reflects light, resulting in images. Some of this light is visible and some is not. Light in the non-visible spectrum with non-visible wavelengths, such as ultraviolet and infrared light, cannot be seen by the naked eye and neither can images that result—but the images are there just the same.

Kind of like God, thought Smokey. That's what her father's friend, Irene Purdy, would have said. You can't see Him, but He's there just the same.

And like God, Boris was all-seeing. He contained a special sensor that was sensitive to extremely faint infrared light. He could convert non-visible infrared images to visible ones, making the invisible visible. But he scavenged these images indiscriminately. You might say he was the garbage man of infrared light. You pointed Boris and he collected. But once Boris captured an image, he couldn't do anything with it. He couldn't share it with you. He couldn't interpret it for you. He couldn't speak your language.

That's where Bella came in. Bella was an image processor, the brains behind Boris. She extracted information from Boris's signals. She manipulated and improved the image with talents such as contrast enhancement, shading correction, and level indication.

Together Boris and Bella were a dynamic duo. In semiconductor inspection, for example, they could work their way through multiple levels of circuitry on a silicon wafer and expose flaws before they caused malfunctions in an F-16 rocket. In fiberoptic communications, they could profile laser beam intensity to ensure better transmission. And in the world of art they could strip away, layer by layer, the series of preliminary renderings underneath a finished canvas attributed to a master such as Rembrandt or Botticelli—or Titian.

Although Boris and Bella had been utilized by the industrial community for some time, their value was only recently being appreciated in the world of art, where they were discovered to be invaluable in proving the authenticity of paintings by the masters. Boris and Bella could detect forgeries and prove that copies, even those most skillfully and artificially aged, were, in fact, fakes.

Initially Smokey had been technology-phobic. When the boxy almond-colored camera first arrived, she would have nothing to do with it. She named him Boris and left him in his crate, along with Bella and the color monitor, which was too dumb to deserve a name. There they stayed, trapped, for weeks.

I should have left you there, thought Smokey now. I could have avoided all this trouble.

Then one summer day the air conditioner was blowing papers around her small office and Smokey opened Pandora's Box. She extracted Boris from his nest of bubblewrap and used him as a paperweight. "There," she said. "At least you're being useful."

He stared at her with his black unblinking eye.

"Don't look at me like that. It's nothing personal. I'm just not good with equipment. Believe me, you wouldn't want me to touch you. I'd probably give you a breakdown."

But it was a slow day and boredom eventually overcame her. She plugged Boris in. She uncrated Bella and the monitor and connected everyone. She flipped through the manual. Then she started to fiddle.

Before Smokey knew what was happening, she was experimenting with contrast enhancement, switchable automatic gain control, something called a white clipper, a shading corrector, a video booster, and external synchronization control.

"This is fantastic!" she cried. "You guys are great!"

Boris beamed.

A week later Smokey made the mistake of demonstrating her new found skills to Randall Moffett. She wrote a paper that was published in *Art Historian*. And before you could say supersonic transport she was on her way to Paris. To the Louvre. To demonstrate. Boris and Bella.

Now here she was, in deep shit, all because of *them*.

"The C2741 is a highly reliable tool for image detection and analysis," said Smokey patiently. "You know it, I know it. God knows, the Japanese know it."

"Let's leave the Japanese out of this. We never should have bought the damn thing from them."

"It was a gift," she reminded him. "A gesture of good will."

"They have an ulterior motive, believe me. They want our Van Goghs or something. They're trying to cozy up."

Clearly the man was nuts and it didn't take an infrared camera to see it. "Why'd you send me to Paris if the camera's so unreliable?"

"I never would have sent you if I'd known you were going to demonstrate on the Titian!" exploded Randall.

Suddenly Smokey understood. He'd known the Titian was a fake all along. He'd passed it off on purpose. To make his career. It was beyond belief. And it was criminal.

"You knew the painting wasn't by Titian," she blurted.

She waited for him to deny it, but he only blinked. Then she saw something in his eyes. Fear. She had him by the short hairs now, she really did.

"I'll pretend I didn't hear that, Miss Haggarty. What I expect you to do now is to pick up this phone . . ." He pointed. "I expect you to call Philippe Tremblant and tell him you made a mistake. You were hasty. You used poor judgment. Say whatever you have to say."

"I will not."

"Then you are fired."

"Fired?" She gulped. This wasn't supposed to happen.

"Fired."

She shot from her seat. She couldn't believe it. She would take her story to the *New York Times,* to the *Post,* to Oprah. She would tell the world.

But who would believe her? Worse yet, who would care? And perhaps worst of all, maybe people didn't even want to know. People like the board of directors of the museum. It would be embarrassing. They would blackball her. She'd never get another job again.

"Miss Haggarty . . . the phone?" He smiled and held out the receiver.

"No," she said. "I just can't."

He told her to bring back the equipment, all of it. The camera, the controller, the monitor. That's when you'll get your severance, he said, and not a moment sooner.

He was holding her money hostage. Very well, she told him. If that's the way you want it.

She stopped at Bull Feathers on the way home and had four jumbo salt-crusted margaritas she could no longer afford. She ate twelve mini-pizzas and fifteen mozzarella sticks dipped in red gunk that remotely resembled marinara sauce. She refrained from having a cigarette. Then she made it to the E Train and threw up on some poor man's shoes. Wing tips, if memory served, leather grillwork with itty bitty holes. When she got to Prince Street she had a sour taste in her mouth and a monstrous headache. She jabbed her key at the lock and missed. On the third try the key hit home. Tumblers clicked, deadbolts slid. She stepped into the cavernous underfurnished loft. Pipes dripped. All it needed was stalactites to make it complete.

"Hello! I'm home!"

Of course, nobody answered. She lived alone.

How am I going to pay the mortgage? she wondered. When Michael died, the airline settlement went for the down payment on the loft. Now she had expenses. She supposed she could let Inez go and clean the place herself. She pictured fingers of black mold reaching up the bathroom walls and strangling her. She felt like crying.

"I hate dirt," she said out loud. "I hate dirt and debris and clutter." Her mind answered back: Perhaps that is why your life is so streamlined. So devoid of human flotsam and jetsam. So empty.

"Oh, shut up," she said.

Her stomach heaved. Please, she told herself, don't get sick. Ignore the floor that undulates like waves. Ignore those gyrating gastric juices. Do something! Anything!

She would check her messages.

She navigated toward the machine, expecting the usual nothing, and saw the flashing red light—make that two red lights, since she was seeing double. Perhaps Randall had called to say all was forgiven. She tried to focus. She pressed the button.

"Smokey? You there? Dodging bill collectors?"

She teetered between a grin and a groan. Oh, Dad.

"How's life in the rotten apple?" continued the voice on the machine.

"Fine. I lost my job." She made a mental note to register for unemployment tomorrow.

"Hey, I never got those swatches you were going to send."

She'd promised her father a custom casket for Christmas. He hated the thought of being laid out on cold satin and wanted plaid flannel. Kane's in Raven's Wing had agreed to do a special order and keep it on layaway. But first her father had to choose between Royal Stewart, Dress Campbell, or Black Watch and looking at a printed page in a *Bean*'s catalog wasn't good enough. Forrest had to have actual swatches in his hand. "After all," he said, "I'm the one who has to live with it."

Now swatches didn't matter. Now he would be wrapped in a sheet because there was no money.

"How can I choose," he persisted, "if I don't have the damn swatches?"

"Don't hold your breath," said Smokey, meaning it literally.

"But I digress," he said.

Digress?

"I didn't call about swatches. I'm up here in Coldwater, Connecticut . . ."

"Hey! I used to go to camp there. With the Girl Scouts. I had the least number of badges. I was a disgrace to the troop."

"I need your help."

What? Her father never needed help from her, or anyone else for that matter.

"You know that gizmo you told me about?"

She looked at the steel suitcases on the floor. Boris and Bella were inside.

"I want you to bring it up here, Smokey. The whole kit 'n caboodle. Things are starting to break, and I think it might be just what we need."

She considered the fact that she hadn't yet unpacked. She considered the chance at a final assignment with Boris and Bella. If she knew her father, it probably involved murder, something she was in the mood for at the moment.

"What the hell?" she said. "Severance can wait."

CHAPTER THIRTY

She leaned on the frame of the doorway in an effort to appear casual. "So," she said, "what'd they say?"

"Not much. They were on their way to the women's lavatory in Sturdevant. Not that it will do them any good."

"Ah. I figured they'd hear about that sooner or later. Duffy must be shitting a brick. I'd like to be a fly on the wall when they talk to him, wouldn't you?"

She plucked the spokes of her chair like harp strings. Plunk. Plunk. Plunk. "Not particularly. You know, sometimes I wonder about you."

"What do you mean?"

"His family loved him." She looked out the window at the pond. Someone was shoveling, someone skating behind. "It doesn't seem to bother you at all."

"Of course it bothers me. I'm just curious, is all. Aren't you? I wonder who called her. His mother, I mean."

"I haven't a clue." Plunk. Plunk. Plunk. She wished Angelique would leave. She was always hovering around, always trying to be helpful, trying to be friends. Deirdre wondered if she had an Uzi hidden in all that hair.

"I kind of thought maybe it was you. I mean, you two were close."

"Not in the biblical sense." Deirdre smirked as though making a joke. Who would believe anybody could want someone trapped in a nest of stainless steel tubing and electronic gadgetry? She might be empty from the waist down, but her mouth was full of wisecracks. This chair has everything I need, even a vibrator. And they'd laugh, thinking she was cool, brushing off paraplegism as though it were nothing.

"It wasn't me, Angelique. Now I have to study, okay?" She gave a spoke a good final snap.

"Is it chemistry? I could help you. I'm good at chemistry."

"No," she lied. "English lit."

Finally Angelique left.

Deirdre lied most of the time and was quite good at it. It was amazing how people thought a physical infirmity somehow made a person more truthful. Touch football, that had been a lie too, and not a very challenging one at that.

What else was she supposed to say? My mother did this to

me, my crazy alcoholic mother? Only it didn't turn out the way it was supposed to, because I ended up in a wheelchair instead of dead.

She never told the real story. Only two people in the world knew, Deirdre and her father, and her father was a pro at lying too.

It was said that at the beginning Arletta, Deirdre's mother, was crazy about Deirdre's father Maxwell. Problem was, she was crazy period, only Maxwell couldn't see it. Diagnostic signals that set alarm bells ringing in clinical settings were well documented in her file. Paranoia, histrionics, voices, delusions. Doctors didn't need to be especially insightful to deliver the damning diagnosis of schizophrenia, a condition that often worsens after the birth of a child.

But Max couldn't see it. He was a nuts-and-bolts kind of guy, the kind who believes craziness is a matter of weak will. He kept telling Arletta to "buck up."

After it became apparent that Arletta's will would not buck into any semblance of sanity, Max fell prey to charlatans who claimed schizophrenia could be cured and who were ready to take his money to prove it. Fortunately—or not, depending on your point of view—Max had lots of money to spend, so the cure phase took a long time, almost long enough for Deirdre to die.

People who know better know there is no such thing as a cure for schizophrenia and tried to tell Max. The demon within might be controlled, they said. It might lie dormant, might be drugged or bullied into syncopation with everyday life—but it would always be there, waiting. And sooner or later it would wake up.

Deirdre, who had seen the demon wake many times, could have told her father this. Time after time she witnessed Mother's transformation from Max's woman—a woman with a quiet doll-like smile—into a raving harridan. And at those times, she was forced to accompany Mother on automobile excursions.

The first time they never made it out of the garage.

Her earliest memory was of exhaust, the sweet smell of it. Strong arms dragged her from the car, away from the garage, onto wet grass. There were sirens somewhere, faces looking down.

"She tried to take her with her, can you imagine?"

"Her own child. It makes me want to cry."

"Someone should do something."

"I tried to talk to the father once, but he . . ."

"I sent her a pamphlet from AA. Anonymously, of course."

They blamed it on booze. She shouldn't drink like that, they said, she has a child to consider. Blaming it on booze was easier, after all, than saying someone was . . . well, you know . . . *crazy*.

After that Arletta always made it out of the garage. Deirdre would sit strapped in the passenger seat, rigid with fear, as houses flashed by, grand ones with tennis courts and turquoise swimming pools, colors swirling, blending, Mother at the big wheel, ruby red lips wrapped around a soggy Chesterfield.

"Give Mother a light, DeDe." And when Deirdre fumbled with the plug-in lighter, "A light, goddamnit, a fucking light! Can't you do anything right!"

When Deirdre turned sixteen she saw salvation in the form of a learner's permit. "I'm going to learn to drive," she announced. "That way I can take you places."

Oh, the places you'll go, Mother! The places you'll go!

"Is that a fact? I'll show you how to drive! I'll teach you!"

She shoved Deirdre into the car—a Mercedes wagon, built like a tank, purchased by Max, who said nothing was too good for "his girls."

"Don't put on that seat belt! Don't you dare!"

Deirdre realized that this was the punch line. Mother was going to kill them both. It had been her intention all along. The other drives had simply been trial runs. Gravel spun and they were off, down the country road and onto the six-lane interstate. The Mercedes rocketed into the fast lane.

Something inside Deirdre realized nothing could be worse

than this. She reached over, wrenched the wheel sideways (thank God for power steering), and dove under the dash.

She heard Arletta scream before the crash.

She awoke in a hospital bed, wrapped in starched white sheets. Her face was stitched, her eyes were swollen shut, her ribs cracked, her pelvis shattered. Her legs she couldn't feel at all. They said Mother was dead.

She replied clearly and distinctly so there would be no misunderstanding: "Good."

They pretended they didn't hear. They said it was shock. There were murmurs. It was the last time she told the truth.

Later she looked into her father's eyes and realized that he'd known all along. He plucked words from nowhere. "I'm sorry, honey. I should have done something. But I promise you this: No one will ever hurt my princess again. Never ever again."

And no one did. Max hired physical therapists. He built a new wing and crammed it with gym equipment. Nautilus. Soloflex. Free weights. He hired trainers, one of which took her to bed. He also showed her how to hurt people, should the need arise. "Use your fingers," he said. "Get them close and . . ."

For two years her legs shriveled and her biceps expanded. Then she decided she wanted to rejoin the human race. She wanted to go to college, wanted to be like normal people. Maybe she would even get a boyfriend.

She really thought it possible back then.

What'd you think, Deirdre? That you could pick one out, like in a supermarket? That a boyfriend could be bought like a trainer? Is that what you thought?

She selected a school carefully, poring over catalogs and watching videos of leafy campuses until she was bleary-eyed. In the end she selected a place called St. Sebastian's. She liked the name, a martyr like she was. The school was small and friendly and far from home. Like Goldilocks and the chair, St. Sebastian's would fit just right.

But the college wrote a letter to Max saying they were unequipped for handicapped students. We don't accept a penny of Federal funding, they said, because there are always strings attached and stipulations we don't choose to meet. Admitting handicapped students isn't one of them, but nonetheless we simply can't afford to accommodate your daughter. Much as we would like to. Bright as she is. We have no ramps, no elevators, no special access.

"Nonetheless." What an asshole word.

And why didn't they write to me? I'm the one who applied.

The world treated handicapped people like dolls, as though they were husks, molded plastic with dead flesh inside. Deirdre hadn't known this but she was learning.

Max explained to the college that he was a man of means, a man who could pay for ramps, elevators, and ways of access they never dreamed of. Draw up plans, he told them, I'll send you a check. You can stuff it in your heavenly access. My daughter will be there in September.

When the acceptance letter came, Max bought Deirdre the fanciest wheelchair money could buy. He also bought a special van. That way, you'll be able to get around, he said. You'll have wheels.

Two sets, she reminded him, and Max told her to "buck up."

The van turned out to come in handy, especially with Kevin. She put her head on the formica desk attached to her chair and wondered if the tears on the inside could show on the outside.

"Are you all right, DeDe?"

She felt a finger touch her shoulder. "Get away from me! Can't a person have a moment's peace!"

Angelique shrank back. "I'm sorry, DeDe." She slunk away, stricken.

Sorry. The whole fucking world's sorry. Fat lot of good it does.

CHAPTER THIRTY ONE

"Here's your coffee, Father."

"Thank you, Sister."

He couldn't believe it. He'd actually cancelled a class this morning, something he'd never done, to meet with these people. He'd gone to the basement classroom and stuck a Post-it note on the door. *Theology 101 cancelled today.* After hearing about what Louise had done, waking students in the middle of the night, making them repeat an inane line, he had no choice but to give this top priority. Because this problem wasn't about to go away. Indeed, he had a feeling things were about to go to hell in the proverbial handbasket.

He needed to collect his thoughts. Should he forbid her to question students in the future? How would that look? And what would the bishop say if he found out? Damn! He sipped the coffee.

"They're waiting outside, Father."

"I'm sure they are," he replied, "and they can continue to do so." He took a sip of his coffee and waited for Sister G. to be gone.

But she didn't budge. She hovered like a dark cloud. "Who would have thought it," she gushed. "Murder at St. Sebastian's."

She sounded pleased as punch. "We don't know that for a fact, Sister."

"True." She shifted from foot to foot as though she had to pee. "Father?"

"What *now*?"

He caught himself. No need to snap at the poor nun. "I'm sorry, Sister. I'm preoccupied. I'm sure you understand."

"Of course. The investigation is playing on your mind. I've been thinking about it too. In fact, I was wondering . . ."

For a wild moment Francis pictured Sister Gabriel selling a story to the *National Inquirer* and running off to Las Vegas to play the slots. Stranger things had happened.

"Wondering what?"

"If I might help. In some way. I know it sounds crazy at my age, thinking I could help. And I'm very fulfilled doing the light housework and the filing, don't misunderstand me. But sometimes I get . . ." She wrung her hands, then plunged on. "Bored, Father. I hate to say it, but I do. And I know it's my fault. Happiness and serenity come from within. But I've had enough serenity for several lifetimes. And now . . . well, now . . . I'm . . ."

"What?" asked Francis, losing patience. "You're what?"

"Bored." There. She'd said it again. "Aren't you ever?"

He stiffened. Good God, did she know? About his flights of fantasy? Had she found Game Boy? Or the racing forms? He only wagered in his mind, but still . . . Perhaps she'd found those brochures about Bali. He never planned to go, of course. Such a trip would be far too costly and without religious purpose as well. It was a mind excursion, nothing more. They had beautiful flowers in Bali, or so he'd heard. He wanted to dream about them, those flowers. And perhaps a naked native with a flower stuck in her . . .

"Certainly not," he said flatly.

She sighed. "Of course you aren't. I didn't mean to presume."

"I understand."

But still she didn't leave. "I could be helpful with this investigation, I just know it."

"What a preposterous proposal!"

"But I could! Think about it, Father. I could escort them around the campus, answer questions, provide them with information about students."

"Student records are confidential."

"With your permission, of course. Nothing without your permission. I understand your dedication to the seminary program, Father, understand and respect it."

He looked at her intently, wondering what she was driving at. Her hoarse voice dropped to a whisper, and he leaned forward to hear. "You're a busy man, Father. You can't be everywhere at once. I could be your eyes and ears. Your eyes and ears."

He was getting the point.

"It wouldn't hurt, would it, to have someone from the *inside* on *their* side? At least ostensibly."

He thought for a moment. "You may have a point there, Sister. Very well. Become part of their team, as it were. But keep me fully informed."

She commenced to bounce up and down as though on springs. "I was hoping you'd see it that way! This is so exciting!"

"Don't look so damned hopeful," he snapped.

The bouncing stopped. "I beg your pardon, Father?"

He hastened to erase the words. "I just meant, don't be looking for trouble that isn't there. This is all probably nothing, Sister. It won't amount to a hill of beans."

"Of course, Father." But clearly she didn't think so. She clasped her hands and practically danced out of the room.

Sister Gabriel brought in Louise, Trevor, Mildred, and Irene. Francis, who had a phone to his ear, waved them into chairs.

"Yes, Bishop, I understand, but we've had Winter Carnival every January for twelve years running. The ice sculptures are part of the festivities . . . Of course . . . Yes . . . But to cancel the entire event simply because one particular sculpture was in poor taste last year . . . All right, obscene. We can agree on the terminology. But Buildings and Grounds melted it down before anyone was offended . . ." He rolled his eyes and covered the mouthpiece. "Except the bishop," he whispered to them. "He was offended plenty."

Irene leaned over to Louise's ear. "Is that her? Sister Gabriel?"

"Yes," whispered Louise.

"Kinda creepy, isn't she?"

Louise was relieved to see that the elderly nun appeared oblivious to the remark. She was probably hard of hearing. Louise mouthed introductions. Everyone forced smiles. Heads bobbed.

Mildred looked to the door. "What's taking Forrest? He said he wouldn't be long."

"He's calling his daughter," Irene replied. "He'll be along."

"In any case, Bishop, it would be a shame to cancel the entire event because of one isolated occurrence. The townies look forward to Winter Carnival—and we both know how much they need something to look forward to. And what with the new element moving in, there's no telling who might show up. Dustin Hoffman. Glenn Close. And that little fellow what's-his-name. Fox, that's it. The carnival promotes good will for the college. The *Hartford Courant* does a feature. We get coverage on Channel 8. I'm talking television, Bishop, *television*." This was Duffy's trump card.

"I give my word that nothing like that will ever happen again . . . Very well." Francis winked and pinched his thumb and forefinger together in a sign of victory. "Thank you, Bishop. And we'll count on you to open the festivities with an invocation? . . . Wonderful! . . . Of course. I'll be sure to inform Channel 8 in advance, Bishop, well in advance."

He set down the receiver gently, as though it might explode. "Mercy! Sorry you had to witness that tempest in a teapot."

"What was that ice sculpture anyway?" asked Irene. "Something dirty?"

"Irene," said Mildred.

"Well, pardon me. I was only asking."

"Something anatomical," he said, then winked. "Let's leave it at that."

While Irene considered various possibilities, Louise introduced everyone to Francis. She had no sooner finished when Forrest strode in.

"It's all set! I left a message. If I know Smokey, she'll be here tonight. With the gizmo. Wild horses couldn't keep her away. Unless she's out gallivanting around. Christ, I hope she's not off in Europe or something."

Francis rose and shook Forrest's hand. "You must be Chief Haggarty."

"Right." A black shape in the corner caught his eye. "And who the hell is she?"

Mildred closed her eyes. "Forrest, honestly."

"Sister Gabriel," said Louise.

"My assistant," said Francis.

Forrest grinned. "You're kidding?"

"I most certainly am not." This man is rude, thought Francis, very rude. "At my request Sister Gabriel has agreed to assist with your investigation."

"Now wait a cotton-picking minute," sputtered Forrest.

"She will function as your guide, provide you with any necessary information, answer questions about the campus and the students and whatnot."

"Oh yeah? And what if we don't want help? What then?"

Mildred tried to keep her voice light, "I don't believe Father Duffy is giving us a choice in the matter, Forrest."

"I wouldn't have put it so plainly, Mrs. Bennett," said Francis, "but actually you are correct. To protect the interests of the college and the students, we must have a representative present at all times. And that includes any nocturnal interrogations." He looked at Louise.

"Since I have classes to teach and masses to say, Sister Gabriel seems a logical choice. I'm sure you'll find her very helpful." He impaled a pink phone message on a spike, as if to end further discussion on the issue, then looked up at Forrest. "Now what's this about a gizmo?"

"We wish to examine a wall," said Louise tightly, still smarting over the remark about nocturnal interrogations.

"The one in the ladies' room downstairs," added Irene.

"With a special kind of camera," said Trevor.

"Infrared," put in Mildred.

"Yeah, infrared," muttered Forrest, still smarting over the intrusion of Sister Gabriel. "It can see under stuff. Stuff like paint. No matter how many layers."

Francis sat very still. "I'm afraid you've lost me."

Trevor tried to explain. "We understand that there is a message about Kevin Cannivan written on the wall down there, Father."

"A death threat," intoned Irene.

"That was painted over," added Mildred.

"We want to see the handwriting," said Forrest.

"I see," said Francis.

Louise looked up from her lap. "Is it true, Francis? That someone wrote such a message?"

"Who remembers? Graffiti appears in so many places. We're constantly repainting."

Forrest leaned forward. "The point is, we've got to have an in-depth look at that wall to find out what's what."

Francis spread his hands as though saying Mass. "I really don't see how this can help."

"It's a clue," said Louise, "that could prove important." She twisted her handkerchief. "The person who wrote such a message could have killed him. It could have been some demented person. We should find out, shouldn't we?"

"Damn right," said Forrest.

"Before someone else dies," added Irene ominously.

"Yeah," said Forrest. "Or the blood will be on your hands, Father."

"Like stigmata," intoned Sister Gabriel out of the blue.

Francis was appalled. "Sister!"

"Forgive me, Father. The analogy popped into my head. It's totally inappropriate, of course."

Irene perked up. "What's stigmata?"

"Never mind," said Mildred. "Sister Gabriel is right. It's an inappropriate analogy."

"But what exactly is—"

"I'll tell you later!"

Francis gripped the arms of his chair. His cheeks flamed. Stigmata indeed. "I can refuse your request, you know. I can call security and have you removed from this campus."

Louise looked up. "Please, Francis. Don't."

"There's no need to panic," said Mildred. "We will work discreetly. We always do."

"No one's panicking," said Francis curtly.

"This thing could happen again, Father," said Irene. "Think of that."

"No, it will not," said Francis. "Because nothing happened in the first place!" He took a deep breath and tried to calm himself. "It was an accident, a terrible, most regrettable . . ."

Happen again? Never. It couldn't, simply couldn't. He needed time to think. Time to consider ramifications. He folded his hands and closed his eyes.

Irene nudged Mildred. "What's he doing?"

"I don't know," she whispered back. "Praying perhaps."

"Maybe it's some sort of spell. I knew a fella once. He'd have these fits, see? Just kind of nod off. Then he'd start to drool. Is that what stigmata is?"

"Hush!" hissed Forrest. Sometimes he felt like screaming. "What'll it be, Father? You going to help us or not?"

Francis opened his eyes and commenced to clean his glasses with a handkerchief. "Very well," he said. "Have your look."

"Now ask him about the rope," reminded Irene.

"The rope? Oh yeah." Forrest reached into his pocket and

pulled out the zip lock bag. "What do you make of that, Father?"

Francis eyed the dangling bag. "What is it?"

Forrest shook the bag impatiently. "The rope found around Kevin's neck. A fancy rope it is, too. Any idea where it came from?"

Francis started to tell them no. Why should he recognize the rope, for heaven's sake? He took the bag and examined it more closely. "It's from the confessional."

"The confessional?" repeated Irene.

"There are two such ropes at each of three confessionals—or there were before that one disappeared. They are used to hold back the curtains when a chamber is not in use."

"Ah," said Mildred.

"Apparently Kevin was the one who took it," said Francis.

"Well the FBI's going to give it the once over," said Irene smugly. "At their fancy lab."

Francis strove for a jocular tone but his voice edged up nervously. "What do you expect them to find? Fingerprints?"

"Who knows?" said Irene ominously.

CHAPTER THIRTY-TWO

They sat in Irene and Forrest's room, which was the most spacious, huddled around the television. A local weather man with a bad haircut was predicting a snowstorm.

"Great," said Forrest. "And Smokey on her way. She's a city girl now, not experienced driving on slippery country roads." He pictured his daughter marooned in a snowbank, the exhaust pipe blocked, dying of carbon monoxide poisoning.

Irene tried to reassure him. "She'll be all right, Forrest."

"How do you know? A semi could sideswipe her right off the highway."

"Smokey is a bright young woman," said Mildred. "She'll put up in a motel if driving becomes treacherous. What you're really stewing about is Louise, isn't it?"

"She sure as hell isn't adding to my peace of mind," he admitted.

"She'll be fine," said Mildred. "Sister Gabriel is with her, after all. And, who knows, maybe they'll manage to track down that mystery caller."

"Well, I don't like it." He looked to Trevor. "And I bet you don't like it either."

"I can't say that I do," agreed his friend. "Louise is obsessed with Kevin's death. I'm worried about her. Frankly, I think we should send her home."

"Already?" said Irene. "We only just got here."

"I know, but her emotional condition may be worse than I realized."

"I'd send her home in a minute," said Forrest, "but she won't go. What are we going to do—hog-tie her and load her on the bus? And then there's this storm to consider. If it turns out to be the doozie they're predicting, no one's going anywhere. For days," he added darkly.

Mildred went to the window and pulled back the curtain. Snow was already swirling in streetlamp lights. Down in the parking lot the Lincoln was becoming an enormous white lump. She dropped the curtain. "Brendan Cannivan called a while ago. Again. He was very short with me. I don't think they're getting along. That marriage is in serious trouble, if you ask me."

Irene licked a finger and turned a page of the *Star*. "Still demanding she come home?"

"Yes. He says Christmas is coming."

"Of course Christmas is coming!" snapped Forrest. "It comes every year at this time. What's he think—we can't read a goddamn calendar?"

"Forrest," said Mildred.

"Maybe I'll call him. Maybe I'll tell him to come get her tonight. See how he likes driving through a goddamn blizzard." He went to the phone and picked it up. It was still working. "Jesus, I wish Smokey would call."

Irene threw down the tabloid. "Listen, let's order a pizza from Rudy's and go over the case. What do you say? It'll keep our minds occupied."

"I guess," said Forrest. "But no anchovies."

They ordered a large pie with everything on it, what Irene called a "gut buster": pepperoni, onions, peppers, meatballs, and, much to Forrest's chagrin, anchovies. They also ordered a small plain pie for Mildred in deference to her more delicate stomach.

"It's all that gin you swill," said Forrest. "All those martinis. They've ruined your digestion."

Mildred set down her drink. "I do not. I have one cocktail before dinner, maybe two, and that's hardly swilling. You're just jealous."

"So what if I am? You think it's fun never having a drink?"

"No."

"Damn right. Trapped in a snowstorm without a good drink. It's enough to make a grown man cry."

"We're all on edge," said Trevor, "cooped up this way. We ought to use the time productively. We were supposed to review the case, remember?"

Mildred sighed. "I don't mean to be a spoilsport, but at this point I don't see that there's much of a case to go over. We'll know more after we examine the wall, of course, but right now we don't have any suspects."

"That's what you think," said Forrest. He washed down a mouthful of pizza with a slug of Dr. Pepper, ripped off the top of the pizza carton, grabbed a Bic and scribbled something on the limp cardboard. "I think better when I write things down . . . There." He held up his handiwork. "Two suspects already!"

They squinted at his chicken tracks.

"Not Cameron!" cried Irene.

"We've got to include him, Reenie. He's got a motive and no alibi. I'm sorry, but he can't be eliminated. Not yet."

"But that's ridiculous," scoffed Mildred. "We all know Cameron is incapable of murder. Of all the farfetched notions."

"No one's incapable, Millie."

"And your other suspect is equally outlandish. Father Duffy. I mean really."

But Trevor saw a grain of logic. "It's not entirely out of the question, dear. I know Louise admires him, but the way she described him troubles me—his adherence to strict doctrine, the intensity of his devotion to the seminary program, his hopeless pilgrimages to all the high schools—he sounds like a bit of a fanatic."

Irene took exception to this. "Just because he takes his religion to heart doesn't make him a fanatic. The world'd be a better place if there were more like him."

"I don't know," said Forrest. "He could have snapped. Fanatics often do."

"What about Kevin," said Mildred. "What do we know about him really?"

"Sometimes the victim can lead us to a killer," said Irene.

"As in victimology," said Forrest.

"If indeed he was murdered," Mildred reminded them.

Trevor rubbed his throat. "The crushed larynx indicates he probably was." He paused, remembering something. "You know Tom Roberts?"

"Sure," said Forrest. "The fella who took over your practice."

"Right. I told him we were coming here and he said he knew Kevin. Not well, but enough to say hello to. Kevin's girlfriend Meg Cravin is Tom's patient. She was in a car accident last spring. Kevin was driving. It wasn't his fault—he swerved to avoid a deer or something. Anyway, Tom said Kevin visited Meg every day at the hospital. Hardly left her side. Tom was impressed by such devotion in one so young."

The phone rang shrilly. Forrest lunged for it. "Smokey?"

The others looked at one other, relieved. Now Forrest wouldn't be rattling about all night and they'd be able to get some sleep.

His shoulders slumped. "Oh . . . uh huh . . . yeah . . . Christ on a crutch, are you sure? . . . Okay, but for God's sake be careful. We'll see you in a bit then." He hung up the phone.

Mildred looked at him in amazement. "She's coming in this weather? Well, your daughter is certainly determined, I'll say that. It must be a genetic trait."

Forrest pulled on his boots.

"What are you doing?" asked Mildred.

"That wasn't Smokey; it was Louise. She and that Sister Gabriel found a witness."

Everyone babbled at once. "A witness to what?" asked Irene.

"To Kevin's murder."

CHAPTER THIRTY-THREE

"Forrest," said Mildred, "surely you're not going out there."

"Of course, I'm going out there. We're all going. You'd best hurry and bundle up."

"You mean she's not coming back here?" said Irene.

"Not now," replied Forrest, as though explaining to a dull-witted child. He pulled on his old parka. He wasn't about to ruin his sheepskin jacket in the snow. "She's taking the witness to Duffy's office. They'll wait for us there. The kid's pretty scared, apparently. This is a break, a real break." He gave the final buckle on his boot a snap and looked up. "Well, don't just sit there! Get dressed!"

Trevor tried to reason with him. "Forrest, you don't expect us to drive in this weather."

"Of course not. We'll walk. It's less than a mile. The snow isn't bad yet."

"But it will be!" cried Mildred, her voice escalating several octaves.

"Not if we get our asses in gear. The worst won't come for hours yet." But their reluctance remained. "Okay, stay, if you want. I'll go alone."

He knew they'd never let him hike up there by himself.

"Father?"

"Yes, Sister." He didn't look up. His nose was buried in the latest financial statement from the accountant. There were a lot of numbers, all of them red. The seminary program wasn't holding its own. It was a financial drain on the college. But that wasn't the worst. The worst was what the president had implied in a chat with Francis just yesterday. He'd dropped hints like bombs, hints that the seminary program actually drove away prospective students. St. Sebastian's wasn't getting its share of national merit scholars, he'd said. They're attracted to more liberal environments. On a campus tour one of them asked who the black shirts were. As though they were brown shirts.

"Christ," muttered Francis.

"She's found a witness."

"Ummmmm hmmmmmm." Maybe they could charge admission to Winter Carnival. It would give the seminarians a chance to shine. And they would select another topic for their ice sculpture this year. Stations of the Cross hadn't gone over well. It didn't make people feel good. It made them feel lousy.

"Did you hear me, Father? She found a young lady who says she saw someone murder—"

He looked up, eyes wide. "What!"

Sister Gabriel started her nervous two-step. "The snow drove the students indoors . . ." She spoke of them as though they were field mice. ". . . and Mrs. Cannivan wanted to do some more canvassing. We were on the one hundred and fifty-eighth student. Over in St. Rosemary's Hall, don't you know. Mrs. Cannivan was knocking on doors. I followed in her wake. Keeping an eye on her. As we agreed." Bounce bounce bounce.

"Yes, yes."

Get on with it, for Christ's sake.

"Well . . ." Sister Gabriel drew herself up dramatically. "Mrs. Cannivan knocked on the door of a single—I wasn't paying attention, I must admit. I was weary. But her determination never wavered. She went on with the routine, I guess you could call it. You know, in which she leads the student down the garden path saying 'Repeat after me'. I was finding the whole enterprise rather tiresome at that point. I doubted we'd ever find the caller—if there even was a caller. Or so I was thinking at the time."

"Sister, please."

"Please what?"

"Get on with it already."

"That's what I'm doing, Father. If you'll just bear with me. So all of a sudden this girl says she saw something—I was hardly paying attention—and Mrs. Cannivan lets out a whoop. Scared the daylights out of me, shrieking that way."

"Who!" demanded Francis. "Who was it!"

Sister Gabriel flinched. "Brandi Beaufort."

Francis sat there, stone faced.

"I know, Father. That girl's been nothing but trouble since she got here. And now this."

"Where is she now, Sister?"

"Miss Beaufort? Why, just outside. Waiting with Mrs. Cannivan."

189

"Waiting for what?"

"For the others. For Mr. Haggarty and Mrs. Purdy and Mrs. Bennett and Dr. Bradford."

She certainly had all the names down pat. "Surely they're not venturing forth as a snowstorm swirls around us?"

"Oh, but they are." She gestured to the window. "As we speak."

He went to the window. He could see them in the distance, four abominable snowmen trudging up the hill. "Jesus," he said.

"You've got that right, Father."

He squared his shoulders decisively. "Get Miss Beaufort's file, Sister. I want to review it before this little soirée."

"Of course, Father." She scurried off.

Francis hardly glanced at Louise and Brandi Beaufort as he swept past to meet his geriatric inquisitors. "I'll be back in a moment," he called over his shoulder.

Louise and the young woman sat stiffly, hardly looking at one another. "Please don't be frightened," said Louise.

Brandi Beaufort stared at the floor. She'd taken off her mittens and placed them on the knees of her jeans. The ice on them was starting to melt. Water was sopping into the jeans and dripping onto the floor as well. "Wouldn't you be?"

"I'm sorry I made such a scene."

"What were you trying to do—get me killed too?"

"No."

Father Duffy plunged thorugh the door followed by four senior citizens. They looked chilled to the bone. They'd left their wet boots somewhere and shuffled along in sock feet. Hair was plastered to their scalps. The taller lady looked like queen bee. She kept primping, trying to salvage her appearance. She kept looking around—for a mirror, Brandi guessed. There were two guys and the one with the beady bald eagle eyes honed in on Brandi like a stealth missile. "You're the one?"

Brandi stood up and backed away. "Now, wait a minute—"

"Sit!" Father Duffy pointed to the chair. "We'll talk to you shortly, Miss Beaufort. First, I have a few things to say to our guests. In private."

"That's fine with me," said Brandi. "In fact, I'd just as soon be going. I'm supposed to be shoveling walks. It's part of the deal on my scholarship."

"Since when do our women students shovel walks?" said Father Duffy.

"Since equal opportunity."

"We don't have any of that here, Miss Beaufort."

Where had he been? "Whatever you say, Father."

"Forget about the shoveling. Just sit quietly for now. You might try saying a prayer or two. Do you have your beads?"

"No."

"Somehow I thought not." He motioned the others into his office and shut the heavy mahogany door.

"What's this all about?" demanded Forrest. "We came here to talk to the girl, not to you."

"You may talk to 'the girl,' as you call her, when I'm ready to give permission and not a moment sooner."

"Permission?" cried Forrest.

"She saw what happened," said Louise. "She was there."

Francis appeared unimpressed by this news. "Did she now? Well, perhaps there are some things you should know before you put too much stock in Miss Beaufort's story." He handed a file to Mildred. "Go ahead, Mrs. Bennett. Read her application essay for us."

"Out loud?" Mildred opened the file. A passport-type photo was stapled on the left. On the right were some sheets of unlined paper jammed with handwriting.

"All applicants are required to submit a handwritten essay," said Francis, "the subject of which is their life story."

"Golly," said Irene, "that's a doozie."

"We get some remarkable responses. They give us insight to a student's motivation and character."

Forrest shifted impatiently in his chair. "Let's get this over with. Go ahead and read it, Millie. Though I don't see the point."

"All right." Mildred snapped open her Dior eyeglasses. "But it seems like an invasion of privacy to me . . ."

CHAPTER THIRTY·FOUR

By Brandi Beaufort:

Nobody really knows your life. You want to know why things happened the way they did. What got me here. You expect me to have answers. Do you expect me to blame God or something? As if I believe?

I'll tell you what I can and maybe you'll be satisfied. I'll tell you about Before. Before I was in this place with chicken wire and glass and flooded toilets and chicken a la king for dinner every Monday.

I lived with the carnival crew. The Yankee State Fair was one place we went to, one of many. We were booked there every October. It was one of the better places, in Fairfield County, the area called Connecticut's Gold Coast. It's full of affluence or effluence, depending on your point of view. It's a place where people think nothing of buying a five dollar chance to win a fifty cent knick-knack. In short, it's a damn good place to run a scam.

The carnival was owned by a lady named Edna. Everyone called her Grandma. She was plenty plump and couldn't bend to pick up her pills when she dropped them. I picked them up for her many a time.

Grandma Edna owned the whole shebang—the scram-

bler, the Ferris wheel, the tents we worked in, the trailers we
slept in, the lights, the power and the glory. She paid every-
one a salary, even kids.

It was like a big family. Auntie Erna was Grandma
Edna's daughter. She kept the books, collected the money,
and handed out tickets. Everyone else was The Cousins. At
least that's what I called them, though most of us weren't re-
ally related. They felt like family to me.

Mildred stopped. "A very peculiar essay."

"I like it," said Irene.

"You would," snorted Forrest.

"Hush," said Irene. "Keep reading, Millie. It's a good story."

Mildred cleared her throat and continued.

Cousin Herbie was responsible for security. He ran off
low life, drunks and scumbags—people who loitered, pick-
pockets, people who made trouble. He always tried to make
things right. Like Rush Limbaugh says, The Way Things
Ought To Be.

Cousins Mary and Marilyn were exotic dancers, very
pretty and graceful.

Cousin Gregory ran the rides—the scrambler and the
tilt-a-whirl and the spinner, a round cage that held you
against the sides as it rotated. One time he cranked up the
speed and a girl threw up and it flew back in her face. Greg
liked nothing better than a good joke.

Cousin Erna, who was Auntie Erna's namesake and
Cousin Herbie's twin, got to run the pig races. That was a
key job because there was gambling on the side, run by—
you guessed it—Cousin Gregory.

Truth was, we survived on that gambling money. The
rest of the carnival hardly broke even. But Cousin Erna be-
came overly fond of the pigs and fed them Twinkies on the
sly. They got so fat they could barely walk, let alone run

around the sawdust track. Cousin Herbie called Cousin Erna 'a bleeding heart who's bleeding us dry.' He also called her a Democrat. Soon Grandma Edna demoted Cousin Erna to supervising the Spam carving contests.

I have good memories until Sweet Sue died. She was my mother. She was the cook and the cleaner. She made each new place home. She cooked the food and served it to everyone in a red and white striped tent. It was like a big family party. Thanksgiving every day. Until Sweet Sue died.

She got a lump in her breast and said it was nothing. A cyst, she said. I'm healthy as a horse. I'm even pregnant. Pregnancy brings out cysts, everyone knows that. Then she gave birth to a beautiful blond baby girl everyone called The Prexter. My sister. I wonder where she is now.

Mildred stopped.

"I've got a feeling this story doesn't have a happy ending," said Irene.

"We'll never know if Millie keeps stopping every five minutes to swallow that lump in her throat," said Forrest.

"Cancer," pronounced Trevor. "That's what it was."

"Don't go saying that!" cried Irene. "It wasn't, was it, Millie? Sweet Sue's going to be all right."

Mildred, who had read ahead, shook her head sadly and went on.

What Sweet Sue had wasn't a cyst, it was malignant. An uncontrolled growth of cells, according to Webster. It grew and grew until it pushed the life right out of her. One morning she was yellow and didn't wake up. The doctor said it had spread to her liver. He said she was in a coma.

They took her to the hospital on a collapsible stretcher with wheels and she never came back.

Everyone said it was a blessing that she had no pain.

They said it was God's will. Well, when I die I have a few questions for God.

They didn't know what to do with me and The Prexter. The Cousins had families of their own by then, babies popping right and left. The Prexter was cute and someone finally took her. But me? Are you kidding? I was way past the cute stage.

I slept from trailer to trailer, counting the days until I'd be grown. I thought it would be better then. But it never was.

For one thing, Boy George came along. That was his name, long before that guy in England came along. Boy George had a freak show and needed a place to roost. Auntie Erna objected. It offended her delicate sensibilities. She didn't want him and his "entourage," as she called it, moving in. She said it would hurt our reputation as family entertainment. There's no telling what kind of riffraff will come to see such trash, she said. People with 'prurient interests.'

But Grandma Edna had a keen eye for business. "Prurient is the way of the future," she said. "Just look at TV. A Current Affair, Hard Copy, Donahue. *Even Brokaw is scraping the bottom of the barrel. Besides, it will be weeks before the pigs are back in shape. We can use the money."*

So they let him in. They fixed me a room between Gator Boy and Electric Woman. Grandma Edna said you'll be fine here. How was she to know?

Everything fell apart after that. I guess you know what happened. I mean, the police told you, right?

Mildred put the papers down.

Irene almost pitched forward from the chair. "Don't stop there, Millie! What happened next?"

195

"Don't tell me," said Forrest. "Let me guess. Boy George made advances and she killed him."

"She ran away," said Trevor. "The police picked her up. They decided carnival life was no place for a juvenile. She was adopted by a well-to-do couple. She graduated from high school and went to college. St. Sebastian's. That's the way the story should go."

"I'm afraid that's all there is," said Mildred. "Brandi Beaufort's essay stops there, rather abruptly I'd say."

"What the hell!" said Forrest. He turned to Francis. "So what happened to this little lady? Which one of us is right?"

"No one."

"Huh?"

"Miss Beaufort," said Francis, "is an incredible liar."

Forrest stared at him. "Get out."

"It's true, Mr. Haggarty."

"Just what we need," he groaned. "An incredible liar."

"Better than a credible one," quipped Mildred.

"Will someone please tell me the point?" asked Louise.

"The point," said Francis, "is that Brandi Beaufort fabricated this entire story. Just as she fabricated that unfortunate tale she told you about seeing Kevin murdered. The point is, you're wasting your time. I'm sorry you came all this way for nothing."

"A nut case," sighed Forrest.

But Louise wasn't about to give up. "We should at least hear what she has to say."

"Right," agreed Forrest, but he feared their big break might amount to nothing.

"Wait a minute," said Trevor. "What's the real story behind Brandi Beaufort? Or do you even know it?"

"Oh, we know her real story," said Francis. "It isn't nearly as colorful as the one she concocted but I find it even more tragic." He stopped and considered his words carefully. "You see, Brandi

Beaufort is what we call a 'high risk student.' She's on probation."

"Academic probation?" said Mildred.

"No. Probation with the law. For burglary."

Forrest threw up his hands. "It goes from bad to worse."

"And she sounded like such a nice girl," sighed Irene.

"Maybe she still is," said Mildred. "Just because she lies and steals doesn't mean she's not nice."

"I don't believe this," said Forrest.

Francis went on. "Brandi stole from houses in her hometown of Devon."

"A nice town," said Louise. "We almost moved there."

"Nice for some, I suppose. Not so nice for Brandi Beaufort. Or for the people she stole from, for that matter—and there were many."

"Why'd she steal?" asked Irene.

"She was living in the park." He saw their disbelief. "I know that sounds bizarre. You think it can't happen in a town like Devon. But it can—and did. Her mother was divorced and had the misfortune to marry a despicable individual. A drinker. A womanizer. A man without inner fiber or moral substance. He cut through her money like a combine and drove her to an early grave."

Louise pictured a farmer, harvesting cash, sweeping it up, baling it, spewing it into a silo. She pictured him driving his wife to a hole in the ground and saying "I know we're early, but step in. It's your grave." The farmer was her father.

"So Brandi was alone," said Irene. "Like in the story."

"Alone would have been better. She was left with the stepfather. To use a description so favored by therapists, it was a highly 'dysfunctional' family. She was treated like a galley slave. She did the cooking, the cleaning, the laundry, and God only knows what else." He let them chew on that for a moment. "Finally she ran away. That's how she ended up living in the town park."

"Didn't anyone know?" asked Louise. "Surely there were teachers, guidance counselors—"

"Guidance counselors in towns like Devon get young people into the college of their parents' choice and that's it. Brandi wasn't a troublemaker, at least not then, so she went unnoticed. She lived in the park for three months, all the while maintaining a solid B average in high school. Don't ask me how. Apparently she went to the library to study. It was across from the park."

"But she needed food," said Mildred, "and warm clothes."

"Exactly. Which brings us to the issue of stealing. She stole money mostly. And food." In spite of himself, Francis admired Brandi's gutsiness. "It just might have worked too. Winter last year was mild, and she could have made it to graduation. But she stole something valuable."

"What?" asked Irene.

"A piece of jewelry. An emerald ring. Later her excuse was that the woman had plenty of others. I'm sure she did. In any event, one of Brandi's classmates recognized it as her mother's and reported it to the police. They discovered her living situation. And her stash. Nothing much—clothes and a few dollars. But they were only too happy to solve the string of petty burglaries that had been plaguing the town. And the ring was on her finger. It had been something she couldn't resist and it was her downfall. She almost ended up in prison."

"My," said Irene.

"And why didn't she?" asked Mildred. "What saved her?"

"A social worker—a young woman named Erna—called me. There was a bright young girl in serious trouble, she said. Returning her to her stepfather was out of the question, and she couldn't be left to her own devices. If a place could be found for her, a safe, stable place, she might get off with probation. If not, the judge would have no alternative but to send her to the women's penitentiary."

"So you took her in," said Irene.

"Not just like that I didn't. We have our standards, you

know. She had to pass her GED exams. She had to fill out a proper application. Hence . . ." he grimaced ". . . the essay."

"A real piece of work," said Forrest.

"Actually, I was rather taken by its creativity. And I liked the dig about affluence or effluence. There was potential there, I could tell. I hoped she'd be an asset to the college. Frankly, some of our students are such dullards. They're comfortable financially and take no pains to hide the fact. They glitter like fool's gold. Girls who wear mink jackets to classes. Boys who twirl about on three-hundred-dollar roller blades." He made a face. "I call them The Hollow Heads. We endure them. Their parents support our scholarship program, of which Brandi Beaufort is a recipient. I suspect she finds it galling but has the good grace not to say so."

"How has she done here?" asked Trevor.

"Not as well as I'd hoped. Oh, her grades have been fine, no problem there. But she doesn't mix well with other students. Frankly, she's somewhat of an outcast. There was an incident . . ."

"Oh?" said Forrest. "What kind of incident."

"Things missing from St. Rosemary's. It's one of our nicest dormitories, completely modernized this past summer thanks to a gift from the father of one of our students. A handicapped young lady. The first we've ever had."

"Physically challenged," corrected Mildred before she could stop herself.

"Hogwash," said Forrest.

"For once I agree with you, Mr. Haggarty," said Francis.

"Is Deirdre Canfield the one you're talking about, Father?" asked Irene.

"Yes. You've met her?"

"Yesterday. Real nice girl. Well adjusted too."

"Indeed. In any event, I pulled strings to secure a room for Brandi in St. Rosemary's, right down the hall from Miss Canfield, as a matter of fact. I thought she deserved something nice after juvenile hall. I thought I was doing her a favor. Ha!" He shook his head. "You know what she said when she saw those luxurious accommodations? She said 'What a dump.' Just like Bette Davis. I almost had to laugh. Such a marvelously perverse attitude! So refreshing! But then possessions started to disappear and I stopped laughing fast."

"How'd you know she was the one who took them," challenged Irene.

"I didn't. But St. Sebastian's is a small community and people talk. Brandi Beaufort was the perfect scapegoat, and her dorm-mates blamed her.

"It was a difficult time, and I hoped we'd gotten through it. But apparently we haven't. She's deceiving Louise—a cruel thing to do."

"But maybe she's not!" insisted Louise.

"So," said Sister Gabriel, "shall I dismiss her, Father?"

"No way," said Forrest. "Liar or not, let's at least hear what the girl has to say. Go get her, Trev."

CHAPTER THIRTY·FIVE

Brandi Beaufort wasn't what Trevor would have pictured. He was a man who couldn't abide prejudice, but all by itself her name would have steered him to preconceived notions. Brandi was a name like Crystal or Bambi or Amber. It was a name for someone who lived in a trailer by a strip mine. Someone who had five children and no husband and ate Devil Dogs for breakfast. Then another image came to mind. A wisecracking, smart-mouthed mall rat with a plug of Bazooka in her cheek. A teenager wearing constricting spandex. A girl with bleached blond hair and fluorescent nail polish.

But the young woman sitting in the chair was none of these. She was frail, with large brown eyes that blinked behind owlish glasses. She wore an oversized Mets jersey. Her brown hair was clean, simply cut, and pulled back in a ponytail with runaway strands that fell around her ears. She wore no makeup. Her face had the anxious, pinched look of someone anticipating the next blow and trying not to show it. The eyes behind the glasses skittered from side to side, as though panning for an escape route.

She saw Trevor and started to get up. Then she sat back down. "I'm not feeling so good."

He went to her and felt her forehead. "Dizzy?"

"Yeah."

"Put your head between your knees." She did so and he pressed his fingers to back of her neck. "Stay like this a moment. You're feeling faint, is all."

She sat back up and bit blue lips. "Do I have to go in there?"

"No." Forrest will kill me, he thought, but so what? He wasn't about to force her. "Not if it's going to make you sick."

She pushed strands of hair behind her ears. "You don't understand. It's his mother in there. She doesn't have any idea. I can't tell what happened. I just can't."

"Was it that bad?"

"Worse."

"You could tell me. I'm a doctor. I've heard it all and then some."

She smiled wanly. "Like a priest?"

"No. I don't have a list of rights and wrongs."

She glanced at the door to Father Duffy's office. "Did he tell you how I came here? To St. Sebastian's?"

He nodded.

"I wouldn't be here if it wasn't for him. I could lose my scholarship. I could go to jail. That's why I didn't tell anyone."

"Not to mention being scared?"

"That too."

"The cat's out of the bag, Brandi. At this point, you'd better tell somebody."

She looked at him. He was so dignified. He had class. He was what she'd want for a grandfather, if she had one. His silver hair was combed just so. He wore a Burberry tweed sports jacket and a ring with a silver crest. She guessed he came from a well-to-do family, a family where fathers wore such rings and gave them to their sons.

"Maybe I should."

Forrest stuck his head out. "What's the holdup?"

Trevor waved him off. "Give us a few minutes, Forrest."

"Jesus night," he muttered but the door closed.

"It happened the night before Thanksgiving break," she began . . .

She ran along the asphalt path, holding an army blanket over her head. It was starting to sleet. Beads of ice melted on her glasses.

She had been surprised when he suggested they meet down here. They had a few classes together. She'd noticed him immediately. He stood out with the head of red hair. Girls revolved around him like satellites. The fact that he was a seminarian seemed to attract them all the more.

He was supposed to be celibate and she wondered if he was. There had been rumors about him slipping out of his room at night. Getting it on with someone. She had learned to distrust gossip a long time ago. Look at what they were saying about her. Thief! Liar, liar, pants on fire!

One day she was walking to class, alone as usual, and there he was. He said he knew she hadn't stolen those things, said it right out. Those girls are just a bunch of twits, he said. Don't let them get you down.

She was taken aback by his directness and at the same time pathetically grateful. They came to a fork in the quad that would take them in different directions. If you want to get together, he said, just to talk . . . He let the words hang.

Really?

Tonight even. I'm free. And you look like you could use a friend.

She was awash with gratitude.

Don't tell anybody, though. It would be awkward. People talk, you know.

So she hadn't told, because who was there to tell anyway?

She crept up the stone steps and pushed open the door. "Hello?"

The first thing she saw were candles, dozens of them, flickering all around. She should have realized it was a strange gesture but she didn't. She danced up the aisle, the blanket swirling around her like a cape. "It's beautiful!"

He sat up in the pew, sleepy eyed. He was wearing the clothes— the bulky black coat, the shapeless wool pants, the black shirt, and stiff white collar. His face flickered in the light. "I wanted it to be special."

She never thought to ask why.

He flipped on a boom box. "I hear you like classic rock." Aretha belted out "Rescue Me."

She glanced at the door. "Someone will hear."

"No one comes down here this time of year. Don't worry. Come here." He ran the words together, c'mere, and she realized he'd been drinking. He patted the pew.

She hadn't pictured things this way but sat anyhow. He wrapped the blanket over them and put his arm around her. He did it smoothly, as though it were routine.

"I thought you were supposed to be . . . ?"

"This?" He pointed to the collar. "It's a costume, nothing more." Aretha's wailing subsided.

She would wait a few moments, then fabricate an excuse and leave. He pulled her to him and told her to relax. "What's wrong?"

Everything, she wanted to say. Then she heard a sound. "What's that?"

"Nothing. You're nervous, is all. Here, have some of this . . ." He brought a bottle to her lips. Jack Daniel's. Sour Mash. Kentucky Straight.

"I don't—"

He shoved it into her lips. "Go ahead. It'll relax you."

She considered pouring a few drops into the cap and drinking that, just to appease him, because she knew that look, knew it very well. But before she could make a move he decided for her. He inserted the bottle in her mouth and tipped. Bourbon burned her throat and dribbled down her chin. She jerked away.

"Hey! That's good stuff! Don't waste it!"

"Sorry," she managed to say. "Don't be mad."

"I'm not mad." But he was breathing hard.

She wanted to leave, but knew it would upset him. She decided to stay just a little longer and hope for the best. When he proceeded to lick the bourbon off her chin, she endured it. He sucked, then bit, her lower lip, stopping just before he drew blood. She didn't know it, but this was his pattern. Pleasure and pain, pleasure and pain.

He kissed her, shoving his tongue down her throat. She tried to pull away but couldn't. Her struggles seemed to excite him more.

He will stop, she told herself. Surely he will stop.

He shoved his hand inside her jacket and ripped open her blouse. "Hey," she cried, "don't . . . don't!"

He unhooked her bra with a practiced flick of the fingers. He grabbed her breasts in both hands. He leaned on her, his boozy breath hot in her ear.

She tried not to panic. "I don't want to do this," she said. "Please."

"Shut up."

He never told her she was beautiful.

He never told her he loved her.

He never even bothered to lie.

He pushed her down in the pew, yanked open her jeans and rammed his hand into her panties. "Like this? Like it?"

His arm was across her throat. She couldn't speak, she could hardly breathe.

"You want it, you know you do."

He moved very quickly, as though she might fall out of some mood. He opened his coat and unzipped his pants. He shoved her face down. "Kiss it. Go ahead, goddamn it!"

"No!"

He squeezed her neck. "Do it or I'll kill you!"

Tears streaked down her cheeks as she did what he wanted. At the end, for the barest instant, his fingers relaxed and she wrenched free. He exploded all over himself.

"Fucking bitch!" He slammed her face with the back of his hand and she fell to the floor. Then he pulled a handkerchief from his pocket and began cleaning himself.

"Get out!" he yelled. "Or I swear I'll—"

She stumbled down the aisle, her eyes stinging with tears. She fled into the woods. Needles of sleet stung her face. She tripped, then clawed her way through a thicket of thorns. She was lost, she realized. Her glasses were gone. Blindly she searched for them, but it was hopeless. The thought of going back to look brought a new wave of tears.

But she had to go back. She had an exam tomorrow. She would fail. She would lose her scholarship.

She stumbled toward the muffled music. Ain't Too Proud to Beg. Finally her feet hit pavement. She hunched down, groping for the precious glasses. When she found them, they were shattered. She held them, brittle and broken, in her bleeding hand.

The man's voice was gentle. "What happened next, Brandi?"

"I heard something inside. A cry."

"Then what?"

"I went to the side of the chapel and looked through a window. It was stained glass, so I couldn't see much. Just fragments. Plus, my glasses were broken."

"But you did see something?"

"Yes. Someone was hunched over Kevin."

"A man or a woman?"

"I'm not sure. A woman, I think. It was a shape, a dark shape. Kevin's head kept jerking from side to side like a puppet."

"And then?"

"I ran, Dr. Bradford. I ran like hell."

In the next room Forrest flipped off the intercom.

Francis glared at him. "I want you to know I object to that eavesdropping."

"It was the only way we were going to hear what she had to say," said Forrest.

"I think we got more than we bargained for," said Irene. She didn't dare look at Louise, who was sitting there, staring into her lap, her hands working at a tissue that was rapidly turning to lint.

"She's lying," she whimpered. "Isn't she?" And she started to cry.

CHAPTER THIRTY-SIX

Gary slowly punched out the number—he knew it by heart now—and waited for the call to go through.

"We're sorry to miss your call. At the sound of the beep, please leave your name, number, and—"

"Shit!" He slammed down the receiver.

It's time, Gary. Time to call in the troops.

But this was *his* case, damnit. *His.* He didn't want to hand it over to someone else. And besides, maybe it really was nothing. If that was so, he'd look like a fool. A crazy ex-cop with splinters in the windmills of his mind.

So what, Gary?

Yeah. So what. Besides, he'd thought of a way to handle this. He punched out a second number.

"Raven's Wing Police Station."

"This is Gary Gonski of the River Bend Police in Ohio. I'd like to speak to the officer in charge."

"Chief Pulaski is in. Hold on, I'll connect you." Moments later a gravelly voice came on the line. "Leonard Pulaski."

"Chief Pulaski, Gary Gonski of the River Bend Police in Ohio. I was hoping you could check something out for me."

"Sure. What?"

"You've got a family in Raven's Wing. Cannivan. Father's name is Brendan. I don't know the street—"

"I know who they are. What about 'em?"

"Their son died recently. An accident up at St. Sebastian's College."

"Yeah."

"The Cannivans used to live out this way. They were good folks. Everyone liked them." And now the lie. "My wife was friends with Mrs. Cannivan." He thought wildly for a moment. "Louise. Anyway, Bea—my wife—has been trying to call her for days and gets no answer. I'm afraid she's worked herself into somewhat of a state over it. You know how women can be."

"Don't I ever," agreed Pulaski.

"I hate to ask, but would you mind checking in on them. Just to see how they're doing?"

"Not at all. Should be getting over there anyway. I try to stop by and see families going through tough times. Sometimes they need help and are afraid to ask. We've got good social service support in this town."

"That would be great," said Gary. "I really appreciate it. You can call me back collect at this number . . ."

Lenny Pulaski set down the receiver. Sounded like a nice guy. He made a note on his monumental Things To Do list and went to get a cup of coffee.

CHAPTER THIRTY-SEVEN

He stared at the page, trying to reread it for the third time. *Readings in Organizational Behavior and Psychology*. Part of the innovative new curriculum for seminarians. *"The primary focus of humanistic organization theorists is . . ."*

"How's it going?"

"Deirdre! You startled me."

"Sorry." She maneuvered to the table and opened a book of her own. "Library's pretty dead, huh?"

"No one's studying. It's almost Christmas break."

"I know. You going home?"

"No."

"Me neither." She brightened. "Maybe we could go out somewhere for Christmas dinner. Not a date. Just—"

"Sounds good. McHugh's staying too. I'll ask him to join us."

She deflated. "Great."

They studied in silence for a few minutes. "You know these people trying to find out if somebody killed Kevin? I wonder if they've gotten anyplace."

"I don't know. They were hoping to see some kind of message on the wall of the women's lavatory. But it's been painted over, so now I don't know what they'll do." He paused. "Of course, they can always pursue the watch."

She swallowed. "What watch?"

He looked her in the eye. "The one Kevin wore. The one with the inscription on the back."

"I never noticed it," she said.

"Oh. Well. I gave it to Forrest. He seemed pretty interested in it. It's the only evidence they've got at this point."

"Evidence?"

"That Kevin was having a romantic relationship—" He stopped. Maybe he'd gone too far. "Deirdre, are you okay?"

"Fine," she managed to say.

Her hand trembled as she turned the page.

CHAPTER THIRTY-EIGHT

"Amazing," said Forrest. "Looks like we're getting a break in the weather."

They were making their way back to the Coldwater Arms. Louise, Mildred, and Irene trudged a few yards ahead.

"A temporary respite. A storm watch is in effect for tonight."

"I hope Smokey has the sense to stay over at Scott's then. She can drive up after it's over."

"I'm sure she will. Forrest?"

He kicked through a small drift. "Yeah?"

"I got a call from Country Home. They have a buyer for the house."

"That's great news, Trevor! Great!"

"I know. But I have to sign the contract. So Mildred and I are diving back this afternoon. Before the storm hits."

"The hell you are!"

"Only for a day or two. I don't have any choice, Forrest. And besides, I can talk to Kevin's girlfriend while we're down there. Meg Cravin."

"Why?"

"Because of what happened to Brandi. If there's a pattern of abusive behavior, it would tend to corroborate her story. She did write a pretty outlandish essay. I don't think she's lying, but she *could* be. Anyway, it won't hurt to talk to Meg. It may give us some insights."

"I suppose so. How 'bout taking Louise back with you?"

"I already asked. She won't go."

"Figures. All right, go ahead and talk to Meg. But hurry back. You're the only one Brandi trusts. She's scared shitless, and frankly I don't blame her."

"She'll be all right, Forrest."

But Trevor was wrong about that. Dead wrong.

CHAPTER THIRTY - NINE

As Mildred and Trevor were en route, New England was hit by the worst blizzard in thirty years. They barely made it back to Raven's Wing. Roads were buried and power lines down. As Forrest had hoped, Smokey had the good sense to wait out the storm with Scott and his family.

Forrest, Irene, and Louise were marooned at the Coldwater Arms, where they passed the time playing cards, reading old magazines, doing crossword puzzles and playing board games. Finally, after five days, Smokey arrived.

"It's about time!" cried Forrest.

"And hello to you too," she laughed, kissing his cheek.

He looked over her shoulder. "Where's Millie and Trevor?"

"Coming later. Hi, Irene."

"Later when?"

"Tomorrow, I think. There was a problem with the contract, and the storm delayed—"

"We can't wait until tomorrow! We've got to get moving now! Did you bring the gizmo?"

"In the car. I thought maybe I'd catch my breath before we get star—"

"Great! Irene, Louise, time to get cracking!"

"That's not fair," complained Irene. "I just got Atlantic, Ventnor, and Marvin Gardens. And you owe me forty thousand in back rent. I'm on a roll. Sheesh."

While Louise and Irene pulled themselves together, Forrest briefed Smokey on the case, finishing up with Brandi's story.

"That's awful," she said. "And poor Mrs. Cannivan. What a terrible thing for her to hear."

Forrest shrugged. "I guess."

"Think about it, Dad. How would you feel if someone you loved did something so terrible?"

"I don't know how I'd feel. It's not high on my list of things to figure out. Your trouble is you're too psychological for your own good. It's that shrink you see."

"I don't see him anymore."

"Good. All he did was stir up trouble. It was natural for you to be grieving. You'd lost your husband, after all. Not that he was real high on my list to begin with. The man had no ambition. Liked nothing better than to put his feet up . . ."

She closed her eyes and started counting. *One, two, three . . .* Let it go, she told herself. Let it go.

". . . Of course, the men you brought home always were a bit off. People in the arts are usually freaks. Not to mention liberal . . ."

"Michael was a pilot. A Republican." *Four, five, six . . .*

"You have such abilities, Smokey. You really could do something with your life . . ."

Seven, eight, nine . . .

"The way I see it, it's probably for the best you got canned. It's an opportunity to do something sensible for a change . . ."

"Ten!"

"What?"

"Never mind!"

He shrugged. Sometimes she was strange. "Soon as Louise and Irene get down here, we'll head for St. Sebastian's."

"Saint who?"

"Sebastian."

A painting came to mind. By Andrea Mantegna at the Kunsthistoriches Museum. Young man en brochette, impaled with arrows, fifteen of them, blood oozing from every wound. "What a grotesque name for a college."

"Never mind grotesque. Here's Irene and Louise. Let's get going."

Twenty minutes later they descended into the bowels of Sturdevant Hall. Forrest blew on his hands. "Jesus, it's freezing down here. What happened to the damn heat?"

"Maybe they turned it down for Christmas break," said Louise.

"At least there won't be a bunch of Nosy Parkers looking over our shoulder," added Irene. "Smells kinda rotten down here, don't it?"

Forrest sniffed. "Dead mouse."

Sister Gabriel materialized at the stairs. "Dead what?"

Forrest glared. "Speaking of Nosy Parkers."

"Mouse," replied Irene. "Morning, Sister!"

"Morning!" She hobbled over. "I don't smell anything."

"At your age," said Forrest, "senses fall by the wayside."

"Ah," said Sister Gabriel. "So that's what it is."

"Forgive him," apologized Irene. "Forrest never was big on

tact." She brushed away a cobweb. "I hate to say it, Sister G., but this place is a pit."

Sister Gabriel became defensive. "Father Duffy specifically told me not to clean down here. He said it was too much for me. He said the janitorial staff would tend to it." She surveyed the musty basement room. "Obviously they've been derelict in their duties."

They slipped down a dark, narrow corridor and crowded into the women's lavatory. Smokey proceeded to set up the array of equipment, fiddling with connections and dials as she worked.

Irene was reading the manual and assumed the role of tour guide. "This here is what they call the 'image processor.' " She pointed to an almond-colored box about two-thirds the size of a VCR and looked at them as if to say How do you like them apples!

The image processor had a power switch, dials marked BRIGHTNESS and CONTRAST, and a port marked MOUSE.

Forrest's eyes were glued on the camera. "So that's it," he marveled.

"Not entirely," said Smokey. "The camera is like you and Irene and Trevor and Mildred—part of a team. What we have here is a continuous system. The camera captures so-called invisible images. Then, through manipulations with the image processor, we enhance those images and see the results on the video monitor . . . here."

"Just like a regular ol' TV," commented Irene.

"Right. Any television will do the job, even black and white. But since this system is for museum applications, it has a color monitor."

Louise put her finger on the VCR. "I suppose you record everything with this."

"Exactly. Plus I can shoot still photographs. Dad, if you want a print of the message when it appears on screen, just let me know and I'll generate one with the video printer . . ." She gestured to another box.

"I'll be damned," said Forrest.

Smokey placed the camera in her father's hands. "For heaven's sake don't drop it."

"I don't intend to. What do you take me for anyway?"

"What about me?" asked Irene.

"You get to watch," replied Forrest.

Irene hung a face, Louise stood by expectantly, and Sister Gabriel took a catbird position at the monitor while Smokey gave instructions to Forrest. "Pretend you're painting this wall with even horizontal strokes." Forrest nodded. "Then just keep going around the room until we find the message."

"Fine," he said.

"I must emphasize that you have to move slowly." She demonstrated, moving at what seemed to be a millimeter at a time.

"A snail's pace," he grumbled.

"I know. It's not going to be easy. And we may have to repeat the process several times while I make adjustments to the processor. This isn't abracadabra quick magic, that's all I'm saying."

"So let's get started already."

Smokey flipped on Bella's power switch and turned the monitor on. "Okay, Dad! Start your paces!"

All eyes watched the screen expectantly as Forrest walked, but the results were disappointing.

"Static," pronounced Sister Gabriel.

"Yeah," sighed Irene. "Like the past few days—nothing but snow. Can we change the channel? Maybe catch *I Love Lucy* or something?" She giggled.

Forrest stood there impatiently. "Do something, Smokey."

"I'm trying." She fiddled with BRIGHTNESS, CONTRAST, and the MOUSE. As she had predicted, it took quite some time. Finally things came together and she was satisfied. "Go ahead, Dad."

"The most boring program I ever did see," said Irene.

Forrest glanced over his shoulder. "Nothing but a white cloud."

"Kind of like flying," said Irene. "At least what I picture flying to be. Never have been in a plane for real."

"In a way it is like flying," said Smokey. "We're moving through space. Minute space, to be sure. In this case, less is more. Nanometers are our universe."

"Nano what?" said Irene.

"Hold on!" cried Louise. "What's that!"

Smokey pressed RECORD on the VCR. "It's really small. Dad, hold up. I don't want to lose it."

The message appeared slowly and they stared transfixed at the screen. Everyone hovered as Smokey enlarged it, then generated the print. She held it up triumphantly. "There!"

They stared in amazement.

"Even better than I hoped," breathed Forrest.

"Better?" repeated Louise. "How can you say such a thing?"

He grabbed her hands. "Don't you see? It's perfect! It's clear! It's—"

"Awful!" She threw down his hands. "That's what it is! Perfectly awful!"

"No it's not! It's *handwriting*, Louise. Clear, legible handwriting."

And indeed it was . . .

Kevin Cannivan, Puddin & pie,

Watch out girls, he'll make you cry.

He'll do what he wants & then he'll lie.

A boy like that deserves to die.

"Now that we have it what do we do with it? Have you thought about that?"

"Of course I have. We find out who wrote it. We find a match."

"Oh. And how do we accomplish that?"

"Well," stammered Forrest, "I don't know just yet, but I'm sure we'll think of—"

"I know!" cried Irene. Louise and Forrest looked at her. "The essays! Don't you see? Everyone had to write essays to get into this place! Handwritten essays!"

"Ah," said Louise. "And how do we . . ." She and Irene had the same idea simultaneously. They turned on Sister Gabriel.

Sister Gabriel backed away. "Now, now. I very much doubt that Father Duffy will allow—"

"Don't tell him," said Forrest.

Sister Gabriel was shocked. "You mean we take the essays without permission?"

"Sure!"

"But . . . but . . . we can't *steal* the essays!"

"Borrow," corrected Irene. "We borrow them. With your help, Sister G."

"Oh, my," said the nun. "My, my, my, my, my."

"Please," pleaded Louise. "Say you'll help us."

Sister Gabriel stood there with a pained expression on her face. "Well," she said at last, "I suppose I could."

CHAPTER FORTY

They were packed up and about to leave the basement, when who should appear at the stairs but Mildred and Trevor.

"You missed all the fun," said Forrest. "How was your trip? Find out anything?"

"I should say," replied Mildred.

"What?"

"We found out . . ." began Trevor. "Phew!"

Mildred made a face. "Indeed. What's that terrible odor?"

"It's kinda ripe, ain't it?" said Irene.

"What'd you find out?" repeated Forrest.

"We found out . . ." she lowered her voice ". . . why Kevin came to St. Sebastian's."

"What was that?" said Louise, who had strained to hear what Mildred was saying.

"Go ahead," said Forrest. "Whatever it is, she has as much right to know as anyone."

"More," said Louise.

"It's rather a long story," said Trevor. "I think it should wait until we get back to the hotel. You know that smell really is re- pugnant."

"We're sort of used to it by now," said Irene. "It's just a rat in the wall or some such. Happens this time of—"

Trevor shook his head. "I don't think so." He followed his nose to some trunks stacked in a corner and put his hands on one. "Give me a hand with this, will you, Forrest?"

Forrest hurried over. "Sure, Trevor. Sure." He lowered his voice. "What's going on?"

"I'm not sure. Nothing, I hope."

They lifted the top trunk. It slipped from their hands and landed with a thud.

Sister Gabriel wrung her hands. "Father Duffy isn't going to like this! He's not going to like this one bit! He specifically told me not to mess with those old trunks!"

Trevor leaned over and whispered. "Ask the ladies to step outside, Forrest."

"Huh?"

"I said ask the ladies to step outside."

"We most certainly will not," said Mildred.

"I should say," sniffed Irene.

"I'm not going anywhere," said Louise.

"Don't say I didn't warn you," said Trevor.

He pulled at the fixtures. "It's locked. Hey look . . . the hardware's all rusted but the lock's brand new."

Forrest pulled out a penknife and wedged it under a corroded hinge. When he pulled the hinge snapped off easily. He repeated the procedure with the second hinge. Trevor withdrew a handkerchief from his breast pocket and held it over his mouth.

Irene looked at him apprehensively. "Why you doing that?"

"I think I should leave," said Mildred. "I really think I should . . ." Her feet remained glued to the floor.

"I think I should get Father Duffy," said Sister Gabriel. But she remained planted in place as well.

"The police," said Smokey. "They're the ones we should—"

Forrest lifted the lid and looked inside. The odor washed over in waves. He could taste it, feel it. He felt his lunch rise up in his throat and turned away. "Oh, God."

"What is it?" demanded Irene. She pressed forward. Her eyesight wasn't what it used to be but her nose worked just fine. "Lord in heaven!"

Dried eyes stared from crusty sockets. The face was a plum-ish purple. A black tongue protruded. The lips peeled back in an incongruous grin. There was a dusting of mold at the hairline.

"Oh my God," breathed Louise. "It's . . ."

"Brandi Beaufort!" blurted Irene.

The baseball jersey and owlish glasses gave it away. The rope around her neck was embedded so tightly you could hardly see it.

Trevor forced himself to speak calmly. "Call the police."

Mildred started to sway. "I'm going to be sick."

"Don't you dare," said Forrest. "Not in here. This is a crime scene!"

Irene, who had seen many dead bodies in her nursing days and prepared more than a few of them for burial, struggled to regain her composure. Trying not to gag, she reached out and touched the corpse.

"Irene!" cried Mildred.

"There's something here . . ." She touched the hairline. "Something strange." Gingerly she peeled away a gelatinous sub-stance. "Oooooaaah! Yuck!"

Forrest stared at what appeared to be sausage casing dan-gling from Irene's fingertips. His voice escalated nervously. "What the hell is that?"

Mildred fainted with a thud.

"I don't know." Irene whipped her hand around, trying to fling it off. "It's disgusting!" Whip, whip, whip. "It's like skin . . . like she had a sunburn and it peeled . . . it's like . . ." She flicked hard and the gelatinous gunk flew free, catching her across the nose and lips.

"Aaaaaaaugh!" She leaned over and upchucked into the trunk.

"So much for protecting the integrity of the crime scene," muttered Forrest.

Trevor cradled Mildred's head in his arms. "Mildred, dear? Mildred?" Her eyes fluttered open.

Irene struggled upright. Gunk still clung to her face. She peeled it off and held it aloft. "Saran wrap!" she cried.

"It's not either!" said Forrest.

"Okay, maybe not Saran wrap. But something similar. A plastic of some sort. Yeah. For some reason someone's gone and covered her face with it." She placed it neatly on the table.

"Total gross out," said Smokey. "Total, total, total . . ."

Irene rummaged around in her pockets. "Does anybody have a mint? My mouth tastes godawful."

CHAPTER FORTY·ONE

"It's late. At least wait until morning, Smokey."

"I'm sorry, Dad, but this is more than I can take. I have to get out of here. Now."

"I guess it is pretty gruesome."

"It's not just that. You lied to the police."

"I did not."

"Well, you didn't tell them about the wall. You didn't show them the photo. You didn't tell them about Kevin Cannivan and what Brandi saw through the window."

He looked away. "They didn't actually ask."

She closed her eyes. "I don't believe this."

"The police are bunglers, Smokey. You can't trust them to do a job right."

"Fine sentiments, spoken by a former chief."

"You could stick around. We could work this case together, you and me."

"You already have your team. Such as it is. And besides, I've got to get back. I've got to find a job."

"Oh," he said. "That."

"Yes, that. Making a living, putting clothes on my back, and food in my mouth. Incidentals like 'that.'" She took a deep breath. "Listen, I was wondering . . ."

"About what?"

"Would you give me a reference?"

He shook his head. "I don't know any museum people, Smokey."

"Not museum people. I was thinking more in terms of the FBI."

"The FBI? Why?"

"International art fraud is a big deal now, Dad. Millions of dollars are involved and the infrared camera is the way to catch the culprits. I could set up a whole new department for them. I just need to get a foot in the door and do a demo. If I do that, they'll hire me in a minute, I know they will."

He seemed to deflate. "Maybe," he said grudgingly.

"Why are you so negative? I thought you'd be pleased. I'd be following in your footsteps, in a way. Come on, Dad, give me a referral. To one of your big shot cronies. I'll be in like Flynn!"

Forrest looked at his feet. "I've got to tell you something, Smokey."

She didn't get it. "What?"

"I . . . I, uh . . . don't exactly have any big shot cronies."

"You don't? But you said—"

"I know what I *said*. What's true is another matter, and the truth is I don't know anyone in the FBI. I never did."

"Oh."

"I was just shooting off my mouth. Trying to impress people. Trying to be a big shot. I'm nothing but a broken-down old cop, not a very good one at that."

"You are not! You're a great cop, you always have been. So you don't know those people. Big deal. I'll tell you something. If they don't know you, it's their loss, Dad, their loss."

"Yeah, right." He felt like a heel, letting her down when she needed him. "I'm sorry, Smokey."

"There's nothing to be sorry about. I don't really need the reference anyway. I'll approach the FBI, and if they don't know a good thing when they see it, I'll pursue other options. For example, I could set up my own consulting business. I made a lot of contacts through the museum. Wealthy people could hire me to authenticate paintings before they buy them. And they'd pay me a lot more than the FBI."

"Sounds like a great idea," he said, trying to appear enthusiastic. Fact was, he liked the idea of her working at the FBI a lot. It would make him so proud if she did that. Not that he wasn't proud of her already, of course.

"Only thing is, I'd have to buy a camera and a processor."

"How much to they run?"

"A total system runs about a hundred and fifty."

"Why didn't you say so? Heck, I can help you out with that. I'll write you a check right now." He reached into his coat.

She looked at him in amazement. He was always so tight. Always said once his children were twenty-one his financial obligation was over. The day after she graduated from college he had refused a collect call. That's the way he was. She hated to spoil this rare gesture of generosity.

"*Thousand,* Dad. A hundred and fifty thousand dollars."

"The hell you say!"

She couldn't help but laugh. "No, I swear. It's true!"

"Well, I'll keep my fingers crossed for the FBI then."

"You do that." She climbed into the 4 Runner. "Take care, Dad."

"You bet. And Smokey . . ."

"Yeah?"

"Keep in touch. Sometimes . . ." He looked away.

"Sometimes what?"

"Sometimes I miss you."

"I love you too, Dad."

She kissed his sandpapery cheek, put the car in gear and drove off.

Forrest walked back into the hotel. Mildred, Irene, Trevor, and Louise sat in the lobby, shell shocked. The police had questioned them for hours, it seemed.

"Well," said Louise, "are you going to tell me?"

"Tell you what," said Mildred hollowly.

"Why Kevin came to St. Sebastian's."

"Louise," said Trevor, "I don't think now is the time—"

"I want to know," said Louise, "and I want to know now. I have a right."

"Very well," sighed Mildred. "You tell her, Trevor. I can't bear to."

Trevor gripped the arms of his chair as though bracing for an unpleasant ride. "Okay," he said. "Mildred and I talked to Megan at the Cravin home on Stoney Brook Lane . . ."

The house was at the end of a street of cookie-cutter bi-levels identical except in color and foundation plantings. Back in the early sixties, Stoney Brook sprouted as an offshoot of Windy Pines Road and sloped down into swampy, undesirable land. In summer the mosquitos were fierce and in spring some of the basements flooded. But it was more affordable than other Raven's Wing neighborhoods and a good place for young families starting out.

Trevor parked the Lincoln, got out and opened the door for Mildred. "Ready?" he said.

"As I'll ever be."

The Cravin household was somewhat unusual in that three generations lived under one roof. Hank was a fireman in the Bronx. Back in the seventies Dot's father Ed gave him the down payment for the house. Ed was widowed and retired, living in an apartment in Danbury. He had always admired Raven's Wing. It would be, he believed, a good place for his grandkids. It was understood that Ed's moving in was part of the deal. The finished basement included a playroom, a bedroom, and a half bath. It would serve as a small apartment, and Ed could take his showers upstairs.

It was Ed who met them at the door.

"Evening, Doc. Mrs. Bennett."

"Evening, Ed. I appreciate your allowing us to talk with Megan."

"Hank and Dot were against it, I may as well tell you. They figure she's been through enough."

"Young people take loss hard," said Trevor. "They haven't learned. They still think life is fair."

Ed looked at Trevor for a moment, as though gauging how much to tell him. Then he shrugged. "No point in digging all this up now, if you ask me. But she's been seeing this doctor. A head doctor. He says she should talk about it, says it does her good." Ed shook his head at this, at a loss to understand head doctors.

Hank and Dot sat perched on the sofa in the living room like birds on a wire. Mildred could tell that the room was used only for special occasions. The brocade upholstery looked new and there were plastic covers on the lampshades. A plate of home-baked cookies sat on a doily in the center of the coffee table.

They shook hands. Hank was strong as an ox but a whole lot smarter. He was taking courses at Western Connecticut State at night, racking up credits toward a master's degree. When his twenty years with the department were up, he hoped to teach high school history.

Dot asked if they would like coffee. She seemed anxious for them to say yes. Mildred complimented her on the cookies and said coffee would taste good with them. Dot fled to the kitchen.

Hank studied the backs of his hands as though they were maps. "I can't say I'm sorry the boy's dead. You'd feel the same way if it was your daughter." He looked at Mildred. "Are you sure you want to hear this Mrs. Bennett?"

"Mildred," she said. "And yes. I'm sure."

"Okay then. For a long time we didn't know what was going on. I mean, Dot was pleased Megan was dating him. He came from a nice family, his father had this big job, they live in a real nice house. You know the place."

Dot handed them coffee in Lenox cups from her wedding set. She gave them little pink napkins with an M embossed on them. "From Megan's sweet sixteen," she said, smiling wanly.

"I didn't say anything," continued Hank, "but I was wary. Megan's pretty—I know I'm biased—but she was two years younger than the Cannivan kid. Only a sophomore at the time. She hadn't dated much. And she wasn't what you'd call sophisticated. She was still into Scouts and 4H. Had a prize pig she raised right in the backyard. Against zoning regulations, but no one complained. She'd walk that pig up and down the street, guiding it along with a flyswatter. Called her Dolly. Never hit her hard, just give her little pats.

"Anyway, my little girl was on cloud nine the day Kevin Cannivan asked her out. Right, Dot? Cloud nine. She couldn't believe he was interested in her. So out she went. They became an item, I guess you'd say, and for a while Megan seemed to blossom. Oh, there were moments when she was moody, but what teenaged girl isn't? And the bruises . . . well, we never saw them. She covered them up with makeup, with long sleeves. If I'd known . . .

"Prom night was when things unraveled. You heard about that? The 'accident'? Honey, go get Megan, okay?

"She's been through a lot, what with the plastic surgery, the orthodonture and everything. She's fragile emotionally. The guidance counselor knew something was wrong. Not what, just something. He recommended a psychiatrist, so that's what we're trying.

"All I'm saying is, don't say you don't believe her; don't even hint it. You voice the slightest bit of skepticism and you'll have me to contend with." He stopped thinking. "Do I think someone killed him? Wouldn't surprise me. And if someone did . . . ? Frankly I hope they get away with it."

"Ah, here she is. Megan, this is Dr. Bradford and Mrs. Bennett. Tell them what happened. Your mother and I will be right here."

Dot hunched up. She reached over and patted Megan's hand.

It looked as though Meg Cravin hadn't eaten a meal since April.

225

Her face was chalk white. She wore black sneakers and a purple sweatshirt intended to make her appear heavier than she was. Her wheat-colored hair fell limply to her shoulders. Trevor wondered if she might be anorexic. When she spoke she kept putting a hand over her mouth. It wasn't until well into her story that he saw the glint of metal and realized she was self-conscious about braces. She looked off into the distance as she spoke.

"On prom night we'd been drinking Southern Comfort. Not a lot. Not enough so the Breathalyzer showed him drunk later. I told him I wasn't going to see him anymore. He didn't take it well. There'd been arguments before, times when he hurt me . . . pulled my hair, squeezed me under the ears . . . here . . . pinched my arms and my . . . breasts. Once he gave me a black eye. I told Mom and Dad I walked into a door.

"If they'd known the truth, they'd have made me stop dating him, and I didn't want that. Kevin was my first real boyfriend. Being Kevin's girl meant I was popular. It meant I was accepted. It seemed so important at the time. And if he hit me sometimes, it seemed a small enough price to pay. Plus I always thought each time was the last. And he always said he was sorry, you know?

"But finally another boy asked me out—not one of Kevin's crowd, but a nice guy—and I wanted to go. So I told Kevin it was over.

"I never should have told him in the car. I should have told him here, or at school. Some place where other people were around. But I wanted to protect his pride. That's important with boys. I read that in Seventeen.

"Anyway, he totally lost it. His face got all red and he slammed his fist on the steering wheel. He said, 'You think you can walk away? Just like that? After I've waited so long?' He got out of the car, came around on my side and dragged me out. I had no idea what was happening. Then all of a sudden he's on top of me. I panicked. We'd never . . . I'd never—

"I fought him as best I could, but he was so strong. I tried, I really did, but he hit me . . .

"With his fist, with the flat of his hand, both. He broke my nose, fractured my cheekbone, loosened my teeth. I could have screamed, but no one was there to hear. And my nose was full of bubbles and my throat was clogged. It was all I could do to breathe. I'm telling you . . . I'm telling you . . . oh God, I'm sorry . . .

"No, I'm okay. Really. After he finished, after he'd done what he wanted, he picked me up and sat me back in the car like I was a doll or something. He smoothed my dress down. He wiped my face with his handkerchief. It was like I was watching a video and it was happening to someone else. I tilted my head back, trying not to get blood on my dress.

"I must have blacked out, because the next thing I know my face is mashed against the windshield. We're crashed into a stone wall. Over on Golf Lane? By the Ward estate? It's isolated there. The whole front end of his father's Audi was smashed in. There's glass everywhere and now he's covered with blood too.

"He said this deer jumped in front of the car and he swerved to avoid it. That's what happened, he said. That's all that happened. He said it like he really believed it. He said everything would be all right. He kept saying it over and over.

"I lay back in the seat bleeding and picking glass out of my face and crying 'You raped me! You raped me!'

"He didn't say anything for a few minutes. He waited for me to stop crying. Then he said no one would believe me. 'Look, Megan,' he says, "I'm bleeding too. We were drinking. We had sex. I was driving you home and swerved to avoid a deer. That's what happened, Megan. That's all that happened.'

"I didn't know what to do. I'm thinking maybe I provoked him in some say. My dad told me that once a man gets started it's hard for him to stop. A girl's got to be careful, he said. Don't put yourself in a compromising situation.

"I was leaning out the door, barfing blood. And behind me he keeps saying no one will believe me. He keeps looking around, like he's afraid the police will come. Me, I'm afraid they won't.

"I wasn't thinking straight but I knew one thing: He was right.

No one would believe me. They'd believe him. They'd say I was a slut. Look what happened with William Kennedy Smith. It would be better, better for everyone, if I didn't tell. And I felt so dirty. I didn't want anyone to know. So I said okay. I'll say it's an accident.

"I just wanted to get away!

"No, I never thought about it happening to anyone else. I thought about me! Only me!"

Dot patted her daughter's hand. "She was in the hospital a week. Him, they discharged the next day. And he visited her all the time, was at her side constantly, making sure she didn't change her story. But I knew something wasn't right. A mother can tell when her child is lying. So I went to Megan's room one night, after he'd gone, and I said 'Tell me. Whatever happened, I'll love you. But please, tell me the truth.' And she did."

"And Dot told me." Hank's hands balled into fists.

Dot spoke up again. "By then it was too late to do tests to prove the rape. By then it was too late to do anything."

"So I handled it my own way," said Hank. "I knew he had a job at Friendly's and I waited for him in the parking lot. When he came out I took him by the arm and said 'You and me are going for a ride.' We got into my car and I drove him to Mamanasco Lake. I took him out on the dock. We had a little chat. And by the time it was over, he took the deal I was offering."

"What kind of deal?" asked Trevor.

"Four years of his life. That's all. Four years at St. Sebastian's Seminary. Four lousy years for what he did to my daughter. Doesn't seem like much, does it? Not nearly enough. But I have a cousin—a priest—who was there years ago, and I knew they didn't take any guff. And there were no girls there, or so I thought.

"Now all of a sudden I hear it's changed. It's like a regular college. But now it doesn't matter because he got what he deserved after all. I'm sorry, Dot, but it's true." He looked at Mildred and Trevor. "I didn't kill him, if that's what you're thinking."

"How did you make him go?" asked Mildred. "He was supposed to go to Yale."

"I held his head underwater. He almost died. Several times. I told him if he didn't go, I'd finish the job. I meant it and he knew it."

Mildred swallowed hard. Trevor leaned back, stunned.

"On the way back he started sniveling about it, giving me crap about Yale, how he's already accepted and what does he tell his folks.

"I said, 'You're a bright boy. You'll think of something.'"

CHAPTER FORTY-TWO

Gary waited until Bea had her coat and boots off to bring up the subject. He and Bea were sitting in the living room, having their wine. "I got a call from Chief Pulaski today."

"Oh?"

"He spoke to the father."

"Good," she said. "So they're fine."

"I don't think so. The father gave him the brush-off. Said the family was coping, thanked him for his concern. But as Pulaski was walking to his car, he met the youngest boy. Danny. Six or seven, something like that."

"And?"

"Well, the kid was fascinated with the police car. Wanted to get in. Pulaski went back, asked if he could take the kid for a ride, the father says sure and off they go. And while they were driving around, the kid starts talking about his mother. How much he misses her. Turns out she's gone up to the college. Someone called her and said it wasn't an accident."

"Oh, God."

"They said she should come up. Chief Pulaski thought it was strange the father didn't mention it, but he decided not to interfere."

"But you will."

"Yes."

Frustration etched her voice. "So now what?"

"I'm going to St. Sebastian's."

"How, Gary? How do you plan to go?" She knew the answer.

"You'll drive me."

"I can't go traipsing off like that. I've got commitments. I'm working two jobs."

"School's out 'til New Year's."

"But not the store. They're relying on me, Gary. I gave my word. They need me through Christmas."

"I need you more."

"That's not fair!"

"I'm sorry, Bea, but I need your help. Without you, I'll have to hire a driver and—"

"We can't afford—"

"Right."

"What about Sally?" she said. Already she was giving in. She always did.

"I've already thought of that. Sally can stay with the Wentworths."

"Is there anything you haven't thought of?"

"What we do when we get there. I'm not sure about that part."

"It's a long drive." She got up. She would pack tonight. "You'll have plenty of time to think about it on the way."

CHAPTER FORTY THREE

Mildred avoided looking at Louise. "It's been a long day. A terrible day. We could all use a good night's sleep."

"No," said Forrest. "Louise wanted to hear the truth and now she has. Louise?"

She stuck her chin out defiantly and glared at him. "I'm still his mother. Nothing will ever change that."

"Of course," said Mildred quickly. "We understand, Louise."

"No matter what they said. No matter what Brandi Beaufort or Meg Cravin said about him, he was still my son. And I love him!"

"I'm sure you do," said Forrest. "And you're entitled. No one is all bad. I'm sure Kevin had his good points."

Irene looked at Forrest in amazement. This was a new twist. Forrest was a black-and-white kind of man who believed you were either good or bad with no in-between. Maybe he was just trying to be considerate. But that would be a new twist too.

"He had lots of good points!"

"Of course he did. But we have to know, Louise. We have to know the truth. Is there anything else? Anything you haven't told us."

"Nothing that relates to this."

"Why don't you let us decide that?" said Trevor gently.

"Because I don't intend to air dirty linen with strangers."

"Strangers?" said Irene. "We're not strangers, Mrs. C. We've been living cheek-to-jowl for days now. We're real fond of you. We assumed you felt the same way about us."

"Well, I guess I do," admitted Louise.

"There's nothing you can say will make us think less of you," continued Irene. "Nothing."

"Protecting Kevin's memory won't help us find his killer," said Forrest. "You still want us to do that, don't you?"

"More than ever."

"So . . . ?" said Irene.

"Very well." Louise took a deep breath. "There was an incident in the last town we lived in. River Bend, Ohio. A girl—a retarded girl who didn't know what she was saying—accused Kevin and two other boys of molesting her."

"I see," said Forrest.

"The charges were dropped. Nothing came of it." No one said anything. "The story was fabricated, I'm sure."

"Is it possible that the girl has a sibling at St. Sebastian's?" asked Trevor.

Louise was taken aback by this. "Well, I don't know. I never thought about it."

"Could be," said Irene. "It's something we should check out at least."

"What was her name?" asked Forrest.

"Poultice." Louise would never forget that name. Never. "The girl's name was Charladene Poultice."

"We'll ask Sister Gabriel," said Forrest.

"They could have changed their name," pointed out Mildred. "Or it could be a cousin with a different name. Or—"

"Then we're back to the essays."

"Essays?" said Mildred. "What essays?"

"We've got the handwriting," explained Irene, "now we have to find a match. So Sister Gabriel is gonna help us get the essays."

"Ah," said Mildred. "Good idea! I'm glad Father Duffy agreed."

"He didn't," said Forrest. "In fact, when we asked him, he refused. He's all shook up about Brandi. He said enough was enough."

"So Sister G.'s going to help us get them," said Irene.

Mildred cocked her head. "I'm not sure I understand."

Forrest explained. "Sister Gargoyle agreed to help but she's afraid to take the essays from the files. She says someone might notice. So you and Irene will accompany her to the office tomorrow tonight—"

"We'll what!" cried Mildred.

"Accompany her to the office. And photocopy the essays."

"But there are hundreds of them!"

"Eight hundred to be exact," said Louise.

"It will take hours!"

"Just copy the first page of each," said Forrest. "That'll save time."

"And what about Father Duffy?" Mildred went on. "He lives in Sturdevant Hall. He's liable to hear us."

Forrest grinned. "Louise has volunteered to keep him occupied."

CHAPTER FORTY-FOUR

Brendan called from the office the next evening. "When are you coming home?" he asked without preamble.

Louise closed her eyes. "Soon."

"What's that supposed to mean? Everything's going to hell here, Louise. Your Mrs. Cranston quit. I think she took some of the silver with her too."

"You think?"

"Do we have service for eight or twelve?"

"Sixteen." It had been her mother's pattern as well as her own. Patience held onto it through all the difficult years, fought tooth and nail to keep it, then gave Louise the place settings before she died.

"Shit! That dirty crook! She watered down the booze too."

"Now that," said Louise, "is really going too far."

"Very funny, Louise."

"Call the police, Brendan. Report the silver."

"The police have already been here."

"Good."

"Not about that. They came before I realized I was harboring a criminal. Actually the chief stopped by. Did you know anyone named Bea Gonski in River Bend?"

"No." Now Louise was thoroughly confused.

"Well, Chief Pulaski seemed to think you did. Somebody from River Bend called him because somebody named Bea Gonski from there had been leaving messages and was getting no answer. It turned out Samantha was erasing the tape."

Louise gripped the receiver. "She what!"

"Don't worry, she's not doing it anymore."

"But you were supposed to check the messages, Brendan! In case whoever called before calls again!"

"Fat chance." He paused. "Calm down, I'm checking now."

"Good. Who's taking care of the children with Mrs. Cranston on the lam?"

"Me."

"You?"

"Yes. I'm taking vacation time, Louise. Some vacation it is, too. Everything's falling apart. Laundry piled sky high. Toilets overflowing. Dinners burned. Pete went to stay at Hank's until you come back, and Marty's with the Hogans. So much for family unity. We need you, Louise. You've got to come home."

"I will. Soon. We're getting close, Brendan, really close."

"Close to what?"

"Kevin's murderer."

He let out a sigh. "That again."

"He *was* murdered, Bren. There was a witness."

"What?"

"A witness. And now she's dead too."

There was stunned silence for several moments followed by: "Are you sure?"

"I saw the body, Brendan."

"I'm coming up there, Louise."

"Don't, Brendan. The children—"

"I'll find another sitter. Somehow. And as soon as I do I'm coming to get you. I'll drag you back bodily, if necessary."

"You better not," warned Louise. "You had your chance." She looked at her watch. "Good-bye, Brendan."

"Louise—"

She hung up. It would be the last time he would ever hear her.

"Ready?" said Mildred.

"Yes," replied Louise.

Irene surveyed Louise's sensible skirt and blouse. "Couldn't you wear something a bit more provocative?"

"I'm not going to seduce him, Irene, I'm merely going to keep him occupied. With conversation."

"Oh." She seemed disappointed. "Here, take this."

Louise took the brown paper bag and looked inside. "Wine?"

"To enhance sociability. I got strawberry."

Louise tried not to make a face. "How nice."

Mildred tried to convince Forrest and Trevor to remain at the hotel, pointing out that the football game was on. But they insisted on coming along and said they would wait in the car.

Louise never thought to mention the calls from River Bend.

The buzzer sounded after the evening news. He wondered who could be at the door. The police, probably. Back to ask more questions. He felt paralyzed with dread. He made his way downstairs as though wading through mercury.

He peered through the beveled glass side panel and saw Louise. She was standing in the snow, holding something in her hands. Relief washed over him. He opened the door. "Louise!"

"I thought you might need cheering up."

"Everything has taken such a dreadful turn." He ushered her inside and proceeded to brush snow off her coat. "I hope you're not angry about the essays. It's just that things have gotten completely out of hand. If I hadn't allowed your investigation in the first place, Brandi Beaufort might still be alive."

"I know. We feel terrible about it too." She handed him the bag.

He looked inside. "Wine?"

"Strawberry. A peace offering from Irene."

"Well," he said, "it was a nice thought. I'm beside myself, absolutely beside myself. I can't stop thinking about that poor child. Dead. It's a horror, Louise, an absolute horror."

"Can we talk upstairs?"

"Upstairs? In my apartment? Oh Louise, I really don't think—"

She took the decision out of his hands by starting to walk. He chased after her. "They think it happened in her dormitory room and that she was moved. The police tore the room apart. They put yellow tape across the door. Crime scene, it says. Can you imagine? In St. Rosemary's Hall. Crime scene!"

She kept climbing. "I know. I'm sorry, Francis, so very sorry."

"Don't be sorry for me. Be sorry for Brandi Beaufort. She's the one who's dead. She's the one who was strangled." He gulped convulsively. "Just like Kevin."

He chattered on. "They don't see any connection yet, but

they will, mark my words. They're asking everyone questions. They're rummaging around the basement and won't tell me why, just said they'd be back tomorrow. Will someone please tell me: What do they expect to find?" His voice edged up hysterically. "Another body?"

"I don't know, Francis, I really don't know."

"No one else is missing. We've checked the entire campus. If only I knew what they wanted, I'd help them. I didn't tell them about Kevin, of course. Brandi's sordid accusation, I mean, and what she witnessed through the chapel window. I didn't tell them about the wall either."

Louise stopped on the landing. "You didn't?"

"No. The seminary program would be ruined. Ruined! There are people out there, lots of people. People who say priests lead unnatural lives, with all sorts of repressed desires. This would be grist for their mill, Louise, grist for their mill."

"I see." She continued up the stairs as he prattled on behind her.

"I didn't lie to them, you understand, nothing like that. But I did skirt the truth. I needed time to think. I've been so preoccupied lately. They'll be back to me, I just know it. I could tell they weren't satisfied. They'll talk to students, to staff. They'll talk to everyone."

"Maybe that would be for the best," she said. "Let the professionals handle it. I'm a mother, not an investigator." They stood before a heavy mahogany door. "Here we are."

"Yes." He turned the glass knob and pushed the door open. Before he could stop her she swept inside, shrugged off her coat and went to the closet. She reached inside for a hanger. It was then that she saw the clothes. She looked at him and he almost lost it.

"My sister's," he said quickly. "She comes to visit sometimes."

Louise continued to look at him curiously.

"It's the truth, Louise."

"I'm sorry, Francis. Of course it's the truth. Things are just crazy. I'm jumping at shadows."

The living room was small and simply furnished. There was a braided rug, two bookcases bulging with theological texts, a small television, an end table, a couple of decrepit lamps, and a flowered couch with split seams.

She settled herself on the couch. There was no place to sit but beside her, which he did. He folded his hands in his lap.

"You look like you're praying."

"I probably should be."

"How about some wine?"

"Strawberry? I think not."

This wasn't going to be easy. "Scotch?"

"I really shouldn't. I've already had—"

"Another won't hurt. I'd like one, Francis."

"Very well." He went to a cabinet and poured two neat. "Ice?"

"Please."

She proceeded to get him drunk. She knew she should feel terrible about it, but soon she was well on her way herself and beyond feeling much of anything.

"I keep seeing her face," he said.

"Brandi's?" She shuddered. "It was pretty horrible."

"I feel responsible. I should have become a monk. It would have been better than this."

"You wouldn't be able to serve Mass."

"That's true."

She clinked her glass against his.

"What are we toasting."

"My lousy marriage."

"Marriage is a wonderful sacrament. I'm sorry I missed it."

"It's like a bus. You can always catch one later."

"Not me. I made my bed. I only sleep in it."

"Maybe the church will let priests marry some day."

"I doubt it. Besides . . ." He took a sip. ". . . I wouldn't ap-

238

prove of that." He had to remind himself. "Why is your marriage lousy?"

"The usual reasons. He lies, he cheats, he steals. He's having an affair with his secretary."

"Nothing too serious then."

"Right. Nothing too serious." She took a gulp. Scotch was a wonderful beverage. It just slid down. "If you could marry, Francis, would you marry me?"

He almost spit out his drink. "Louise, really!"

"No, I mean it. Would you?"

"You're already married."

"But if I wasn't would you?"

He smiled at the thought. "Yes, I suppose I would."

"That's the nicest compliment I've had in a long time."

His face darkened. "But my life as I know it is over."

"Francis, things are bad but life will go on."

"Not for me. Everything I have here—everything I've tried so hard to build—at St. Sebastian's—is finished."

"That's not so, Francis! Even if the accusations about Kevin come out, even if the seminary program closes, the church will find a place for you. You've done good work. You've been loyal." She nodded knowingly. "The church takes care of its own."

He eyed her skeptically. "They'll take care of me, all right. They'll find a place for me. In Latin America or some other miserable continent. Doing missionary work like that poor bishop from Ireland who had the misfortune to fall in love and bear a son." He got up and poured himself another, spilling some in the process. "Want some?"

"Don't mind if I do."

He took her glass. "That bishop was weak. Just as I am weak. He failed. Just as I have failed. But worst of all, he embarrassed the church. That's the kicker. The sin the church won't forgive."

"It's not the place of the church to forgive." She felt unbelievably intelligent. "It's God's place."

"God's not here to protect me."

"God is everywhere."

"Ha!" He stopped, stunned that he'd said such a thing. "I didn't mean that. Of course He is."

"Damn right."

"Damn right." He sipped some down. "But the church holds all the cards. What's going on at St. Sebastian's is embarrassing the church, you can be sure of that. A young lady dead, packed in a trunk, sprayed with plastic. The tabloids are already sniffing around. Next thing you know there will be satellite dishes set up in the quadrangle.

"It's terrible and tragic. But worst of all, it's scandalous. And it happened on *my* watch. I'm responsible." He gazed into his glass as though it held the ultimate secret of life. "Yes, the church will find a place for me. Not a very nice place." He downed what was left. "But then, I can find God anywhere. At least that's what I've always believed."

They were silent for some moments. "Funny," he said. "Once I thought I was destined to be a bishop, maybe even a cardinal."

"What happened?"

"I made mistakes. Put myself in compromising situations."

"Situations like what?"

"Situations like this."

"Oh."

"I don't know. For some reason, women have always been attracted to me."

"I can believe that."

"I never encouraged them. But wherever I was assigned, there were rumors. My superiors didn't like it. Whether or not they were true didn't matter. They were embarrassing, and that was totally unacceptable. So they shipped me to St. Sebastian's. It was supposed to be my last chance. A safe place. There were no women here then. Not even nuns."

"I remember you saying that."

He sighed. "It doesn't seem so safe anymore."

"You've done a marvelous job here, Francis. You've kept the seminary program going long after it would have closed otherwise."

"I made the best of things. I tried to build the best program anywhere. If I couldn't be a bishop, I would take satisfaction in educating those who could. And I did too. Some of our boys have gone off to accomplish great things." He poured another glass and took another swallow. He looked at her, his eyes suddenly full of sadness. "I'm sorry, Louise. So sorry about your Kevin. You're a good person. I wish . . ."

"Francis?"

"Yes?"

"Hold me."

"Louise, I—"

"Just hold me, that's all. Nothing more." She started to cry. "I'm cold, Francis . . . and so scared."

He sat down and held her. She put her head against his shoulder.

"Everything's going to be all right, Louise. I promise."

But Francis was wrong. He offered Louise compassion and nothing more. He tried hard to play by the rules. And in the end it wouldn't matter.

CHAPTER FORTY · FIVE

"What took you so long?"

Louise climbed into the car and eased the door shut quietly. "I couldn't leave too abruptly, Forrest. That would have raised suspicion."

"Yeah, but did you have to stay four hours?"

It was now past eleven. Mildred, Irene, and Sister Gabriel had finished copying the essays an hour before. Since then, Forrest, Irene, Mildred, and Trevor had been waiting for Louise in the Lincoln—in the dark, with no heat, behind windows crusted with ice. Forrest hadn't wanted to attract attention and wouldn't allow Trevor to idle the engine.

"If you must know," said Louise, "we fell asleep."

"Ah," sighed Irene. "The afterglow."

"I hate to disappoint you, Irene, but there was no afterglow. I fell asleep. So did he. In the living room. With our clothes on." Louise scratched away ice on the window. "So how'd it go? Where's Sister Gabriel?"

"It went fine," replied Mildred. "She's up in her room." She glanced toward the tower in Sturdevant Hall opposite the one occupied by Father Duffy. "It wasn't easy for her."

"I'll say," agreed Irene. "She was nervous as a flea on a griddle."

Trevor thought of her quivery voice and trembling hands. No liver spots on those hands. No plumpy ridges of purple veins, no parchment-like skin. He dismissed these thoughts and started the engine. "When folks get on in years, they don't cope well with stress."

"At least our mission was a success," said Mildred. She patted a stack of manilla envelopes on her lap. "We copied all the essays."

Soon they were climbing the front steps to the Coldwater Arms. Everyone was weary. Irene yawned. "I can't wait to hit the hay."

But sleep was the last thing Forrest had in mind. "Forget it," he said. "We've got to get started comparing the essays to the photo."

"Now?" protested Mildred. "But we're all tired, Forrest. We can hardly see straight."

"Go to bed then. I'll do it myself."

Damn him. Why did he always do this! "No," she sighed. "I'll help."

"Me too," said Irene.

"Count me in," said Trevor.

"And me," said Louise.

"Good."

They went inside and settled in the lobby. Irene took the liberty of brewing a pot of coffee in the kitchen. "I'm sure Loretta won't mind," she said. "Heck, we're practically family by now."

Forrest gave them each a copy of the print along with a magnifying loupe purchased at the photo shop down the street. Louise distributed the copies of the essays submitted by students with their applications to St. Sebastian's. Mildred, Irene, Trevor, and Louise each got two hundred.

Irene looked at Forrest. "How come you don't get any?"

"Because I'm supervising."

"Oh," she said. "How could I forget?"

"Now study the essays carefully," he instructed. "Compare the writing of each to your copy of the rhyme. If you don't find a match, toss the essay aside."

Mildred poured murky cups of coffee, and they began.

Two hours later they were bleary-eyed and frustrated. Despite their best efforts, matching essays to the writing had proven fruitless.

Mildred tossed aside a sheaf of papers. "I give up."

"Don't say that!" bristled Louise. "Just because we didn't find a match doesn't mean we're giving up. Maybe we overlooked something. We should look through the essays again."

"No way!" barked Irene. "I'm tired!"

"Look," said Trevor, "there's no guarantee that the person who wrote the message actually killed Kevin anyway."

"True," said Forrest. "But it seems mighty coincidental that a threat like that would appear and then he dies. Mighty coincidental. Whoever wrote it obviously knows *something.*"

They sat there glumly, ruminating.

"There is something we could do," said Irene at last.

"What?" asked Forrest morosely.

"I personally think whoever wrote the rhyme killed Kevin."

"So?" said Mildred.

"So maybe it wasn't a student."

"Of course!" cried Louise. "It could have been a faculty member."

"Or someone on the custodial staff," added Trevor.

"Or anyone!" exploded Forrest. "That doesn't help, Reenie! You've only made things more complicated! How do we get samples of all their writing?"

"We could approach all staff members individually, of course," said Irene, "but that would be time consuming. Besides, Duffy probably wouldn't allow it. So we pursue another angle. We analyze the handwriting. Handwriting tells a lot about a person. A whole lot. What we need is a handwriting *expert*. Someone who's trained in the fine points of handwriting analysis."

Trevor spoke up. "That's a fine idea, Irene. But we don't know any such person." He turned to Forrest. "Unless you have a source at the Bureau."

For a moment Forrest looked downright crazed. "No! I don't!"

"All right, all right," said Trevor. "I was only asking."

"I can't be bothering my contacts about every little thing. They're busy people."

"Okay, okay. It was just a thought."

Irene smiled. "We don't need those Bureau folks! We've got an expert right here in Coldwater!"

"Oh yeah?" said Forrest. "Who?"

"Miss Monique."

Mildred cocked her head. "Miss who?"

"Monique. The lady down the street. She's got a shop."

"Christ," groaned Forrest, "I should have known."

"I don't get it," said Louise. "Who's Miss Monique?"

"A con artist," said Forrest. "They should throw her ass in jail."

"She's into all kinds of exotic things," said Irene. "She's got crystals. She reads palms. She does seances." She rummaged around in her purse and dug out a card. "It's all right here . . . Oh—COLOR COORDINATION—I forgot all about that. She'll tell you if you're a summer, winter, fall, or spring and which colors are right for you. Ain't that something?"

"Give me that." Forrest snatched away the card. "Yeah, right. Look what else she does. ROLE PLAY. Do you have any idea what that is, Reenie?"

"Something like charades?"

"Yeah! If you like to play naked."

Irene grabbed the card back. "I don't care. It's what's on the bottom I'm talking about. In the fine print." She thrust the card in his face. "HANDWRITING ANALYSIS!"

"We'd have to be pretty desperate to resort to something as harebrained as that."

"But we *are* desperate," said Mildred.

"I'm telling you, Forrest, Miss Monique is no fly-by-night floozie. She takes it very seriously. She has lots of books on the subject. I saw them myself."

"Oh really? And when was that?"

Irene looked momentarily uncomfortable, then thrust out her nonexistent chin. "When I was there. Having my palm read. I'm not ashamed of it neither. She was right on the mark with my palm. She said I was involved with a cantankerous old fart."

Forrest's nostrils flared. "Then you must be involved with someone else besides me!"

"Aw, come on, Forrest. Don't be so stubborn. Give Miss Monique a chance."

"Handwriting analysis is a legitimate science," said Mildred. "It's called graphology."

"Perhaps Irene is right," said Trevor. "After all, we don't exactly have a plethora of options."

"Right," said Irene, wondering what the hell a plethora was.

"I say we give it a try," said Mildred. "After all, we have nothing to lose."

"Wanna bet?" said Forrest. "Hold on to your wallet, Millie. Hold on to your wallet."

CHAPTER FORTY·SIX

"You expect me to work with this?"

Monique Yoblonski waved the photo. Plump and cherubic, she swirled about like a dervish in a billowing purple caftan. Red corkscrew curls bobbed about her shoulders as tiny feet encased in pink plastic jellies danced across the essays on the floor.

"This is what we got," said Forrest in a take-it-or-leave-it tone.

Monique paused and remembered the enticing fee Mildred Bennett had offered. One hundred dollars. A tidy sum for very little exertion on her part.

"So what's the problem?" asked Forrest.

She could lie. She could simply make up some gruesome characteristics. It would be simple enough, and no one would be the wiser.

But Monique hated to lie. The crystal ball crap was one thing—who did it hurt, after all? But this was different. Here you had well-intentioned older people trying to help a grieving mother. And Monique knew all about grieving mothers, having been one herself.

Twelve years before, Monique had lost her children because she had been declared unfit.

The word still stung. She hadn't been unfit; she had merely been trying to care for her children the only way she could. How many options did a woman like her have, after all? And besides, *he* had driven her to it. Driven her to behavior that, on the surface perhaps, might appear unfit. To some. But it wasn't. Wasn't at all!

His name was Gerald Yoblonski. He was her ex-husband and never paid child support or alimony. Never paid for orthodonture, music lessons, or summer camp for the kids. Never paid nothing. Not one red cent.

Every Friday night Monique would hold her checkbook in one hand and a fistful of bills in the other and tell the kids things didn't look good. "There's no low-income housing in Westport," she would remind them. "We may have to get jobs. We may have to move. To Bridgeport."

Did her little darlings offer to get paper routes? Did they offer to mow lawns or babysit? No. Three surgically corrected noses turned up in unison. As though jobs and Bridgeport were four-letter words.

"There are things you could do," said Babette. "To earn money. If you really loved us."

"Things like what?" asked Monique, who was open to suggestions.

Babette peeled up the hem of her tube skirt and raised an eyebrow.

"That's not funny! Where do you get such nasty ideas!"

"You could be a mule," said Ricky helpfully.

"Thanks a lot."

"I mean a courier. You know, someone who swallows coke, then flies in from Colombia."

"Coke?" She doubted he meant Coca-Cola.

"You put it in condoms. It's very safe."

"Enough!" Monique pressed her hands to her ears.

Suddenly an idea came to her. It was illegal, but it was also just. She would steal money from Gerald. But it wouldn't be stealing, not really, because the money would be what he owed her. No more, no less.

On their next weekend visit, the children lifted a book of Gerald's checks from the very bottom of the little cardboard carton. ("That way, he won't know it's gone for months and months," Ricky pointed out.)

From then on, Monique simply wrote herself a big fat check on the first of the month. The checks covered exactly what Gerald owed her and they never bounced. Gerald had plenty of money. He was just busy spending it on a new, glass dome house on the Sound, a forty-foot cabin cruiser, and a blond bimbo named Desiree. Or maybe it was Desire.

Things went smoothly for a while. Then Jessica demanded riding lessons. Babette was caught shoplifting and sentenced to counseling. Ricky had to enter rehab. Twelve years old and the kid was sneaking shots of vodka from the liquor cabinet. Monique became reckless with worry and started writing checks for larger chunks of cash, money she wasn't, by law, entitled to have. And still it wasn't enough. The children always wanted more. They were conspicuous, consumerous little gluttons. Babette demanded private school. A fancy-pants place called Laycock, a disgusting combination of words to Monique's way of thinking. But what Babette wanted, Babette got. Monique was afraid to say no, lest the child's shrink—a diminutive monkey of a man with hairy knuckles—label Monique a Bad Mother.

What would a Good Mother do?

She would use a talent God had given her, that's what. By now Monique knew she had a flair for signatures. She had mastered her ex-husband's with ease and could master others as well. She wrote a business plan and started a housecleaning service, not for the money she was paid, which was paltry, but for the access it afforded her to checkbooks in homes of Old Greenwich, Darien, Westport, and Southport. The children were horrified, not so much by the notion of forgery as by the fact that their mother was working as a—God forbid—domestic.

"How can you do this to us?" they cried.

With a sinking heart Monique realized she'd spawned a bunch of insufferable little snobs.

As it turned out, Monique had a gift for forgery, and people along Connecticut's Gold Coast had so much money they didn't miss a few thousand here or there. At least not for a while. But then one day her house of checks collapsed. Gerald discovered the missing checkbook and took his nose out of the bimbo's snatch long enough to examine his bank statements. A dowager in Greenwich died and the executor of her estate noticed unusually large payments to the cleaning lady. A bond trader in Darien went bankrupt and the checks Monique had written against his account punctured a hole through the ozone layer.

As George Bush would have said, Monique was in deep dodo.

Gerald came over while she was grilling baby back ribs on the patio. He threatened to have her declared unfit and take the children. Monique felt faint. Everything swirled around her— the ribs, the fire, Gerald's fat florid face . . .

When the police came, she explained that Gerald had fallen onto the barbecue fork.

They turned off the gas grill. The ribs were ruined.

The children were sent to live with reluctant relatives and Monique went to county jail, where she was assigned an incompetent public defender. The district attorney couldn't face trying yet another murdering housewife who claimed to be psychologically battered. He offered her a deal: An open-ended term at Soundview State Hospital for the Criminally Insane or go on trial and risk doing serious time in the women's pen.

"The pen was what got me into this in the first place," muttered Monique. She wondered what they meant by serious time. Was there such a thing as funny time? Maybe that's what Soundview State offered.

Her attorney coached her like a college admissions counselor. "Go for Soundview State," he advised.

The idea of prison was not appealing. Monique pictured herself being gang-banged with broomsticks and opted for hospitalization.

At Soundview State a young doctor with a facial tic encouraged her to pursue her talent in handwriting. "Turn a lemon into lemonade," he said cheerily. "It could be a whole new career for you, Monique. Personnel screening is very hot right now. Companies are afraid to make a mistake when they hire. There are a lot of loonies out there." He winked.

She took his advice and poured herself into the subject. She read books about graphology and books about psychology and melded the two into a science called psychographology. She disdained working at the loom and instead studied alone in her cell. She honed her technique by analyzing the handwriting of everyone on the ward and found the staff to be more abnormal than the patients, which did not surprise her. She used her time of incarceration to perfect her craft. And ten years later when she left for a halfway house in a jerkwater town called Coldwater, she was a CHA—Certified Handwriting Analyst.

As it turned out, no corporation would hire her.

She took this philosophically, opened up shop, and threw in palm reading, tarot cards, and role play as draws. The kids were adults now, accomplished felons in their own right. They visited on holidays. The shop did all right, what with new money moving into town, and life wasn't so bad. Actually, she'd never been happier.

She studied the photo again. No, she wasn't going to lie to these people.

"I wish I could help, Mr. Haggarty."

"But what?" said Forrest. "Either you can do it or you can't. It's nothing but a con, right? Graphologist? Ha!"

"*Psycho*graphologist."

"You got that right—a graphologist who's psycho."

Monique's eyes narrowed. She drew herself up. "I'll pretend I didn't hear that remark. I will endeavor to educate you. A psychographologist applies psychological principles to the science of graphology."

"To get clues about character and personality," added Irene.

Monique blessed Irene with a beatific smile. "Exactly."

"So go ahead and do it," challenged Forrest.

"It's not that simple," protested Monique. She clutched the print to her bosom. "This sample flies in the face of basic rules."

"Rules such as?" asked Mildred.

Monique took a deep breath and proceeded to rattle them off. "Rules like not using a single sample of writing but, rather, two or, better yet, three. Using handwriting written in ink and on unlined paper, never mind a wall, never mind a glossy photograph of such a sample. Moreover, each specimen should be long enough to contain all letters of the alphabet, a good range of capitals, and plenty of *t*-crossings and *i*-dots."

"Could you give it a try anyway?" put in Mildred.

"I think it might be sufficient," conceded Monique.

"So do it!" challenged Forrest.

"You make it sound like a piece of cake, Mr. Haggarty. Well, it's not."

Louise spoke up. "Isn't there anything you can tell us?"

Monique looked at Louise, and her heart went out to her. Clearly the woman was desperate. "I'll try."

"Great!" cried Irene.

But Monique held up her hand. "Calm down. I'm not promising miracles. I'll do my best. It will be a tremendous challenge. So much so that . . ." She paused.

Forrest looked at Mildred. "Here it comes."

"Working with such flawed material will require an adjustment in terms of compensation."

"There!" he cried. "You see!"

Forrest turned on Monique. "Mrs. Bennett retracts her offer. She's too free with her money. We're not paying you a dime."

"Well!" huffed Monique. "If that's the way you're going to be, I'm leaving." She swivelled on her pink jellies and headed for the door.

"Hold on!" cried Mildred. "For heaven's sake, Forrest. I told her I'd pay her, and I will. If she wants a little more, that's fine. How much can it be, after all?"

Monique stood there, poised.

"Monique?" said Mildred. "Monique?"

She turned. "Yes?"

"How much did you have in mind?"

Monique didn't bat an eye. "Five hundred."

"Two-fifty," countered Irene.

"Sold!" said Monique.

CHAPTER FORTY-SEVEN

Monique pinned the rhyme to the wall and studied it.

Kevin Cannivan, Puddin & pie,
Watch out girls, he'll make you cry.
He'll do what he wants & then he'll lie.
A boy like that deserves to die.

"How large was this writing?" she asked suddenly.

"Tiny," said Irene.

"My daughter had to enlarge it to make it readable," added Forrest.

"I thought so."

"Why?" asked Trevor.

"The hand of an abnormal person is usually extreme one way or another. Overly large or extremely small and cramped. In addition to which, negative people tend to write small, and this person is certainly that—negative. See how the last word of each line drops? When the last word in many lines drops, it's a clear sign of melancholia. Sadness."

"Well, I'll be darned," said Irene.

Forrest didn't give a damn if the person was melancholy or not. But the business about being abnormal was another kettle of fish. "You think maybe this person is crazy?"

"Crazy, I don't know, but abnormal, most assuredly. The wandering baseline is a dead giveaway."

Mildred looked puzzled. "Wandering baseline?"

"Take a look. Every line weaves and wavers. That's a wandering baseline. It indicates out-of-control emotions. Writing of this nature is characteristic of someone mentally ill. Someone who can't be trusted to follow a controlled standard of conduct." Monique's own writing had been this way when she was at Soundview, a tidbit she left unmentioned.

"Mentally ill," breathed Irene. "Lordy."

"Oh, it gets worse," said Monique. "I see something else in this writing. Something very disturbing."

They all leaned forward.

"I see deceit. A deceitful person with a high degree of tension and frustration."

Mildred clutched her pearls. "Not a good combination."

"No indeed. And there's more. There's emotional coldness. A lack of feeling or empathy for other people." Monique couldn't help but shudder.

"Good gracious," said Mildred. "You make the person sound like a psychopath."

"A distinct possibility," said Monique.

"Bah!" said Forrest. "How can you be so sure? Deceit. Frustration. Tension. Coldness. It all looks like plain letters to me."

"Oh, I'm sure," said Monique. "Quite sure. Here's why: This writing displays a backhand tendency, plus it's angular. Backhand angular writing, especially when there are low stems on the small *d*'s, is characteristic of a deceitful person."

"Lookie there!" said Irene. "All the *d*'s are chopped off!"

"Precisely," said Monique. "And as for frustration—there's a disturbance in the rhythm of the writing and the small *a*'s and *o*'s are tightly closed. In addition to which, the tendency toward exaggerated capitals, as well as *i*-dots made like commas, indicate a high degree of tension. Frustration and tension. A dangerous combination, very dangerous indeed."

"Why's that?" asked Irene.

Monique looked to Trevor. "Can you enlighten her, Doctor?"

"I'll give it a try. When a person is extremely tense, Irene, she concentrates so strongly on her own acts that she forgets the rest of the world around her. It reduces what is called the margin of safety. Such a person may drive faster, drink more, eat more, and so on. Psychologically and physiologically she's out of control and moving toward a fatal collision."

Monique beamed. "Very good, Dr. Bradford. I couldn't have said it better myself!"

"What's so good about it?" said Mildred. "This is terrible news."

"What about the coldness you mentioned?" asked Louise. "How do you know that?"

"Backhand writing in an angular hand goes hand in glove with deceitful indicators and implies emotional coldness as well."

"This is all well and good," said Mildred, "but can you tell us anything about the person that would provide a noticeable clue? Something on the outside, rather than the inside?"

"Aw, she can't do that," said Forrest. He turned to Monique. "Can you?"

Monique almost preened. "Actually, I can. Your health affects your handwriting. This person, for example, is definitely nearsighted. Nearsighted people always begin a line of writing so it slants at a different angle than the one preceding it."

"No kidding?" said Irene.

"I never kid about handwriting, Mrs. Purdy. And another thing—look at the loops. On the *l*'s, the *h*'s, the *b*'s."

"What about them?" asked Mildred.

She looked at them with a loupe. "There are little gaps in them."

"We'll take your word for it," said Irene. "So?"

"Rifts or catches in loops and curves above the line indicate a breathing deficiency."

"You don't say!" said Irene.

"Indeed I do say."

Forrest peered closely at the print. "So what are you telling us here? We have to find a nearsighted person with hiccups?"

"Or asthma or sarcoidosis or whatever," said Monique. She studied the print and became lost in thought.

"What I want to know," said Forrest, "is this: Is the writer a man or a woman."

"That I can't tell you."

"Damn it all!"

"Forrest," said Mildred.

"No, Millie! Damn it to hell! That's important!"

"I'm sure it is," said Monique. "But one can never be certain about the sex of a writer because people are blends of masculinity and femininity."

"Ah," said Mildred.

"There is, however, one thing I'd bet my shop on."

"What's that?" asked Forrest glumly.

"You're on the right track with this rhyme. Whoever wrote it is capable of murder. The combination of characteristics leaves little doubt."

CHAPTER FORTY EIGHT

"Boy, that Monique sure can pack it away," said Forrest. "Did you see all those enchiladas she ate?"

Mildred held onto Trevor's arm and stepped carefully on the

icy sidewalk. They had tried a little Mexican restaurant down the street for dinner. To everyone's surprise, Forrest had invited Monique along. "I wasn't counting, Forrest."

"Six. Not to mention those refried beans. I'm glad she's not staying with us."

"You're a fine one to talk," said Irene. "Ordering a beef burrito when you know you're supposed to have chicken."

"You managed to wrest away the sour cream," he replied dryly. "Nearly broke my wrist in the process too."

Trevor walked on the outside of the sidewalk to protect Mildred from splashes of nonexistent cars. He observed manners and niceties that most people didn't bother with anymore, and she loved him for it.

"Are you all right, Louise?" he asked. "You were awfully quiet during dinner."

"Oh, I'm fine." The words were automatic. She seemed to be tuning them out more and more. She wished she could talk to Kevin and ask him why he'd done those terrible things. The boy she loved wasn't terrible. He read to his little brother at bedtime, put a bird feeder up at the Senior Center for his Eagle Scout project, served as an altar boy when one of the regulars got sick. "I could name a dozen things," she said absently.

"What, honey?" said Irene.

"Nothing."

Now she was thinking about Francis all the time too. He was such a nice man. Decent. There was a song she halfway remembered . . . something about meeting the right person at the wrong time . . .

"Louise?" Trevor touched her sleeve. "What is it?"

"Oh," she said. She tried to recoup and started walking as though nothing had happened. "Nothing. I get teary sometimes. I don't know why."

Irene hooked her arm in Louise's. "It's to be expected, honey. You're a trooper, you know that? A real trooper."

"Hold up," said Forrest suddenly.

"What is it?" asked Mildred.

He looked up at the hotel. "I saw a light. In our room."

"Aw, go on," scoffed Irene. "You did not."

"I don't see any light," said Mildred.

"Neither do I," said Louise.

"It was a beam. Like a flashlight."

Trevor scanned the row of black windows. "You're sure?"

"Of course I'm sure!"

"What should we do?" whispered Mildred.

"You and Trevor take the front door. Irene—you and Louise position yourselves out back. That way whoever it is can't get away."

Mildred's voice escalated nervously. "But what if they try? What are we supposed to do? Tackle them?"

"Yeah," said Irene. "And what about you? What're you gonna do?"

"I'm going up there."

"You are not!" cried Irene. "You'll get yourself killed."

"No I won't. Look, it's probably nothing. Probably just Loretta snooping around."

But Irene was unconvinced. "Don't do it, Forrest. Please."

"I'll be fine. I've got this . . ." He reached into his sheepskin jacket and withdrew a plastic box the size of a pack of cigarettes.

"How's a TV clicker going to help?"

"It's not a TV clicker. It's a stun gun."

"A stun gun," gasped Mildred. "You don't mean it."

"The latest kind. Neat and compact. But it packs a helluva wallop, let me tell you. Anyone gives me trouble, they'll be sorry."

"Good Lord," said Trevor. "Put that thing away."

"I will not. I'm not going up there unarmed. That would be foolish. Now don't go looking at me like that, Trevor. A stun gun won't kill anyone. It'll just take them out of commission for a while."

"Unless they have a heart attack," replied Trevor. "Or a

stroke. Or any one of a dozen other complications I could mention."

But Forrest was already at the front door. "Go on," he said. "Assume your positions." Then he slipped inside.

He wasn't particularly worried. Hell, it probably really was nothing. He wasn't absolutely sure he'd seen a light. But the possibility of a confrontation got the old juices going. At the very least, this would be good for drill.

In the lobby a single light cast an eerie glow. Loretta wasn't at the desk, and he didn't expect her to be. She'd be in her room, a room Forrest had already visited on one occasion.

But never again, he told himself, never again. It had happened in a moment of weakness. Loretta had caught him unawares as he strolled down the hall in search of a forbidden cigar. She reached out from her web and drew him in. Invited into her room. For a glass of sherry, she said.

It had been years since a woman did any such thing. Decades even.

He told himself he didn't want to hurt her feelings, told himself a glass of sherry wouldn't hurt, told himself they'd just chat.

Who was he kidding?

As it turned out, they did a lot more than chat. Forrest had never experienced such acrobatics. He almost threw his back out. Then, to add insult to injury, Loretta had the nerve to ask him for fifty bucks. "I thought you understood," she said. "I mean, wasn't it obvious?"

He stuffed five tens in her hand and left, humiliated.

But that wasn't the worst. The worst was the guilt. Every time Irene looked at him, he felt like a heel. They weren't married, but he tried to be faithful just the same. Plus all those diseases around today provided extra incentive to be true. After his slip with Loretta he started to fret. He examined his penis repeatedly. He felt a burning sensation whenever he made water. He remembered those films they showed in the navy of wart-covered private parts. Finally in desperation he went to Dr. Ramírez (he couldn't face Trevor) and confessed. It cost him another fifty to hear he was fine, plus he had to endure a film about sexually transmitted diseases.

Fooling around just wasn't worth it.

He pulled off his boots and started up the stairs.

"Uhhhhhhhhhh."

Forrest's head swiveled round. "What the . . . ?"

"Uhhhhhhhhhh!"

The sound was coming from the desk. He tiptoed over and looked behind it. There was Loretta on the floor, trussed up like a Thanksgiving turkey.

"Loretta? What the hell are you doing down there?"

She rolled her eyes at the ceiling and gnashed her teeth on the handkerchief in her mouth. *"Hun hie eeeeee owwwwwwww!"*

He guessed the translation was *Untie me now!* but had no intention of doing so.

She swung her head from side to side.

"Are they still up there, Loretta?"

"Hun hie eeeee! Hoant hust hand hare, hu hun huva hitch!"

Son of a bitch?

"Fifty bucks," he whispered. "That's what it'll cost you, Loretta. To get untied." He turned and left her there, pounding lacquered hair on the carpet.

He reached the second floor and peered down the dim hallway. Never had it seemed to long. He held the stun gun before him like a holy grail and started walking. When he came to the suite, he pressed his ear to the door.

Someone was in there all right. He heard papers being shuffled, drawers being opened, objects thrown about. They were tossing the room. His room! The nerve! He threw the door open.

"Freeze!"

The intruder beamed light into his face, blinding him. He waved the stun gun wildly, aimed, fired . . . and zapped himself in the stomach.

"Ooooooooooooh!" His burrito was twice baked. His knees

buckled. He crumpled to the floor, limbs thrashing. He was dimly aware as someone stepped over him. "Reenie . . ." he groaned. "Trevor . . . Millie." The names slipped from his lips. He let out a weak sigh and was gone.

Outside on the back porch Irene was busy reassuring Louise. "Believe me, honey, this is nothing. Forrest saw a reflected headlight, is all. Ever hear of a hunter with deer fever? That's Forrest. He's so eager, he sees what he wants to see. He gets himself all worked up. And for what? For nothing. You just watch. Any minute he'll be down, all disappointed, telling us the coast is clear."

"But you seemed so worried," said Louise. "You said he'd get himself killed."

"Sure I did. Why spoil his fun?"

At that moment someone came crashing down the stairs. "Forrest?" yelped Irene. "Forrest, honey?"

But it wasn't Forrest. It was someone in a ski mask who crashed through the door and shoved them aside. Louise flew backwards off the railing and landed in deep snow. Irene clung to to banister and managed to swing back.

"Hey, you!" she yelled. "Stop!"

Whoever it was ran toward a waiting van. Without thinking, Irene gave chase. When he yanked open the rear doors and hurled himself, Irene was right behind him.

"What are you?" he yelled in disbelief. "Nuts?"

He wasn't a man; he was a woman. Irene could tell by the voice. This gave her courage. She lunged and wrestled the woman to the floor.

"Drive!" screamed the masked woman. "For God's sake, drive!"

Drive? There was someone else in the van?

Irene never got to ask who. The clutch popped, tires spun, and before she knew it they were careening down Main Street at breakneck speed. The van swerved from side to side on the icy road, back doors flapping all the while. Irene clutched the

woman to her in a bear hug. "Now calm down," she said, "just
. . . calm . . . down."

The ski mask spat in her face.

Irene hauled off and popped the face with her mittened
hand—*I can't believe I'm doing this*—then popped it again. The
mitten cushioned the blows. The mask laughed. Then the creature broke free and kicked Irene in the stomach.

"Ooooooomph!" Irene clutched her midsection. "That
wasn't nice," she gasped. "That wasn't nice at all."

The driver braked, then accelerated abruptly, trying to dis-
gorge the unwanted cargo. The creature kicked again, this time
hitting Irene squarely in the jaw.

Irene felt something crack. She yanked off a mitten and
touched her mouth. Her dentures were broken! She was so mad
she could have spit nails. "That does it! That really does it!" She
grabbed hold of the creature's foot and climbed up to her throat.
She engaged her in a choke hold, an illegal maneuver she'd seen
demonstrated on *Cops*! The eyes under the mask looked at her
quizzically, then the body went limp.

"Oh, my God," gasped Irene. "What have I done?"

The van slowed.

"Don't die! I didn't mean it! Honest!"

The van stopped.

"Wake up," she pleaded. "Please!"

The eyes fluttered open. "Jesus," groaned the creature.
"Where'd you learn to fight?"

"Praise God," said Irene. She pulled off the mask, unleashing
a bundle of weirdly wired yellow hair. "Are you okay? Are
you—Hey! I'd know that hair anywhere! You're . . ."

The woman rubbed her throat.

". . . Angelique Whiting! Yeah, that's it. You're the one who
gave Mrs. C. the flyer. The one who Forrest calls a Feminazi.
"And you!" Irene barked at the driver. "Who're you!"

The driver turned around in the seat as best she could and
removed her ski mask.

"Heavenly days," marveled Irene. "You can drive?"

Deirdre Canfield flexed her gloved fingers. "Of course I can drive. What do you think I am? A damn cripple?"

Irene looked at those fingers and felt a chill.

"You think I killed him or what?"

"Dede, don't," said Angelique.

"Well, she does. I can see it all over her face."

"No," said Irene quickly. "It never crossed my mind."

Until now.

CHAPTER FORTY·NINE

"There's not much I can do," said Trevor. "Try tea with honey. That will be soothing."

"It only hurts when I swallow."

Actually, it hurt like hell. But Irene Purdy, the lady with the arm of steel, looked so miserable that Angelique almost felt sorry for her. She kept standing there, wringing her hands, her lower lip jutting out as though she were going to cry.

"I'm okay," Angelique assured her. "Really."

"I'm not upset about you!" snapped Irene. "I'm upset about my teeth! They're expensive. I can't afford a new set. I'll have to put them together with Krazy Glue."

"I'll buy you new ones, Irene," said Mildred. "For Christmas." It would certainly be the most bizarre gift she'd ever given.

"Thanks, Millie. You're a peach."

Now it was Angelique's turn to be concerned. "How's the old man?" she asked.

"His name is Forrest," answered Mildred. "Mr. Haggarty to you."

Trevor snapped his bag shut. "He'll be all right. He's more embarrassed than anything."

"I just looked in on him," said Louise. "He's sleeping peacefully."

But Mildred wasn't about to let it go with that. She addressed Angelique and Deirdre, her face shifting from one to the other like a tennis ball. "He could have died. Turning that stun gun on himself. He has a bad heart."

Angelique tried to apologize. "I'm sorry. I didn't mean to hit him. I panicked when he threw open the door."

"Sorry doesn't cut it," snapped Louise. "Why did you ransack our rooms?"

Angelique plucked at her hair nervously and looked to Deirdre.

"All right, all right. She did it for me, okay? She was looking for something. Something I gave Kevin."

Trevor Bradford reached into his pocket and withdrew the watch. "This?"

"Yes."

"You're the one who gave it to him?" asked Irene.

"Of course I am. Don't pretend like you don't know. My initials are on the back."

"No they're not." Mildred took the watch from Trevor and held it out. "As you can see, the initials of the giver have been obliterated."

Deirdre snatched it from her and looked closely. "I don't get it. Cameron said . . ." She stopped. What had Cameron said exactly? He said there was a watch and he'd given it to that guy Forrest. And that's all he said. So Cameron may have suspected who gave it to Kevin, but he didn't know for sure. He'd been testing her. "Shit," she muttered.

"What'd Cameron say?" asked Irene.

Deirdre slumped into her chair. "Nothing. I read him wrong. I thought my name was still on it. I thought he knew.

And I thought you were all trying to build a case against me. Damn. I've really blown it."

Trevor sat next to her. "Did you kill him, Deirdre?"

"Are you crazy?" blurted Anglique. "Look at her, for God's sake!"

But Deirdre didn't seem to hear. She smoothed the abraded area on the watch with her thumb and struggled with conflicting emotions. "Why did he scratch out my initials?"

"He told Cameron he was going to sell it," said Trevor.

Angelique was triumphant. "See, Dede? He didn't care about you. You gave him a gift, something he was supposed to value for sentimental reasons, and all he cared about was the monetary value."

"Shut up!" cried Deirdre. "He cared about me! He said I was special! He said—"

"That he loved you?" she sneered.

"Yes!"

"You and everyone else, Dede. Love didn't mean anything to Kevin Cannivan. That message on the wall—"

"You, of all people! I knew you wrote that, Angelique! I knew all along!"

Angelique's eye's widened. "You don't think I—"

"Damn right I do." Deirdre turned to the others. "*I* was the one who painted it over."

"Why?" asked Mildred.

"Because I cared about him!" Her shoulders slumped. "I used White Out. It was all I had. But she—"

"It's a lie!" insisted Angelique. "I never wrote anything!"

"Indeed she didn't," said Mildred.

Deirdre did a double take. "What?"

"Angelique wasn't the one who wrote the message."

"But her handwriting is—"

"Similar," finished Louise. "Not a match. We compared a sample and an expert concurred."

"But if she didn't write it," said Deirdre, "then who did?"

"That's what we're trying to find out," said Mildred.

"What was going on between you and Kevin?" asked Louise.

"We . . ." Deirdre stopped, then took a deep breath. ". . . had a relationship. A caring relationship. You find that hard to believe, I suppose, but it's true. We tried to be careful. We always met in the van. I had the windows tinted black so no one could see in. But we could see out. And we saw her. Lurking outside. Watching."

"I was not!" cried Angelique.

But Deirdre went on. "You were the pathetic one, not me. We'd joke about you, you know that? We'd laugh."

"Stop," whispered Angelique. "Please."

"You're nothing but a goddamn queer."

Angelique flinched and looked away.

Irene touched her arm. "Angelique . . . could you have been . . . you know . . . jealous of Kevin?"

She sighed hopelessly. "Yes. But I didn't kill him, I swear it. I was only trying to protect her. I knew he would hurt her. I could tell."

Louise spoke up. "But someone hurt him instead."

"So we're right back where we started from," grumbled Forrest.

They were seated in the lobby, trying to think how to proceed. Deirdre and Angelique were long gone. Forrest was shaky but determined to join in.

"Don't get discouraged," said Trevor. "We're better off now than we were four days ago."

"You sound like Ronald Reagan," said Forrest.

"Well, it's true," put in Mildred. "We've got more suspects, Forrest."

Louise rattled them off. "Cameron, Angelique, and Deirdre all had motive and opportunity."

"I think we can eliminate Deirdre," said Mildred. "Considering her condition. I mean, really."

"There are paved walkways to the chapel," Louise reminded her.

"And a ramp up the steps," said Trevor.

"And she's awful strong," added Irene. "She works out on those muscle machines, don't forget."

"And maybe she was the one who was jealous," said Louise. "Maybe she saw Kevin and Brandi together and followed them. When Brandi ran, she killed Kevin. Later she killed Brandi. It makes sense."

"Then how did she get Brandi Beaufort's body into the basement?" asked Mildred. "There are stairs. And narrow hallways too."

"There's a service elevator," replied Louise. "She could have used that."

"Maybe she can walk!" said Irene excitedly. "Maybe the wheelchair is nothing but a disguise."

"That seems rather extreme," said Mildred.

"Disguise," repeated Irene. She closed her eyes and started rocking back and forth.

"Quit that," snapped Forrest. "Don't go getting clairvoyant on us."

Irene stopped. "I suppose you have a better idea?"

Forrest ignored her and spoke to the others. "Maybe Angelique and Deirdre are in cahoots. Maybe they both did it."

"Or," said Louise, "maybe it was Cameron."

"No way!" insisted Irene. "I say a woman did it. Don't forget, Brandi thought she saw a woman."

"She *thought*," said Mildred. "She wasn't sure."

"And she thought wrong." The voice erupted from nowhere. "Dead wrong."

Ken Pressman, Coldwater's lone police officer, bellied his way into the lobby. His crew cut hair was spiked with stickum in

267

front and his belly hung over his belt. Essays crunched under his feet as he walked.

"Watch it!" barked Forrest. "You're stepping on evidence!"

"Sorry," said Ken, though he wasn't really. Mostly he was pissed. The state police had taken over the case of the dead girl in the trunk. His case. They said it was too much for one man to handle and came to his office to "give him a hand." "Go ahead and clap," Ken had joked. "I'll take applause any way I can get it." But the joke was on him. Before he knew it the troopers had taken over. They shoved him to the periphery, reduced him to running errands. Like this one, telling the old folks the case was solved. Telling them to butt out.

Irene spoke up. "What do you mean she was wrong?"

"It wasn't a woman who did it. It was a man."

"Oh yeah?" said Forrest. "Who?"

Pressman hitched his thumbs in his belt. "Father Francis Xavier Duffy. He killed them all."

Irene's jaw dropped. "You don't mean it!"

"I certainly do. He fooled everyone. Who knows, maybe he was in drag. We're searching his apartment."

Louise looked stricken. "He had women's clothes in his closet."

Mildred was thoroughly confused. "I don't understand, officer. You said he killed 'all of them.' Only two were murdered—Kevin Cannivan and Brandi Beaufort. Not that two is nothing, of course, but it hardly merits the adjective 'all.' "

"Adjective smadjective" said Pressman. "Three were killed, not two." He ticked them off with thick fingers. "Brandi Beaufort . . . Kevin Cannivan . . . Kathleen Finn."

"Kathleen Finn?" blurted Irene. "Who's she?"

"The housekeeper. Disappeared last summer. Duffy was having an affair with her." He leered. "Can you believe it?"

"How do you know all this?" demanded Forrest.

Ken Pressman proceeded to tell them.

CHAPTER FIFTY

Charley McCarthy popped another Maalox. This was not going well. The guy hadn't made fun of Charley's name, which ordinarily would have been encouraging. But not this time. This time a little teasing would have been preferable to the steady unblinking glare the priest was giving Charley. The man was so upset he was just about catatonic. If he kept on that way, his eyes were going to dry right up. It gave Charley the willies.

He decided to give it one more go before calling it quits for the night. "Please, Father. Francis. Or would you prefer I call you Frank?"

The priest eyed him stonily.

"Okay, not Frank. We'll keep it formal. But please, I can't help you if you won't talk to me, Father. Now if you'd just tell me what happened . . ."

Charley tried not to let his impatience show, but at this moment he wished the firm didn't have the archdiocese as a client. Ordinarily it was easy money. The church paid a monthly retainer and asked for little in return. When trouble arose—and it rarely did—someone from McCarthy & Hornstein stepped in and arranged quiet compensation to the supposedly injured party. Like the time Gloria Molinaro slipped on a cat's eye marble on her way to communion. Probably planted it there herself. What the hell was a marble doing in the aisle anyway? But the church didn't want trouble, so they paid Gloria off and now she was living high on the proverbial hog down in Florida.

But this was no marble. This was murder. Multiple murder. Three of them. The number loomed large in Charley's mind.

Charley had told the bishop that his firm was not the best choice for a criminal case. "Real estate is our bailiwick, Bishop, real estate, trusts, and tax. Of course, we can handle a traffic ticket on occasion. And if one of our clients wants to fight a DUI, we can manage that too. But this?" Charley threw up his hands. "This is way out of our league."

The bishop's eyes were ice. "I didn't know we were talking baseball here, Charles."

"No, Bishop, of course not. It's just that—"

"Father Duffy has been accused of heinous crimes."

Charley nodded gravely.

"Heinous unspeakable crimes. But people *will* speak about them, won't they, Charles?"

"I'm not sure I follow what you're sa—"

"You've noticed the reporters camped on my doorstep? The minicams? The little satellite dishes?"

Charley sighed. "Yes."

"This is a horror. An absolute horror."

"I agree," said Charley quickly. "One hundred percent." The bishop was preparing to work himself up into one of his frenzies and Charley hunkered down for the siege.

"Things can only get worse. From what I understand, it looks bad for Francis. The police have assembled compelling evidence, have they not?"

"I guess you might say that, Bishop."

"I might and I will! They have assembled compelling evidence!"

Charley gripped the tapestried arms of his chair.

The bishop took a deep breath in an effort to compose himself. "Much as I might like to, I can't simply transfer Father Duffy to another diocese or to a mission in Latin America. Like we did with that fellow—what was his name?"

"Giambelli." The one with the penchant for altar boys. Good God, why did he bring that up now?

"Yes." The bishop's face clouded at the memory. "Well. We can't send Duffy down there." He looked at Charley thoughtfully. "Can we?"

"No," he blurted. "I mean, they haven't set bail yet, but the figure flying about is high, very high indeed, and when bail is met, he can't just go traipsing off to—"

"How high?"

"Bail? Well, the district attorney mentioned a figure of a million two."

"A million two!" The words erupted like a sneeze. "We don't have that kind of money!"

"But surely the church does," said Charley hopefully. "Only one-tenth is required."

"To a bondsman? A hundred and twenty thousand down the toilet? Never!" The bishop pressed his fingers to his temples. "Christ, this is one godawful mess. We can't leave Father Duffy in that jail, Charles. It's unseemly for a man of God to be in the county jail."

"I'll argue in court for reduced bail. There's a good chance we'll get it. After all, Father Duffy isn't a risk for flight. I don't think he'll try to go anywhere."

"Oh, but wouldn't I like to send him! I'd like to send him to the fucking moon, Charles, the fucking moon!"

Charley bit his lips.

"But I won't send him to the moon. You know where I'll send him?"

"No."

"I'll send him to Great Barrington." He held up his index finger. "Now there's the place."

"Great Barrington?" repeated Charley. There was a ski mountain there. Butternut Basin. He pictured Francis Duffy schussing down moguls, a spray of incense behind him.

The index finger remained aloft. "The church maintains a facility in Great Barrington. A sanitarium."

After the bishop's remark about the fucking moon, Charley hated to say the next thing. "I'm afraid he can't go to Great Barrington, Bishop."

"Why the hell not?"

"Because Great Barrington is in Massachusetts."

"Of course it's in Massachusetts! It's always been in Massachusetts!"

"Francis Duffy can't leave the state. It will be a condition of his bail. It always is in cases like this."

Now the bishop looked like death itself. He fixed ice pick eyes on Charley.

"It's not my fault, Bishop. That's just the way things are."

"Not my fault!" mimicked the bishop. "The way things are! We pay you a hefty retainer every month, and you have the nerve to sit there imparting worthless pearls of wisdom. Saying that's the way things are! Must I do everything myself!"

"I'll defend Francis Duffy to the best of my ability," babbled Charley, "to the very best—"

"You will not!"

"—of my—" Charley's head snapped back. "I won't?"

The bishop straightened up. "No. I'm rethinking our strategy, Charles. It is my responsibility, my *primary* responsibility, to minimize the impact of undesirable publicity on the church."

He's going to fire me, thought Charley. He's going to get better, more capable counsel. Counsel with experience in public relations. It was probably for the best. Actually, it would be a relief.

"What I'm talking about, Charles, is damage control. Do I make myself clear?"

Charley nodded sagely. He had no earthly idea what the bishop was talking about.

"There will be no bail, Charles."

"No bail?"

"No bail. If Francis remains incarcerated, he will be out of reach of the press."

"But I don't think that's a good idea. We have to prepare a defense, and I hear he's . . ." He stopped.

"Crazy?" said the bishop.

"Well, yes."

"That's all to the good. You'll plead insanity or some such thing. If I'm not mistaken there's a verdict called 'guilty but insane' or something of the like." Though the bishop waved his hand vaguely, he knew exactly what he was talking about. He researched the defense the night before in his collection of law books. He wasn't about to rely on some asshole with a degree from Fordham to tell him what was what.

"But . . ."

"But what?"

"What if he didn't do it?"

The bishop bridged his fingers together and spoke as though addressing a dull-witted child. "There are larger issues at stake here, Charles. I have the seminary to consider. I have the college to consider. I have the church to consider." He spread his hands like Christ in Rio.

"I see," said Charley carefully. "And Francis Duffy is last on the list."

"I wouldn't put it that way, but one must be practical. You make a deal with the district attorney, Charles. A deal."

"What kind of deal?"

"I don't know. You're the lawyer. Plead guilty but insane or plead Francis guilty to some lesser crime. I believe it's called copping a plea."

"Lesser crime?" blurted Charley. "What lesser crime? Shoplifting? Loitering?" His voice escalated hysterically. "Indecent exposure?"

"That's enough! You will enter a plea and the district attorney will move expeditiously to wrap up this sordid little affair with a minimum of public fanfare. He doesn't want a trial any more than we do, believe me."

"And what happens then?"

"Francis will be dispatched to some facility."

Dispatched. As though he were a parcel to be picked up by Federal Express. Charley felt bile rise in his throat. He would speak his mind.

"It won't be a nice place, Bishop, believe me. It won't be like that Great Barrington place. No T-bars or hot tubs, no indeed. It will be a hospital for the criminally insane. Soundview State Hospital, if I had to lay odds, Bishop. Soundview State."

"A fine place," said the bishop.

Charley felt sick.

"Francis will be in good hands there, Charles. And meanwhile? Meanwhile people will forget this unfortunate incident as new atrocities come to the fore. I've seen it before. These murders will be forgotten. Rather quickly, I'd wager." He folded his hands. His ruby ring gleamed. "That's what damage control is all about."

"But what if Father Duffy didn't do it?"

"Believe me, Father Duffy would be the first to agree that we should proceed in the manner I have stipulated. The very first! Francis loves the church more than himself."

"Maybe we should ask him," said Charley evenly.

"If you like." The bishop smiled.

When Charley got to the office, he tried to convince Josh to handle the case. Josh laughed in his face. "Me? Defending a priest! Come off it, Charley."

"I think it would be better, Josh. Really. I think you'd be more . . ." he groped for a word ". . . objective. I'll be too intimidated by him. I'm a product of Catholic schools, don't forget. Put me alone with a priest and I'm liable to start confessing myself." He tried to laugh.

"Forget it, Charley. He'll feel more comfortable with you and you know it. You've got to establish a rapport with the client, especially in a capital case like this."

"The bishop wants us to cop a plea."

Josh tipped forward in his chair. "What?"

"You heard me. He told me he wants to get this cleaned up as quickly as possible. He thinks the DA will go for a plea of guilty but insane."

"But they'll put Duffy away forever."

"I know."

"Talk to Duffy," said Josh. "It's his decision."

"The archdiocese pays us a nice chunk of change every month, Josh."

"I know. But if Duffy wants to fight it . . ."

Charley felt a glimmer of hope. "Yeah?"

"If he wants to fight it, I'll help you. I'll give it all I've got. We'll work together."

"It'll cost us, Josh. It'll cost us a lot."

"So we'll move to cheaper quarters. I never wanted a glass palace anyway. I could live on less. The money we make's excessive." He opened his eyes wide and laughed. "I can't believe I just said that!"

"This is way out of our league, Josh."

"No it's not. I worked for Al Dershowitz before coming here, remember?"

"Yeah . . ." Charley thought for a moment. It was true. Josh had experience in criminal law. And, like Charley, he was bored with mundane lawyering where an occasional nasty divorce provided the only excitement. "Jesus, Josh, do you really think we could?"

"Yeah, Charley, I really think we could." Josh paused. "Plus, there's another aspect to this."

"What's that?"

"If Father Duffy didn't do it . . ."

Charley's stomach did a flip-flop. "The murders might continue."

"You got it," said Josh.

CHAPTER FIFTY-ONE

"But I can't believe Father Duffy did it," said Mildred after Pressman left. "I just can't."

Forrest got up and stretched. "Believe it, Millie. The police have it all figured out. He had an affair with Kathleen Finn. She was pregnant, Pressman said so. She must have gone to him. When he didn't respond the way she hoped, she became difficult. Maybe she threatened to expose him. And he killed her."

"But he seemed like such a nice man," said Mildred.

"Yes," said Trevor. "And what about Kevin? Why kill him?"

"He's a fanatic," replied Forrest. "He killed anyone who threatened his little world. He'd already killed the Finn woman, remember, a woman who threatened to destroy his life at the seminary. When that accusation appeared on the wall about his prize student, was Duffy going to ignore it? I don't think so. Maybe he confronted Kevin, and the boy lied—or worse, laughed at him. We know Kevin was no angel."

"Then he snapped?" said Mildred.

Forrest nodded. "Stranger things have happened."

"But then who wrote the rhyme?" asked Irene.

"Damned if I know," said Forrest. "But does it really matter now?"

"Maybe not," answered Irene. "But I still want to know."

"Maybe Duffy wrote it," said Trevor.

"In the women's room?" Irene shot back. "Get out!"

"He could have dressed as a woman. There were women's clothes in his closet, remember. And the physical clues Monique mentioned hold true: Father Duffy is nearsighted, plus he has a breathing disorder—emphysema. He told Louise."

"More nails in his coffin," sighed Mildred.

"One thing that gets me," said Forrest, "is how he killed Kevin. The only way I can figure it is he followed him and Brandi to that chapel and killed him after she left. It must have been real spur-of-the-moment, you know? It shows quick thinking on his part. Ingenuity too."

"Honestly!" sputtered Mildred. "It sounds as though you admire him."

"Well, in a way I do. And I'm not wasting any time mourning Kevin Cannivan. Good riddance to bad rubbish, I say."

"Shhhhhhh," said Mildred. "Louise will hear you."

"Don't worry," said Trevor. "I gave her a strong sedative."

"She sure is taking it hard," sighed Irene.

Mildred glanced at the door. "How is she, Trevor?"

"Not good. I don't know what her relationship with Father Duffy was, but she's very upset. We're taking her home. Tomorrow."

"Tomorrow?" blurted Forrest. "But tomorrow's no good. I want to talk more to that Pressman fella again. I want to talk to Duffy. I want—"

Trevor lost patience. "What you want doesn't matter, Forrest. Louise matters. Tomorrow we're leaving. In my car. And if you want to stay here, that's your choice."

Forrest gave in. "Oh, all right. What the hell—the case is solved. That's the important thing. But I'll tell you something: This is the last time we involve a member of the victim's family in an investigation, the very last time."

Loretta hovered in the doorway. "Excuse me, folks."

"Don't worry," said Forrest, "we're not going to skip out on the bill."

"Oh, it's not that." She waved a blue and white envelope. "The postman just dropped this off."

Forrest grabbed it. "Holy Christ, it's from the FBI."

The others scurried to his side. Irene beamed. "You sound so surprised. I knew your friends wouldn't let you down, Forrest. I just knew it!"

"Open it!" said Mildred excitedly. "Even though we know who the murderer is, it will be interesting to see if the FBI was on the right track."

"Right," agreed Irene.

Trevor put on his glasses and peered over Forrest's shoulder.

Forrest stepped away. "Just hold your horses, okay? It's addressed to me. I'll read my own mail, if you don't mind." He broke the seal and withdrew several sheets of paper.

"It's a letter," he said. Not an official report, a plain letter. Handwritten. Not even on letterhead. "It's from a fellow named Peter Bolling." No one Forrest had ever heard of.

"An agent?" asked Irene eagerly. "Someone important? The head of the lab? Or one of those fellas who write the books?"

As Forrest read the opening paragraph his heart sank. Peter Bolling wasn't anyone important, not by a long shot. He made it clear in the first paragraph that he was a lowly technician, someone who did little more than wash test tubes and file tissue samples. *"I shouldn't even be doing this, but I found your letter in the trash . . ."* The trash! *". . . and I got curious."*

It was downright humiliating. Forrest held the letter close so no one else could see.

Mildred was on pins and needles. "Read it aloud, why don't you?"

"Well, the first paragraph is mostly personal stuff. About mutual acquaintances at the Bureau and so forth." He hoped the rest contained something . . . anything . . . please Lord . . . "Ah!"

"What?" said Irene.

"Bolling says the rope's from a company called O'Daniel's Religious Supply out of Boston. One of three such companies that distribute church regalia, he says."

"Big deal," said Trevor. All he wanted to do was get Louise home. He hoped this FBI report wouldn't upset the applecart.

"There's more." Forrest flipped through two more pages. "Remember that Derma Color stuff? Bolling writes all about it."

"Why don't you just give us the salient points," suggested Mildred.

"Okay." He straightened up and took a breath . . . " 'Derma Color is a highly effective camouflage cream manufactured by Kryolan . . . designed mainly for street wear for both men and women to cover skin discolorations like birthmarks or uneven pigmentation . . . also used as stage makeup . . . as a foundation over the entire face or applied only to discolored areas.' "

"Maybe he used it on his beard," said Irene.

"Bolling goes on to say that he tested the rope. Looked at it under some kind of microscope—"

"Scanning electron," said Trevor.

"Yeah, and—get this—Derma Color was on the rope. One end of the rope, where the murderer's hand was—not the center third of the rope, where Kevin's neck—"

"We know," said Mildred quickly.

Forrest looked thoughtful for a moment. "Wonder why Duffy had makeup on his hand?"

"From smearing it on his face," answered Irene. "Does he say anything else?"

"No, that's it."

Irene's stomach rumbled. "Why don't we hash it out over dinner. Anybody hungry?"

"Me," replied Mildred. "There's a new Italian place down the street. My treat."

Trevor cast a worried look at the door of the adjoining room.

"She'll be fine, Trevor," said Irene. "We'll only be gone an hour or so. What can happen?"

As it turned out, lots of things could happen. And did.

CHAPTER FIFTY-TWO

Louise pressed the partially dissolved pill between her fingertips and waited for them to be gone. Thoughts whirled in her head.

Francis didn't wear makeup. She was sure of it.

Maybe he wore it when he killed Kevin. And he did have those clothes in the closet.

No. Francis couldn't have done it. He couldn't have!

Think, Louise. Think . . .

What would Francis want to hide with Derma Color? And if not Francis . . .

A thought occurred to her. No. It was too bizarre.

But maybe, just maybe . . .

She leapt out of bed, went to her suitcase and withdrew a shoe box. She turned on the light and dumped all the cards on the rumpled covers. There were dozens of them . . . *In your time of sorrow . . . Our thoughts are with you . . . You are in our hearts . . . Sometimes we don't understand* . . . She rummaged through the pile and withdrew a stiff linen note.

Clutching it tightly, she slipped into the adjoining room. She put it next to a print of the rhyme.

She blinked hard. No.

Yes!

But why?

She sat down, still holding the photo and the note, and wrapped her arms around herself.

It didn't make sense!

She ran to her room and threw on some clothes.

On her way out, she scribbled a note and left it at the desk.

CHAPTER FIFTY-THREE

"Cigarette?" said Charley, wondering why he was bothering. Clearly it was hopeless.

Francis nodded and took a Kent from the extended pack.

Thank God, thought Charley. He lit Duffy's, then his own, and exhaled a stream of blue smoke. Never mind he was trying to quit. This was more important. He tried to act calm, like talking was no big deal. "Okay, Father, let's go over what they've got."

Let's not, thought Francis. Let's just let me die.

"They have a strong case, Father. The stuff in your closet—the ropes, the bucket of latex, the Derma Color, Kathleen Finn's clothes . . ."

Francis took a deep drag. Emphysema be damned.

"The Finn woman was covered with plastic, just like the Beaufort girl. And pregnant. Did you know that, Father?"

Didyou-didyou-didyou? Francis closed his eyes.

"They're saying that's why you killed her. The autopsy revealed she died from a blow to the head. It could have been an accident, Father. You had an argument . . . she slipped . . ." Charley kept feeding him lines.

Killedher-killedher-killedher.

"The police know Cannivan was blackmailing you. They found notes in your desk, in his handwriting. Rotten little bastard, wasn't he? No one would blame you if you lost it with him. We can deal with it if you did. You were under a lot of strain. You were . . ."

Francis blocked out the words.

Charley got up and began stuffing papers in his briefcase. "Fine," he said and snapped it closed. "It's your funeral." He headed for the door. He pushed the call button for the guard.

"It's for the best," said Francis.

"Look" said Charley desperately, "is there anyone, anyone at all you'd be willing to talk to?"

Francis mumbled something that might have been a name.

"What?" said Charley. "What did you say?"

"Forrest Haggarty."

"Where can I find him?" said Charley.

As it turned out, Charley didn't have far to go. Forrest Haggarty was out in the lobby, raising Cain because they wouldn't let him see the suspect.

"I'm not leaving 'til I see him!"

"Visiting hours are over," snapped Matron Ellis, her large nose looming like a monstrous spoon reflection. "Besides, you're not even on the approved list."

Charley stepped forward. "It's okay. He's with me."

"I am?" said Forrest.

"Yes."

"And who the hell are you?"

"Father Duffy's attorney. Now if you'll just come this way." Charley gripped his arm.

Forrest looked at the man in amazement and didn't budge.

"He says he'll talk to you," said Charley urgently. "Only you."

"Oh," said Forrest. "Right. I would have expected that." Which was a big lie, but he wasn't about to quibble with this opportunity. "My friends didn't want me to come," he added, "seeing how the case is already solved. But I couldn't eat. It kept sticking in my craw about Brandi Beaufort. Duffy liked her. He liked her gumption. He wouldn't have killed her. But if he did, I want to hear him say it to my face."

Charley hoped Father Duffy wouldn't do that. Confess. If he did, it would be a disaster. Old Haggarty might testify, and that wouldn't do at all.

"Mr. Haggarty," said Charley gravely, "I am making you an official member of our defense team."

"But we're leaving tomorrow."

"No matter. Just so long as you understand that, for the purposes of this meeting, rules of confidentiality apply."

"Oh, sure," said Forrest. "Don't you worry. I can keep my mouth shut." Another lie, but what the hell.

They sat at a cracked table. The surface was pockmarked with cigarette burns. Francis stared at it gloomily.

"Now," said Charley hopefully, "shall we try again?"

"Let me handle this, okay?" said Forrest.

"I'm only trying to—"

"I know. But you had your go, now let me have mine. Father Duffy here asked for me, after all. Isn't that right?" He looked to Francis, who nodded, almost gratefully it seemed.

"Did you do it, Father?"

At least Haggarty had the courtesy to ask. Everyone else, including this McCarthy fellow, seemed to have concluded that he had.

"Did you?" pressed Forrest.

"No."

"Well," said Charley happily, "that's a start."

Forrest eyed the priest. Was he lying? Probably. "Okay then, tell me what happened. Maybe I can help."

"No one can help," replied Francis. "But I'll tell you what I know, what happened with Kevin Cannivan . . ." His voice dropped. ". . . what happened when I—"

"You'll have to speak up!" barked Forrest. "I'm seventy-five years old!"

"All right." Francis bit off each syllable clearly and distinctly. "He was a problem almost from the start. No sooner had general freshman orientation begun, then rumors surfaced about his involvement with a female student."

Forrest pulled out a pad and started making notes.

"I'm responsible for the seminarians. They aren't supposed to develop romantic attachments. We make that quite clear before they enroll."

"Right," said Forrest.

"In any event, I confronted him." He stopped, remembering. "I expected him to deny it, but . . ." His words trailed off.

"But he didn't?"

"No. He didn't even bother. He said he was 'getting it on' with someone, an important student too. Someone whose father was a benefactor to the school. I realized instantly whom he meant and I was horrified. He wasn't apologetic either. Far from it. He was proud as a peacock! Arrogant, that's what! I was shocked at the transformation of character. It was as though a mask had fallen away. It gives me chills to think of it now."

"You had a glimpse inside his soul, Father."

"It was the devil before me."

"What happened then?"

"He became verbally abusive. I can still remember his words. He said 'You're sticking your own . . . dick . . . where it doesn't belong.' He said I was . . . I was . . . 'humping the housekeeper.' " Francis looked physically ill.

"And it was true?"

Francis couldn't look at Haggarty. He looked away and nodded, almost imperceptibly. "Miss Finn and I had . . . a relationship . . ." He gulped. ". . . for several months. It started last spring. I don't know . . . it just . . . it just . . . happened! I don't know how! Dear God, I never intended for it to! Never intended for her to . . ."

284

"Become pregnant?" finished Forrest.

"I never knew she was, I swear it! Kevin Cannivan said coming to St. Sebastian's wasn't his idea. He said he'd been forced into it. Blackmailed, he said. And now he wanted compensation. If he had to endure four years in a 'shit hole' like this, he said, he wanted something in return. Money. As if I had any!"

"So what'd you tell him?"

"I didn't know what to do. I told him I had to think about it. He wasn't very patient, I must say. He sent vile notes. I gave him what money I could, but it was never enough. Finally I had to tell Kathleen. I had to tell her that someone was aware of our friendship."

"How'd she react?"

"She took it hard. Oh, she didn't cry or become hysterical or anything like that. She was a sweet person. A quiet person. Nice. She just sat there. She said absolutely nothing about any pregnancy. She got up and left. And I never saw her again."

"Weren't you worried about her?"

"Of course I was worried! I'm not devoid of feeling, Mr. Haggarty. I tried to find her, but she was gone. She simply disappeared. I was distressed about it, terribly distressed. But upon further reflection and prayer I decided that perhaps it was for the best."

"Right," said Forrest.

"I had no idea she'd been murdered! Dear Lord, that poor woman . . . and the poor child . . . my child . . ." His voice broke. He put his face in his hands.

"All right, Father, all right. Get a grip on yourself. It's a terrible thing, but now we've got to think about you. We've got to concentrate on saving your life."

"Don't bother."

"I will too bother! You're not the only one whose life is at stake. There's a crazy running around. Someone else might get killed."

That possibility had never occurred to Francis. "Surely this can't go on."

"I hope not, God knows I do. But honestly? I just don't know."

Francis dumped his head back in his hands.

"So Cannivan was blackmailing you, and Kathleen Finn disappeared. Later, Cameron came to you with the watch."

He looked up. "And I was forced to side against him."

"I see. What about this?" He pushed a copy of the message from the women's room toward Francis.

"Vile, perfectly vile," said Francis.

"You didn't write it?"

"Certainly not! I told Mr. Brooks to paint over it. He did an inadequate job too."

"So you painted over it again after we arrived."

"I had the maintenance people repaint the lavatory, yes."

"You must have been relieved when Kevin Cannivan died."

Duffy's face flushed. "Yes. I hated myself for it, but I was. I thought it really was an accident, you see. The way the medical examiner described it made sense. And considering the liaison with the student, the message on the wall, *and* the blackmail, it seemed rather . . ." What the hell. ". . . a perfect penance."

"Penance isn't supposed to kill a person, Father."

"I told you—I never dreamed he'd been murdered. I thought it was an accident."

Forrest drummed callused fingers on the table. "None of this looks good. The police figure you killed Kathleen Finn because she was carrying your child and threatened to expose you. The fact that Kevin Cannivan was blackmailing you provides a perfect motive for having killed him. And Brandi Beaufort too because she saw what you did to Kevin. It all makes perfect sense."

Father Duffy sank in his chair. "I know."

"But just because it makes sense, don't necessarily make it so. Tell me something, Father . . . Is there anyone who would want to hurt you?"

"No one I can think of. Why?"

"Because it's all too pat. Too perfect. It smells like a setup."

"But I don't understand," said Francis. "Why would anyone set me up?"

"I don't know. Maybe you were just convenient." He narrowed his eyes. "Like Kathleen Finn. She was convenient too."

"I don't understand."

Forrest thought for a moment. "Who has access to your apartment, Father?"

CHAPTER FIFTY·FOUR

She knocked softly, and the door swung open. Clothes and books were strewn about the room.

"Mrs. Cannivan! What a surprise!" The elderly nun struggled to her feet, then waved her arms. "Look at this—the police have trashed Father Duffy's apartment. It's a shambles! I could just cry. I'm trying to straighten things up as best I can." She wiped her hands on her habit.

"Oh, really?" said Louise.

"He'll be needing things—clothes, a few books, that Game Boy gadget he plays with. Is something the matter? You're looking at me very strangely, I must say." The nun peered through her thick glasses. "Don't you believe me?"

"Maybe I don't."

"Mrs. Cannivan, what are you talking about?"

Louise thrust the note in her face. "This! This is what I'm talking about!"

Sister Gabriel appeared momentarily befuddled. Her eyes

blinked rapidly and she sputtered as though she were a chain saw getting started. "Wut, wut, wut—"

"You know very well what it is. It's the condolence note you sent."

The nun stopped and smiled. "And so it is."

"Your handwriting matches the rhyme on the wall, Sister, matches it perfectly. Kevin Cannivan, puddin' and pie! Watch out girls, he'll make you cry!"

"An apt rhyme if I do say so myself."

Louise stepped toward her menacingly. "Who are you, Sister? Who are you really?"

"Now, now, you're upset. We'll talk about this in detail soon. First let me pour us a cup of tea. You like herb tea, don't you? Why, of course you do. I gave you a cup when you first came here, and you drank it right down. I have a thermos here somewhere . . . Now where did I put it . . ." She scanned the rubble strewn about the room. "Ah, here it is, right where I left it!"

"What are you, deaf?" cried Louise. "I want an explanation! I want—"

Louise saw a flash of silver before the thermos crashed into her skull. There was the faraway thud. Her eyes opened wide in stunned surprise and she crumpled to the floor.

Sister Gabriel glared at the body. "Does that answer your question?"

She wiped the ribbed surface of the thermos with the hem of her habit. She was pleased to see that the blood and hair blended in with the fabric. There would be no stain.

"Such a naughty girl. Naughty, naughty, naughty! To make me do that."

She gave the sand-filled thermos a shake. Now the glass inside was broken and the outside had a nasty dent besides. She sighed. It had lost its original purpose.

"Just as I've lost mine," said Sister Gabriel to no one in particular. "No matter. Now it's a weapon and it works just fine."

CHAPTER FIFTY-FIVE

"I demand to know where they are!"

"Look, Mr. Cannivan, you can demand all you want. They went to dinner, I'm not sure where. You can try Pearl's or the Tex Mex place down the street or there's Chink over at the mall." She tapped a lacquered fingernail on a pink message slip. "Hey, wait a minute. Here's something."

Brendan could see Louise's handwriting.

"Doesn't say much. Just—"

He plucked it from her fingers. " 'Sister Gabriel.' That's all it says."

"Hmmmm. Maybe your wife went visiting. Sister Gabriel's a nun at the college—the only one. Does housekeeping and stuff. Lives in a tower in Sturdevant Hall—hey, where you going?"

Loretta shook her head as the door slammed. This place was getting weirder and weirder. She sat down and went back to perusing the *Courant*. She was on Ann Landers when the chimes on the door tinkled. She looked up. "Back alread—" She stopped. It wasn't Mr. Cannivan; it was a man and a woman.

"We're Gary and Bea Gonski," announced the woman. "We have a reservation."

Brendan knocked authoritatively on the door. What was it with this Sturdevant place? It seemed to be deserted. The front entrance had been unlocked and it *was* a public building of sorts, so he'd walked right in. He then made his way to one of the two towers, the wrong one it turned out, since no one was there. He hoped he'd have better luck here. The door swung open and he faced an elderly nun. "Sister Gabriel?"

"Yes?" She eyed him nervously. "Are you the police? I thought you were through here. I'm in the process of cleaning up."

"The police? No, nothing like that. I'm Brendan Cannivan. I'm looking for my wife, Louise. She left a note back at the hotel with your name on it, and I thought—"

Her face lit up. "Brendan Cannivan! Why, this is a surprise! Do come in! Louise isn't here just now, but I expect she'll be along shortly."

He stepped inside. The room was a shambles. "What happened here?"

"This?" She waved at the mess. "Nothing. Just doing spring cleaning."

In December? "You mentioned the police?"

"Oh. Them. Well, they were here, yes. Looking for something, I don't know what. But they're gone now. Have a seat, make yourself comfortable. I'll fetch some tea."

He sat and eyed her curiously. "You're sure my wife will be along?"

"Yes, very. Now where did I put that thermos . . ."

Loretta met them at the door. "Something weird is going on."

"At least let us get our coats off, Loretta," said Mildred.

"No, I've got to tell you *now*. Mrs. Cannivan's husband is here."

"You're kidding," said Irene.

"No I'm not. First he comes and demands to know where his wife is. Well, I thought she was with you all. Then I find a note on the desk from her saying 'Sister Gabriel.' "

"Sister Gabriel?" repeated Mildred.

"That's what it said. In toto. And off he goes."

"Well," said Trevor, "I suppose that's all right. Obviously

Louise was upset and decided to talk to Sister Gabriel. When Brendan finds her, perhaps they can settle their differences."

"I think it will take more than one chat," said Mildred.

"So then," Loretta continued, "this man and woman show up. The Gonskis. And—get this—he's *blind*. Has the white cane and everything."

"What's that got to do with the price of fish?" asked Irene.

"Before Mrs. Gonski can take her husband upstairs, he starts in about Mrs. Cannivan too. Wants to know if she's staying here. Says its urgent." She lowered her voice. "A matter of life and death, he says."

Trevor looked at her sharply. "What did you tell him?"

"Not much. I told him she was staying here but out at the moment. He's waiting in the lobby. Real agitated too. Look, I don't need any more crazies here, know what I mean?"

The man stood up and reached out a hand when they entered the lobby. "Mrs. Cannivan?"

"No," said Trevor. "She's not here just yet. I'm Trevor Bradford. Irene Purdy and Mildred Bennett are with me. We're friends of Mrs. Cannivan. Can we help?"

The hand dropped. "Oh God. Where is she? She shouldn't be alone. What you people are trying to do is very dangerous. She could get herself killed."

"Killed?" echoed Mildred in horror.

"What's this all about?" demanded Trevor.

The man replied in an exhausted voice. "My name is Gary Gonski. I'm with the police in River Bend, Ohio. Or was, before I lost my sight. I've got to talk to Louise Cannivan. I've got to warn her."

"About what?" asked Irene nervously.

"About Edwin Poultice."

"Didn't Louise mention someone named Poultice," said Mildred. "The retarded young lady—"

"Yes!" cried Gonski. "Poultice is after her. He's going to kill her!"

Despite the chill in the room, Gary Gonski's face was beaded with perspiration. His color was pale. Irene sought to reassure him. "It's all right. She's safe. She's with a nun."

"But—"

"Believe me," said Trevor, "she's not in danger anymore. The police have everything under control."

"They do?"

"Yes," replied Trevor. "Maybe you better sit down."

"Maybe I better," agreed Gonski. "We've been driving for two days. My wife . . . she's upstairs, resting."

"Would you like something to drink?" asked Mildred. "A soft drink? Brandy?"

"No thank you, I'm fine."

They all sat around him. "Now please," said Mildred, "tell us what's going on, Mr. Gonski."

"Yeah," said Irene. "You tell us your story and we'll tell you ours."

Gary Gonski took a breath and began talking. "There was a fire last June in River Bend . . ."

Sister Gabriel surveyed her handiwork. She hadn't been able to find the damn thermos. The room was such a terrible mess that the minute she put it down it vanished in the rubble, which was vexing indeed. So she had to make do with the beads. She'd unhitched them from her waist and strangled Brendan Cannivan with them one-two-three. He put up a bit of a struggle, kicked and flailed and twitched for some time. But she was behind him and there was very little he could do.

She straightened him up and folded his hands in his lap. She turned his chair so it faced the window.

"Now stay there!" she instructed.

She would leave the beads exactly where they were.

292

* * *

"I suspect," continued Gonski, "that he's killing them all. The Prescotts, the Boardmans, and now the Cannivans. He's a master of disguise."

"I knew it!" cried Irene.

"He ran a beauty parlor back in River Bend, and he wasn't any run-of-the-mill beautician either. He was brilliant with makeup. He'd regale the ladies with stories about days when he did makeup for famous people—Bette Davis and Joan Crawford in *Whatever Happened to Baby Jane,* Dustin Hoffman in *Tootsie,* and that guy—the one who grows old in the Mozart movie, I forget his name."

No one spoke for some moments.

"Derma Color," said Irene finally.

Gonski looked at her curiously. "I beg your pardon?"

"Derma Color," explained Trevor, "is theatrical makeup. Camouflage cream. It's used to hide skin discolorations and uneven pigmentation."

"Poultice underwent chemo and radiation," said Gonski. "It could have discolored his skin."

"What kind of cancer was it?" asked Trevor.

Gonski pointed at his neck. "Throat. He's not going to recover either. That's the only good thing in all this. He doesn't have much time left."

"People who have nothing to lose are the most dangerous of all," shuddered Mildred.

Trevor turned a thought over in his mind. "The cancer—did it affect his voice?"

"I don't know. Probably."

Mildred looked at Trevor. "Surely you're not thinking . . ."

"My God," he said. "Why didn't I think of it! The latex!"

"Latex?" blurted Irene. "What about it?"

"Liquid latex is used in the theater—for creating the wrinkles and texture of age."

293

"Lordy," she breathed. "You don't mean . . ."

Trevor looked at Gonski. "You said he was a master with makeup. Could he pass as a woman? An old woman?"

"Mr. Poultice can be anything he wants," replied Gonski. "Anything at all."

"Oh, no!" cried Irene. "Louise!"

Everyone started moving at once. "Hey!" cried Gonski. "Where are you going?"

Mildred pulled on her boots. "To catch a murderer, Mr. Gonski."

C H A P T E R   F I F T Y · S I X

He sat in the rocking chair, waiting, knowing they would come.

The apartment was tidy now. Everything was in its place . . . the books back on the shelf . . . the priest's personal effects back in the drawers . . . Louise in the bathtub and Brendan at the window.

The pistol was in its place too—a nickel-plated .25 caliber Hawes semiautomatic that fit neatly in his palm. His hand was dry. He wasn't nervous. The gun was a great equalizer.

They would come looking for Louise, of course. It was only a matter of time. Time was something he was running out of, but there would be more than enough for what he had to do. He toyed with the convex silver heart on his chest and resisted the urge to pick at his face. Just a little while longer, he told himself, just a smidgen.

He wondered about Charladene. Had she eaten her dinner this evening? Had she thrown it on the walls? Could she remember him? Would she? And would she ever understand that he'd done all this for her?

At first the killing had bothered him, but he was past that now. Murder is an acquired taste, but addictive nonetheless.

He heard the shuffling footsteps on terra-cotta floors. They were coming!

You don't have to kill them, you know. Your work is over.

Not entirely. There were children back in Raven's Wing. Children who needed tending. Loose ends, as it were.

So he would kill these people first. They were old. It would be easy. And then he would kill the children.

The door swung open. He uncrossed black high-top sneakers under the voluminous habit and Sister Gabriel stood up.

He smiled, revealing teeth artificially brown with age. He kept the pistol hidden in the habit and gestured grandly with his free hand. "Come in, come in! Mr. Cannivan has been waiting for you."

They hesitated, so he had to show them the gun. The doctor's cheeks lost their ruddiness then. "What have you done with Louise and Brendan, Mr. Poultice?"

"Ah," he said, "you know who I am."

Mildred Bennett made the mistake of being snippy. She looked at Poultice as though he were a turd on the carpet. "Indeed we do. And put that toy away."

He fired a shot. Mildred looked down at the bloody hole in her boot and fainted.

"Good God!" cried the doctor. "What have you done?"

"Don't be dense," Poultice replied. "Clearly I've shot her. Don't just stand there! Bring her inside! And be quick about it!"

Trevor and Irene struggled to carry Mildred into the living room. They lay her on the couch and Poultice shoved a dish towel at them. "Tend to her. I don't want her bleeding on the carpet. If she does, she goes in the bathtub with Louise."

"Louise?" cried Irene. She started toward the hall.

"Sit!" screamed Poultice.

"Do as he says, Irene," said Trevor.

Irene looked for a chair. Her eyes found the motionless figure seated by the window. She wondered why he didn't turn around. "Who's that?" she whimpered.

"Brendan Cannivan. He's forgotten his manners." Poultice went to the chair and wrenched it around. The body fell sideways and he shoved it back up. "Say hello to these people!"

Irene stared, wide-eyed. "He's . . . he's . . . he's . . ."

"Dead!" snapped Poultice. "As a doornail! Now sit, damn you, sit!"

Irene crumpled to the floor and buried her face in her knees. "Hail Mary, full of grace—"

"Shut up!" snapped Poultice. "I'm so sick of that religion crap I could vomit."

"The Lord is with—"

"Irene," said Trevor, *"please.* Don't provoke him, okay?"

She looked at Trevor with crazed eyes. "Okay," she whispered. "Okay, okay, okay."

Trevor removed Mildred's boot and wrapped her foot in the towel. The bullet had gone clean through. He hoped it hadn't splintered bones along the way. He thought of the walks Mildred liked to take with her dog Winston and felt like punching Sister Gabriel in the chops. He had never hit a woman—or a man either, for that matter. And that's what she was, of course—a man. He told himself not to forget it.

Mildred moaned, and Poultice plucked the handkerchief from Trevor's breast pocket. "Here. Stuff it in her mouth."

"For God's sake, there's no need for that." He put his face close to Mildred's and whispered softly. "Mildred, honey . . . it's okay. Just take it easy. Everything will be all right." She blinked back tears and managed to nod.

Poultice positioned them in a row on the couch, facing the gun, with Mildred's injured foot propped on the coffee table. Blood was starting to seep through the towel. Mildred tried not to look. She also tried not to look at Brendan, who was staring at the ceiling. She stared at the ceiling as well. Her mouth flooded with saliva and she fought down nausea.

"Where's Haggarty?" demanded Poultice.

"Wouldn't you like to know," shot back Irene. She patted Mildred's hand.

Poultice put the pistol to Irene's cheek.

"At the jail!" shrieked Mildred. "Visiting Father Duffy!"

"Oh, he is, is he? We'll just wait for him then. Somehow I think he'll be along."

So there they sat. The antique steeple clock on the mantle ticked away minute after excruciating minute. After many such minutes Irene could stand it no longer. "Is Louise dead?" she asked in a small voice.

"Quite," replied Poultice.

He's crazy, Trevor realized. Crazy as a loon. "Look, Mr. Poultice . . ." The nun glared. "I mean Sister. We're not going to hurt you. Let's talk this over. I'm sure if we hear your side, we'll understand."

"You think talk solves everything," said Poultice. "Well, it doesn't. I tried talk and talk didn't work. Sometimes a person has to do more than talk."

"Why don't you tell us about it?" He was desperately trying to buy time. He didn't know what the hell to do. He'd never felt so helpless.

Poultice brightened. "You really want to know?"

"Oh yeah," snorted Irene. "Really."

The sarcasm was lost on him. He had an audience, a captive one at that, and he loved it. It was better than the stage. "Well now, let's see . . .

"Ah, yes. It started out simply enough. After what happened to Charladene—" He stopped. "You know about Charladene?"

Trevor nodded.

"She was my daughter. I was both mother and father to her.

297

Charladene's mother left shortly after she was born. After she realized Charladene wasn't what you'd call one hundred percent."

Irene forgot her fear for a moment. "Sometimes those children are the sweetest ones on the face of this earth."

"Charladene was like that," said Poultice. "Sweet. Anyway, after her ordeal she became totally unmanageable, and I had to have her institutionalized, something I'd tried so hard to avoid. They said she was well treated there. They were lying. I visited her many times and she was always there in the day room right where I'd left her the last time. Unresponsive, to be sure, but there. In any case, I put the blame squarely on their shoulders."

"The institution?" said Trevor.

"No, you twit! The boys! The boys who raped her!"

"Of course," said Irene quickly.

"I had to set things right. I didn't want to hurt anyone, not in the beginning. I only wanted some satisfaction. First, I wanted them to say they were sorry. That was all."

"Sounds reasonable," said Trevor.

"Of course it was reasonable! A sense of remorse is important, don't you agree?" He cocked his head and waited for theirs to nod in unison. "Of course it is! And it would have been enough, back then. They could have had it easy.

"But they didn't want it easy! They wanted it hard! They were spoiled little brats, that's what! Spoiled brats protected by everyone—their parents, the police, the school, the whole fucking system! They had never been held accountable before! The very concept was alien to them."

"Calm down," said Irene nervously.

"Calm? You expect me to be calm? Would you be calm? Well, would you!" He pointed the gun at Irene's face once again.

"No!" cried Irene. "I wouldn't!"

He lowered the gun just a bit. "Of course you wouldn't. Now where was I? Oh yes, at the beginning . . . Well, when it became obvious that no one would listen to me, least of all the brutes themselves—or their parents—or the police—I began to despair. Then Charladene went to the hospital, and I had time on my hands. I decided something had to be done. I started killing them then."

"Killing," repeated Irene dully.

He pointed the gun. "Wouldn't you!"

"Yes!" she cried. "I would!"

He directed the gun at Mildred. "And you?"

Mildred bit her lips to block the pain and managed a nod.

"I started with the Prescotts—down the falls they went— and moved on to the Boardmans en flambé, then made my way to the Cannivans. I was running out of time. You can imagine my dilemma when I discovered the little shit was off at some seminary. But I managed to cope. I devised a plan."

Trevor nodded. "A brilliant plan."

"Damn right. I fooled everyone! Even Father Duffy! Of course, he was easy, not knowing much about women. And Kathleen Finn, she was easy too, a naive little mouse scurrying along toward spinsterhood until I blocked her path and stove her face in."

Mildred started to cry softly, but Poultice hardly noticed.

"I really had no choice. What else could I do?"

"Nothing!" agreed Irene hysterically. "Nothing at all!"

"That's right, Missy! Nothing!" He stopped and looked at them expectantly.

What are we supposed to do, wondered Trevor. Applaud? Instead he nodded encouragingly without revealing his revulsion. Then he glanced at the empty doorway. Surprise registered on his face. "Forrest!"

Poultice turned and Trevor lunged from the couch. He flew over the coffee table, upending it in the process. Mildred's foot crashed to the floor. She screamed in pain.

"Why, you little sneak!" screamed Poultice. He aimed the gun and fired.

Somewhere Trevor thought he heard Irene saying that someone had been shot. But who?

He split into two people, one pondering the implications of Irene's words, the other driving himself like a linebacker into Poultice's midsection. The moment Trevor hit Poultice the two people coincided. Pain burned through him. It was like nothing he'd ever felt before, an excruciating ball of fire that plunged through his chest.

"You miserable dirty bird!" screamed Poultice. "I'll kill you! Kill you deader than a doornail!"

"Dive for cover!" barked Irene. "Get down, Millie! Down!"

Mildred remained tranquil. "Bullets are flying," she said. "Nothing can save us." And she fainted again.

Trevor grappled with Edwin Poultice but was weakening fast. His vision clouded. It was difficult to breathe. He coughed, spewing blood on the white wimple.

"Dirty, dirty, dirty!" Poultice cried.

Irene tried to intervene, but she couldn't tell where Trevor ended and Poultice began. She danced around frantically on the periphery, waving her arms.

Though he was terminally ill, insanity gave Poultice the edge on strength. He hugged Trevor to him with one arm and fired wildly with the other. A stunned look appeared on Irene's face and she looked down in amazement as a red stain spread across her stomach. She groaned and collapsed to the floor.

"Two down, one to go!" cried Poultice.

Trevor clawed at the blood-spattered wimple. He ripped it away, exposing a mottled skull. He raked his fingers down the wrinkled face. Gelatinous latex and wads of cotton came away in his hand.

But Trevor was losing consciousness and Poultice slipped from his grip. He gasped. Air seeped through the ragged hole in his chest. He tried to cover the wound with his hand. "I wish," he said dreamily. "I wish—"

His head fell back and he stared into the distance with un-blinking eyes.

Edwin Poultice struggled to his feet. His chest heaved and his face was bathed in perspiration. Tufts of cotton clung to his cheeks. He surveyed the carnage. Two of them would die soon without any further help from him. But the one with the foot needed a little encouragement.

He went to Mildred and put the gun to her temple.

"Don't! For God's sake!"

Poultice held the gun in position. "Come in, Mr. Haggarty. Join the party."

CHAPTER FIFTY-SEVEN

He could have run, but didn't. How could he, when his friends lay there bleeding, maybe even dying? Mildred looked at him with terrified eyes. Irene lay curled in a ball. He couldn't even tell if she was breathing. And Trevor . . . Trevor was the worst of all. He lay on his back with a hole in his chest, staring into space. It looked like he was already gone.

Forrest blinked back tears. He could cry later. "Give me the gun, Mr. Poultice."

"I'll give it to you, all right! I'll give it to you after everyone is dead, you included! I'll put the gun in your hand! They'll say you did it!"

Forrest tried to keep his voice even. "You don't really believe that."

"Oh yes I do! And what will it matter anyway? You're old. Life isn't worth living for you either!"

"It's worth even more when you're old. Or sick."

"So what if I am!"

"Just hand it—"

"Don't move! I'll shoot her!"

Forrest saw something move behind Edwin Poultice. He stood stock still, scarcely breathing. Yes. Someone was creeping down the dark hallway, inching forward ever so slowly. The movement was pained and jerky like a wind-up doll off kilter. He shifted slightly to see who it was.

"I said don't move!"

"All right, all right. Please, Mr. Poultice. It's over. Hear those sirens . . . ?" He babbled. There weren't any sirens. Where were the damn police! Gary Gonski was supposed to . . .

And then he saw her . . . the hair matted with blood . . . the face purple with bruises . . . one eye swollen shut. My God, it was Louise. Forrest nearly lost it then. Christ, look what he did to her.

She moved slowly, relentlessly, her good eye fixed on the back of Edwin Poultice. She held something in her hand, he couldn't see what. She inched closer. There wasn't much time. Forrest doubled over and started to cough.

"Hush!" said Poultice. "I don't hear any si—"

It happened so quickly, Forrest had no time to react. Poultice heard Louise and swung around. "You!" he cried. She plunged the screwdriver into his chest.

He stood there, wearing it like an ornament.

Louise hadn't anticipated the silver heart on his chest. It had served as a shield, deflecting the shaft away from his heart and into his lung.

"Nice try," he whispered and fired into her face.

Later Forrest would remember seeing Poultice smile before he fired that last shot. By the time Forrest lunged, it was too late. Louise fell forward. She reached out blindly. Brendan's body toppled from the chair. Louise grabbed hold of Poultice and thrust him against the casement window.

"Louise!" screamed Forrest. "Don't!" The window gave way, and Forrest watched helplessly as the two of them tumbled toward the icy cobblestones below.

Louise fell through shards of glass bright as stars. Somewhere Forrest was calling her name. She tried to look back, but he was too far away. She wanted to tell him not to worry, wanted to tell him that everything would be all right.

I'm fine, she wanted to say. Just fine. And then she hit the pavement.

She blinked. Edwin Poultice lay beneath her.

She stayed there for some moments, taking inventory. Everything was in working order.

I'm alive!

She got up, dusted the snow off her clothes, walked into the woods and didn't look back . . .

When the ambulance arrived, the bodies of Louise Cannivan and Edwin Poultice were still warm. They lay together like crumpled dolls, so tightly entwined the medics had to pry them apart.

Those who didn't know might have thought they were lovers.

A squad member leaned over one, then the other, and shook his head sadly.

The crew unfolded two zippered bags. They slipped a body inside one and lifted the other to do the same.

"Hey, wait a minute," said one of the men. "Jesus, Jack! This one's still breathing!"

"There was nothing more we could do, Gary."

"I know." They'd stayed longer than planned—a whole week longer—unwilling to leave Dr. Bradford while he was still critical. A man his age, taking a bullet like that. No one thought he would survive. But somehow he was going to. "I keep thinking about Louise Cannivan."

"I know."

"If only I'd—"

"Stop, Gary. Let it go. You did what you could. If it weren't for you, her other children would probably have been killed too."

"I know." He looked out the window, imagining scenery, trying to forget. "Where are we? Pennsylvania?"

"Not exactly." She paused. "We're taking a short detour."

"Huh? Where?"

"Know what day it is?"

He thought for a moment. "Christmas?"

"Yes. We're going to pick up your present. In Morristown."

"Morristown?"

"Her name is Dinah. She's a golden lab. Graduated at the top of her class."

"Bea, I thought we agreed. I threw that application away."

"And I retrieved it. Don't be mad, Gary. She'll be great. We can take her into restaurants even, did you know that?"

"Yes. But this won't work. They don't just hand over a dog.

I'd have to go through training. I'd have to *live* there for a week or more. We can't afford the time."

"I can't, but you can. Besides, it would be rude to decline. She's a present from the guys in the department." She reached over and flipped open the glove compartment. "Along with this." She tossed something in his lap.

"What's this?"

"Your plane ticket home. After the training."

He held the thick envelope in his hands. "I don't know what to say."

"How 'bout Merry Christmas?"

He pictured himself going other places, lots of places. With that dog. Dinah. Suddenly things seemed remotely possible. "A golden lab, you say? Really?"

"Mildred! Wake up! Time to take your temperature!"

Mildred eyed the nurse with disdain. The woman was entirely too familiar, using her first name like that. And she was an overbearing martinet, always barking orders.

"Merry Christmas to you, too," muttered Mildred.

Ruth Petrie slipped the paper strip into Mildred's mouth. "Guess what?" she said. "You're going home soon."

"Thank heaven for small blessings. Yesterday wouldn't be soon enough."

"Close that mouth!" Nurse Petrie wrapped the constricting band around Mildred's arm and proceeded to take her blood pressure.

"What about me?" asked Irene. "When do I go home?"

"Not for a while yet. You're not even on solid food."

"Don't I know it. I'm getting mighty sick of this intravenous, let me tell you."

Petrie made a note on Mildred's chart, and plucked out the thermometer. "Pressure's fine, so's your temp." She wheeled the contraption over to Irene, who opened her mouth and stuck out her arm. "Doctor says we can try tapioca tomorrow."

"We?" repeated Irene sarcastically.

"You."

"How 'bout ice cream? Or a milk shake? Or a banana split!"

"Don't press your luck, Irene." She ripped off the arm band, made a note on Irene's chart and swiveled to leave.

"Nurse!" cried Mildred. "Nurse!"

She swiveled back. "What now?"

"Would you pour me a glass of water. Please."

"You're supposed to start doing for yourself, Missy."

"If they'd unstring my leg, I'd be happy to. But as long as I'm in this blasted traction—"

"All right, all right." She lumbered over and poured. "Anyone ever tell you you're a prima donna?"

Mildred took the cup and glared. "Isn't your shift about over?"

"Not for a while. Now if you don't mind, I have other patients to tend to, ladies."

"Say hello to Trevor," instructed Irene.

Petrie gave a mock salute. "Will do."

She left patients Purdy and Bennett and walked briskly down the hall. She glanced at her watch. Damn. Visiting hours already! The old coot would be wandering her floor, poking his nose into this and that, checking medications, voicing opinions and ignorance about every blessed thing. She stopped at Dr. Bradford's room. Sure enough, he was already in there. She stood outside, listening.

"Do you want to see my Christmas present for Irene?" asked Forrest.

"Sure," said Trevor listlessly.

Forrest thrust a little box in Trevor's face and snapped it open.

"Good Lord," said Trevor. "It's beautiful."

"Ain't it though? It belonged to my grandmother. Queenie wore it too. Think Irene'll mind having Queenie's ring?"

"No. I think she'll be ecstatic."

"I hoped this news would perk you up."

"Oh, it does, it does. It's just . . ."

"Louise?"

Trevor looked away.

"We all feel bad about her, Trev."

"Yes. Well." He cleared his throat. It was painful and took effort. Outside, Petrie had to resist the urge to run in with a tissue. He was adamant about doing for himself. When he finished coughing, he went on. "So when's the big day?"

"I don't rightly know. I hope this ring'll hold her for a while, if you know what I mean. I believe in long engagements."

"How long?"

"A couple of years at least."

"I see. So you're going to forget about the plaid casket then."

"Smokey doesn't have the money now, and besides, I'm feeling pretty chipper. Hell, I'm the healthiest one of our bunch."

"Not saying a heck of a lot," said Trevor.

"True," agreed Forrest. His voice turned serious. "But seeing Reenie like that, lying on the floor in a pool of blood, made me realize what's important. It made me realize . . . how much . . ." He stopped.

"How much you love her?"

"Yeah."

Petrie almost wiped away a tear.

"Not to mention you!" blurted Forrest.

Petrie stepped inside. "Mr. Haggarty, kindly lower your voice."

"I didn't know you cared!" laughed Trevor.

"I don't mean that! I only mean you gave me a real scare, that's all. And don't do it again!" Forrest turned to Petrie. "I thought he was a goner. They were on the verge, the very verge of declaring him dead! There was no heartbeat, no pulse."

"The two go hand in glove," said Petrie. Trevor started to chuckle, then lapsed into a coughing fit. She rushed to his side and patted her favorite patient on the back. "There, there, Doctor. Easy, easy."

"If I hadn't insisted they zap him one more time," continued Forrest.

"Let's not talk about it," Trevor managed to say. "It's over."

"Thank God."

Petrie straightened up. "I'll be back in a few, gentlemen."

"Where you going?" asked Forrest.

"ICU."

When she got to Intensive Care, Petrie walked up to Gloria Dennison and tossed her head in the direction of the beds. "No change?"

"Nada," replied Dennison.

They gazed into the windowed room.

"What is it with him anyway?" asked Petrie. "He never leaves. Just sits."

"I know."

"I wish someone cared for me that much."

"I know what you mean. You're sweet on that doctor, aren't you. The one with the chest injury."

"Not really. He's a nice man. A little long in the tooth, but nice. But what am I talking about? Even if I did have designs on him, it wouldn't do any good. He likes Miss Prim."

"The Bennett woman?"

"Yes."

"Oh. Well, there's always the guy who visits."

"Forget it!"

Somewhere in the distance Louise heard a Hail Mary. She struggled and managed to open an eye, and Francis swam before her. "Francis?" she whispered. "Francis?"

His head snapped up. "Louise!"

"Francis, where—"

He held a finger to his lips. "Don't talk. I'll get the nurse."

"No. Wait. Where am I?"

"The hospital. You've been in a coma for seven days."

She tried to reach for her face.

He stopped her hand. "Don't."

"What . . . ?"

"They couldn't save your eye, Louise. The bullet—"

Suddenly it all came back. "Poultice! He shot everyone!"

"Yes, but don't think about that now."

She was terrified. "Oh, my God. Where—"

"Dead, Louise. He's dead."

She closed her eye. "Good." Another thought emerged. "The others. What about—"

"They're fine, just fine."

"Good." But it wasn't. She remembered something else. "My children. Brendan," she whispered. "Are they okay?"

"Brendan came looking for you. He was there after you. And . . . I'm sorry. There was nothing they could do."

She tried not to cry.

He reached through all the wires and took her hand. "I've been waiting, Louise, waiting for you to wake up. I knew you would."

She pushed a word through her tears. "Faith?"

"Yes. I wanted to tell you."

She had expected this. "You're going away." He nodded. "Where?"

"Ecuador." He saw her expression. "I *asked* for the assignment, Louise. I want to serve God where people need me the most. Here . . ." He gestured vaguely with his free hand. "Well, they just don't need me very much."

"They need you," she whispered. "They just don't know it."

He smiled sadly. "Whatever."

"I never . . ." Her voice trailed off.

He leaned over. "What?"

"I never . . . should have . . . done this."

310

"No! You did the right thing! You saved your children's lives! Poultice was going to kill them! There were other families, others he—but never mind. It doesn't matter now. What matters is you saved them. And you saved my life too. In more ways than one."

She pressed his hand to her heart. "Thanks."

"What will you do now?"

"I don't know. Recover?" She managed a weak smile. It was a long process, one she started the day Mildred Bennett showed up on her doorstep. Now it was time to go home.